CHRISTOPHER ZYCK

The Glass Planet

First published by CJZ MEDIAISLAND 2022

First edition
ISBN: 979-8-9868928-2-5

DEDICATION

Dedicated to the patriots in humanity who fought for and fight on for the liberty, freedom, and 'wellbeing' of the human condition with due respect eternally to the Lost Souls of the Forgotten Sacrifices

FORWARD

"You should not honor men more than truth." ~ Plato

"Poverty is the parent of revolution and crime." ~ Aristotle

"All cruelty springs from weakness." ~ Seneca

Contents

DEDICATION iv

FORWARD v

PART ONE ~ METAPHYSICAL *ix*

What Bugs Me 1
Showtime 15
Unveiling Layers 25
Minister of Intrigue 33
Spark Creation Genesis 41
Interrupted 45
ZS Indoctrination 51
The Star Gazer Angel 61
Mars Runner Hook Up 67
Political Entropy Wins the Day 79
De ~ Tourist 87
Chasing Down a Dream 97
In a State of 'Wellbeing' 101
Windfall Effect 111
Keeping Pace In Space Travel 127
Refugees Like Us 131
Setting the Stage 135
Two Paths Taken 143
Sponti Goes Viral 153
First Impressions 157
Making Acquaintances 161

PART TWO ~ EXISTENTIAL 179

Debrief Belief 181
ACRES Cares 191
The Short and the Long of it 211
Old Blackmailer Picnic Party 235
Soiree 243
Two Ends of Population Management 249
Then, Now, and Date Night 255

The Styling of Nature 263
Space Trucking and Racetracks 281

PART THREE ~ TRANSCENDENTAL 297

A Natural Progression 299
Sling Shot 309
Three Engagements 315
Graduation 333
Same Truths 341
JJL JO ETHW SSN TRAGEDY 347
Hidden Money, Terrible Horror 353
A Fly in the Ointment 361
Uniquely Zealot Sentinels 371
A Toast to Goodbye 381
Sabotage War 391
Mars: A Fight to the Death 399
The Dark Eagle Strikes 405
The GPPJ Counterattack 417
A Balance of Liberty & Sacrifice 423
How Pathetic is War to be Had? 431

THE END 443

What is Metaphysical? 444
What is Existential? 444
What is Transcendental? 444

ABOUT THE AUTHOR 445
Connect 446

I

Part One

METAPHYSICAL

1

What Bugs Me

It is not every day one wakes up in a cave. My day begins, or my life resumes, as this may be the last of many countless days I have slept here, sitting up choking, dry heaving in musty stale dirty air to exhale while coughing up granular sand. I gasp for oxygen holding air in my lungs to keep consciousness as I do not remember ~ I do not remember any previous days to this point I can say I have lived.

As I gain my feet, I am struck by the cave walls around me, there is no explanation for this! It is like waking up with the worst-ever blackout and being deprived of your bearings, unable to find clarity.

Curious is the bed of moss cushioning me from the rock surface; it is ideal for my body size. A thick moss, Broom moss, grows on rocks.

Fine moisture in the cave glistens in areas where the sparse sunlight shines in from an opening a short distance above me.

My skin feels cold and clammy, I whisper to myself, "This is strange."

"Isn't it?"

My heart jumps into my throat from the voice in the back of the cave. If it were not a familiar voice, my response would be more defensive.

"Hello?"

"I agree, this is strange," a middle age well-built man smiles at me with a boyish grin and joyful eyes, giving off an intense warmth of personality, a bond I feel tracing into his eyes.

"What is going on here?" I respond without hesitation, "Have you been watching me for very long?"

"It appears we have gained consciousness simultaneously," he says. "When I heard your movements just now, I opened my eyes. Hearing your voice, I feel not so lonely."

The wind gusts hot, dry air into the cave carrying with it a slightly sweet odor.

"Do you smell that?" He asks while drawing in deep breaths.

"The fragrance of Gardenia flowers." I notice it undeniably as Jasminoides, "Let's take a look out there, come on!"

He smiles looking at the short distance to traverse, "A little rock climbing, get the blood flowing into these stiff joints. I'm in."

Blood rushes to my head as I exert physically a surge of adrenaline pulsating through my muscles elevating my strength upon contact with the rock surface as I establish that I have the agility of a trained athlete as I scale the rock steadily.

Rock climbing is not as demanding of a challenge as I anticipated it to be. It is more like I have rock climbed often. My hands are callous, and my fingers and forearms are muscular. My shoulders and legs are ripped in muscular definition having carried my weight the most.

I look back to see how this guy with the baby blue eyes is getting along. He is a familiar face to me. If not for the fact we found ourselves in a strange, mysterious place, we otherwise have zero knowledge of how we got here. His looks intuit our mutual bond, it is curious to share a sense of trust on our faces, as if our past has a long thread together.

"The first mystery to crack is why are we wearing unmarked khaki brown flannel shirts and pants, wearing jungle boots, and without any identification?"

"It could be, we hooked up last night at some costume beach party, and imbibed way too much to black out!"

He has a penchant for sarcasm.

"Without feeling the effects of a hangover," I simply point out, my bafflement is curbed by the presumption, "this will be explained soon enough."

A wind whirls dirt in from the cave entrance overwhelming me to have a dry cough. The high pressure exhaling in the process of clearing my air passages led me to near fainting.

"Are you going to be, okay?" He asks with severe concern.

I wave my hands palms down indicating, "I will be fine in a moment." I am forced to whisper due to a dry scratchy throat.

"Who would have ever thought," he remarks, "I would wake up in a cave next to a gorgeous woman nonetheless, and not know where I am or how I got there."

"I'd be surprised if this is the first time."

"But we don't know each other, it's weird."

"I'm sure that's never stopped you in the past," I tease him further. "Would you like to know the where?" As I reach the cave's opening, I invite him to join me outside.

A jungle. There is a vast jungle before us.

The temperature is sweltering with heavy vegetation growth all around us, some flowering, most of it green, thick, and lush in health. The Gardenia flowers as Jasminoides are a subtropical shrub with billowing lobes, white and pale yellow.

From our elevated position, we gain a view of the landscape within ten miles of visibility. It's a hazy view, yet an open tundra I presume exists. The heated vapor rising distorts the visibility of the horizon. Amazon rain forest, only "Amazonia" has the vastness.

"What did you say? You just whisper something?" He chuckles, "No-secrets-between-us, okay?"

He wears his sarcasm like a toothless smile, easy to appear foolish, and sometimes ugly.

"It looks like going west is our best bet," I recommend. "Sunlight is behind us now. We can get the most out of the daylight and put a camp together while the Sun sets."

"You're the romantic type?" He is delighted to ask. "Good plan but we still must get down from here to get over there. Ready to move on?"

"Yes, let us move. 'No' to the crass comment; it has nothing to do with being romantic, I'm being practical."

My regard for my integrity prompts me to make myself clear, "We have no idea where we'll be when the Sun goes down and I'm not sleeping vulnerable in the open air."

"I'm in. We better get on with it."

We are free as humans can be in this environment of the wild. Yet we do not know how we got here, but we are free. I feel we may be intimate, not that I would object, but not knowing the why of either circumstance makes such thoughts extraneous.

It's a beautiful hot, humid day under the fractures of sunlight rays shimmering through the dense broad-leaf coverage above. We identify with the Sun, as we identify with the Earth, the prospect of water, and everything natural from what we've seen, this is a world familiar to us.

Time is different from our innate experience, and we feel out of place like a dream is out of place, out of reality. We know this as a fact especially as the sky is dotted with tremendously fast, low-flying air traffic zipping across the atmosphere; and floating higher above are space stations so massive they are clearly visible through the crisp clean atmosphere; further, beyond the exosphere above all satellites, we can make out misshapen space stations as they orbit the Earth!

We continue to descend from our vantage point and explore what is before us. Although we are defenseless against the wildlife on the terrain, we know how survival is; to contend with adversities in fight or flight scenarios and avoid poisonous plants and snakes. We continue to trek down the side of the hill, we work to brace and secure each other over the steep rocky terrain, our every touch offers a hand in a growing trust.

As we scale down onto some level terrain we share smiles, giddy with fascination, and it becomes evident there is a trail to blaze intuitively. On the jungle floor, we find it difficult to traverse without the use of a machete to cut through heavy plants with strong thick roots.

We know it is helpful to make aware of our presence in the wild, to put the wild on notice. With a stick in hand, I advise my fellow explorer to search for a walking stick.

"Good idea. Three points of contact would be useful in a flytrap like this. They keep tripping me up," he replies, noticing my expression of anticipating more, he exults, "or for self-defense too!"

"Yeah, I'm not talking about the abundance of insects. I would not underestimate the veracity of a wild boar or a jungle leopard."

"Could be." He looks around into the trees, "Or hostile indigenous tribes."

Interesting he would think about indigenous tribes, I think with all the apparent advanced technology in the sky, the prospect of primitive tribal communities seems meek at best.

The animals are in fear of us, as evidenced each time we cross paths with a forest floor dweller. The plants shake and rustle from near to far as marsupials scamper away from us.

"The density of the underbrush is receding . . .," I observe before he anticipates my words finishing my thought.

"We're going to need to collect some of this to use as kindling later," his decisiveness reflects his need for certainty. This assertiveness does not offend me as a woman, even when he talks over me, given the circumstances, anything said or witnessed could bring a significant memory to the surface.

"What is your name?"

He looks at me curiously, "I was thinking the same thing."

"What do you mean? Do you not know your name?"

"No, I do not. I feel like I should. What is your name?"

This question startles me, and I hesitate to think, "I don't remember my name. Isn't that strange? I feel as though I know you intimately, however, I do not remember who you are either. I somehow did not realize I do not know my name."

"I'm certain we are experiencing amnesia for some reason. Probably hit our heads on the cave rock."

"Transient global amnesia ~ usually due to emotional, neurological stress ~ it's my best thought." I do respond with a nod of my head not as certain as he is, "We better figure out where we are so perhaps, we can find out 'who' we are."

Once into the depths of the jungle, we are afforded continued relief from the heat of the Sun by the shade of the leafy canopy above us from a variety of trees ranging from Kapok to Rubber to Brazilian nut.

"Doesn't this seem familiar to you?"

"Yes, there is a certain quality of déjà vu again!" He laughs cavalierly towards his remark, for some reason it strikes me as cliché.

I stop to speak my serious concerns, "That's right, I mention it as we are not walking in circles! At least, I'm not walking in circles."

"Good point, sensible thinking." His demur reply is more appropriate for the circumstances, "Let's see if we can find a freshwater source."

"Do you think it's a good idea to get the attention of these 'spacecraft' overhead?" I wave my arms in futility under the lush leafy branches made dense with the growth of epiphytes on top of the plethora of tree variety.

"No," he asserts, "We don't know who is flying them. I think we need to determine what the hell is going on. It will be more of a problem to hide than to get their attention, but we must find a way to get closer to the civilization unnoticed."

"If this is Earth and they are human, then maybe we can blend in," I suggest with a lack of conviction as his mind was made up, he is already marching on ahead.

"We can move faster on this terrain," he shouts once on solid ground without turning his head back to me, "We need to find a water source before the end of the day!"

For hours as we traverse the jungles' difficult terrain, we discover a cornucopia of digestible insects and worms, stopping on occasion to snack on grubs and termites in rotted-out tree trunks. There are many other edible insects, millions of insects within the rainforest no doubt, but most surprising is the immense variety of insects from different regions of the world.

We may not be on Earth after all. Finding dozens of varieties of species of insects from everywhere except Antarctica. If this is the Amazon Rainforest, then why are there significant African insect populations too?

"Hey!" He raises his voice measuredly, "Here's a rock formation!" He cups his hands around his mouth as he begins speaking, he realizes he is a little further ahead of me than he thought.

My forward progress is impeded by my curiosity about the unique ecosystem revealing itself to us. At least it is interesting to me anyway, he is driven to find more reliable sources of water before sunset. The abundance of life is evidenced enough to me that water is not a scarce resource. He must be going 'by the book' not to realize this simple, obvious fact.

Finally, we stop to examine the crevices of a rock formation for fresh water when I present him with the facts, "You know," I start in to gain his full attention, "intelligent inhabitants are plant breeding and bioengineering the ecosystems."

He arduously works his fingers into and through the rock crevices, "Yes, I've noticed that too."

"The 'Army ant,' 'Bullet ant' and the 'Blushing Phantom,' a clear-winged butterfly, are known to be from South America! The 'Bombus Traversalis bumblebee' is specific to the Amazon Rain forest."

"Bombus Traversalis is an underground nesting bumblebee unique for the 'protective dome' over the entrance to provide added protection against the rainfall."

"Correct. They also have a few bees guarding the entrance from predators' approach. That's when they introduced themselves to me."

"I was aware of the fact; they went for me as well," he rebuttals defensively, "What has you so concerned?"

"There are insects from other regions like the 'Comet moth,' 'Goliath beetle' and the 'Dancing Jewel damselfly' are from Africa. It's astonishing the variety we've encountered all at once."

"What's a 'Comet' moth?" He asks.

"The Comet moth, once hatching, has no mouth, no ability to feed, it only has a week to find a mate and reproduce."

"Talk about hard times. Why is it a 'comet' moth?"

"Other than the nature of its life span, each of its' tail wings resemble comets."

"Yeah? You know, I had a 'Ulysses butterfly' nearly fly into my face earlier. Those are from Southeast Asia."

"See what I mean? As long as it was not President Ulysses Grant."

"Right, hallucinations would not be a good~" he pauses for a moment in contemplation, "Wow!"

"Wow, what?"

"There was a 'Brachydiplax' dragonfly resting here, causing me to think there is water on this rock formation!"

"How does that elicit a 'wow' reaction?"

"The 'Brachydiplax' dragonfly is known to exist near pools of standing water from Queensland, Australia."

"I don't think we're in Australia, do you? Do you realize both insects you mention are prevalent in Southeast Asia? Why is it you are familiar with them?"

"I don't know, but I know the 'Brachydiplax' dragonfly lives nearby water sources."

"It most likely does, as does the 'Dancing Jewel' damselfly I found earlier, lives by lakes and rivers in Africa."

It doesn't occur to him moisture is abundant in the Rain forest. His expression of anticipation raising his eyebrows makes me wonder what experience in the wild he has. His internal fascination is a curiosity I find as affable as his gentle smile reveals.

Through our way, as we follow the Sun westward, we find more sustenance in the form of nuts and flowering vegetation. The volume of varieties at peak form of this cross-section of plants, trees, and vegetation from around the world, is enough to deduce methodical plant breeding. I spot a 'Plukenetia Volubilis' plant native to much of tropical South America and is known for its star-shaped fruit Sacha Inchi. Stepping closer to prune a few off, my boots sink into an increasingly muddy area.

Looking out through the top of the plants there appears to be a clearing where fewer trees exist. The mud is ankle-deep, and it cools my feet. He walks toward me seeing I have ceased.

"What's going on? Did you find something?"

"I found these Sacha Inchi and walking over, I found my boots sinking in this mud, ~"

"Water? Where do you think it's from?"

"There appears to be a clearing over that way." I point to my right extending my arm and shaking my right hand. He's looking in the direction and runs off like a jaguar toward unsuspecting prey.

Before I can slop my way to firm ground, I hear his jubilant cries.

"Water, it's fresh water!"

It takes my breath away to view the large pond of water, calm and pristine except for the algae and lily pads prominently floating a few feet from the edge around the pond. He is looking urgently around for something.

"What are you doing?"

"We need to find something to parcel some water in to boil before we drink it."

"Oh, is that all? You may have kindle, but there is no dry wood stock to be found to generate friction to coax the smoldering charcoal needed to create fire. There's no time to spend on creating a fire now. Not to mention we don't have access to a kettle or any containers for storage."

"I'll have to risk it and try soaking my sleeve then squeeze the water into my mouth."

"Really? We're not at severe risk; at least with what we've consumed in plant moisture and in tree trunks, condensation in rock crevices, ~"

"Okay, I got it. I should have been looking for something to transport water with."

"Do not get down on yourself. We're going to be okay."

"I could shove a bamboo rod up my buttocks and perform a water enema or colonics."

"What for?"

"To hydrate. It's safer in the end."

"Sarcastic to 'the end,' are we?"

"Figuratively most of the time, in this case literally!"

The heat of the Sun is made tolerable caressed by a series of subtle breezes gently revitalizing our senses as we approach a breach line fifty or so yards ahead of us. The bright sunshine demarcates the perimeter of the jungle where just beyond is a drastic change of terrain as we take notice of drawing nearer.

The open plain of tall grass is dotted with trees indigenous to the African Sierra and Australia. Perplexing as it is to encounter this stark contrast in terrain, we soon realize our sudden exposure to the Sun is damaging to our survival! Much worse is our exposure to the suspect aircraft continuously zipping overhead.

Crouching to find cover in the tall grass, as our clothing is a shade duller than the brown-beige tall grass, we crawl our way toward the nearby copse of mauve-crimson bottlebrush trees some one-hundred yards away.

The breeze across the plain alleviates the oppressive heat, a dangerous distraction as we relax our awareness while we rejuvenate ourselves.

We observe the sky traffic as we close in on the bottlebrush tree coppice when up to ten feet away from us appears the mane of a lion! We see through the blades of tall-grass three lionesses accompanying the male lion. Our rejuvenation is draped over in caution by the dominance of their presence.

We freeze in place. Unbelievable how this pride did not detect us by smell, and if so, they do not attack us within this threatening short distance.

The three lionesses continue past us a few yards before coming to a full stop!

We look at each other, my right hand gripping his left forearm.

The large head of the male lion parts the tall grass to the side of my friend, and I thought 'this is it!' The baked breath from the lion overwhelms us with the odor of rotting flesh.

My friend, startled, rolls over onto me keeping my body hidden from the roaring majestic beast.

The lion, as if put to ease by our frightened reaction, gingerly steps forward and licks my friend's face with his thick wet tongue graciously.

Then the lionesses came upon us sniffing, licking, and laying to rest around us.

"They're going to eat us," he whispers.

"I don't think so."

"Why not?"

I don't know why other than the wild beast's calm demeanor is counter-intuitive to an attack, "Because they are purring."

In an instant, the group's attention is drawn elsewhere. A rumbling is felt on the ground prompting the pride to their paws sensing a pending threat. Their keen awareness alerts them to flee!

Suddenly a crash of rhinoceros and herds of wildebeests and zeal of zebra charge by perilously close. The pack of frightened quadrupeds creates a slight alteration of their path to purposefully avoid stampeding us.

The sudden chaos motivates us to push forward crouching in cover as we scamper on. For all we know the excitement could be due to a sandstorm, but the air is heavy with moisture and the Sun of this bizarre world stretches orange-red bands of sweltering heat rising, distorting the horizon from the surface in waves of evaporating moisture.

We keep our pace despite growing fatigue once entering a desert, as ahead of us appear pools of water in the not-too-distant desert sands. With every hour passing our frustration grows, desperate for nourishment in our approach to the water source and the seeming lack of progress to arrive at these pools of water, and our senses are taxed to make a rational observation of our surroundings.

The Sun hovers above the desert sands at the four o'clock hour. The dehydration of our bodies is becoming severe as I feel my tongue swelling, salty to taste, and the soles of my feet scorched through my boots in the unbearable hot sand. Our sleeves are cuff to wrist to protect from sunburn.

We press on, every minute becoming more momentous than the last. We share the urgency of finding a location for a campsite subsiding to our dire need for finding an oasis. The temptation of mirages we haplessly expend energy to reach is discouraging to us. We find in our ignorance we've been played by the charade of the deserts' devices. We begin to experience the increasing desire to quench a burning thirst every few minutes gasping in heavy stifling hot air.

I swear the better choice is to draw attention from above. We are fully exposed now and there is no apparent concern about us, an absolute loneliness pervades.

Succumbing to delusion undermines my consciousness again as the flow of rushing water in the near distance arouses my attention.

We lost our heads in contemplation toward the sound of softly crashing waves. In a few breathless, adrenaline-fueled moments we scale over a mound of sand and into a gully sliding down on the loose sand to the edge of a riverbank!

Reaching the river, we dive in immersing ourselves in flowing fresh water, reinvigorating our mental and physical strength, euphorically splashing wildly about. He cups water into his hand sniffing it then in one motion drinking it. He is too quick for me to interject caution. He appears uncertain of the potential of ingesting bacteria-laden water. In a moment he is confidently refreshed and the both of us begin to take in copious gulps.

"It is advised to purify fresh water in rivers and bodies of freshwater before consumption," I remind my risk-taking friend.

"Are you serious? This water is as clean as a baby's bum!"

"It's too late now, we'll know better in the coming hours!"

"Yes, we will," his left hand emerges from the water gripping the dry kindle, now soaking wet, he holds it in his open hand between us. The recognition of losing out on this precious resource at the expense of currents of water is now profoundly humorous to us.

He brings me in closer placing his right hand around my back on my left shoulder blade.

He could have kissed me for every circumstance up to this point has dealt with the anxiety of isolation and with the probability of being outcasts to society, but his play on me is for his sake only.

"Please, no," I place my hands on his muscular biceps, "Until we know who we are, I will not be subject to intimacies."

He releases his caressing hold on me and shakes his head in understanding. His embarrassment is flattering and heart-warming to an extent. He's not lacking in self-confidence, or self-respect for sure.

He speaks with his chin down, "I'm obviously experiencing feelings for you. You said you thought we were intimate together?"

"Yeah, I did, I did," I offer reassurance to him, "Due to the circumstances it would be better to refrain from such advances until we know better. What if we are brother and sister? Okay with you?"

"That would be embarrassing."

"That would be disgusting!"

His crooked smile turns smooth when looking into my eyes, "Sounds like the right direction to me. I'm in!"

Revitalizing our hearts and spirits, we came to the same conclusion to traverse upstream in search of inhabitants living off the water source.

The river water is so clean the distinction between slippery rocks and areas of stable footing on the bottom of the riverbed is discernible through hip-high levels. I kept cupping water in my hands sipping it along the way.

Moving steadily, we exit the stream of waves intending to run along the sandy riverbank edge increasing our rate of speed. We spot a pipeline a mile in the distance appearing desolate. We decide not to venture out on the desert floor again with the Sun within two hours of setting. The temperature will drop rapidly near the desert. We need to build a camp around a fire, and I am intent on sleeping elevated from the ground to avoid the hazards of poisonous critters and desert foxes.

A wind gust provides an unexpected odor.

Coconut oil?

The scent thickens in the minutes before we halt given two humanoids upstream about one hundred feet. In reflection of our mutual concern for remaining undetected, a prudent observation is advisable to approach without alarming them.

Scantily clad we see there is one female accompanied by one male.

"Wait for a second, are they exhibitionists?"

"Indeed, in the middle of nowhere," he spoofs me. "What are they doing? I see quite a remarkable female."

"She is, her aura glistens, it's amazing."

"Like I said, 'remarkable female.'"

He smiles at me. Where does this guy learn his manners?

"Oh yes, her too, so far away," his smile beams without a care in the world. "You're blushing!"

"What did we just now discuss about making advances?"

"No advances. Sorry, sometimes I cannot help myself."

"No excuses either," I held my ground continuing, "and I am not blushing. Shush ~ look at what's happening."

"Should we be looking, what about respecting other people's privacy?"

"They don't seem to have a problem with the air traffic viewing them ~ maybe they're nudists?"

Standing opposite one another on either side of the river, they proceed to perform motions in synchronization that evolve into a beautiful form of performance art once the water elevates from the riverbed. As if by their command, in a collage of shapes and animated forms, the water alternates in various states of liquid, gaseous, and ice.

There is a sense of technological bones creating the illusion of a miracle, a splendid enhancement of reality, orchestrated by human ingenuity.

Rivulets of water float above them in the air as if minuscule prisms separating sunlight into an array of colors projecting extended rays of the spectrum. It feels like we are witnessing an intensely intimate engagement.

A flock of thousands of birds of various feathers commands

my attention flying in droves and populating the sparse tree-tops upriver tweeting harmoniously ~ the tree limbs begin swaying, shaking despite the wind gusts subsiding minutes ago, and we hear an escalation of primal screams. "Look on the branches. Are those monkeys?"

"Yes, I'm speechless!"

This mesmerizing magnificence of affection on display is a transcendence at the core of what it means to be human. This is an aesthetic true to love. A celebration of the soul. We watch in amazement the defying of physics, the calming truth instilled by the powers of nature.

A terrifying noise, a siren of sorts, at deafening decibels forces us to crumble to our knees before collapsing to the ground entirely.

Seeing the ritual is abandoned and we suffer the anguish of our motor functions being paralyzed, our brain capacity to rationalize deteriorates from this mind-bending audio, also incapacitating us from physical movement.

Appearing from the horizon downstream is a pack of immensely large wolves racing toward us. From a closing distance, the horrifying spectacle reveals its' true origin as these are not animals but artificial life forms intent on our capture if not our destruction.

My companion stares at me helplessly, a distorted expression of pain equal no doubt to my own as we remain paralyzed, unable to flee, and in anticipation of our certain demise.

As the pack descends relentlessly towards us, we manage to maintain our focus on each other's eyes realizing the imminent release of our souls soon to occur.

Nearing unconsciousness, the penetrating, disabling sound is silenced. A spacecraft hovers directly above as energy tickles our senses and hoists us off the ground and into the apparent safety of the craft's cabin.

2

Showtime

Silence prevails as we stand there is no sense of the crafts movement from inside the cabin walls.

The view from any window in the cabin proves the opposite as the craft makes a steep and rapid ascent into the exosphere, a spectacle to behold.

As the craft enters orbit at seventeen-thousand-five-hundred miles per hour, our bodies float in weightlessness. Seeing my friend visibly unnerved, I move to offer him a hug of reassurance, "What is happening?"

"Damned if I know," he responds rattled by the circumstances. "I thought you said no advances?" He chokes a broken laugh, "My bad, I couldn't resist."

"We almost . . .," I feel at this moment disconnected, "you're right, I did say no advances. Sorry."

"No worries, I'm only listening to you. I say, 'go ahead,' what the hell do you have to lose?"

The view from the port side confirms the terrain we were on is Gaia, Terra mater, and Mother Earth, the nature of which is recognizable, however, the landscape is blended with incomprehensible feats of engineering beyond any reasonable explanation we can muster. The view confirms Africa where the jungle is, and where the vast Sahara Desert used to be. The 'Amazonia' is flooded by the ocean water and where there is turf it is prominently developed into villas and resorts.

A glimpse of North America reveals equal amounts of the natural environment and industrial technologically advanced structures and the prominent development of cities formed on the accumulation of those structures.

We float from port-side to starboard where the view of a vigorous community of crafts moves much faster in outer space and is equally as wondrous as it is beyond description. The variation of technological achievement is on display with these structures, from city-designed space stations with skylines to the apparent resort structures with all the grandiose embellishments of a Las Vegas destination. Many of these space stations are so large they must be designed for recreational, high-volume use.

Attention is drawn through the bizarre design of a multitude of crafts varying in size and rate of speed. The humongous freighter behemoths, the understated low-key appearance, and pedestrian rate of motion are so more breathtaking up close compared to plain sight on ground-level earth.

I turn my head as the cockpit door transforms from a solid state to a translucent glow as two figures take shape and appear.

"Oh my God!" I am breathless as the entities reveal themselves as the couple whom we witnessed moments ago along the river, "Thank you so much for rescuing us."

They stand looking at us quizzically.

My friend asks, "Who are you? What year is this? Is this some parallel universe to our own?"

They remain to examine us without a word or sound uttered by anyone. Then a perceptible wave of energy fills the room, a rhythmic clutter of incoherent languages transmitting in our heads.

This incursion is as disabling as the strange paralyzing audio alarm was, but in an overwhelming soothing manner. It feels like we are in a radio wave lulling us to semi-consciousness and near complete physical immobilization. In our present state, the two hosts urge us with gestures to communicate by miming instead of opening their mouths to speak to us. Is it the incoherent voices speaking inside my head a form of telepathic expression originating from them?

At this moment the male motions to the starboard of the craft, a soft high-pitched sound as he moves closer to the female standing by her side. Their lips move as they vocalize sounds, we are incapable of interpreting.

My friend queries, "What are you saying? Can you speak the English language?"

At this point, they hand us a device indicating we place it in our ear.

"This is a communication link," I suppose as we insert the thin layered synthetic material against the ear drum.

They begin to speak, albeit in English, different words.

"We hear you both, but please one sentence at a time," I reply.

They react exasperated by my request before again speaking this time simultaneously, this time the same words synchronized down to the syllables.

"What do you have in mind concealing yourselves from us?" Their voices together emphasize their alarm, "Whom are you working for?"

"No one," my friend states definitively, "We are lost!"

"We traveled along the river hoping to find our way to civilization," I earnestly state our situation.

With that explanation, their heads shift from curious into cocked positions revealing twisted eyebrows. They are communicating extensively through their facial expressions, gesturing with subtle movements of their heads.

The male speaks to us with gentle inquisitiveness, "You are refugees seeking entrance into the GPPJ?"

"What's a GPPJ?" My friend responds.

"The Glass Planet Population Journal," replies the female flatly in concern of our ignorance.

The male offers what sounds like plausible insight, "You're not equipped with the GPI, then you must be from one of the vivarium communities?"

"What is a GPI?"

"Glass Planet Interface for operations."

"Excuse me?" I blurted out, "Vivarium communities?"

"Yes, what Vivarium are you from?

"I don't understand, what do you mean?"

The female exchanges a look of confusion with the male, then speak to us in unison, "Where do you come from? How did you find yourselves in the desert plains?"

My friend speaks with measured caution, "We only know we woke up in a cave. We then made our way through a jungle."

They continue to speak in unison, "Why were you in a cave? Where were you before that?"

I find this line of questioning frustrating and our answers potentially incriminating. "Listen, we don't understand why or how or where we came from. All we can tell you Is that we worked our way west through the rainforest from the jungle until we reached the plains."

They again look toward each other and seem to be holding a conversation without speaking until returning their focus to us, "Now we understand why the painted wolves were alerted, you would be exposed by any number of surveillance insectebots."

"Insectebots?"

"Yes, utilized to monitor the jungle for refugees from the vivarium societies."

My friend queries, "Vivarium societies?" His eyes wince as he sways his chin in confusion.

"You must know what that means, otherwise who are you people?" The female retorts.

Without any understanding of their implication I clarify, "I'm sorry, are we talking about confined environments for the observation and study of life forms?"

"Interesting response," the male states.

"Yes, it is a most interesting response."

"Not that I am particularly inclined to be detained for observation, but at the risk of sounding sarcastic, are we not all human beings?"

They ask, "You are primitive humans? Where do you live?"

"I'm an American from Colorado," he responds, surprised by his statement.

"I was born in Texas. Dallas-Fort Worth area?" I reply unexpectedly leaving me wondering if I am answering the question or asking it.

"We will help you, although your shared ignorance we find puzzling. What are your identity coordinates?"

"We don't know our names," I said with great certainty. "Do you mean social security numbers?"

"If you have no names without identity coordinates, then you are from pre- Twenty-third century. You refer to pre- Twenty-third century when you speak of social security; social security became an antiquated system in the twenty-second century."

We look at each other stunned by this statement before he says to me, "Did they say 'pre- Twenty-third' century?"

"They did."

"We must be in an alternate reality." He turns his head to look curiously at our hosts, "What year is it now?"

They stare at us before nodding heads to each other, then speak in unison, "This is the year Twenty-three-thirty-nine."

"What was it we encountered? Those mechanical beasts and the siren?"

"You were detected by population control," the male explains.

"Due to your lack of modernization," the female adds.

My friend turns to me, "We were incapacitated both cognitive thinking and physically unable to defend ourselves."

I turn to our hosts, "Can you tell us why such harsh, aggressive tactics?"

They answer in unison, "You are life forms outside of the population journal." Noticing, or anticipating our confusion they continue, "Any anomaly in the population journal indicates potential criminal or rebellious activity, and the security robots are terrifying in appearance to those unfamiliar, but they are made to stand out to ward off the animal population."

This answer is marginally helpful in understanding our present circumstances. "Then why did we experience a similar effect on this ship?"

"You lack modernization. Your sensory abilities are not supported by the GPI."

"How does the GPI affect us?" We ask simultaneously, I am annoyed by our unified response.

The male speaks independent from the female, "The infrastructure of the Space Station Network, also known as the SSN, is reliant on the centralized operations of The Glass Planet to provide an interface of complete cognitive skills and tools to utilize the entire comprehensive database of the complete recorded knowledge of all human existence. It helps individuals discover passions to pursue in living a fulfilling life."

"Included are an integration of communications via brain circuitry," the female has a subtle accent I can't place, "promoting the transmission of visual and emotional sensory directly to the 'human will' is what you know as money. It follows the ETHW, the Economic Theory of the Human Will: What will you do without it; What will you do to get it; What will you do when you have it?

"This concept of reciprocation is the basis of modern civilized morality, the intertwining of human experience with the unfettered abilities of nature. The technologies in place are what sustains The Glass Planet connecting us all."

"What about us? Can we be modernized?" I ask.

"We appreciate your enthusiasm. Yes, as I said, it is the first issue we will address." They assert, "We can help you cross the bridge to The Glass Planet, then we will have to administer a cell cleanse for revitalization and to enhance longevity before we can begin our research to determine who you both are."

"Or who we were," my friend utters.

"My name is Qyxzorina, and this is my husband, Marcel."

"Nice to meet you both, especially since you saved our lives!"

"What are your names?" Qyxzorina asks.

"We don't know our names."

They look at us with suspicion.

"We honestly do not know!"

Marcel approaches and places sensors on our pulse and pressure points, "We are ready to begin."

Qyxzorina handles an ultra-thin control pad placing settings before stating, "While this process takes place you can relax and learn more about our present-day world environment."

"Sounds amazing," I comment continuing, "but I was wondering about nourishment. It seems like I haven't eaten in centuries!"

The laughter we share at this moment, I say is a watershed moment, to me, our common humility reveals a warmth of intuitive mutual survival.

"A famous saying: 'Humility and Humor put the 'Hu' in Humanity,'" offers Marcel.

"As you cross the bridge both of you will be fully hydrated. After this process, we can visit an eatery in a city with a lot of history you do not know about." Qyxzorina points out, "It is a city unlike any other in the modern world."

Qyxzorina and Marcel leave us strapped in comfortable flight chairs.

Moments later my friend and I are in what Qyxzorina describes as a holistic virtual reality, suspended in space, between Jupiter and the asteroid belt, an expanse of one-hundred-forty-million miles. Quite an expanse to be adrift in outer space.

A sound of music, Ravel's 'Bolero' begins as our bodies become buoyed, floating in weightlessness, closing in on the asteroid belt.

An amazing sight as every terrestrial planet with its moons and the Sun are viewable from within the belt; a giant virtual display of our inner Solar system is before us. We are informed a handful of large asteroids are inhabited by humans in buildings and various utility vehicles transporting valuable rocks, minerals, and metals from the asteroid mines to cargo ships destined for the Dark Nest SS.

The asteroids are hundreds of thousands of miles apart from each other, some are large enough to have their own moons. They are mesmerizing as the random floating of multitudes of asteroids ranging in size from a mouse to a house surrounding us in open space!

Emerging from the asteroid belt a jumble of lights, both natural and artificial in source, are taking shape as the design of the Astro outpost called "Dark Nest SS" spelled out in all its' enormity on the hull. Atop, cradled in the "Dark Nest SS," is a vessel displaying the moniker "Dark Eagle SS."

Despite the heavily armored reinforced sharp contours, the Dark Nest SS is a vertical design easily two Empire State Buildings in height. Barely perceptible to the naked eye, incredibly, the cargo ships haul the precious rocks to the lowest quadrant where docking bays convey the loads into storage. The stockpiles are transported to Earth every ten years.

The whole presence suggests a beacon to the Milky Way, if not the entire Universe; the Dark Eagle SS is no doubt a center for discovery and communications.

'Bolero' continues to build momentum as each sequence heightens in intensity matching the visuals as we encounter them!

Mars, the Red Planet, its' two moons in orbit around a cloudy atmosphere, water wistfully floats down red rock mountains, through valleys, and carried by the slight winds into resting lakes and seas encased by synthetic barriers protecting from extreme levels of radiation.

The prevailing theme of Mars Metropolis City contains the fusion of a homage to the Roman God of War in color scheme hues of yellow, brown, orange, mauve, crimson, and red depicting images of Mars, chariots, and vivid scenes of ancient instruments of war on the architecture of the buildings. With columns and arches of the classical age prominently flaunting designs consistent in an art-deco style reminiscent of the motion picture industry era famous for depictions of mythological Martians from space travel and speculation of life on distant planets.

How a planet half the diameter of Earth and about fifteen percent its volume, formerly a desolate, lifeless landscape is now a thriving ecosystem of life forms and activity rivaled only by Earth's modern cultures is astonishing to the eye.

Five space stations gracing the expanse around Mars are each wildly resembling the head of Medusa with her talons of snakes for hair, actual robotic metallic appendages used while in orbit of Mars to protect the surface from rogue space rock impacts.

Once leaving Mars's gravitational pull there is an expanse of ninety million miles minimum before reaching the SSN extending a few hundred thousand miles from Earth!

A web of corridors connects several of the space stations, exuding an aura of excitement, in a network of interchanging colorful designs and architecture.

A good deal of insect-inspired engineering is pervasive from the hulls and protective walls of numerous structures floating in space.

The flashing, bright lights on the oval-shaped space stations are positioned like pedals on a flower. Each pedal is opaque revealing thousands of revelers participating in multiple dance parties, robust evidence of a roaring enthusiasm for celebrating life. The revelers are dancing, I can determine this by their bodily movements even from a mile or two away.

Other structures appeal to more intimate pleasures of life's lusty romance, provoking an emotional curiosity for recreational sex.

These establishments are in stark contrast to the elegance and stylish motifs of fine dining and performance art venues orbiting as if Lincoln Center was uprooted from its concrete foundations and hoisted into orbit, minus the Revson water fountain.

Somehow a majestic water fountain is functioning in the main hall station, exhibiting compliance with the laws of gravity.

This is as gratifying as it is disturbing to be able to understand so much while knowing so little of what is informing us.

As I view in front of me hundreds if not thousands of crafts of all shapes, designs, and color schemes joining together latching onto a configuration of platforms, a synchronization of form as an impromptu space station gathering, a wedding reception is taking place, as the revelers are in a kaleidoscope of the color of individual crafts linked to form conceptual beauty with the utility function to celebrate party styling.

Amid the adventurous danger of living in space, there is a softness of dreams fashioned by human desires. The prevailing sense of bravado in the face of perilous sudden permanence of death is apparent on the Moon with a population of six billion, the infrastructures are sheltered communities sprawling with multi-colored lights, evidently to prove some devotion or remembrance worthy of the mesmerizing spectacle.

The popular Fra Mauro crater Lunar City consists of a few large structures constructed on the rim of the crater surrounding an elegant, sublime backdrop to the fluid environment of human activity from dune buggies kicking up moon dust while towing surfers along courses exhibiting competitive racing. Events are promoted on brightly lighted signage for concerts at the Lunar Hall performance arts center exhibiting a vibrant culture of entertainment. Multiple solar panels designed for solar energy use and projected shields resembling beetle shells to deflect most sizes of space debris away from the Moon's surface provide examples of the aesthetic of architectural beauty combined with engineered functions.

The Moon Is the ultimate vacation destination! A series of thin canopied structures cover a large segment of the Moon's surface, a controlled environment for social gatherings.

A group of hundreds of individuals hovers in open space, and a sign clarifies below on the surface: 'Terrain Walkers.' I see they are tethered together and anchored to the surface as they leap off various structures to glide back down to the surface once again. Gravity-free bungee cord jumping into the Moon's deepest of its millions of craters sends a chill down my back.

Traveling toward Venus, the space station network ends about two-hundred-fifty-thousand miles from Earth.

On the outskirts are massive rectangular encasements made of solar panels to harness the sun's energy into solar coil cells charging in unimpeded sunlight. Spacecraft resembling forklift trucks extract and secure the solar coil cells for transport to Earth and the Moon supplying energy. The encasements remain while the charged coil cells are extracted and replaced with exhausted coil cells in need of recharging.

Then we enter empty space on approach to Venus. Hot, humid, and windy typically describe enjoyable weather conditions, but on Venus, these conditions are too extreme for human life to exist, historically speaking.

Known for its robust atmosphere and vibrant color, expected as orange or yellowish, Venus has now become a marble of blue and brown! Scientific breakthroughs creating chemical and biological engineering advancements transformed sulfur dioxide clouds and the formerly carbon monoxide-rich atmosphere into an ocean planet of fresh water and rocky shorelines. Venus is another gem of a planet for scenic tourists and is presently an abundant resource of fresh water supply for tens of billions of human beings throughout the inhabited Solar system.

The celestial calm is short-lived in these parts of the Solar System.

Mercury and the Sun are a classic juxtaposition of opposites in exertion. Mercury is so close to the heat of the Sun, that its tiniest rocky surfaces rich in sulfur cover its iron core composing seventy percent of the planet's mass.

While the Sun, the source of life-supporting energy, curls in fire, blooms in immense gaseous explosions and delights in its legendary force.

We want to avoid looking directly at the Sun; We are fixated on the spectacle of boisterous flares of flame, nuclear size explosions appearing impressive but at a safe distance.

The Sun is for everyone. No one owns the Sun with its unparalleled powers. A force of nature speaks its truth in its purposes, has its jurisdiction, shares its warmth, its catalytic powers.

We jettison toward an area of space stations orbiting close to Earth's atmosphere and specifically one elegantly designed station with several enclosed viewing decks. Satellite dishes and beacons of varying sizes are situated facing multiple directions indicating a primary function for communications. The insignia on the hull reads The Glass Planet SS.

We are informed it is primarily sourcing a utilization of computer-generated illusions of environmental autonomy under atmospheric vector shields in constructing terrestrial boundaries isolating barbaric societies from interacting with one another. It provides a separate but equal lasting peace principled by the Economic Theory of the Human Will in support of the categorical imperative of the 'wellbeing' of the human condition.

This information is fantastical, and beyond our understanding.

Then descending upon all the wonders of the world we are aware of, and marvel at those we are to become aware of as we pass the bridge noticing personnel on board it is apparent the importance of the enormous space station as the vital link between Earth's operations and the communications informing the entire SSN.

3

Unveiling Layers

Upon descent to the surface, Qyxzorina enters and with a wave of her arm she engages us in conversation: "What do you think of the presentation, I hope you liked it? How do you both feel?"

I try to answer but I cannot vocalize any words through my mouth.

"Good to know you are amazed by the overview of present times," apparently Qyxzorina reads minds.

"That's exactly what I was trying to say! Wait a second. Did I just . . . Qyxzorina, can you hear me?"

She turns to gaze directly into my eyes and without moving her lips she says, "We all can hear you."

"You mean just me, you, and Jürgen only, not all of the population?"

Qyxzorina smiles while responding, "Just us. And Marcel too. He is setting our porting cues to receive a proper rebooting."

"What are we doing communicating like this? Are we engaging in telepathy?"

She peeks up at me as she moves to stand at the rear of the cabin, "Yes, but a bit above your learning curve at this moment. There are various settings for how you communicate. If you want to speak via vocalization, just think about your intention first. We can also arrange for our designates to communicate with, just think it."

"And if I want to reach out to a stranger?"

"If it's a public greeting or small talk is your intent, you think of awareness, and thought is sent to gain attention before you speak. The intent is always the first thing to be stated. You should excuse yourself, introduce yourself unless you know the name of the person you are speaking to first, and always make your intent clear, otherwise, you may unintentionally include people whom you do not intend to," she amuses herself with that emitting joyous laughter, "Let's share some fresh air."

Marcel emerges from the cabin and proceeds to step out with Qyxzorina.

She motions swaying her hip toward us before turning to exit for us to follow her.

As I move one step forward a hand caresses my shoulder, "You called me Jürgen."

"I know. That is your name. Do you know mine?"

"Catherine is what comes to me. What do you think?"

"Relieved. I think I like it, 'Catherine.' It's a start at least. I think we are beginning to communicate better now that we don't need to move our mouths."

"True," Qyxzorina interjects from the hatch, "greater brain activity will arouse recollection of memories over time."

Stepping out of the rear cabin onto the grassy field is as natural an experience except for a brief sensation of weightlessness mid-step emerging from the craft.

"Marcel, is there some gravitational alteration exiting the craft?"

"To reduce friction. Also, the 'craft' is better known as 'Blister,' as in the Blister movement to promote access for all classes to visit the Sun. The name is intended to be a play on words."

"We just visited the Sun!" Jürgen alerts us, "'Blister' seems a harsh reference for a tourism operation?"

Qyxzorina informs Jürgen, "You experienced a simulation just now, but we may visit the Sun together someday. I agree with your assessment on the name; my choice is 'Star Gazer,' but Marcel chose 'Blister.'"

"Theoretically speaking," I respond to the prospect of commercial tourism to the Sun, "or theoretically thinking?"

"A test program is in place and 'Blister' seems an appropriate name until the technology is developed to withstand the drastic elements at close exposure. Optimistically, travel for the masses is anticipated in the next decade or so," retorts Marcel. "Then, for marketing purposes, a name change can be considered."

He projects an aerial Image of a distinctive, uniquely reusable energy source city, "We will go to a most important location: Nativa City. With the twenty-first-century demarcation of the separation from the 'old fossil fuel-based industries' to the evolution of the ecologically potent technologies of today, Nativa City holds the distinction of being the first of its kind in human history to be an independently sufficient city operated on solely clean energy sources."

Qyxzorina adds, "The moniker of Nativa City is 'Only the Beginning.' Two additional cities were invested and constructed in the twenty-first century as well. The boom in construction coincided with the development of the space station network and by the middle of the twenty-third century, it was by twenty-two-fifty-six when all of Earth's populations found their place in the new world order."

As we begin to walk in pairs euphoria overcomes me from breathing in fresh clean air. The beauty of nature surrounding us, and clarity of mind connect inside me to spark a question, "Why do I feel so confidently curious and eternally safe from harm?"

Jürgen is quick to add, "Almost complete invincibility."

Our hosts courteously reply, "Welcome to The Glass Planet."

A mass transit shuttle arrives at the platform as we are approaching. The platform is one of several positioned along the shuttle 'track' that is more of a series of kinetic energy panels the shuttle 'floats' on. These platforms are for access to and from privately owned transports parked in solar-constructed garages.

Entering the shuttle, the translucent surface is as transparent as I am, "How long is the ride into the city?"

I can hear odd voices expressing mundane conversations from the other people on board the shuttle. It is an intriguing ability to hear other peoples' thoughts only to discover how boring common people's ideas are.

A dozen travelers turn their heads to me as they exclaim in unison, "We can hear you!"

Jürgen is grinning as if he knows any better.

My embarrassment, a feeling representative of the expressions on Marcel and Qyxzorina's partially obstructed faces, each with a hand over their brows, they share in my pain.

"Sorry everybody, didn't check my proximity setting."

Marcel proceeds to exit the shuttle, "As I say, 'Humility and humor.'"

Qyxzorina holds widely opened eyes toward me, "We are already at our stop! Proximity setting?"

Her laugh and a touch of empathy with the humor settle my anxiety.

Our hosts lead us to a three-dimensional map simulation diagramming the layout of the city. Several landmarks are highlighted and when we touch each location on the map an automated description details the point of interest's facts and functions Qyxzorina selects an open-air restaurant located on the edge of a beautiful park.

"We can ride, or we can walk, what is your preference yons?

'Yons' is synonymous with 'friends' or 'best friends,' I will assume as I acquiesce to Jürgen in wide-eyed anticipation of his response.

"Walk, let's definitely walk."

The walkways are designed to harness solar and kinetic energy during an afternoon of pedestrian activity. The energy is sufficient for supplying pedestrian escalators, elevators, trolley transit, and public lighting systems overnight.

Marcel walks next to Jürgen, "You are not going to smoke a cigar or cigarette on a nice couch, are you? Then why smoke on the Earth right? In terms of manufacturing, fuel production, and mass consumption the destructive burden of harmful emissions has been lifted off the Earth," Marcel reveals adamantly.

Jürgen notes, "So that is why the air quality is sweet and every breath feels nourishing like a sip from a cool glass of water?"

"All of the materials used in the construction of every aspect of this corporation is made from self-sufficient reusable energy sources," according to Qyxzorina, "From kinetic energy stored in battery cells as electricity to the use of water, wind, solar and ecologically friendly technologies ranging from dams to precipitation converters to human waste recycling to algae cultivation. Every mode of pedestrian activity sustains the corporate resources to provide low cost, high quality of living, ensuring vitality in its citizens and reliability in safety and security ~ and all cities are centers for commerce.

"When this city and others like it were built in the mid-twenty-first century, the business contracts were bid out to young, talented, aspiring entrepreneurs to begin the spread of opportunity and wealth amongst the masses.

"Technology catalyzes this economic integrity binding all engaged in employment throughout the city."

"And their successes were undoubtedly passed down to family generations?"

"No Jürgen the world has evolved quite significantly since then, now providing for the human population sustenance completely. Longer life spans encourage various alternate disciplines during one's lifetime," Marcel explains as we all slow to a stop, "Here it is, 'The Rotunda on The Green.' After you."

We enter through an atrium galleria featuring the Great Seal of South Dakota affixed to the ceiling.

The interior design is centered around a variety of sculptured depictions of Mount Rushmore accentuated with light to dazzle the eye and panoramic views of the city green featuring structures near and from afar surrounding the park's confines.

We are escorted to one of the tables with a breathtaking window view.

"Here the food is gelatinous, at high-end eateries like this, we eat without using utensils. Infusion, no confusion, the cuisine is contemporary reinventions of classic inspired recipes," Marcel relates with an air of expertise.

"You got that memorized, don't you?" Qyxzorina quips.

"Exquisite dining for those who can afford it," remarks Jürgen.

"How large is the human population?"

"Overall, twenty-two billion and growing by a billion every ten years."

"How?"

"How what?"

"How is it possible to maintain the 'wellbeing' of so many billions of people?"

"The Glass Planet offers all the education and opportunities to fulfill dreams, both real and fantasy; to master several disciplines in a life span and change occupational responsibilities as self-awareness allows. Everyone contributes and everyone receives due to the mining of precious metals and minerals from the Asteroid Belt expanding the wealth for all law-abiding GPPJ to thrive.

"And as you may recall from the overview of the SSN, six-billion people populate the Moon, with two-billion more throughout the SSN and populations on Mars."

"People reside in the SSN?" Jürgen asks for clarification.

"Mostly secondary residences, offices, and resorts," Qyxzorina courteously offers.

"What makes it possible for such individual growth? How long is the average life span?" My questions go directly to the agricultural resources about the individual's responsibility for their destinies.

"The average life expectancy in the event of a natural demise is five-hundred-fifty-nine years of age. There is some genetic engineering allowed, but there is one procedure that remedies the toxicology buildup in the various cells of our bodies."

"There are seniors with wrinkles on their skin and thinning gray hair. Are they the oldest?"

"Gray heads are late recipients of the medicinal technology, so although they appear feeble, they are physically the equivalent of a twenty-five-year-old. However, yes, they are the elders of the tribe. Sadly, their population is dwindling due to aged brains leaving them vulnerable to terminal disease."

"How are they treated?"

"What do you mean?"

"As the first generation to realize the expectant extended life span, are they revered in any public display or treated with special attention?"

"They are collectively known as 'Mother Generation.' Just treat everyone the same, in the way as if you would want to be treated," Marcel's face expresses doubt, "It is curious why some who, in advanced age when the Condorcet procedure is administered, have opted to remain with their elderly appearance."

"I don't get it if there are cosmetic procedures available."

"Most definitely . . .they can alter their appearance as they wish, but they choose not to. Others of the 'Mother Generation' are progressive 'gray heads' who use cosmetic and corrective procedures. They embrace their re-awakening youth enjoying healthy sexual relations and are curious, engaging, adventurous ~,"

"Continually reaping rewards of emotional, intellectual, and creative growth," Jürgen interrupts on cue to finish someone else's thought.

"While the traditional 'gray heads' are choosing to continue living in a perceived reality rather than embrace actual reality. It is a pity they are clinging to the anticipation of death's arrival. Many feel ashamed of their physical prowess, as they prefer the frailties, the diminishing attributes of both body and mind."

"It is an experience of life, a sort of conditioning of valuing the imminent certainty of death and a reminder of how cherished living is; how life's precious frailty, the memories of lives lived as time diminishes, are to be cherished in the later stages of ones' existence in reflection."

"Jürgen," Marcel has a moment in contemplation, "Now that you put it from that perspective it makes sense. Still, if you ask me, old-fashioned thinking and feelings prevent their individual growth as humans. It would be a scientific breakthrough to affect their attitudes towards progress."

"You're either dying to live or living to die!" Jürgen states having been taken aback by Marcel's response.

A chance for me to change the subject.

"Why is the Sahara Desert now mostly a jungle?" I direct my question to Qyxzorina.

She smiles placing a hand on my shoulder, "Due to the global warming damage, the watermarks swell over many shorelines. To reverse this, technology was engineered to transport the overflow water into the vast deserts. Natural filtering of the saltwater took place creating volumes of fresh water into the water shelf, hence transforming inhabitable lands into nutrient-filled soil suited for sprout in unlimited forms."

"Wow! Would the salt do the opposite and make the soil infertile?"

"The soil is treated the same way the soil of the Mesopotamian dealt with salt build-up; by leaving salty fields fallow to recover. In a matter of three or four years of growing barley gradually the land becomes nutrient enriched.

"Deserts were once ocean floors; it is required to saturate the sand in abundance. Today the oceans are cleansed of artificial debris apart from some piles of plastic manufactured hundreds of years ago, over time made into artificial reefs by the sea life. Many more coral reefs were created through bioengineering."

"I listen intently, as this sounds incredible. Just these topics alone baffle me."

Jürgen is quick to agree, "Yes, why are we here? What for?"

"How, what and why." I add lightheartedly, "'How' will tell us everything we need."

"We know the where, when and who, right?"

Jürgen's playfulness is infectious, but I am not to be outdone.

"Well, maybe the 'where' and 'when' are certain, not all of the 'who' though."

Jürgen points a finger toward himself.

"Yeah, I'm talking about you!"

He looks at his finger and rotates it to face me before tapping me on the nose affectionately.

Marcel is unable to contain himself, "Are you both feeling all right?"

Qyxzorina adds her concern, "You are, okay?"

Jürgen replies with an innocent smile.

"I think so, we are having a mild identity crisis is all!"

Qyxzorina is visibly relieved, "Understandable, don't worry about it over dinner. What's in a name that can define you as well as your actions? Find yourself in the ever-constant spontaneous instant and take the control to define yourself."

"That's right, we will help you research your prior lives," agreed Marcel, "To clear up this 'identity crisis!'"

Expressing my dumbfounded reaction as my jaw hit the floor, "Jürgen, we had prior lives."

Jürgen says displaying a splashy smile, "I sure as hell hope so!"

His reaction startles me, "It is discomforting, I mean what if we don't like or understand who we were?"

"Not so much. I'm just saying we've been here only moments compared to the physical age span of our bodies!"

He winks at me as though he is thrilled by the prospect of the rediscovery of our identities, "There must be something we accomplished to be proud of? We must be important in some way relating to our current circumstances."

This guy is continuously hitting on me. Why? I wonder. Is he experiencing a feeling we once shared, but I have forgotten?

"Jürgen?"

"Yes?"

"Why do you," I pause choking on my words. "How do you feel about us?"

He turns his head at an angle fashioning a clever pleasant expression on his face. Placing his right-hand forefinger crossed with the thumb over his chin he replies, "Have you been drinking? Again?"

"And what's that supposed to mean?" I keep a firm gaze into his eyes. "I see, you think I'm being unfair to you?"

"I think you are insidiously attempting to manipulate me."

This remark makes perfect sense to me. I discouraged the several advances he made in the past, and he is now adjusting his mind toward me by denying his impulsive urges to show proper respect for me. Suddenly I'm aware of my stupidity; prying into his emotions towards me is pure conjecture, a farce at best.

4

Minister of Intrigue

Shoes kicked off, bare feet suspended above head level, as laying on the spacious leather recliner is often the way Patrick Riverstrike culminates his workday, "Ah, these development projects are more holiday than work!"

Above his abdomen he cradles a three-dimensional transparent simulation of his proposal for his next engineering design layout of space stations extending beyond the asteroid belt, "Almost there, one move here, this station here, and a few quick touches for tidiest display."

He wiggles his left forefinger across the display before setting his coordinates, "Walla!" With a wave of his hand, the display closes, and he stands to his feet crossing the expansive office linoleum granite floor to stand before the fifty-foot from floor to ceiling plate diamond encrusted synthetic transparent wall with a view of Jupiter not too far off, some two-hundred-seventy-million miles, but on a hyper-magnified scale created by the Dark Eagle SS, a mere forty-million miles for dramatic effect.

An overlay of the display he tediously managed is now projected in space from the station to a distance approximately two-hundred-thirty-million miles short of Jupiter's gravitational pull, or thirty-two million on the scale.

"What do you think?"

"I believe the word is 'Voila' and not 'Walla.'"

"No, no. 'Walla' is the term of my preference. What do you think about my Proposal?"

"Impressive," is the response from the man shadowing Riverstrike, "When do you plan for these stations to be constructed?"

"Ah yes, obviously funding is the thing when there's a need for work to sustain the GPPJ. That is when the will of the masses comes full circle to value my vision."

He stands in admiration of his space station model laid out before him, and in retrospect, he relishes his prior successes in persuading the will of the masses to support his visions.

"Why should there be any disconnect with the vision of expanding space station construction and planetary colonization in the good name of facilitating a growing human population? With my savvy futuristic point of view, my humorous and charismatic personality, the disarming aura, perhaps being the best-ever-thinker, orator of words, and unquestionably the greatest deal maker ever!"

"Understood, Sir. Speaking of the masses . . ."

"Oh, what is it now Simon? An emergence, mysteriously no less, of two more human life forms, not of our present time?"

"Yes Sir, then you are aware of the incident occurring just hours ago?"

"I have felt the ripple effect. How could I avoid it, they're all the buzz on the GPI." He sits at the monitor table, "What recon do you have for me to look at?"

"The only images capturing the escape are from the painted wolf-pack's pursuit once alerted; the suspect's movements were recorded earlier by nanobots within the rain forest."

Simon privately discloses his passcode to access the security footage.

An image appears in a three-dimensional sphere, "A woman and a man briefly immobilized by Audio Fragmentation Suppression, on their backs along the riverbank. The painted wolves were in the closing distance just as the craft hovers above, boarding the refugees before making a rapid exit."

"Ah, so there are conspirators involved with extraditing these suspects from the AFS! What information do you have on that craft?"

"The craft is titled 'Blister.'"

"Who claims ownership of 'Blister?'"

"One Marcel Etrion."

"Have you located and apprehended him yet?"

"No, the suspect remains at large, as do the non-journal refugees."

"Why is this the case, Simon?"

"It is unknown exactly why Etrion cannot be located as he is fitted to The Glass Planet."

"Ah, Simon, run scans for any cloaking or jamming activity within The Glass Planet. Investigate every aberration until he and that craft the . . .what is it called?"

"Blister."

"Blister. Why does the name sound so familiar to me?"

"It is the working title of the enterprise Etrion is developing for educational tourism around the Sun."

"Ah yes, the tourist ship voyages to the Sun; conceived in response to the immense backing of the will of the majority for every human to experience their celestial star."

"Once in a lifetime."

"Yes, a once-in-a-lifetime visit! This Marcel Etrion is an intriguing move with the entrepreneur ambitions so massive. He comes from humble beginnings does he not?"

Simon checks a dossier from his wrist assistant. "Yes, minister. He was in the Colombian military as a teenager in the early twenty-first century."

"He is a Colombian citizen, indigenous?"

"No, actually identifies as Jamaican, Haitian, and Creole."

"Then what in hell was he doing in the Colombian military?"

"He was a mine and improvised explosives engineer assigned to special operations with the Hoover's."

"Also known as a 'sapper.'"

Simon stands in place as he summons an accurate dossier on Marcel, "If it were only imagined, the man spent four years in hospitality training and another six years in aerospace engineering and propulsion. After that, he has primarily worked in aerospace engineering and jet propulsion firms, designing prototypes on the side for his Blister Sun Star Tour ships along the way."

"It would be perceived as an act of benevolence to assist him. First by changing the name Blister! I do not care for it."

"There is an application on file to formally establish the company, naming one Qyxzorina Astraea as a trustee."

"Qyxzorina, I know that name, how could I ever forget it!" He stands exuding a surge of enthusiasm, "Qyxzorina is a rock star in the fashion world, but just as a runway model for most people. A few billion people are aware of how her designs have influenced the GPPJ over the past one hundred years."

Simon displays images of Qyxzorina in various official career publicity releases, wearing stylish clothing of her own making.

"Will you look at these," Riverstrike states admiringly. "You can see from these images why she is the best of her generation. She was born in Nigeria, but her eclectic family tree has a substantial percentage of descendants of French Moroccan, and Egyptian; A half-dozen indigenous tribal populations, all masterfully reflecting the history of her lineage in her designs."

Riverstrike paces about in contemplation, "The will of the masses certainly are misguided on this one. Take the time and expense to design, develop, and operate a service providing every human being, despite their economical worth, an opportunity for an instant sun tanning." Riverstrike shifts his focus to his plans on display, "Or choose fair expansion to facilitate the 'wellbeing' of the human condition in this majestic plan! What lies before us, Simon?"

"Economic opportunism on your part? Sir."

"Wait, consider the Economic Theory of the Human Will: What will you do without it? What will you do to get it? What will you do when you have it? You are familiar with this golden rule, the law against immoral transgressions and greed against the vulnerable, disadvantaged masses?"

He pauses to gauge Simon's level of awareness.

"If you're not, you should be," he takes a seat on the chaise lounge, "Economic opportunism? The benefit of everyone's participation in every human being's benefit, not just for a once-in-a-lifetime experience, but for greater simplicity and ease in day-to-day experiences.

"This 'Blister' scheme to view the Sun? What ~ Riverstrike emulates a clownish personality shaking his hands irresolutely in the air ~ Up close and personal? My goodness, what can that lead to?"

"Blindness?"

"Or worse, or much worse." Riverstrike whimsically smirks, "Ah yes blindness in two ways: One from not seeing the massive waste of resources to realize this concept, and secondly, from the damage to the billions of retinas it will cause!"

He is quick to refrain from his amusement adding, "However, I would invest in the concept if any financial return were expected."

Riverstrike gesticulates waving his hands in the air, "Why to travel ninety-three-million miles to the Sun when on a good day they very well can blind themselves from Earth without as much of investment as to stare at the Sun?"

He grows silent, suddenly deep in thought upon reflection of this statement he spins to stand from his seated position to face the overlay, "We are easier to achieve the growth of the human population than the economy needed to support that growth."

Marveling at the overlay depicting the result of the top-secret classified Spark Creation Genesis mission, "Interstellar colonialism is a concept that time has come to be implemented and utilize to facilitate an economy to support population growth."

Riverstrike's attention is diverted by the subtle reflection in the overlay screen of a silhouette entering the conference quarters from behind ~ he surmises, "They go hand in hand. What do you say Janalake?"

"I suppose they do. It is a noble cause you plan!"

"Yes, it is." He takes a moment to check his breath by cupping his right hand briefly over his mouth and blowing. His hand quickly lands on his side as he turns to face her. "Do you know Janalake what I like about you most?"

"No, not what you like most about me," she speaks with authority as the commander of the Zealot Sentinels, "I only know what you expect from me."

"Good," Riverstrike replies coquettishly, "One thing at a time, but it's the increased stimulation of my circulatory system, literally and metaphorically."

"You reference to maintaining the gain of monetary units as circulatory?"

"Yes, that is particularly good Janalake. The analogy does not escape you. RAKLAV was first created three centuries ago to collect data on the populace to define the wants and needs of individuals to better understand and reap the rewards of the consumer debt slaves they are."

Riverstrike is pacing around studiously admiring her as he speaks, "And now RAKLAV must maintain accountability of our 'human capital' by indoctrinating and conditioning all of our Glass Planet Population Journal, and refugees from the vivarium societies who hope to defect from their controlled environs and to join the GPPJ."

"Have I not performed up to your expectations Minister?"

"Most certainly you have Commander Janalake," Riverstrike stops pacing positioning himself directly in front of her. "For now, we expect you to detain a pair of refugees not enrolled in the GPPJ."

"Where to find them?"

"The problem is they emerged from the Sahara Jungle and were detected by surveillance, but before the painted wolves were able to secure them, they were assisted and made their escape."

"Should be no problem tracking them down. Who intervened to prevent detainment?"

"A craft called 'Blister,' as to imply the effects of soaring past the Sun at close range. I know, pathetic, but extraction of refugees from The Glass Planet population journal would cause an uproar!"

"I understand, but I wouldn't foresee any problem if executed covertly."

"No, of course, you wouldn't," Riverstrike rescinds his expression of his emotions by releasing muscle tension flexing his back, shoulders, and neck. Closing his eyes, he breathes in deeply, then slowly exhales.

Janalake is looking on curiously for she knows nothing of the GPI being a refugee herself fitted with the oppressive Zealot Sentinel interface better known as ZSI.

The ZSI allows for awareness of her assigned orders and only how to execute them. The ability to experience emotion is curbed limiting her inventiveness, as tactical thinking and enforcing the will of Minister Riverstrike is all that is required of her.

"What I need from the Zealot Sentinels is the reconnaissance on one Marcel Etrion's course of action and of equal importance, to obtain the refugees under the guise of population journal to be fitted and accounted for in their roles."

"As Zealot Sentinel inductees?"

"Congratulations Janalake, your deductive reasoning skills are impressive. I wish you to keep up the excellent work."

Janalake acknowledges with a slight nod of her head before turning to exit. She uses every inch of her backside to arouse Riverstrike who reveals a salacious smile in the belief that his desire for her is not to be long delayed in satisfying.

Riverstrike's infatuation with Janalake derives from his envy of her human nature. To claim the title 'Commander of the Zealot Sentinels' is not in name only. The confidence, trust, and her biography offer broad appeal as a proletariat whose rise from obscurity has earned devotion from a large portion of the ZS ranks.

Vulnerable for multiple reasons, foremost her prolonged lack of intimate relations involving love; Patrick is the only source of admiration she has ever known, at least the only one to leave a lasting impression on her.

The anguish of her current longing is unclear to her as her understanding of what it means to be a woman, the component of giving and receiving love is lost upon her, as is any expectation of awareness of child rearing and childbirth. After indoctrination to the Zealot Sentinel interface her heart and mind are conditioned toward servitude and obedience, in any aspect, way, or form to Riverstrike's desires.

From her point of view, in the limited scope of awareness restricted by the ZSI and her prolonged isolation from the real world, her activities are a routine performance of her duties in her livelihood of control as commander of the Zealot Sentinels.

"Besides," she would console herself, "My expenses are paid."

"Will you require my presence at this time?" Asks Simon who has been standing silently off to the side of the room.

Riverstrike shows no feelings in addressing his most senior aide, as he is lost in lusty thought when Simon burst in with this question.

"Simon? You said the painted wolves were activated for the search and apprehend of the refugee subjects by nanobots?"

"They were detected by surveillance Insectebots in the Saharan rain forest. These reconnaissance images are from one of our 'Bombus Traversalis bumblebee' models. An image of the woman's face is in complete detail."

As the image constitutes a three-dimensional capture the display is of a blonde hair female whose facial features include a stunning bone structure, perfect contours from the jawbone, high cheekbones, a petite nose, and full lips.

The Minister is awe-struck, "She's stunning; Can you bring up the image of the male subject?"

"Yes, but it is at an angle as he never truly stopped in place with his face in a straight-on position to the surveillance Insectebots."

"Not once, in how long of a time?"

"The Insectebots are maxed out after five minutes of content capture."

"Five minutes? What century are we in?"

"The decision was made by you twenty years ago."

"Why would I say, 'Five Minutes,' it's ridiculous."

"To the contrary. That decision has diverted trillions over that time into the ETHW. You were motivated by the rarity of refugees appearing in the middle of the Saharan jungle, opting for a presence over the quality of surveillance."

"Ah, yes, of course, I remember ~ it's still paying dividends, originally gave me a tremendous boost as an influencer."

The image of the male provides a vividly detailed profile of his face. The Minister views the image and smiles with pure delight in the recognition of the male's identity.

"Do you see Simon, do you recognize the bone structure of this man's face, the physical stature, the way he carries his gait?"

"He has a slight resemblance to my own Minister, except his stature is 'scrawny.'"

"I forgive you for your bias because this is an incredible circumstance! It is, in the end, the female I am taken by; she is whom I am most invested in, Simon."

"Yes, Minister, if you say so."

"Simon, oh Simon my boy, you're lucky you have me to credit for your existence! You cannot understand what I am feeling at this moment as emotions are too complex for you to handle."

"Yes Minister, I do recognize your excitement."

Patrick shakes his head in annoyance, "Come on Simon, let's have a look at our SCG mission."

5

Spark Creation Genesis

Standing above the 'Spark Creation Genesis' mission control room on an observatory deck with a deep space telescope positioned to track Prometheus One, the highly classified into non-existence status 'God Particle' delivery vessel, Riverstrike views the 'space zero' event area two light years away. "Over twelve trillion miles away and we have an outstanding view from right here in our Dark Nest!"

They descend from the observatory platform to locate the captain assigned to oversee the one-thousand-fourteen-hundred current Prometheus probes missions and the tens of millions of ZS operations staff located in both space stations and the RAKLAV and ZS Mars HQ.

There are three-dimensional video display hubs receiving images from deep space orbs monitoring various nebula, comets, celestial bodies, and planetary solar light systems.

Riverstrike is especially interested in 'Prometheus One' as an achievement rivaling the purpose and function of 'the God particle.' Capable of elements to be powered by nuclear fusion in the cores of Stars, mostly converting hydrogen into helium and releasing vast amounts of energy, under the umbrella of the 'Spark Creation Genesis' mission, Prometheus One is expected to explode into a medium size star three times less massive than our own Sun.

Intended to provide a more local outpost to accommodate travel to Alpha Centauri from Earth's Solar system, the newly manufactured Sun will have a space station network in place achieving a suitable temperature for surface water to remain liquid and a circular orbit sustains a distance necessary for the development of plant-based food sources. The ecological systems are developed with natural elements of oxygen, carbon dioxide, nitrogen, and hydrogen provided by the two hundred years of mining the asteroid belt for minerals essential to

Terra-forming intricate planetary designs.

Technologies involving interdisciplinary sciences from biology to physics allow the creation of self-eradicating structures from roads to houses to atmospheric enrichment monitoring apparatuses. A complete societal infrastructure for immediate economic activity will require some assembly, but the essentials for survival will be firmly established.

It Is one thing to launch and navigate the Prometheus orbs through space, but to hazard many landings in distant solar light systems throughout the Milky Way is to invite chaos and the form of the complete unknown. To provide a road map for future generations to explore as a logical next step after the establishment of the SSN, then the enormously popular Fra Mauro crater Lunar City on the Moon, and out to the Martian Metropolis including the ZS headquarters on Mars, provides evidence to human capabilities to confidently explore, expand well into the Milky Way for the Next Millennium. Ultimately travel to all points beyond the asteroid belt leading to real estate development, and both terrestrial and gravity-controlled space cities spanning twice the Earth's capacity to support life will gain popularity and the support of the GPPJ. The case of sustaining human populations in deep space must be proportionate to the size and strength of the economy that allows for a successful operating infrastructure.

Riverstrike gestures to Simon waving two folded hands pointing the way down from the operations control room platform to the operations deck.

No sooner do they get to the bottom of the stairs when an officer walks over to greet them.

"Hello Minister, the pleasure is mine."

"Knock off the bullshit junior. Have you prepared to give me an update son?"

Captain Patrick Riverstrike Jr. better known as 'Captain Junior' for clarity's sake, is a slight edge taller than his father, with a slender build in comparison to the Minister's stout, broad shoulder frame.

"Nothing has developed in the past twenty-four hours. Other than minor glitches in several communication link feeds, and the occasional malady caused by weather events such as sandstorms or radiation field disturbances. I'm sorry father, there is nothing significant to report."

The Minister is always solemn in the mood when there is a lull in discoveries. Meaningful discoveries can take years if not decades to register. Many of the fourteen-thousand-five-hundred-forty- three orbs are dozens of light years away, and transmissions sent decades ago will be received unexpectedly without notice of pending arrival. The tens of millions of staff members comprising ZS personnel work in shifts around the clock meticulously operating signal receptors.

Captain Junior is second in command to the staff senior officer Admiral Barcarui, responsible for controlling the SCG mission reconnaissance and data evaluation.

The Captain is a wire-thin man with a boyish look of twenty-one because he received the Condorcet procedure prematurely in the initial phases due to being Minister Riverstrike's only offspring.

His father was aged sixty-five years when the initial phase was administered. Benefits from the Condorcet procedure had an immediate effect on his libido. The Condorcet procedure was unable to do the same for Junior's mother Lauren, the Minister's estranged wife, leaving her to die of natural causes. Eligible on her eighty-fifth birthday, she benefited from a prolonged life span of one-hundred-eighteen years, passing away in Twenty-One-Zero-Four.

Her aged brain was spotted with patches of plaque. On her brain tissue, the plaque debilitates the motor functions first. She was paralyzed from the chest down for the final ten years of her life. Her internal organ function began to fail, and life support left her clinging on to sustain internal organ regeneration function.

She may have survived if her vital organs were cloned, but her brain was neurologically deteriorating with total loss of cognitive capabilities. Vital organ replacement would only prolong the suffering. Minister Riverstrike made certain for her to sign the divorce papers on her deathbed in a barely legible, feebly faint sprawl of a signature.

She died before Captain Junior had a chance to say goodbye.

6

Interrupted

It was once just a dream to think humanity should become a close-knit tribe of twenty-two-billion strong! Without extreme divisions in social-economic classes, the world is abundant with opportunities for life experiences realizing capabilities, and talents, and exploring passions as freedom permits an unlimited potential to create anything imagined.

"With this unlimited potential comes great responsibility. As famously said by revolutionist Thomas Paine, it is the preeminent qualification: 'The World is my country, all humankind are my brethren, and to do good is my religion.'

"The Glass Planet community, the technological biological organism connecting our minds, our hearts, our honor, and our fortunes towards the advancement, preservation, and unbridled pursuit of fulfilling our mutual promise to share freedoms from tyranny, greed-fascism, and hatred."

The Chief Administrator for the World Organization for Children's Health (WOCH) is addressing thousands of families in an outdoor amphitheater, broadcast to all corners of the GPPJ.

"It is the protection against any oppression of human rights enforced by spirit alone. The spirit in the faith of the cycle of life, a common interest all societies embrace: To create aesthetics supporting civilization to span eras or not, with the eventual erosion of these aesthetics being imminent, the eventual demise of an invention portraying nature as itself, cannot defy the rules of nature.

"Therefore, a metric of truth emerges with each creation, with each erosion. Every outcome registered in the GPPJ from an individual's life experience will impact their station in life, and more importantly, the metaphysical health beyond existence.

"Of course, three hundred years ago the introduction of toxic cell reduction methods, known as the Condorcet procedure, was designed for treatment and cure of internal organ damage caused by disease or abuse as well as to correct genetic imperfections, therefore playing a significant role in eradicating illness and disease from human existence. The result is a vivid example of the benefits of cellular health.

"Being a poor, uneducated peasant from Colombia, scrounging for scraps to survive on, living hand to mouth for basic survival did nothing to promote my chances of receiving the life-extending anti-aging treatment.

"It was twenty years later when I was age forty-seven-years old before the Condorcet procedure was available for mass application. The adverse effects of global warming at the time were threatening all existence on Earth and only then under dire circumstances did the self-determined entitled ultra-wealthy elitist decide to make available the procedure for the entire world population, for better or for worse.

"The hope was that the Earth may be saved with longer lifespans and genetic engineering of nutrition. If not saved, then in desperation to acquire and retain information over hundreds of years anticipating a rapid succession of scientific and engineering breakthroughs.

"What response from this comment elicited twenty-two billion GPPJ the impulse of love, harmony in thoughts shared with satisfactory enlightenment and awareness of innate human beauty.

"Two initiatives were mandated for the creation of the vivarium societies. Mandate One: Reverse the climate hazards footprint created by 'fossil fuel' technologies as quickly as these hazards developed within. Mandate Two: Engineer technologies to transform marginally similar planets to Earth's composition vital statistics inhabitable for humans to populate.

"I flourished despite the fact I was forced to wear the pains of anguish, humility, and shame on my face caused by the prolonged exposure to unrelenting poverty defining the penultimate station in civilization, second only to death itself.

"Truths, as with time, prevail over liars, machinations, deceitfulness, and all human corruptions. It cannot be repeated enough. The source of contempt toward human fellowship is revealed through their permanence, the persistence of truths, and inexhaustible time merely being.

"It is avarice, rapacity, and covetousness. It is greed, the antithesis of what makes living a whole healthy cycle of life for all of human existence possible.

"Greed is counter-intuitive to the reliance of trust on each other for mutual security, enrichment, and procreation with stern emphasis on learning empathy, compassion for the frail, hungry, thirsty, ignorant, diseased . . .in dire need of a roof to sleep under like I was three-hundred-years ago in the time of fascism's decline.

"It was at that time I took this pledge: 'My name is Roberto, and I am willing to commit myself to contribute all of my industry in every waking moment in support of the 'wellbeing' of the human condition.' The 'wellbeing' cannot be repeated enough if we are to live in a just society, in concert with our passions equally."

Roberto's transmission holds Catherine and Jürgen in reflection, his experiences speak to the context of a fellow Twentieth Century citizen.

Marcel and Qyxzorina have disengaged from the platform to focus on signals of an incoming transmission.

"Qyxzo, there's a priority communique."

"Got it," she noted as she placed her security pass code to receive the message privately.

Jürgen has a puzzling expression on his face, "Marcel, correct me if I'm wrong, but hasn't the first mandate already accomplished?"

"It has, for the most part," Marcel responds casually, "The technologies are in use, yet require an unyielding operation."

"He mentions that 'mandate two' involves engineering technologies to transform marginally similar planets to Earth's composition. What is being 'done' exactly? I am annoyed by the vagueness of the description."

Marcel offers a relaxed smile, "The objective has been achieved with the Terra-forming biophysics developed in the last seventy-five years. The capability to transform alien planets can be conducted with pioneering probes guided to their destination planets from the Dark Nest space station."

"That is tremendous for the expansion into I space. What a genuinely amazing prospect. If the reason for the vivarium societies is achieved, then why do they continue to exist?"

Qyxzorina breaks in, "Marcel?"

"Yes?"

"RAKLAV Agents are tracking us."

"What does 'RAKLAV' mean?"

"We have visitors from 'Reconnaissance Assessment of Knowledge for Legal Authorized Validation.' The bureaucracy monitors the population control and oversight of the ZS. They want to process the two of you."

This talk of the process has a demeaning quality with the air of nonchalance in her tone, Qyxzorina and Marcel are holding us hostage for ransom, futuristic pirates trafficking time refugees, like us, to ransom for a considerable wealth boost.

Marcel in his aspiration, or desperation to launch Blister Sun Star Tours can be undermining the 'wellbeing' of the human condition by selling us out? What if given our station in life as refugees, we are being marginalized from equal treatment?

There is only one way to get straight answers: direct questioning.

"By the way, we were meaning to ask ~," I ask fervently, "Why did you rescue us? Or did you abduct us?"

Qyxzorina receives the question with mild disappointment, "No abduction, only rescuing took place."

"We should get a move on! We will be compromised by RAKLAV tracking our current position."

Qyxzorina expresses confidence by appealing with open eyes and raising her palms, "There is no reason to run Catherine."

I think she is patronizing me, "Why not?"

"Your situation is not uncommon to us," Qyxzorina offers further reassurance, "It is explainable, but right now we need to get the two of you refitted from The Glass Planet to an earlier 'Zealot' model."

"Zealot? Sounds wonderful. Why Zealot?" Jürgen is agitated by the sudden occurrence placing him and myself into another disturbing circumstance.

Marcel consults Jürgen, "If I point to show you the Sun, do I have to tell you it is yellow?"

"RAKLAV agents are engaging us in suspicion of criminality against the 'wellbeing' of the human condition."

"Of what?"

"Or of the conspiracy theorist," Qyxzorina resolutely states, "Against what many view from the fascism of change." She laughs whimsically.

"Call it what it is," Marcel reiterates, "The last bastion of fascist oppression is where the culpable can be found!"

"The last bastion of fascist aggression?" This statement reminded me of one thing, "The 'Dark Nest' Astro outpost positioned on the edge of the asteroid belt?"

"Astute perception," Qyxzorina praises, "The Council of Space Station Governors are always subject to a conspiracy of greed-fascism has given their control over expansive jurisdictions."

"Operations of the space station network for one," Marcel warns, "They can do worse. They dictate the business opportunities based on kickbacks, greed-fascism."

Jürgen is bewildered, "Bloody hell this sounds corrupt, typical enough. 'Two-face' politics beholden science, the special interest."

Marcel is pleading his case to Jürgen, "The moral value system is heightened for greater self-responsibility and loyalty to the law in respect of the 'wellbeing' of the human condition. Financial corruption is a direct offense to the 'wellbeing' of the human condition. It is most vile of betrayals in all of humanity, greed-fascism."

I find Marcel's passion for his underlying convictions in earnest, "Will they be after us for punishment?"

"No, Catherine, punishment is not plausible," Qyxzorina consoles me, "We will protect you, just do as we say."

"How does the refitting affect us?" Jürgen's agitation is reaching a new level of defiance, "Can you at least tell us that?"

"For one, you will have no recollection of the knowledge you have obtained," informs Qyxzorina.

"Great, amnesia all over again!" I offer a smile toward Jürgen to ease his anxiety.

Marcel gives solace, "Your knowledge is available once you are refitted and re-formatted to The Glass Planet."

I look at Jürgen face to face, "Feeling surreal?"

Jürgen sheds a nervous laugh, slightly faltering as if his legs were made of rubber.

"Qyxzorina, will we be aware of our feelings, and emotions?"

Marcel initiates, "Your emotional and creative intelligence will be compromised. Your ability to reason, rationale, and assertion of thoughts intact ~ but suppressed."

Qyxzorina offers Marcel a look of incredulity on her face staring at him as if reprimanding him for his careless exaggerations.

She moves her left arm around my shoulders speaking with calm wisdom, "You will not be able to express empathy or compassion for others' suffering. You may witness some terrible actions toward innocence where your deepest source of feeling in your heart may cry if not altogether break."

"What's the next part, Marcel?" Jürgen's voice spikes as his anxiety exasperate as if facing inevitable doom.

"You will be subject to obey commands and unwillingly relinquish free thought to acquiesce to security protocol. You will become a Zealot Sentinel, while in the process of your knowledge assessment."

"That's just great!" Jürgen throws his hands up in disgust.

"Allowing complete mind control to access everything we know is alarming. It's not even the dignity of 'allowing,' being violated is more like it. What could be so important about our mundane existence to merit such a violation of our personalities? This is unquestionably fascist disregard for human decency."

"What do you know?" Qyxzorina reasserts, "The good news is you will know nothing that will incriminate you. Unless the process locates memories stored in the deep recesses of your brain, and this information is withdrawn for interpretation."

"Why? Truly, what is it they expect to withdraw from us?"

"Catherine," Qyxzorina uses her actual voice soothingly, "No need to worry, this bridge is inconvenient but will prove significant."

"Will it? Is that what you consider 'inconvenient'? The violation of my subconscious, an unwilling participant in this Zealot processing of human identities to verify we fit into the Glass Planet roll calls?"

"Population journal," Marcel awkwardly offers in clarification.

"You are not in the GPPJ yet to enjoy all rights; it is so once you pass over and return from this indoctrination. I understand your concerns about the violation. Act in deference, this is a different reality based on evolving attitudes associated with the growth of knowledge collected over the last several centuries."

The next moment my mind is aloof, fading as I view Jürgen lying beside me already unconscious of our formatting to the ZSI.

I am at ease as I fade into the darkness.

7

ZS Indoctrination

The Mars Simulator Facility is of top-secret classification and therefore is constructed on the most desolate of Martian deserts, half a world away from the urban areas.

This facility is an intricate division of the Zealot Sentinel HQ and an adjoining training facility.

A RAKLAV cruiser, red is the current color of the design of the cruiser resembling a shuttle, but unlike a shuttle that is incapable of travel beyond the exosphere, a RAKLAV cruiser performs high-velocity speeds, six-hundred-thousand-miles-per-hour in zero to sixty minutes, without running the elevated risk of disrupting the SSN. The RAKLAV interplanetary cruisers can change color schemes and shapes of cosmetic elements due to a physical metallurgy technology affording the chameleon activity.

This cruiser is a medical shuttle, the first responders always have cutting-edge cruisers and transports in general. The patients on board are the time refugees whom Riverstrike desperately seeks.

The medical cruiser lands effortlessly on the landing platform illuminated to a one-mile radius around the landing platform. The gurneys levitate out of the cruiser and into the awaiting ATV transport caravan, readied to maneuver into the HQ for express access to the indoctrination blocks.

The bay doors of the warehouse-size indoctrination block slide open in a blink. The interned subjects are escorted through the primary entrance. They are placed there until other refugees to The Glass Planet will undergo the same trans-formative conditioning.

There are hundreds of other capsules placed in the warehouse-sized hall designed to break one's will of dignity, self-respect, and self-identity to become malleable personalities to conform to the understanding of their existence serving at the will of the Supreme leader Minister Riverstrike and Zealot Sentinel Commander Janalake.

Only if they knew how fragile their lives are, how life is under the weight of daily adversities. It makes no difference when it no longer matters to them, and this indoctrination intends to have them continually move on with one purpose as the defenders of the GPPJ.

The capsules are of a lightweight utility design perfect for mass use with a sleek metallic-charcoal-gray color on the exterior, there is a sound like the undoing of a plastic zip lock bag as the capsule lids recede into the body frame revealing a one-size-fits-all contoured interior.

After injection into the capsule, a hyperactive steroid rudely awakes the occupants from their induced slumber.

I am jolted into awareness by a sudden surge of adrenaline, and I view Jürgen gasping to gain his breath as I howl at the moment my body convulses to an upright posture. The dry heave and sneeze tickle my nose forcing me to squeeze it cutting oxygen off to my brain momentarily. Hearing him taking in oxygen copiously is something to rejoice about.

Regaining his bearings, Jürgen leads us to the oddly luxurious contoured units.

Our attention is drawn to another refugee in terrible distress, "No, I won't go!"

I see a woman being coaxed by several other refugees to enter one of the diagnostic modifier cells.

Three drones arrive taking positions around the woman.

A command is made "To break up this insubordinate behavior. You are all subject to severe discipline."

A command is heard to "move out of the capsule and into the diagnostic modifier."

There is a loud distinct cracking sound and to our horror the insubordinate becomes laid out, slain before our eyes, then carried out by the drones, floating the motionless cadaver out of the cell block.

"You're a mindless scourge, you have twenty seconds to obtain a seat and secure yourselves." The male voice is stern and emotionless, "Do not fail this command or else lose your life, as worthless as it is, you all should be very grateful for these twenty seconds of mercy."

Most refugees react in dire panic to obtain a seat and strap themselves in.

One very anxious and confused refugee is desperately trying to fasten into a cell gurney, but the frantic soul screams as a pathogenic sedative are emitted within the cell. Once penetration of the skin is achieved and makes its' way into the cerebral cortex the frantic soul transitions into a docile man.

A profound display of impermanence as his body is rapidly lifted above all others on its way out of the cell block onto who knows where?

The stern, emotionless voice of a male warning against 'any level of insubordination is to be dealt with the termination of your life' bellows through the cell block in sound-like flooding waters flowing until bodies are submerged underwater in fear.

There is a series of panels with a suspended platform where a man appears wearing a face disfiguring mask. It is a clear, transparent mask with qualities of distorting the appearance and voice of the one who wears it.

"Each of you contributes to the one, and no one of you is an individual."

There are smatterings of disgruntled murmurs and echoes of dissent in the form of indiscernible words from the compromised refugees.

"To not be misunderstood by you vile, insignificant scum of the Earth, your choice is simple: Accept subordination or accept death."

He pauses as he surveys the refugee recruits.

"Ironically it is not your choice, as the pure definition of your subordination is that you have no choice; Refugees like yourselves are a burden to society to suspend highly fulfilling, uplifting, fortuitous lifestyles to be troubled by the needs of barbaric, complaining in ignorance displayed in your beliefs, from more primitive eras in human history? Worthless ill-fated imbeciles, who seek acceptance from delusional entitlement."

My neurological system is under attack. Pain pierces every portion of my body as though needles and knives are thrusting into my feet and my hands. The muscles in my legs knotted in a wrench, the very muscles twisting themselves. I can hold out no longer as my screams tear through the chamber.

Jürgen convulses and writhes in pain from crippling electrocution. His body soaks in dripping sweat, and he displays the tell-tale symptoms of physical dehydration and signs of the searing assault on his mental abilities from the added trauma to his nervous system.

Janalake stands in an observation room viewing the secretive indoctrination process. A robotic painted wolf is by her side to be activated and deployed at her discretion.

RALKAV is more than a domestic census bureau, a mere cover for their actual purpose to conduct operations and analytics of personality profiles to determine consumer debt slaves from those who demonstrate an ability for upward economic mobility.

This analytical-driven approach is consistent with maintaining the security of the Glass Planet Population Journal by preventing the infiltration of refugees with the potential ability to perceive weakness and jeopardize the sanctity of The Glass Planet. The system is a scandalous venture and rebelling against it by disrupting the consumer debt slave establishment will expose to the GPPJ the code of greed-fascism Riverstrike and the economically elite governors of the SSN operate under.

Although she values her role as the senior authority official, she has experiences of reticence, lack of empathy, and compassion for refugees instilled in her by the ZSI.

The several hundred innocent humans writhing in excruciating unrelenting merciless torture churn a fire in her heart. The passion for this fire in her heart is ignited by her anger, sourced from a truth of nature she identifies with emotionally, but quickly subsides with the oppression of her feelings by the ZSI.

The refugees are accepted as Zealot Sentinels in training these recruits dwindle the concepts of individual freedoms into malleable wills, blank slates for personality replacement, impressionable as what Riverstrike describes as "a new generation of babes being ushered into the physical world via the reproductive gaits of women." Though it makes her all warm and fuzzy about her involvement, having heard Riverstrike use the phrase "via the reproductive gaits of women," she is entirely unaware of the meaning or purpose of the statement.

Riverstrike often compliments her, so she believes him, and with good reason. Patrick considers her special, why else would he entrust her, a refugee herself, to perform classified missions regarding societal control for economic exploitation and population safety?

Janalake supervises the fitting of the Zealot Sentinel interface on all recruits and administers the physical branding on the foot soles with encrypted scarring.

Simon monitors the progress of the conditioning to the Zealot Sentinel interface dutifully ensuring proper implementation before he makes his way over to Janalake.

"Anything wrong here?"

"No Simon, nothing is wrong. These are the two refugees the

Minister is looking for."

"Surprisingly easy to break them down, as if, let's say for supposed scientists they offered no objection to their oppressive conditions."

Janalake looks away from Simon dismissing him to carry on with his duties, turning her focus to Jürgen, she notices something very familiar about him.

Now fitted with the operational ZSI, he and I will only know one expectation of us, 'What are my orders?'

An announcement: "While embodied in the Zealot Sentinel interface any attempt to be heard, to speak out of turn, to struggle will intensify to pain and suffering."

Janalake must think of Pavlov's dog every time the edict is announced, inducing pain without the pleasure of positive reinforcement. Twisted.

"You are vicious liars, very disgraceful, born to lose I have never seen the weaker pathetic waste of flesh than we have here." Simon approaches close to Jürgen's head, "Let's go for a bit of resistance."

Jürgen holds a steely expression, not at all willing to speak.

"No? Not up to it? Let's see, I know, how about some heat on the feet?"

Simon swings Jürgen's legs from suspended in the air to the default position on the floor, except Jürgen's feet are placed in a footlocker that fills with acidic chemicals causing unbearably excruciating pain in scarring the soles with encrypted branding. Jürgen's shrill screams eerily manifest into a guttural, inarticulate cry for mercy.

"Yes, there we are. Make sure we get in between the toes. Yes, there it is," Simon humors himself.

The pain renders Jürgen semiconscious in a state of exhaustive shock.

Simon moves to take his seat on the platform, "Until the pain turns to pleasure, only then is complete subservience achieved!"

His focus turns to me, the tilt of his head with a sprawling spiderweb smile seen through his mask reveals my turn to be branded is next and will be equally as abusive.

Jürgen and I recover from the branding without visible scarring. We are in the company of six other recruits standing in pairs by the four edges of a square sparring arena in an otherwise vacant hangar facility.

A Zealot Sentinel comes marching into the center of the facility. He is of a large muscular frame and assumes a position in the center of the sparring arena.

"I am Sergeant Gian," he stands rubbing his hands, stretching his fingers, "We are to conduct battle in the center of the arena. Prepare to attack me with the intent to kill me."

At once the six other recruits take on a posture of physical preparedness, Jürgen and I are at the ready with fists up while maintaining a solid grounded position. Where the instinct to, or even the knowledge of how to use our clenched fists is beyond me.

None of the combatants are armed with weapons and we are confined to movement within the arena.

From opposite sides, two recruits approach to engage Sgt. Gian in battle. They sprint to thrust into an attack, one receives a grasp to the neck and under the strength of one arm, the hapless recruit is raised above the Sergeant's head.

The second recruit approaches Sgt. Gian's blind side to leap legs first targeting the right knee joint, the recruit bounces off him landing on his backside.

The Sergeant uses the recruit in his grip as a 'tenderizer' and heaves him over his shoulder and down onto the other recruit pinning both under his body then takes a seat on the two smothered recruits.

The four other recruits, two from either side of the Sergeant, are released into the battle arena.

Jürgen and I witness the other four remaining recruits circle around and attack at once from all four positions.

As they rush toward him, Sgt. Gian maneuvers to leverage the floor executing roundhouse kicks rotating on his back foot taking out their lower legs, disabling them one at a time with knockdown force and rebounding to clasping each by their ankles. Swinging them around, one at a time knocking out the four attackers before flinging their bodies carelessly across the arena.

Sgt. Gian turns to focus his ire on Jürgen and me, "I WILL CRUSH YOUR BRAIN!"

Commander Janalake emerges from the control room, "Sergeant Gian cease the training exercise."

Sgt. Gian walks off the platform grunting his frustration along the way as he exits the arena.

"I spare you from the futility of this exercise, as no doubt you would prove to have an insignificant effect against the dominance of Sgt. Gian."

We are escorted through dimly lit corridors connecting to nodes where there are entrances to several corridors leading in multiple directions. Within the first node, the Zealot Sentinels divide us into two groups of four leading each group in separate corridors. We dare not speak unless we are spoken to and the ZS are not interested in open discussion as they maintain expressionless faces.

The security main entrance is monitored by security cameras discreetly placed above either side of the door panel that is a lighter shade of gray in contrast to the wall panels and steel flooring of the corridors. The door becomes translucent as the ranking ZS approaches it and marches through leading us into the living space.

The environment is a bit more inviting with high arching ceilings throughout a communal area divided into various platforms designed with specific functions and activities in mind. As we march through, we view people lounging about in comfortable furnishings, on other platforms, people engage in interactive entertainment, or it is a form of training station where a hundred people stand in small groups from four to eight persons as multi-colored orbs pass between them. The participants grasp, examine or merge with as though some energy, perhaps knowledge is absorbed into the ZSI shoulder mounts.

It is a bizarre scene as participants seem to enjoy the interactions while others appear sad, others are still in a state of anxiety, and crying and some are screaming in madness.

The enormity of the facility is gradually revealed as we continue our march into several subdivisions. Hundreds more people fraternizing, gauntleting to spar with each other as on foot or hovering about assisted by nothing other than gravity-defying boots. There appears to be excitement over the apparent testing of a body suit that endures flame and ice, while allowing the adorned participants superhuman strength by bending rods of steel and then inserting them, smashing them into walls resembling space station fuselage interior.

The codex projections of topographical depictions across Earth, atlases of the Solar system's planets, also the SSN, and anatomies of life in all its forms present an ambitious training regimen.

Announcements are overheard summoning groups of trainees to the task. Updates of activities of ZS operations occurring throughout the Solar system within the asteroid belt and the inner terrestrial planets and the three moons, Earth's moon, and the two small ones around Mars. Atmospheric music provides a meditative mellowness.

Our escorts lead us to a hovercraft located at the mouth of another spacious corridor. We are instructed by hand gestures to board and take seats in the first row of ten seats across. The hovercraft has about twenty-five rows. The walls on either side of the corridor have a series of columns alternating with arched doorways of classical Roman design.

In an instant, the hovercraft speeds off into the corridor vacant of any people and within a minute the destination is reached. We are instructed to follow. There is a large accessible area surrounded by at least two hundred dwellings on floor level. This architecture design is replicated vertically for dozens of stories above us.

The six ZS guards march us to a lift platform encased in a synthetic, hard Plexiglas material that upon jettisoning upward my heart jumps into my throat!

The lift continues upward for sixty-two floors before coming to a halt and the lift door opens allowing us to follow the instruction of the ZS guards down a very cozy passageway with door entrances every ten feet of wall between them. A door to our left becomes translucent and the four of us are ordered to enter.

Once inside the entrance the door solidifies behind us and we are left to explore the four rooms split division trainee living quarters, each furnished with a single bed, standing shower, private toilet, sink, and a beverage courtesy bar. The common room features a meal dispenser, and four workstations to complete daily assignments as indicated by the three-dimensional monitor globes' compendium index of disciplines.

I look around me and the room is empty in any other aspect, the walls are bare, the floors are a steely riveted mess and there is nowhere to sit other than in front of the globes where there is the basic metal chair without cushioning.

The four of us are standing in place observing one another without any effort to communicate, even with our eyes. We view each other, but like statues, we are non-respondent and cold. Some time passes as we remain in place without invocation to each other or any thought of hope beyond our present being. We stand in place for a lengthy period. There is no knowing for there is no observation of a timepiece, and we are dormant to calculate in our brains.

Feeling anxious, with no urgency or passion to realize how time is passing, it is to 'be best' to subjugate ourselves that we are captive to the limitations of our diminished cognitive skills that make us subordinates.

I recognize Jürgen, tall, with broad shoulders, blonde hair, and blue eyes, like me, our physique is well-toned muscle definition, healthy complexions and our teeth are white and square.

The other two with us are timid, having poor postures and haggard faces, dimly lit eyes with sagging jowls absent of many teeth.

Just then four faces appear, one in each of the four globes, drawing our attention we move closer to observe. A male speaks.

"Unlike a prison cell, there is a solid wall where jail bars would normally be and access is not restricted most hours of each day, of each week, of each month, of each year. Not much room as you can see. I am the Zealot Sentinel known only as Parsiak. I am your group leader."

A second head speaks, a woman with consoling brown eyes, "I am Sula. Your training is mostly physical, but there is the indoctrination into the Zealot Sentinel interface, as the means of achieving a conscience toward civilian life, understanding, empathy, compassion, awareness of intricacies and these are my primary objectives in your progress toward complete assimilation into the Zealot Sentinels, and the GPPJ. The clothing is standard issue utility uniforms supportive to the ZSI, and a complete cruiser suit with certification badges is the extent of our clothing, other than quality undergarments and footwear. The information and diagnostic learning will be daily for the time you remain here and there will be no deviance from your participation in the coming days, weeks, months, and years."

A third head speaks, a bald male with steely silver eyes, "I am Xiang Li. When we are activated, we train to fight. Hibernation occurs to gain sufficient sleep and maintenance of the healing of our wounds. Many fellow Zealot Sentinels could engage in combat training, therefore learning skills we find our proficiency in multiple fighting techniques in rapid acquisition as our bodies' muscles are properly conditioned to perform unlimited motions and maneuvers with great force. Maintaining stamina by exhibiting unlimited endurance and being capable of withstanding extreme physical abuse from physical assault are attributes necessary to obtain in completing the training successfully. You will acquire the stealth, the discipline, the wisdom, and the tenacity associated with the deadliest of martial arts known to humankind: Brazilian Ju-Jitsu, Silat, Muay Thai, Sambo, and Krav Maga with an intensity unmatched by your opponents' physical stature, you will achieve tactical dominance over them in the coming days, weeks, months, and years."

The fourth head speaks, "I am Janalake, I am the Commander of the Zealot Sentinel corps totaling nearly nine-hundred-fifty- million troops throughout the Solar system. We provide the security of humanity, against all threats foreign and domestic, whether to defend against aggression between entities or negligence to harm the GPPJ from their hand, we are sworn to our duty to protect the 'wellbeing' of the human condition at any cost, willing to sacrifice our own 'wellbeing.' When you are committed to gaining citizenship to the GPPJ, you must first prove yourself worthy of the trials and tribulations of ZS training. Only upon successful completion of your training will you be able to seek the good graces of the GPPJ and pursue the fulfillment of the promise for human preservation.

"Finally, you are subject to the scrutiny of Minister Riverstrike who presides over your destiny if you are deemed essential to the operations of RAKLAV, may it be to your honor and privilege."

Three of the four heads close leaving Parsiak to speak, "It is time for transcendental hibernation, you must take to your beds. When you awake you will find you're adequately prepared to execute your daily assignments. Over time, achieving capabilities in all disciplines will be essential for successful growth and assimilation into the GPPJ community.

"Thank you Parsiak," we offer flatly. The others proceed to their quarters. I turn to leave the room and proceed to lay on the single bed in my quarters.

No further preparation is required for hibernation, the nutrition is intravenous, and the entire training sequence is programmed for automated progression.

'Relinquish the heart and the mind will follow,' is my last independent thought before I descend into hibernation.

8

The Star Gazer Angel

This allegiance with Riverstrike will lead to launching the Star Gazer Sun Tours providing us with an ultra-capitalism rank!"

Marcel expresses through GPI reviewing files on the brain screen, "Riverstrike is inviting us for a meal of great consequence."

"Marcel, you have worked so focused for decades to develop this enterprise, it is amazing! And I am happy you decided on 'Star Gazer' instead of 'Blister' for the name."

"Thanks to you! I could not have made it this far without you Qyxzo!"

"I always knew you would make your dreams a reality. Now we can provide financing to the WOCH, and ACRES where orphans are provided sustenance, education for any discipline, and opportunities for adoption."

Marcel is attentive to the landing process of the Blister cruiser, but this distraction cannot shield him from revealing his vulnerability, "We could easily retire for thirty years and raise five or six ~"

Raising her eyebrows to this audacious suggestion, "How do you expect to get away with that? Let's start with one. Remember mister, ambitious accomplishments come with many responsibilities. The first two natural born, then any more we decide to adopt will be dependent on us for the most crucial years of their lives."

Marcel carries a tune in his heart nodding in appreciation to the woman who completes him, "I do love you."

"As I love you," She speaks affectionately, "The time has come, Marcel, to engage in giving the love back to the twenty-two-billion."

Marcel and Qyxzorina land the Blister Cruiser on the Innovation SS and proceed to walk through the docking corridor hanger; walking is an option; a kinetic conveyor belt is default if needed.

They enter the outer lobby and board a taxi auto and indicate their destination, the Surface restaurant.

The Surface restaurant is popular for brunch and business meetings. A formal solid color base interior design with comfortable rolling office chairs sporting bucket seats at glass tables.

Subdued neon lights with a range of colors from lime green to orange, pink, purple, yellow, and light blue swirl in projection.

As they enter the restaurant an 'orb' host guides them to Riverstrike's table location where he is seated in anticipation of his guest joining him.

Riverstrike sips from his whiskey glass and smiles toward them, "Qyxzorina and Marcel Etrion, a magnificent pleasure to have you dine with me."

Qyxzorina smiles graciously, "It is our honor to be invited by such an esteemed personality of The Glass Planet."

Marcel shakes his head in agreement, "We appreciate your interest in our endeavor."

Riverstrike smiles in pleasure at his guest's expression of gratitude, "You may call me Patrick. I prefer it."

Marcel, "Yes, Patrick."

"I thank you for your innovation in creating a transport with heat stress endurance, not to mention stress caliber of the Sun in its gravitational pull."

Marcel wholeheartedly agrees, "Yes. One of the primary benefits of the Star Gazer program is the slowing down of time while subject to extreme heat temperatures."

"Wait, you said 'Star Gazer' program? What happened to 'Blister' as the name?"

"'Blister' was a working title for the program. I decided," Marcel notices Qyxzorina's stare at him, "We decided to use 'Star Gazer Sun Tours' as the official name."

"Very good, 'Star Gazer' is a much better brand name. Congratulations on that. What is the secret to enduring the extreme heat temperatures as the Sun's gravitational pull slows time?'"

"Patented panel design with lithium nuclear coils transferring solar energy into creating extreme subzero temperatures to maintain structural integrity."

Riverstrike is taken aback, "Ingenious. To use the immense solar power to energize the coolant refrigeration design to sub-zero freeze neutralizing the extreme exterior heat?"

"Yes, it is, in so many words." Marcel gleams a smile, "The

sub-zero freezing is assisted by vents releasing any pressure and preventing undesired overheating of the coils."

"Creating a barrier," Qyxzorina interjects, "The frozen coils maintain the integrity of the exterior panels while maintaining room temperature in the cabin."

Riverstrike folds his arms pressing his right index finger over his lips in deep consideration, "The exterior panel's efficacy in heat deflection and radiation resistant material design is not compromised?"

"Never. We have hundreds of successful trials in research and development to engineer state-of-the-art advancements," Marcel passionately asserts, "That was the primary concern in the slow orbit induced by the Sun's gravitational pull. While aligning from a required distance allowing adequate resistance to the extreme conditions."

Qyxzorina pointedly suggests, "Have a look at a file I'm sending you Patrick."

"Received," he confirms concentrating on reading it completely before speaking, "How is the concept going to work without jeopardizing detrimental effects such as the lack of losing your ability for sight?"

"Great question." Marcel exhibits adamant confidence, "Viewing from the observation deck offers two options. The primary option is the specially designed windows with filters to protect from ultraviolet rays and heat density ratings three times above the Sun's temperature. The filters include glare reduction for viewing Mercury in its orbit. Option two is the use of monitors, on the deck and in each cabin room."

"We obtained all necessary patents, certifications, and verification of product performance ratings."

Riverstrike takes little time in verifying the information as legitimate, "Yes, you have my support, Marcel. With the prototype, I can see the potential."

Marcel is vociferous in his reply, "We have escalated the development from prototype to actual certified commercial tour ship specifications."

"How many tour ships are operational?"

"Currently twenty-three of the proposed sixty-four tour ships are in some stage of developmental construction." Marcel is fired up, "With your support, the remaining work on the twenty-three tour ships will be completed before the scheduled inaugural launch."

Riverstrike raises his eyebrows before he speaks, "What is your service schedule plan?"

Marcel becomes boisterous, "Each ship will travel an average speed of three-hundred-seventy-six-thousand-five-hundred-eighty-seven miles-per-hour."

Riverstrike is bothered by this statement, "There will be sixty-four shuttles, each with a capacity of . . .?"

"Two-hundred-fifty-thousand tourist and a crew of twelve-thousand-five-hundred one-time employees per tour."

"Why one-time employees per tour? I would think it would be beneficial for the employees to gain experience?"

"The skill level is menial; the Star Gazer Tour Ships are functionally independent of constant human monitoring. The revolutionary safety technology is innovative."

"No doubt, how long is the round trip?"

"Twenty-eight days plus two days around the Sun," Marcel announces precisely, "The average journey will shorten in time with propulsion upgrades over the two-thousand scheduled launches!"

Riverstrike touches on humor, "Certainly. It will take what, a launch every other day for five- or six hundred years to transport the current population of The Glass Planet?"

Qyxzorina gives her projections, "Four-hundred-fifty-five years, three-hundred-twenty-five days to serve twenty-two-billion people and that doesn't include the twelve-thousand per orbit one-time crew employees."

Riverstrike sits in reticence for a moment before lifting off the chair enough to pull on his blue velvet robe to stretch out wrinkles and 'dapper up.'

"We're talking two-thousand trips. There are many potential hazards to consider, and it is not a commitment taken lightly," Riverstrike raises his concern, "Everything would be on the line for all three of us."

"The benefit and reward will be legendary in contributing to the 'wellbeing' of the human condition," Marcel makes his strongest case. "With your investment, expect eventual tours around Venus and to Mars."

"Right. Nonetheless, Marcel, there's no immediate payoff in it for me. Once this becomes a bonded agreement, I may be put into a position of paralysis on other projects I need to build a public consensus for."

Riverstrike's voice reveals his depth of concern as he strains his vocal cords on the slightest breath, "In return for my long-term commitment I require the two of you to help me in confirming the origin of our mysterious fugitive friends."

Marcel and Qyxzorina exchange tepid expressions. Riverstrike gulps his beverage to quell the scratchiness in his throat.

"When will they complete the Zealot Indoctrination?" Qyxzorina asks, "It's already been five years."

"It all depends on the identification of their origin. They have excelled in their training, but for the life of me, there are no memories stored in the deepest recesses of their brains. I have tried all known techniques and technologies to reveal their path into this world; we see at first memory they were in a cave, but RAKLAV has not been able to confirm where despite narrowing the location to the square mile; Nothing known other than their first names and birthplace."

Qyxzorina would rather avoid addressing this issue if not for her concern about their 'wellbeing,' "Then you plan to detain them indefinitely?"

"I'm glad you asked," Riverstrike is put at ease, "I appreciate your empathy for them and will release them to you effective immediately. If the two of you can somehow gain identification of their origin, in the end, it will serve you in pursuing expansion of Star Gazer Sun Tours."

Qyxzorina grows curious, "Patrick, what is the relevance to you in confirming their identities?"

"It is related to extremely sensitive material dating back a few centuries," Riverstrike leans forward while placing his hand's palm to palm, "I can say an identification will be a game changer."

Marcel yields, "You've piqued my interest; in what way Patrick?"

Riverstrike consumes the remainder of his Wild Turkey whiskey, "In the way of monetary profit and preservation of the human race."

Marcel and Qyxzorina are startled by this assertion.

"Please, excuse my poor manners! I have my drink and have yet to offer you to place your orders."

Marcel defers, "Well, that's okay. Qyxzorina?"

Qyxzorina looks at Riverstrike's drink and points as she squints her eyes, "What are you drinking Patrick?"

"It's called Wild Turkey whiskey, a longtime friend of mine."

Marcel is disapproving of Qyxzorina, "Go ahead if you want."

"Too late. I just ordered a round for everyone."

"What the hell," Marcel turns jovial, "We should mark the occasion with a toast and a little old-fashion inebriation! I'll try one!"

"I have never known you to consume the hard liquor. I apologize to you in advance Patrick, we will be entering uncharted territory with Marcel momentarily."

"Why not? The sky is no limit!" Marcel boasts.

The drinks are served by a service Bot.

Raising their glasses Marcel dedicates a toast, "Cheers to the 'Star Gazer Sun Tours.' Our team will provide safety and security to the Sun!"

"And back again!" Qyxzorina quips already feeling tipsy from the initial sip of whiskey. She breathes in deeply to center herself then steadily exhales, "And back again."

"Cheers to that sentiment," the Minister tips his glass toward his lips, "and with that success, we can open Venus tours and then a line to Mars!"

Marcel expresses with full enthusiasm raising his drink, "Hear, hear, to that Patrick!"

9

Mars Runner Hook Up

Spontaneous Instant is grateful for the Moon Orbiter, the 'Clipper,' his parents gifted him for high school graduation last year. At nineteen, it is his first chance to venture off into weightlessness on his way to a four-month Moon vacation with fellow graduates a year ago.

This, a full year after graduation, was standard practice in observance of a coming-of-age celebration. There's a law prohibiting anyone under nineteen years of age from zero gravity exposure. He promised his parents he would not violate the law. He landed the 'Clipper' observant of The Innovator SS protocols, patiently taking his place in line behind other orbiters and business shuttles arriving before him instead of attempting to cut the line and causing havoc.

"Why does society pick on young yons with all these stupid laws?" Spontaneous Instant clamored to his closest friend and lover Gingi Grind, "You want to know what the reason is Gingi? I will tell you, it's the stuffy old shirts thinking we would be better off as Earth-landers so they can cram their lessons into our ears and assign us perpetually on field trips to study nature, agricultural history, migration history, and history this and that history! We haven't even scratched the surface on advanced quantum physics."

"I don't know Sponti, maybe we're not cut out for regular schooling."

Spontaneous Instant stops in his tracks, "What, damn straight we're not cut out for this imprisonment. They only put us through these diversions to keep us down, thinking we're too irresponsible to be trusted, like bouncing around space stations in orbiters all hours of the days of the weeks of the months of each year!"

"Ha! You are flowing now," Gingi noticing the boyish charm of her intimate other, "In six short years, we will be eligible for the

Condorcet procedure, and two hundred years from now this hurdle will be long forgotten and most certainly irrelevant."

Spontaneous Instant takes off in a full sprint to the Mars Runner prepared for departure located on the Innovator space station central launch pad for their new employer Star Gazer Sun Tours.

"What are you doing?" Gingi is fully aware of these sudden, unexpected actions from her boyfriend, "Don't take off without me!"

He reaches the interplanetary cruiser and enters via the crew door, into the navigator's chair fastening the flight harness properly placing his forearms on the armrests and gripping his hands to them.

"This board is intense," his face lights up like a pinball machine, "Why does this console read three-hundred-fifty-thousand-five-hundred miles per hour top speed?"

Gingi boards via the crew door to quickly seal the vessel's hatches for launch, "Don't plan on going that fast."

"No? Why not?"

"Marcel has a flight program set for the journey. Three-hundred-sixty-five-thousand-miles-per-hour is the speed limit given our inexperience."

"What! That is provocative."

Gingi is mildly amused, "Sponti, this is our first real assignment working for this awesome start-up company. Do you think they are going to entrust the two nineteen-year-old newcomers to travel the distance to Mars and back in like four weeks in a cruiser that can exceed traveling three-hundred-fifty-thousand miles-per-hour? This trip is sixteen days each way Sponti. It's better to keep distracted and leave the heavy mileage to the autopilot."

Spontaneous Instant laments, "The saga of the perpetual oppression on the youth from a cynical, conceited civilization if you can call it a civilization."

"Okay, I know it pains you Sponti, but at least you can examine the controls and get familiar with the procedures and protocol of navigating a commercial grade cruiser."

"True Gingi, that's why I love you," they pucker up and connect for a simple kiss. "Besides it takes an official commercial training program to get your interplanetary travel license first!"

The flight program prompts the occupants of the shuttle for the final time to fasten their harnesses to prepare for launch in T-minus thirty seconds.

"This is exciting," Gingi exclaims, "I cannot believe we're going to Mars!"

The countdown has reached launch initiation. The cruiser hovers twenty feet above the launch pad. They turn to smile anticipating the launch!

"The most amazing launch ever," shouts Spontaneous Instant as the nearby satellites surrounding the nearby space stations are visible for two-tenths of a second before they witness one-hundred-forty-thousand-miles of the SSN as a steady blur for fifty minutes more.

Then everything came to a halt, or at least it seems so.

Gingi looks down at the console to see the cruiser is rapidly gaining speed at two-hundred-seventy-thousand-miles-per-hour and climbing. "Sponti, look at the perspective: We're still accelerating tens of thousands of miles per hour although we can't sense any movement at all."

The view from the cockpit is a quiet, motionless star-scape reminiscent of the many nights they spent together in the past year looking at the stars from the Moon's surface.

"I want to go again please," exclaims Spontaneous Instant whose facial expression grew from 'awesome bewilderment' to 'ecstatic' once he eyes Gingi, "Was that too magnific?"

Gingi remains awestruck by the spectacular view of the Milky Way. "Yeah, it was great, but what do we do now?"

Spontaneous Instant thinks quickly, "Whatever we dam well want to do, who is to tell us otherwise?"

A few minutes later they are embracing in their birthday suits floating in weightlessness within the anti-gravity chamber.

Once the novelty of every young person's desire, the act of making love in weightlessness provides for unlimited versatility in taking positions, the limbs flexible and the joints malleable, without strain or muscle cramps. With experience over time, the novelty becomes an indicator of the two lovers' level of emotional commitment.

Their exertion of energy creates perspiration that beads up leaving contact from skin individually, droplets, spheres of moisture hundreds of them floating, they eventually collide forming fewer, but larger droplets of mass until at the end the one mass of perspiration floats above them as a blob of body sweat.

They dive into the sphere of sweat using their bodies to wedge the voluminous mass into two wobbling, shimmering balls of moisture.

Spontaneous Instant flails his arms about through one of the floating balls of sweat creating dispersion droplets momentarily suspended in separation before gravitating into one large ball again.

Gingi reaches for Spontaneous Instant's hand to lead him out of the anti-gravity chamber.

They communicate through their GPIs.

"That was quite a first," she comments. "I say not bad for a training facility."

"You know they have one of these chambers at the space station engineer technical center."

"Oh yeah? Mechanics always perform the required maintenance in space after making several 'practice' runs in one of these chambers."

"Gingi, you can perform repairs on the Mars Runner?"

"I have the certifications to repair cruisers, shuttles, and orbiters, but my permit is limited to 'in shop utility.'"

"What does that mean?"

"I'm not trained for 'in orbit' repairs. Now that I am nineteen, I can take the training to get certified. Marcel offers the training at no cost to employees."

"Hey, I'm hungry. You want to get some grub, Gingi?"

"Sounds good. Let's have snacks and bring them into the recreation hall for a round of 'Tangle Web.'"

"Yeah, let's game. With the physical environment, effects turned way up!"

"Oh, that will make for quite a mess."

"Isn't that what 'Tangle Web' is all about?"

"Not so much. This is more of a journey back in time," Gingi coquettishly implies. "It's about a way to better bridge the emotional experiences of people from all eras of human history."

They saunter from one recreation room to another until they enter the food dispensary area and pour thirty-two-ounce gelato shakes, falafel with pita, and couscous is served on a float-tote dining set hovering by them as they set down a different passageway.

Through a series of slide doors, they step into a lounge with a 'cocktail-organic' supplement dispensary. Tables with fifty-two chairs, four chairs to each table, are ghostly under the low lounge lighting in the quietude of a vacuum-sealed room in a cruiser traveling over three-hundred-thousand-miles-per-hour heading into deep space.

A few steps across the Milky Way graphic floor design leads straight into the recreational gallery.

"I enjoy parsley on the side." Spontaneous Instant grazes on the garnish he does have. "Hey Gingi, are we going to be okay on autopilot without being in the command deck?"

"The alerts are created at a radius of a half-million miles, detected from hundreds of thousands of miles out. We would have, I don't know, but I think one hour to respond ~ sounds right to me."

The Tangle Web is a plain, bare space. Gingi Grind comes over with a compatibility device to plug into their GPI for full bodily involvement, "From engaging the brain, the respiratory and the nervous systems, muscular and cardiovascular systems, as dictated by the inventions of our dreams." She sits on the floor urging 'Sponti' to join her, "The enlightened understanding of the intricacies and intimacies of people from past generations, and the stimuli of the society of their day are representative of a full emotional life in this holistic realm."

The space before them reveals an energy field in the form of a ten-foot-wide by twelve-foot-tall rectangle subtly pulsing, a gentle, relaxing source of energy.

Spontaneous Instant notes, "This looks like there's some potential here."

Gingi looks towards the rectangle, "Where to start is the point of interest, and let us say nineteen-fifty-six?"

"I'm not so sure, the year would be the birth year of the male. What's his name?" Spontaneous Instant gets the answer from the GPI, "Jürgen."

"Here is the premise," Gingi points a forefinger to the air. "Family life has changed dramatically over the past several centuries, at least for the GPPJ, within those who create enough fortune to live to nearly six hundred years old.

"The law to have only two natural born children. The tendency for most people to have their first child is from one-hundred-twenty-five years to one-hundred-fifty. The child will be legally dependent on their parents for survival, intellectual, physical, creative, and mental health wellbeing until the eighteenth birthday. The final seven years of development concentrate on civil issues, the introduction to opportunities in most needed employment skills like the mechanical engineering fields, and anything to do with the SSN.

"The family scene played out in set circumstances, with selected family members, in a place that all ties into an emotional life vicariously experienced by us to evoke the mindset, emotional states, rationalizations, decision-making influences, outcomes from a particular time in human history.

"Look at the millions, billions of examples of family life and the many personalities intertwined in one family as in all families. In the past, before the Condorcet procedure, children were born fifteen to twenty children or more in a clan. Include cousins and uncles and aunts and a family became quite a clan.

"You could be four years old and have a baby as your younger sibling."

Spontaneous Instant makes a reasonable point, "In those days few people lived past one hundred years. The economy of everything has grown into something else."

"Sometimes I wish I had siblings to grow up with. A second child today is typically born somewhere around the mother's two- hundred-fiftieth birthday."

"Watch this," Spontaneous Instant folds his hands over his chest, closing his eyes in meditation. "A simulation of a family from the period those so-called 'time travelers' are from."

"The mid-twentieth century?"

"Homing in on the nineteen-sixties," he whispers enthusiastically.

"Not nineteen-fifty-six?"

"It's too early in Jürgen's life, and the woman . . ."

"Catherine."

"Right. She was born in nineteen-sixty-six. Jürgen will be ten years old by this time."

Gingi bursts out in laughter, "They are so old!"

"Ha, and probably the most ignorant people we will ever meet." "Not if you're counting the Appalachia Vivarium. Gun toads take the cake in ignorance and stupidity!"

The programming is complete, and the game simulator begins with an image of the skyline of Denver and Dallas-Ft. Worth from the twentieth century.

Basic statistical information on population, industry, place in migration, ecological stats, cultural elements, and events surface, major political movements were as momentous as the cultural movements and impacted the world as well as the United States of America.

"Unpopular wars of the time are a surprise to me Gingi," he points out. "I thought any war is unpopular?"

Gingi repositions herself from sitting cross-legged on the sofa seat to stretching them in front of her spreading her toes while yawning in a full gentle volume of air. "The world was emerging from the age of barbarism, the epoch of Pisces." Gingi yawns quickly, "It was the communication age proceeded by the information age and followed by the personal persuasion age when humans around the globe were unable to escape or resist the complete awareness of every human alive, and from the beginning of RAKLAV in the early twenty-first century, the masses were no longer just another number on a stat sheet, but with technology, growing generations became players on the stage of life and everyone would be held accountable for their actions."

"Well, obviously it has led to our society where you're either on the GPPJ or you are a citizen of a vivarium. Either way, you are accountable for every action you do or anything you speak about. It is only in the brain, with our thoughts for another one-hundred-years before the GPI allowed for cognitive articulation from a thought in one person's head being transmitted to an intended recipient who hears the thought, visualizes the content."

"The Glass Planet being the first recreational space station features the capability of relaying radio waves as well as thoughts from and back to Earth."

"Isn't it funny to think the GPI is like the glue that holds the people together?"

"The 'wellbeing' of the human condition became tantamount to all. And all of the transition from the age of selfish, greedy barbarism to the age of space inhabitation and the Economic Theory of the Human Will make the start of the epoch of Aquarius, one of human unilateralism with equality, love, and respect for the sacredness and miracle of life."

Gingi's face expresses confusion, "If the rumors are true that they disappeared from Earth in the summer of two-thousand-five, then where did they go to arrive in the year twenty-three-thirty-nine?"

"And without aging a second," Spontaneous Instant pauses for effect, "disappearing a good thirty years before the Condorcet procedure was first introduced to the wealthy monetary harvesters."

"Does that mean they're from the greed-fascist class?"

"It doesn't matter."

"Of course not. What matters most to you Sponti?"

"Gingi, it's you, I don't know if I can love anyone more than you."

"I wonder what life will become as our time passes by?"

"We will make enough capital to invest up to six-hundred years for both of us and our first child when we reach the time a little more than a hundred years from now."

"Then what?"

"You know Gingi, raise the kid to be a bad ass, multifaceted artiste, a renaissance man."

"Or a girl?"

"Renaissance woman," Spontaneous Instant wags his forefinger at her, "Shifty of you, I see what you're doing."

"What am I doing?"

"You wanted me to say renaissance girl instead of a woman. Trying to make me into a chauvinistic pig?"

"The gender of our firstborn is not my sincerest concern."

"No? Then what is?"

"When our firstborn arrives, I want to welcome our second child three years later."

Spontaneous Instant flashes a smile toward her in reflection of this orthodox statement.

"You do realize the potential financial risks are momentously high? Most couples want one hundred years to have proper capital to invest in their offspring's longevity."

Gingi reaches for the programming pod and corrals it to her stomach, "These days everyone is consumed by investing and purchasing their longevity, living impeccably moral lives when it comes to observing the 'wellbeing' of the human condition to remain in favorable status to the GPPJ. The GPPJ is a population of people whose values are displaced from a true bonding family unit. Watch this."

She activates a program simulation of young children, four of the siblings interact as siblings would from the newborn baby, then the second child is a two-year-old, the third child is a four-year-old and the fourth child is a six-year-old. So many times, mini-dramas, humor, humility, and life lessons that no longer occur in organic undisciplined ways today have to disconnect us in some ways from our natural, primitive instincts less we become reliant if not interdependent on technological intrigues.

The program illustrates a lifetime spent by siblings from birth to natural death. The files in the program include millions of examples of nuclear families with siblings in unlimited varieties of DNA make-up and the number of male siblings to female, gay, lesbian, bisexual, queer, and transgender, to every combination of ambitions, achievements, activities shared through life as siblings in various degrees of relationship.

"You see Sponti, unlike our lives without siblings, growing up together allows for unique bonds that inform the human condition in ways of emotional fullness. We are lost when your only other sibling is one-hundred-twenty-five years apart in age."

"I get it; the thing to do is adopt!"

"It's not quite the same thing."

"Maybe to you it's not. The newborn baby and the adopted baby will not preconceive themselves not to be siblings. Even if they bear no resemblance whatsoever. The exception is for Doppelgangers."

"Is it equally financially worth it to you?"

"Of course, we do not have the same responsibility to set our adopted child up with more than the standard one-hundred-fifty years. If we bring the kid up ETHW correct, then after eighteen years with us, the kid will have one-hundred-thirty years to extend the Condorcet procedure. No worries at all!"

Gingi sits up with her knees knocked, folding her arms with her elbows resting on her knees and her hands cupped over her nose with her forefingers pressing the bridge of her nose.

"That's bias thinking, Sponti."

"Or it could be having one-hundred-twenty-five years separation from siblings forces us to be independent, solitary, learning to cultivate an internal reserve of intellectual, emotional, and creative curiosity. These are traits for extended space exploration. Just a thought."

"Sponti, you are something. Thoughts? What do you think? Are they training grounds for ideas?"

"If you're trying to make me, think, Gingi Grind, it's a bad idea right now."

"Everything you communicate is at least a thought, Sponti. A thought can be a promising idea or a bad idea."

"Or an unbelievable idea, or a benign idea. I get it, so what?"

"So what? It makes all the 'what' of a difference. Learning values, insights into the truth of nature, to the structure of civilized life and livelihood is the awareness of ideas shared as the collective unconscious deems permissible toward living a prosperous, peaceful life, respectful to the categorical imperative of the 'wellbeing' of the human condition."

"Yes, it is the backbone of our morality, it is universally known."

"Not universally recognized, as there are humans who reject thoughts of civilized coexistence and by closing off the sunlight of knowledge they choose uninspired livelihoods, where ignorance and resentment reign true in relying on their naturally barbaric minds.

They lack basic skills of reasoning and rational thinking."

"You know Gingi, I'm feeling a bit barbaric right now." Spontaneous Instant lets loose his barbaric yawp.

A vigorous rocking of the Mars Runner has the two shaken out of their meditation as emergency alarms sound off.

They rush out of the Tangle Web studio and make their way to the main concourse above one level. The Mars Runner is responding to a close encounter as if crossing in the wake of a passing speed boat.

The sound of thousands of space pebbles pelting the exterior of the Mars Runner is heard from within the fuselage. The alert analysis detects an asteroid twenty times more massive than the cruiser soaring within mere miles of the defenseless ship.

Gingi is first to the flight deck taking a seat in the harness of the flight chair. Turning on visuals on a three-hundred-sixty-degree panoramic view.

"Scanners display a massive object, an asteroid undoubtedly had a near miss with us! The particles pelting the exterior shed from the asteroid as a cloud of space dust."

"This near miss on our first day into deep space? This trip is a little more cursed than I would have bargained for!"

"Sponti, think about it. The Mars Runner on autopilot evaded an asteroid, traveling way faster than us, easily over three-hundred-fifty-thousand-miles-per-hour and we are barely scratched."

"Think about it," he mimics her tone of voice, "The Mars Runner evades an asteroid approaching from the starboard side. Barely scratched becomes 'smashed to atoms' if the next asteroid approaches head-on."

In her most pragmatic sensibility, "Sponti, what's the point of thinking about it?"

He visibly transforms from an apprehensive state into relaxed confidence.

Gingi smiles in adoration, "There Sponti, stay in the moment, let it go. There's nothing to be gained by feeling trauma and worry."

He mindfully disciplines his breathing from tense to relaxed and deep flowing.

"Better, now let's get more baby-making experience in the anti-gravity chamber."

Outside of nutrition breaks, they spend most of the remainder of the journey crawling all over each other, in the spirit of exploration, in between hours of binging on a variety of entertainment in the cruiser's digital library and recreation suite.

Marcel included timed alerts synchronized to notify the crew of the expected arrival time to the Mars Zealot Sentinel Training Facility. The journey is fifteen days, twelve hours one way.

With this itinerary, the two lovers must transition back into professional work mode and press their attire, cleanse their bodies, and attend to proper hygiene every few days to stay in practice.

10

Political Entropy Wins the Day

Riverstrike is addressing the General Assembly including all Space Station Governors in virtual person across the SSN transmitting from the Dark Eagle Nest SS. In the past, he has advocated for the governors to form a coup to dominate the economy and control the direction of the future behind the staged scenes of a democratically free society and portray a false sense of security.

Fortunately, for many decades the council of Governors disagreed with and would keep Riverstrike in check from realizing his tyrannical ambitions.

Overtime Riverstrike has significantly increased its popularity index within the GPPJ, while creating innovations of technology impacting human development, such as housing adapted for adverse climate conditions and the tremendous vision for expanding the SSN, to the unprecedented, classified mission so vital to receive the designation of a 'non-existent-project' titled 'Prometheus One' under the guise of the SCG mission. Within his deepest desire is an ultimate achievement, to be like Prometheus, the Greek Titan who as a trickster, and an advocate for humanity, betrayed Zeus, and the mythological world of Greek gods to provide humans the mastery of fire.

"GAUDIUM ET SPES," is the way the Minister greets his fellow chairperson's heading the watchdog federations of the comprehensive study of all disciplines.

"Joy and hope to you as well, Minister." The chairpersons reflect his greeting with determined optimism. Nobody needs to feign their honest feelings here.

"These momentous achievements, these benchmarks of engineering, architecture, land cultivation of space science, and the overall passion of creating projects designed to protect and procure humanity, to be inclusive of all. Endeavors in Divine Providence toward the realization of the 'wellbeing' of the human condition during the last few centuries of human evolution have served us well."

Applause is given for these noble statements from within the Hall of Chairs to the reticent masses of the terrestrial Earth lander and every citizen of the GPPJ in the balance of learned and emotional responses pondering the truth inherent to nature.

"The great expansion into our Solar system through the commitment of the governments of all the world in these past few centuries, led by the spread across all Nations for the fervor of democracy born in the United States of America, and the 'reeling in' of a fledging Capitalistic economy that burst into an economic system unrivaled in the history of humankind, to an extreme of riches for the few created by the exploitation of the many, to ultimately find balance, fairness out of inequity and the economic abuse commonly referred to as 'Greed-Fascism.'

"This gives evidence of the immense virtue, common respect, and overall love of our mutual participation in this theater of miracles and genuine faith in each other to commit to our part and parcel in the continuing progress of overcoming adversities to strive for a more comprehensive peace in a world order of preserving the 'wellbeing' of the human condition."

His will is embraced by the amassed will of the GPPJ, therefore in economic terms, 'thy will shall be done.' Riverstrike's monetary worth cannot benefit from an address in his political position, as all monetary gain by politicians in their role to serve the people is prohibited since legislation passed forbidding special interest lobbyists from using their wealth generated by the masses is not to be used to perpetuate lies to persuade the masses in the form of disinformation in media.

"Democracy reigns supreme over the undemocratic institutions of corporate greed-fascism. The Economic Theory of the Human Will is the fountain pen used in writing these philanthropic measures into law designed to even the economic playing field relying on a strong dependence on ethical, moral, and empathetic values shared in the collective consciousness of healthy human minds defined by common virtue.

"The vivariums contain populations, who due to their beliefs, choose to remain earth-bound and can exercise archaic beliefs and practices not necessarily conducive to the 'wellbeing' of the human condition. Many populations who follow millennial old traditions developed to sustain their survival have no interest in the world beyond their confines and carry on within the protective shield over their vivarium's nurturing environs.

"Others, like Gun Toads, do not promote the 'wellbeing' of the human condition but insist on maintaining firearms despite a codified law prohibiting them from use in the GPPJ network. This arrangement clarifies societal transformation from the age of barbarism in the epoch of Pisces to the emergence of the epoch of Aquarius and the advent of a new age of Enlightenment."

The growth and health of the GPPJ are threatened by the greed-fascism alliance of Riverstrike and the thirteen Governors; more people than not accept this as fact.

The space development assembly, in its most corrupt form, is required to maintain the carnage after the destruction from a super-mega-hurricane, or a devastating epidemic if not a pandemic, and to bring about uncertainty, hopelessness, and downright despair upon the Earth lander.

"Vivarium is inspired for creating biospheres that maintain while confining cultures relic to the age of barbarism that is forever earth-bound due to their beliefs. This leads me to a case with top-secret confidentiality.

"This is a case dating back more than three hundred years ago, in a remote location in Colombia, South America. The location of interest is Mosaic Caverns, near where I was stationed at the time when I was a Captain of covert classified operations.

"My command concerned taking out the cocaine drug trade manufacturers and sustained through the fascist-terrorist crime organization at the time. Our efforts in the cause were exceeding diplomatic expectations, as I lead my men on the search and destroy missions."

"We are all too familiar with your history of serving for freedom's security. A consensus response from the General Assembly indeed reveals a show of support for your leadership Minister."

"The technology we encountered inspires the current computer compilations that generate the vector shields to construct isolated biospheres for divisive cultures into virtual realities maintaining peace while they enjoy the freedom of security to live as they desire.

"It was the one mission that destroyed my command. A lot of good men died that day in that basin, some assholes too, but my good men are of my concern. There is one question that haunts me right up to today."

"Interesting. Would you please share with the General Assembly what that is?"

"There were two archaeologists with an expedition team allegedly running around the area and may have contacted whatever was living in the crevices leading into the dark depths of our sacred planet's geographical diversity.

"These images are of our recent refugee celebrities. These images are Catherine and Jürgen." He crosses to the center of the circular conference room. He looks around the room at the faces of the General Assembly, "I believe our celebrity refugees are those same scientists. I know for certain one of them is."

He pauses before summoning, "Simon Noir."

He gestures to Simon to stand for everyone to see. Loud gasps are heard throughout the room.

"This is my assistant Simon Noir. He is not the man who calls himself 'Jürgen,' he is however a clone of Jürgen, created from a DNA sample found in a sleeping bag left in a tent from the American Archaeologist Society camp sight circa two-thousand-five."

General assembly members whisper among themselves in alarm over Riverstrike's assertion.

Minister Riverstrike, in officially introducing Simon, explains how he constantly affixes a distortion mask over his face for anonymity, "The mask allows for Simon to perform as my advisor and confidant while remaining free from potential bribery or corruption. A Zealot Sentinel interface leaves Simon vulnerable to persuasions and concealing his identity when in public enables Simon to blend in effortlessly with the GPPJ. This necessity is so he will not be pressured by solicitations for my favor."

Chair Shinnok rebuffs this assertion, "Lobbying for special interest's sake is against the rule of democratic law for two-hundred-fifty-years, you know that Minister. Fascism serves greed, then greed delivers fascism, both are immoral practices, each is anti-democratic, and both exclude the 'wellbeing' of the human condition in general.

"For each exists for the accumulation of wealth and power, hatred is fascism, greed is fascism, and fascism is immoral. This is the essence of the 'Common Sense of Protest for Fairness of Income and Wealth Act.' You may want to consider reading it for your edification."

Chair Utle of the 'Wellbeing' of the Human Condition Council asks, "How are you so certain of your assertions about a 'subhuman species living, hiding in the dark crevices, in the shadows of the homosapiens advanced cities and all countryside's of the great populations around the planet,' as you say?"

Riverstrike's resting face at this moment is one of mild disgust perturbed by the questioning of his integrity.

"I was there. I was the man who discovered the evidence at Mosaic Caverns."

Chair Utle reads loosely from Riverstrike's career history and statements logged on the record, "The outline of a creature vaporized against a cave wall, during a covert mission that you commanded as a captain rooting out cocaine production facilities and operations in the Colombian jungle."

The Minister's eyes glazed over, and his hearing ceased externally as his thoughts commanded his attention and the sound is heard from within his head: "We found those dam UFOs; we're monitoring their probes. These things are designed by an unknown subterranean population. And I think our 'time traveling heroes' have information based on their firsthand experience about that sub-human, subterranean race."

"Minister, the probes they created are far beyond the technologies of the day created by homosapiens. How can you refer to this supposed subterranean as sub-human if their technological prowess exceeds human innovation by leaps and bounds?"

"Because we have exploited their existence and have adopted their technologies of the vivarium gateway and the Prometheus projects probes sent across the Milky Way demonstrate our implementation of their successful probe technologies, they utilized to gain an understanding of our advance intelligence."

"For their edification towards mutual survival?"

"For their ability to subjugate the human race to do their bidding."

The Minister emerges from his ruminations to hear Chair Utle's growing impatience with the balking Minister.

"I will ask you one last time. Were you forced to retire in two-thousand-eighteen, as a one-star General?"

"To hell with the purpose of my involvement. All that matters is the 'wellbeing' of all citizens. This means a basic living platform to allow the most unfortunate, impoverished, to have the essentials afforded to them to pursue and build a life from liberty and in the pursuit of happiness." Riverstrike holds a pregnant pause before offering, "I tell you there is a hidden threat to be aware of."

Chair Utle asks again, "Please answer the question, Minister

Riverstrike regarding your early retirement, why were you forced to retire as a Brigadier General?"

"I was not forced into early retirement; I chose to retire into private business. My military position limited my abilities, and my reach as I have never located any further evidence of the subterranean existence. I determined I could be of greater effectiveness working in the private sector with RAKLAV. I retired voluntarily to take the CEO and COO for the then start-up organization.

"I believe the periodic arrival of humans from the past is reason enough to indoctrinate them into ZSI. This is a reasonable way to create a file, and reconnaissance for the acquisition of knowledge to ensure the refugee is compatible as a legal, authorized, and valid candidate for inclusion in the GPPJ. The key is maintaining a 'safe place' for the best opportunity to overcome their prejudices, ingrained intolerances supported, many times enforced by the cultures they were raised in."

Chairperson Shinnok interjects, "And what is 'this safe place' for refugees to have as they are indoctrinated, conscripted into the Zealot Sentinels?"

"The Zealot Sentinel training facility on Mars is capable of housing hundreds of thousands into the millions of refugees for training if necessary. This process will acclimate and prepare the refugee to understand the advancements in all aspects of life. It will also save the GPPJ from the prospect of increased accidental incidents due to human error."

The council attendees include legislative bodies designated for specific needs across the space station network. Opportunities for economies in each segment of society from the sixteen billion Earth population to the six billion with permanent residence from the SSN to the moon and Mars. Specific needs are usually logistical issues for supplies.

"Minister Riverstrike, what do you have to say regarding reports of harsh, prison-like accommodations in the Martian training facility used for torture in mind control followed by remediation barbarism from their belief system?"

"Minister Riverstrike's main presentation is to announce his association with, and support of the Star Gazer Sun Tours must be deleted from this session's itinerary. The time he used is considerably over his maximum," Simon addresses the General Assembly. "The good news, for the space station Governor's with us today, is the Minister knows how to get what he wants. To get the message across for the need of four-hundred-fifty-quadrillion monetary units and the requested budget for the development of sixty-four Star Gazer Sun Tour ships, the Minister presents a budget plan for each member of each of the General Assembly's members."

The General Assembly members begin reviewing the digital packet on their GPI devices.

"This budget to be raised from sales of cabin reservations and a large slice of the monetary assets from the mill of the ultra-wealthy to rise-up-and-above expectation by furnishing two-hundred-twenty-five-thousand-quadrillion units. This will be a return on investment as the voyages take place. The incremental graduated returns are projected based on the boarding capacity of two-hundred-fifty-thousand tourists per tour ship."

Minister Riverstrike has made his exit moments before Simon Noir concludes the session by disengaging the communications link.

Simon turns to face the Minister who is emotionless in his expression remaining seated in apparent contemplation.

"Did I execute the conclusion of the presentation effectively?"

"You did, most assuredly the General Assembly will be swayed to decide for granting financing for the Star Gazer Tour ships."

"In light of the impending subterranean uprising. Do you think you convinced them?"

"It is not the intent to convince them Simon; the intent is to plant the seeds of discontent by exploiting their deepest fears and historically ingrained prejudices. The expected thought process is to favor the deep space travel progress over the bondage to human barbarism on Earth and the self-destructive toxicity of traditional mythologies cause rise to perpetual conflict."

11

De ~ Tourist

The flight plan alarm for final approach sounds off bringing Gingi and Spontaneous Instant to ready themselves, preparing as if getting up in the morning for work wearing radiation suits and helmets designed to protect against the radiation exposure on Mars' surface.

They harness the cockpit navigator chairs taking in the flight program landing approach. The first impression of Mars is its' two moons and the five Medusa class space stations orbiting in a pentagon formation around the planet. The sprawling wonders of space engineering float majestically, reminiscent of jellyfish luminescent floating atop the oceans equally diverse in spectacle juxtaposed to the starry night, in position to intercept meteorites and rogue asteroids from impacting on the Martian surface.

Gingi 'thought activates automation for description' of the space station's activity and purpose doting about Mars circumference:

Medusa space stations are defined by the dozen talons connected to the oval shape hull extending out thousands of miles with the ability to be positioned in any direction to deflect threatening space rocks from an impact trajectory.

The hull of each of the Medusa space stations offers living space for several thousand people whether in permanent residences for Martian citizens, Zealot Sentinels, or luxury accommodations for ultra-wealthy tourists. Live entertainment includes dance clubs, restaurants, a performance arts center, museums, music lounges, and an assortment of unique galleries and self-wellness spas for relaxation in serene tranquility. Traveling past the jaw-dropping engineer design of the Medusa's near and far, the prominence of the Martian surface magnetizes your attention to the dimly lit, yet majestic beauty in tactful aesthetic usage of the urban neighborhood grids with the commercial areas in the center of the one major city on the planet suitably exhibiting a 'God of War' motif.

There are several domed sports stadiums used for enthusiasts of various competitive sports leagues for the participation of the general population. All structures within the Martian Metropolis are no more than three stories tall, where, like the bottom of an ocean, lifeforms scuttle for survival. The sports stadiums feature domes with the Martian color palate.

"Oh, look Sponti, I just noticed the atmosphere! Look quick the sunlight is fading!"

He pivots his head to his left and leans forward, "I see it, sort of a low ceiling."

Although there is little oxygen and the air pressure is low, the water transported from Venus fills the enclosed reservoirs under controlled air pressure providing for sustainable bodies of water like the huge lakes surrounding the Metropolis.

"Yeah, the storage encasement is made of 'High-Z steel-steel.' It's a metal foam mostly stainless steel with a fraction of tungsten. It keeps the water protected from the radiation emitted from Mars' surface." Gingi poses a question, "Did you know when water is introduced into the Mars atmosphere it instantly freezes and boils at the same time? Isn't that freaky?"

"Heck yeah," Spontaneous Instant reacts with wide-eyed caution, "Make sure to never take off your radiation helmet!"

The landscape goes dark as they coast to the other hemisphere desolate of public community where the ancient Martian terrain provides a measure of isolation for the operations conducted in and around the RAKLAV administered Zealot Sentinel headquarters.

On the quieter side of Mars, there are structures built to eighty stories, half underground. The above-ground structures are imperceptible by design utilizing the absence of potent sunlight.

The Mars Runner begins to descend a mile away from the ZS training facility. Made distinctive by the illumination of the landing port in front of the main entrance, the layout resembles a welcoming mat.

"There's the destination landing pad. Nice to see they went through the trouble to display 'Welcome Star Gazer Tours.'"

"That's cute," Spontaneous Instant states under his breath skeptical of the level of sincerity behind the cordial appearances.

Thirty seconds later the Mars Runner lands, and Spontaneous Instant emerges squeezing an information chip between his forefinger the thumb of his left hand.

Three figures appear at the front entrance with two cargo items. They enter the front lobby as the interior door is secured, and the three figures and the pods become buoyant. They exit towards the cruiser, and he enters the front lobby where the doors are secure and pressurize for safe entry. He approaches a RAKLAV officer who is waiting for him in the rear lobby.

"Hello, my name is Spontaneous Instant. I'm with Star Gazer Sun Tours."

"Yes, those are the cargo pods you are here for." Commander Janalake states, "The three Zealot Sentinels you just passed by are loading the two pods onto the cruiser."

"That's it? Great. Oh, this is my first time on Mars; Is it okay if my colleague and I scope out that major city, what's it called?"

Janalake realizing she is talking to a near juvenile feigns courteousness, "It's called 'Martian Metropolis' and you are welcome back anytime, but don't you think your employers would like to see you carry out your official business first?"

"I would guess so, but I'm into the privileges of youth and I don't know when the next time I'll be out here, so."

Janalake is ready to smack this insolent guy in the chops, "What is your name again?"

"Spontaneous Instant," he responds thrown for a loop by her tone, "I'm sorry, I didn't get your name. Are you hitting on me, Ma'am?"

"You have two live bodies in induced comas as cargo on your ship and I'm certain your flight program will not include a detour for tourism to Martian Metropolis. I'm giving you an order Spontaneous Instant, make like your namesake and be gone in an 'instant.'"

"Right on," he replies as he offers an awkward hand salute before he steps into the pressurization lobby cabin. The exterior door opens, and he takes six low gravity bounds to the Mars Runner.

He gets to the navigator chair to secure the harness for launch.

"Wow, she's an authoritarian type if I ever met one!"

"What was going on out there?" Gingi sits in an adjacent flight chair.

"Not much, I thought we might have some time to party in Martian Metropolis and she tells me there are two bodies in those pods without GPIs."

Gingi laughs in response, "What a fabulous story Sponti ~ you asked her for permission to party ~ I love it!"

Spontaneous Instant is surprised, "I thought you'd know?"

"Know what?" Gingi asks.

He releases from the navigator chair and directs her to the cabin where the hibernation pods connect to the Mars Runner interior power source.

"Our cargo is the time refugees," he states excitedly.

"What?" Gingi is elated, "In those hibernation pods?"

"I understand why you don't believe me."

"I believe you Sponti, I was expecting cognizant, conscious people. I was looking forward to sharing time with them is all."

"You have to help me revive those people and," he reaches into the center panel storage compartment to display two GPI, "suit them up."

Gingi sits down reeling from the unexpected request, "We should stop and freshen up, take a 'look-see' at the Mars Mall. It's going to take hours for them to revive, then most of the trip to waken from their induced comas. We need PTO before we journey back, okay?"

His eyebrows raise in eagerness, "Have I not said it from the start? Let's go!" He helps Gingi stand with a hand to jolt her out of a bucket seat in the cabin. "Thanks, Sponti, kiss?" Gingi asks and he is more than willing to oblige briefly lifting their helmets to lean over to plant a firm, but soft and gentle touching of their lips.

"The hibernation pods are properly plugged into the interior energy reserve, and we are linked to receive monitoring over their vitals, so we can leave them on their own for an hour while we have a drink or two in the Martian Metropolis." She flashes a devilish grin; the iris of her eyes reflects one orange and the other yellow.

"Amazing, it's instant 'night on the town in Martian Metropolis' for you with your little device."

"Thank you Sponti, love. It's a cosmos of cosmetology stored in our RNA, released and manipulated to temporarily alter genetic makeup. I have the patents for the device in place, in just a few more years of 'R & D' and we will be able to secure a millennium of Condorcet each."

"You are bad ass Gingi," Spontaneous Instant praises her with confidence for the occasion.

They proceed into the cockpit to prepare for lift-off.

Gingi is feeling centered now and is smiling in anticipation, "Sponti, do you think you can fly the Mars Runner? I mean you do know Marcel has the autopilot flight plan. Can you override it?"

"Yeah, does it need overriding?"

"He locked the voice and thought commands. You must fly manually, can you?"

"I have the skills. Watch me!"

Gingi warns him reaching her hand out, "Be careful. Anything happens to prevent us from completing this transport mission and we are stardust!"

"The low gravity on this planet helps to prevent hard landings."

"The spaceport has cool architecture and is filled with art inspired here by deep meditations."

"Art? You can do that; I want to see what kind of drinks they make! This spaceport is not even three minutes away."

Gingi looks out from the cockpit window and see's the woman Sponti called a fascist. She is amazing, the women's aura exudes self-confidence, elegance, and strength. She's talking to a man standing just inside the translucent doorway of the Zealot Sentinel training facility. She is issuing orders as the uniformed man listens intently, bows his head, and steps away with purpose.

The woman startles Gingi by locking eyes with her, piercing through the obstacles of one hundred feet in distance with the reach of her magnetism, her intensity is in no doubt focused on her orange iris and yellow iris.

The Mars Runner begins to hover breaking Gingi's sight line with the RAKLAV Commander of the Zealot Sentinels.

"Got this big boy to lift off!" He is childish in his excitement, "Pull back on this switch and up we go!"

The Mars Runner lifts slowly and steadily.

"This palm ball navigator is magnific in its control of this thirty-five-ton interplanetary class cruiser. Slide your hand forward on the ball, slowly forward."

Gingi places her left hand on the ball navigator, "Pushing forward!"

The Mars Runner begins to accelerate forward.

"Faire la-Fête. The traction control on this makes it a smooth motion."

"The good life, Le bon vie ~ accélérâtes ~"

"How?"

Spontaneous Instant is reviewing step-by-step instructions, "Why is the only source of operation manual on this ship in French?"

"It must be locked in the flight program to keep us in check."

"Whatever, Marcel and Qyxzorina, what is a translator?"

"They are old, like dinosaurs just not extinct." Gingi thinks of a common expression, "Twentieth Century Dinosaurs."

"TCD they are true. Press down on the palm ball in the direction you want to go, it should keep accelerating until you release the pressure."

"There it is the spaceport!"

"Okay, let me try and land this thing."

Spontaneous Instant places his right hand on the palm ball, softly caressing Gingi's hand. As the Mars Runner gets above the spaceport landing pad, she retracts her hand as he grips the palm ball with his four fingers and thumb to direct the cruiser to hover.

He flips the switch to hover down to the landing pad.

"A perfect landing!" Gingi ecstatically announces with great relief.

"Don't forget to insulate your suit, it's about negative seventy degrees out there!"

"Yeah, but there's no wind?"

"The atmosphere is too thin in these parts to worry about the wind. C'mon."

They exit the Mars Runner and dash over in five unintended but animated leaps to the entrance corridor about an eighty-foot distance.

"Whoa, Sponti!" Gingi reaches to anchor him, "Too little gravity!"

They step loftily inside and enjoy floating in between steps.

The architecture and complimenting artworks make an intimate impression on them.

Spontaneous Instant is typically skeptical in tone, "Red lava lamp theme going on here."

"Mellow vibe for sure," Gingi is intrigued, "Sponti, does Mars have volcanoes?"

"I don't think so. I heard they have oil though."

"They found oil on Mars. When?"

"Maybe they're just really optimistic about some sonar reading."

"Old news Sponti, like two-hundred-years-old news!"

As they continue out of the spaceport via an enclosed walkway, the wind kicks up to a whisper.

Inside they encounter a kiosk at a juncture of corridors.

They take off their space suits to fold them into their helmets for convenience and to use as cushioned seats if necessary.

Their analysis of a unique space bar leads them to one destination: 'Romulus & Remus rhythm and blues bar.'

"What do you think it is Gingi, not R&B?"

Gingi spreads her arms out for emphasis, "Why not R&B? The sign says so, it's in the name."

They head through several desolate walkways before they enter a retail mall where the galleria is attended by Martian Metropolis citizens enjoying shopping, eateries, and gaming.

"Should we?" Gingi asks in contemplation of purchasing Mars-themed party social attire.

"There will be consequences!"

"Good call Sponti."

"But what the hell? You're only twenty once!"

"Yeah, but we're twenty-five for one thousand years!"

"That's what I am talking about! Privileges of youth!" He grabs her hand and pulls her inside the store.

A 'welcoming jingle' rings upon entry. The automated tellers or the human cashiers will assist you and wish you goodbye.

Automation caught on for decades, but there is a natural innate relationship that humans share that is irreplaceable, therefore profitable.

"The billions of people in the GPPJ are largely solvent. There is one-tenth of one percent of the population suffering in ways of lack of opportunity, poor mental health, prevalent depression, anxiety, and worry to no end! The gene therapy techniques reverse these adverse affectations, but positive support through human interaction is reinforcing the emotional bonds developing healthy minds.

"The growing distances of the GPPJ into interplanetary habitation deepens the vastness of societies' ubiquity. Lonely when measured in finding your way dealing only with machines, or robots in your life, idle time can become a living torment for a sizable percentage of the GPPJ. These impulses for a better life propel the human experience as the root of the economy, the need to compensate others for their part, as much as any wants to be compensated fairly for contributing to the 'wellbeing' of the human condition. It is morality treasured by all that fuels the ETHW.

"On the other hand, there is a percentage of GPPJ who prefer the isolation, albeit not inherently healthy for humans in general to live lives of seclusion, but for some with the inner reserve to occupy the mind with skills of creativity, they are satisfied with the simple comfort of solitude. Am I getting too analytical?"

"Yes Sponti, have some fun, loosen up! Try this on!" Gingi hands him an intriguing style of long sleeve shirt with Mars red paisley patterns and a deep red-orange solid vest stitched directly onto the shirt.

"This goes with your eyes. What is it, a shirt, or a vest or both?"

"It reminds me of a decoupage."

"Excuse me, did you burp?"

"No, but the price of this work of art is eighty-two thousand units."

"All right," Spontaneous Instant strips the clothing off, "This item is available on Earth for an affordable thirty-five-thousand units."

"What do you say, time for a drink?"

They bounce and float their way through several corridors to arrive at the bar within ten minutes.

A bartender is approaching them at their bar stools, an older, middle-aged man, "How are you fine young folks doing this evening?" He sets a menu in front of them.

"Live music?" Spontaneous Instant is jazzed up seeing instruments on a small-scale proscenium performance stage, "What is a popular Martian drink?"

"A request? Okay, I can recommend," the bartender says, "I thought you may be new to Mars."

Gingi wants to speak to the bartender, "We are first-time visitors!"

"Visiting? Not too many people 'visit' Mars this time of year."

"No?"

"Young lady, you either live here in Martian Metropolis or your business is with RAKLAV. The tourist season starts three months before Earth and Mars are at the closest distance between their orbits."

He rubs his portend belly in part to meditate on a recommendation, and to wipe his hands dry from wet ragging the bar top.

"I know, I will make you 'Martian Comets.' Do you like a fireball and Curacao rum?"

"Yes, I do. You up for one Gingi?"

"Sure. What is a Martian comet?"

The bartender is mixing the drinks, "Have a few of these, take a ride on a land rover and you will see as many Martian comets as you like, even more so with each one you consume."

Gingi listens to his explanation, "That must be a trip to ride on one of those in low gravity?"

He is amused by her naivete, "Land rovers are engineered for keeping traction to the terrain, and they top out at about twenty miles per hour. Alternatively, if we had dune buggies, we may be able to lift off into orbit, but you wouldn't want to do that either."

"No, we wouldn't," Gingi's eye is on the fiery blood sweet orange Curacao and whiskey drink being poured into a high-ball glass after being shaken over ice cubes, adding a blood-orange slice on the rim as a sexy garnish. The drinks are served in chilled cocktail glasses and placed on mauve Mars-like oval coasters.

They receive their drinks and toast to "Faire la-Fête on Mars!"

Sudden rousing jubilation from the corner of the bar drew their attention. Loud with joy and happiness are members of two baseball teams who are rejoicing over cocktails and food. They are throwing leather fielder's gloves at each other like pillows; everyone is disheveled, some with Mars soil on their baseball uniforms.

Each uniform is heavily worn as if thousands of ball games were played over the years for each. Also, they were all gray heads; each team, each player, and the coach looked to be in their seventies or eighties, both females, males, and no doubt all persuasions of sexual identity included.

Gingi smiles delightfully surprised by the positive energy they exert. "They are having fun!"

"Hey, what's the deal with our walking?" Spontaneous Instant is tipsy after gulping at his drink a few times already.

"It's gravity, but not so much, you know," Gingi is feeling the buzz by laughing, "It's one-third of Earth's gravity."

"Hey, bartender? What's your name?"

"You can call me Larry."

"Hey, Larry!"

"What can I do for you?"

"This is Gingi Grind and I'm Spontaneous Instant, nice to meet you, Larry, ~"

"You rock Larry ~no, you red rocking it Larry with these Martian Comets!"

"I like your smiles Gingi Grind. I bet you hear that a lot."

"We want to go out on your dune buggy, Larry!"

"I don't have a dune buggy. There are land rovers available, you can get one for hourly rental."

"That's our last drink!"

"Sponti, leave Larry alone."

"Hey Larry, you understand, I want to rent a land rover~"

A large hand grips his right shoulder tightly.

"Hey, now!" He folds at the knees to the pain of the pressure on his rotator cuff. His tormentor flips Spontaneous Instant around to face him.

Spontaneous Instant must look up two feet to meet the eyes of Gian, the Zealot Sentinel Sergeant addresses them, "You must go! Your cargo is overdue."

Sergeant Gian grabs Spontaneous Instant and Gingi Grind by their necks and escorts them toward the exit of the bar.

"Excuse me, they haven't paid for their drinks yet!" Larry demands payment.

Sergeant Gian turns his head sideways to speak out of the side of his mouth, "Put it on RAKLAV TAB!" Sergeant Gian grunts and exits taking the two twenty-year-old Star Gazer Tours employees to the spaceport and the Mars Runner for their immediate departure.

In a few minutes later the cruiser hovers for several seconds before it thrusts forward and upward on its way back to Earth.

12

Chasing Down a Dream

The minds and hearts of the masses awaken to the crude temporary shell of society and the mere conception in its then 'present state' in an age of barbarism in behavior, immorality, and tribalism dating back to the pre-dawn of civilization ten thousand years ago.

The vision took over my senses, a pre-dawn of civilization when early homosapiens lived nomadic lives. Nature's purest existence hundreds of millenniums in the making has me transfixed while flying over an arrangement of island masses along an ancient ocean coastline. The islands are pristine, unscathed by human interaction, and free of any human ecological destruction.

The speed of flight is rapid, to begin with as my flight, with my arms fully outstretched, accelerates in speed to a hypnotizing blur.

A perpetual floating in and out of molecule waves comprise the air while having microscopic perception able to sense the waves of energy, its particles swirling around, folding in multiple directions as the tiniest molecules are visibly identifiable pumping, throbbing, flowing endlessly, relentless in some mystical, cosmic junction of subatomic rivers pervasive through time and space.

I know other humans are in trance communicating their collective unconscious into the collective consciousness. I see the jungle from the sky knowing it is for all of us, as is the rest, visible as is invisible.

The energy is of us, it is free to use in ways for freedom for all. Nature in truth holds the definitive answer, truths build the aesthetic of survival, of the 'wellbeing' of the human condition.

The minds and hearts awaken to the idea of truth afforded by nature a definitive answer: It is not idle death; It is nurturing life!"

I encounter a connection to my past incomplete, but not unclear for the truth resting inside of me as part of my being within the cosmic fabric intertwined with all of existence.

My past connects to the present.

Is this the final truth in the human experience to never know completely the fate of natural existence?

Doomed always, for unyielding adversity is to overcome and in the gradual understanding, perception resulting in achievement will coax us into believing knowledge is growing.

In truth, as it is nature, the more we awaken, the more adversity defines itself and a whole new host of ignorance is imposed on human intellect. The image of ancient humans, before the advent of an agriculturally based society, toasting life as meaningless, yet death carries its worthiness by leaving humans to ruminate and ask 'why?'

The female innovates for survival in ways complementary to male innovations. The female is more often in acceptance of the tides of adversity, the male in defiance of the tides of adversity.

The female forging unity in diversity, expanding inclusion; The male accepts diversity in unity, expanding inclusion.

The environs lighten as I gain consciousness. The light is blurry white, and I view the outline of someone sitting next to me.

It is strange to me when I notice my breathing for the first time. The functioning of my lungs jolts me into sitting up gasping for air. I view a young woman coming into focus with strawberry blonde locks, a smiling young face with nose jewelry, sitting by my side to hear me exclaim, "Necessity is the Mother of all invention!"

"Hello there, parent," the young woman is pleasantly surprised by my arousal.

"What?" I find her claim confusing. Who is this young woman, possibly my daughter?

"You said, 'Mother'. It is appropriate to say, 'Parent of all invention.' No worries, you are emerging from an induced coma. My name is Gingi Grind, and this is my dear friend Spontaneous Instant."

I nod my head in understanding. Disorientated initially, I realize this must be a medical clinic, "What an odd and unfamiliar anesthetized clinical facility."

Spontaneous Instant informs, "You are fitted with the GPI now, after having a reconditioning."

"My name is Catherine. Have you met my associate Jürgen?"

"I'm over here Catherine," Jürgen is connected to a medical analysis system monitoring his vital functions, "How are you feeling?"

"Lethargic but well rested in a way. Do you know what is going on?"

"We've been refitted with the Glass Planet interface."

"Good. Who are these people, and where are we? Jürgen, why can't all of this be in my dreams?"

"Strangely, you mention dreams, I recently had a series of dreams where I was in a Jungle terrain, South America it seemed to me as if I participated in some discovery."

"Did you dream of islands?"

"There was a coastline, may have been a wide river too. I was flying too fast, I needed to land on the pristine island, where I could find solace, off the grid."

"My sentiments exactly. I am closer to my soul. Something is percolating up."

Gingi interrupts gently, "Catherine let me help you up so you can, you know, walk around, and clear your head."

I take her hand and the young man extends his hand to assist me, "Thanks." I grimace at the young man, "What did you say your name is?"

"Spontaneous Instant, at your service ma'am."

"Spontaneous Instant?" I reiterate. "Where have I heard that before?"

"I wouldn't know, have we ever met ma'am?"

"No, and please stop calling me 'ma'am,'" I say considerately, this being our mutual introduction.

"What is it we can do Catherine, more research from archived data footage sourced from South America?" Jürgen is bewildered, "It's a hunch, but it is somewhere to start."

"What about this for a hunch," I lean into Jürgen to ensure privacy. "We visit that mysterious Mosaic Caverns with the ancient curse of 'forgotten sacrifices?'"

"What ancient curse of 'forgotten sacrifices?'"

"I found it in several media streams. This location was the epicenter of ancient civilizations, Inca sacrificial offerings are the preeminent notion. Military operations against drug trafficking were intense, and locals described a great fireball that shook the ground for a hundred miles setting the jungle ablaze; In the year two-thousand-five."

"You are suggesting we visit this site as if our destiny awaits us?"

"You know Jürgen, I'm not one to wait for my opportunity as if it were certain to come by, but what if it never comes and you're left waiting? We must seek out our opportunities and shape our destiny, it is the will of the individual to decide for themselves."

Jürgen raises his eyebrows as he expresses admiration with a tension-releasing laugh, "What can I say? I'm in."

Spontaneous Instant and Gingi Grind continue to initiate dialogue with us.

"Interested in getting to know you, and in turn, having you get to know us better too," Gingi smiles in sweet vulnerability.

"Absolutely Gingi, thank you for your hospitality."

"Absolute hospitality, no issues," she tilts her head increasing her smile's shine via her device.

"What she means is we want to invite you to go bar hopping with us," Spontaneous Instant doubles down on the invitation.

"Well, Jürgen, can you use a drink? We can start research tomorrow."

Jürgen appeases with open hands, "As I said, I'm in!"

13

In a State of 'Wellbeing'

Gingi Grind is mixing drinks for a willing if not captive audience. "This is a rental flat, if you were to have any suspicions, we cannot afford a permanent residence in the SSN. Speaking of rental flats, the Sea Foam condominiums are perfect for the two of you. A suitable place for privacy for celebrities of your status."

She speaks philosophically, "We are imperfect, and time is infinite, so technological performance will always be flawed no matter how well conceived and designed its intended use is." She gathers a bucket of chopped ice and proceeds to pour the chopped ice into pint glasses, "You will find the Sea Foam condominiums representative of the transition times from the passing of the Pisces epoch into the current age of Aquarius."

"Sounds nice Gingi, where are they located?"

"Miami Beach of course," she replies with great enthusiasm, "What do you think Jürgen?"

"I think it will be revitalizing. I'm in!"

"The world, the universe is chaotic, often unpredictable and vastly unknown," Spontaneous Instant chimes in. "Therefore, impossible to fully comprehend, providing eternal ignorance to the human experience."

"What if the universe world, which we are a part of, is meant to function and thrive in chaos, imperfection." Jürgen states the obvious, regurgitating under his breath, "Must be a strong drink he's drinking."

"While the theoretical development of space to create artificial solar light systems," Spontaneous Instant stops to have another sip of margarita, "The Sun, moons, and planets to live on would be morally questionable to do so if human colonization results in exploitation of natural resources."

Gingi Grind sips the margarita through a straw, "There's no morality to it. The chaos and unpredictable nature of the universe world is the erosion of the aesthetic. Like rain and wind on Gaia's surface cause unpredictable chaos eroding the present aesthetic. Humanity builds its aesthetic in response to this constant force of erosion as adversity often presents."

"Everything, Gingi Grind, you say is spoken like the 'true poet' you are," Spontaneous Instant gushes praise over her like water out of a fire hydrant on a sultry summer's day. "She has a CQ of significant import."

"It is a shocking abuse of ignorance!" Gingi scolds abruptly.

"Gingi scolds anything she views as against the 'wellbeing' of humanity," Spontaneous Instant explains, "as a ~"

"It is a shocking abuse of ignorance!" Gingi's rage is a controlled, contemplative harshness.

Jürgen looks to me, as do I to him taken aback by her amateurish outburst.

"What is a shocking abuse of ignorance?" Jürgen whispers calmly to Gingi.

"Not to be able to prevent erosion wherever possible, of course."

The room stood silent as we provided calm for the young lady who epiphanies emotionally and stirs our thoughts within us from her impassioned plea.

Spontaneous Instant proffers to me a screen embedded in the tabletop depicting a logo of a pharmaceutical organization, "Some think you're from the past because you were alive to be the prototypes for aging regression therapies and genetic alterations."

"As if from a secret governmental study?" I skeptically suggest.

"Kind of," Gingi has a seat joining us, "Except there's no research data or a second of any declassified experiment reports. Human genetic manipulation is ethically questionable and morally suspect."

Jürgen is relaxing to the onset of inebriation, "Well good, it all was beginning to sound like a conspiracy theory."

Spontaneous Instant turns a corner on the topic, "Yes, we suspect another 'developer.'"

"Who?" I toss it out for anyone's guess.

Spontaneous Instant drives the point home, "An ancient culture of the old homosapiens family tree."

"I'd like to know what you're smoking?" Jürgen regains his sarcastic form to appeal to the anti-establishment instincts of our youthful friends.

Gingi is near to taking offense to Jürgen's question, "Smoking? Nobody smokes anymore, except Earth-landers. Here you can have one of these supplements. Suck on it."

Jürgen receives the gum drop size 'supplement.'

"Hidden where?" I query.

"That's what we're guessing on," Gingi shares, "Evidence from ancient human cultures lends credence to discovering who or what caused you to survive the prior age before the Condorcet procedure was created, and we need to find out why."

"You need to find out why, when, and where," adds Jürgen.

"How about who and what about us?"

"When did we disappear?"

Spontaneous Instant is getting tipsy, "Due to your mutual unfamiliarity of RAKLAV, at least before the year two-thousand-fifteen when it was founded. There came a time when fascism was finally characterized as a crime against the 'wellbeing' of the human condition."

He stops again, this time tossing a green pill in his mouth followed by another gulp of margarita, "Fascism is also greed and greed is also a crime against the 'wellbeing' of the human condition and is punishable by years-long exile reconditioning on Mars at the ZS training complex."

"A prison of sorts?"

"Were we not interned there?"

"They say it's ZS training, but it is a front for RAKLAV as a vetting facility. The organization evolved from an information analyzer for purposes of consumerism, marketing to individuals tracking where they go, revealing a 'personality profile,' compiling intimate preferences to achieve a unique signature to be exploited by private, commercial and government agencies." Spontaneous Instant stops to finish his drink, then holds up his glass, "Gingi, can we have more margaritas?"

"No Sponti, we are going bar hopping and you just popped a green flurry."

Jürgen shows signs of inebriation indicated by the slouch of his shoulders and flailing limp wrists, "Are you familiar with the term 'collective consciousness?'"

Gingi is disgusted, "You mean 'collective unconsciousness.'" She rolls her eyes and flickers her eyelashes in a sign of incredulity, "The cornucopia of creativeness; The bone marrow of the soul; The proverbial subtext of the orgy that is life."

"Also, the 'collective consciousness is the arbiter of ethics in genuinely knowing what morally correct consensus among the masses is!" Jürgen is adjusting well to the attitudes of our present hosts.

Spontaneous Instant finishes his margarita with one last gulp, "Jürgen, you're exciting me with your enthusiasm! Please don't. Don't stop, please, I mean stop. That is exactly why you have a large credit account." Already beyond sobriety, his demeanor turns lusty, "Jürgen? No question is inappropriate?"

"I would say 'okay,'" Jürgen stumbles in his response. "I mean to say no question is inappropriate."

I see Gingi approaching me slowly crisscrossing her legs as she approaches with her arms open and extended out, "Hugs? What is this, some kind of a come on?"

Gingi smiles receptively, "Yeah, come on. Follow me. Your entire experience with The Glass Planet has been filtered by Qyxzorina and Marcel. Until now, you have a limited scope of perception of the population.

"They shared that the ambition amongst all of the population is the 'wellbeing' of the human condition dependent on the physical manifestation of the human will. The need to bond with a kaleidoscope of personalities and those of varying ambitions is the spine of the ETHW."

"Variations occur and are recognized as the 'varieties of currency' of the human will; as it is most positive and beneficial for the GPPJ."

Spontaneous Instant laughs heartily, "Apparently, not yet for you guys, as you will see the variety is endless; And so is the loyalty to one another is endless, it is the cyclical nature of life, we have learned to embrace, emulate to strengthen our human bonds in a constant cycle of birth, awakening, discovery, innovation, creation, erosion, deterioration, demise to extinction to the proliferation of growth again in cyclical form."

"It continuously rises again," I pitch in. "First Law of Thermodynamics ~ Energy cannot be created or destroyed."

"As it always has for countless generations," Spontaneous Instant points out, "Now loyalty has supplanted greed and not loyalty to one ultimate reigning power, but loyalty to the 'wellbeing' of the human condition."

"Loyalty and greed can be mutually inclusive and often are!"

"You speak of the combination of the two, well three for that matter, this is known as fascism."

Jürgen slaps his left hand on his left knee, "Damned right it's fascist!"

Gingi and I break into laughter over his ridiculous reaction. "I'm talking about the creation of matter, where it is lost it is created in another form to keep equilibrium within the cosmic fabric."

"Nice thought Catherine," Spontaneous Instant focuses mentally. "I call loyalty as it is for the 'wellbeing' of humanity; all of us are loyal to that commitment. Greed is avarice against the 'wellbeing' of the human condition and is akin to fascism."

Bar hopping is an all-time favorite of mine. What better way to plunge yourself into the environs of the culture, learning from inebriate loose lips and tired tongues, some liars revealing secrets from their embellishments while boasting of delusions of grandeur, all of them shining stars at the local tavern or bar.

Spontaneous Instant takes hold of my hand, "You're about to take a journey; It will change the way you feel about yourself."

"Jürgen?" I reach out to him, "What do you . . .?"

The rigid landing of the craft quieted everyone as a hum resonated throughout the cabin.

"What do I 'what?'" Jürgen replies.

An array of color blots fills the cabin.

Spontaneous Instant peers over his shoulder and smiles at us, "Let's go now!"

The cabin opens entirely to a murkier mesmerizing array of color blots, each demarcating an entrance to a world of physical stimulation or relaxation, brain massages releasing volumes of endorphins relieving pain and stress at exponentially exhilarating rates of speed. The serotonin release focuses us to calm happiness.

We float freely through realms of color each offering stimulating intoxicants sending us into fits of madness and moods of laughing, use of nonsensical sounds as verbiage correlating a definition of the elation exuding in our present emotional states.

Spontaneous Instant exclaims, "Now that we're all fluffed up! Let's hop the hopper!"

Jürgen looks at me having begun a story about how everyone is, "Everyone is beautiful in their unique expression. Vibrancy, of the excitement of seeing all happy, healthy humans."

"Yellow aura?" I ask him with precision.

Jürgen smiled at me, though not directly, as he smoothly replied, "I came across one beauty who caught my eye and I asked, 'How old are you?' 'Three-hundred-forty-three-years-old' she said behind experienced eyes so informed they made me feel naked somehow. The tone of her voice reflects tremendous knowledge through that wealth of experience, yellow aura, and all. She speaks in a vocabulary of proverbs."

Spontaneous Instant dancing his way over to a high point from where we started our journey, as we follow dancing in air through this tubular fuselage on our way over to join him. He circles a wide toothy smile at us before using his hands to spread open the narrow slit of light, waving with one hand urging us, "Go, go, a-go-go!"

Jürgen bullets through the meager opening, as I follow him into a splash of diamonds. All at once the four of us become immersed in a pool of floating diamonds!

The sensation of the finely polished bright jewels in countless abundance is as dazzling as seeing the sun up close.

Jürgen spins around revealing a large diamond he secured with his toothy jaw. Sparkles of refracted light throughout the floating diamonds bleed colors as a psychedelic tapestry light show.

"Music is like molasses, if it's pure, slow, sweet, and undeniable to the soul, then both enlarge the heart." Spontaneous Instant playfully continues.

"Music is like lightning in a bottle, as it penetrates reality with insight, both enlighten the spirit of life," Gingi offers to posture her hand for Jürgen to hold on to, "They exhilarate me when I find I'm in rhythm with them."

She takes hold of his hand and wraps her forearm around his before diving into a whirlwind spin bringing the diamonds into a swirling motion that grows gradually to fill the room with spinning diamonds.

"Diamonds undergo immense pressures for millions of years to become the hardest, rarest, most desired gem," Gingi states in the fascination of the thought.

"Elements replicated to form these!" Spontaneous Instant's head unexpectedly pops up before me out of nowhere, "Bulbous re-creations."

"So, these are not diamonds, they're replicas? Like from the twentieth century?" I ask in growing disappointment. "Are these made of wood ash?"

He waves his face left-to-right and back again, "The conditions under which the diamonds are created are much more advanced in replicating the billions of years' quality. These diamonds are very real! Just not really old but are valuable! These are equally as hard and are used in synthetic materials across the SSN, from windows to meteor shields!"

"That sounds fine, but I beg to differ, replicas are known to have little resale value. Although utilizing various manufacturing of vital infrastructure is worthy."

"Well, twentieth-century replicas," retorts Spontaneous Instant, "Old diamonds are for old jewelry. Jewelry highly appraised is reserved only for access to the 'welfare for the rich club.'"

In a blink of an eye, the four of us are in a private lounge.

"How did we get here?"

"We have never left. There are many settings to enjoy ourselves in a virtual environment," replies Spontaneous Instant. "The effect is like a 'disco ball,' popular in your day, I believe. It would have been interesting to live in the twentieth century, primitive but charming in many ways."

"I wish I could tell you exactly, but perhaps a more detailed look back to my era might jar some memories!" This is a simple revelation now that I verbalize it, but it stands to logic to examine the possible sensory memories.

"We can do that, there is an archive we can access," Spontaneous Instant notes, "Were you, hippies, by any chance? I always wonder what a counter-culture lifestyle would be like?"

"Welfare for the rich? Did I understand you correctly?" Asks Jürgen. "And you want to know what a counter-culture lifestyle is like?"

Spontaneous Instant, realizing in our faces we may find this statement as an oxymoron giggles in response, "If you are famous for contributing to 'wellbeing' or if you are a celebrity for bringing inspiration to significant entrepreneur endeavors, inspiring significant populations to innovate, invent, administrate to popular favor of a mass concentration with a swelling will of support; then the escalation of wealth beyond one-billion fiat per year honors the individual with carte blanche access to all of the most expensive services, crafts, resorts, anything their heart desires."

"Short of excess, that is," notes Gingi Grind uncoiling like a kitten emerging from a nap, stretching her limbs, flexing her hips while arching her back, and straightening her bare, shapely legs, "the best things, in life, are free."

She catches Jürgen staring at her as if a zombie in ecstasy, a brain freeze overtakes his senses, and he momentarily appears like a coldblooded lizard in diapause.

As she uses her free hand to caress his chin and then slides her hand gently down his neck, her fingertips touch lightly to his chest seductively before he abruptly places his chin on his chest in embarrassment.

"Poor Jürgen," she says consoling him. Reaching her arms spreading wide at shoulder height speaks of complete willingness to relinquish her heart, "Fortunes and ostentatious display lie beyond what the healthy heart truly desires."

Quite mesmerized at this point by her luminous seducing aura, Jürgen whispers aloud, "How is that 'welfare?'"

"There is no ownership, only public trusts for the ultra-profitable corporations."

"No ownership?" Jürgen basks in growing wonder.

"Ownership is the entry-level into the slippery slope to greed addiction. They're known in today's world as 'money harvesters.'"

Gingi posits, "And there are no private banks either!"

"Wait, how are all these facilities run? Corporations in general?"

"There are boards of twenty-year terms, open for anyone with proper aptitude in qualifications enough to . . .," Gingi transforms with redhead slick hairstyle, adorning body gems adding sparkle to the color range scheme of a cosmic theme cocktail dress with constantly changing illumines levels, ". . . fill the 'opening?'"

Spontaneous Instant smiles before expressing a jovial laugh, "Gingi, no, my lady. You are a villainous voracious vixen of voluptuous vitality. Your qualifications are enough to provide responsible stewardship."

"Stewardship, as in taking grip of the wheel of destiny and twisting to appease oneself?"

Spontaneous Instant remarks expectantly, "I gather those are terms our guest can understand?"

Jürgen gulps, "Yeah, I think so."

Gingi transforms into a platinum dominatrix wearing a purple leather body suit and adorning accouterments, "Outlawing greed-fascism proved not the final fascism."

I am listening all along with little import to the conversation until rattled by Gingi Grind's statement, "What was the final fascism?"

Spontaneous Instant postures a hand to chin in an Auguste Rodin 'The Thinker' inspired pose, "Gingi, love, you make the world go around!"

Gingi rolls her eyes, "Sponti, have you shown them?"

He waves his head left to right and back again.

"You show them Gingi Grind!"

I smile and offer a laugh due to the carefree nature of our exchange. Jürgen is equally amused finding himself aroused and folding his legs over it while standing uncomfortably.

Gingi smirks at Jürgen indicating as she clasps her hands to her knees, "Come here little puppy dog, poochie, poochie, poochie!"

She stands by a plate diamond encrusted glass window with Earth on full display, the scars of rapid CO2 buildup in the atmosphere with the loss of ancient rain forest massive transition in a fleeting period, "Mother Nature is the final fascism out of equilibrium. The fascism of undeniable truth."

Her clothing changes into a blue and white checkered farm dress with a low collar undershirt and her hair is jet black ponytails.

Jürgen moans in pleasure drawing everyone's attention, "Right, so righteous. Gingi, how do you do that?"

Flipping Jürgen off with a rolling of her eyes quickly flicking her eyelids, "It's amazing how rudimentary the idea, the migrating of the ocean waters into the deserts was naturally effective in reducing sea-level and in lowering surface temperatures."

"We missed the pipeline structure in the desert sands when we first arrived. Then it is visible as we ascended into orbit."

"When you first arrived? How? From where?" Gingi asks innocently enough.

"It was out of a cave," Jürgen states plainly.

"A cave? In the jungle?" Gingi asks skeptically suggesting the improbability of her delivery. "Do you think you can lead us there?"

"We don't know where it is. It was where we believe to be transported somehow," I suppose this is a logical statement. "If we look for it, we may recognize the area."

"Transferring ocean water to the desert reduced the sea level, increased fresh water supply, nurturing the foundation of Sahara Desert to become fertile from the bottom up."

"Fascinating revolutionizing technology!

Whose innovation, was it?" I stand firmly as a rush of adrenaline bolsters me to my feet.

"An eleven-year-old girl, maybe she was eight, two-hundred-seventy-five years ago. Her engineering dream was a game-changing environmental saving technological mechanism."

"We visited Nativa City as well. Fascinating history there too!"

"As it is a green energy population," Gingi is set to announce, "a landmark for the first settlement incorporated, designed, and established specifically for the ecological age, the Age of Aquarius."

14

Windfall Effect

Constant-spontaneous-instant is the new Declaration of Independence," Gingi exclaims, "bearing all the principles democracy stands for, plus accelerating the marketplace of ideas by turning away ancient prejudices and harmonizing reality and common sense to enhance the 'wellbeing' of the human condition." She plays with the imagery. "The constant-spontaneous-instant is not ineptitude, intuition, or a gut feeling dredged from ignorance or superstition. The constant-spontaneous-instant is fruition born from natural genius informed by a myriad of experiences, perceptions, and adversities.

"Swimming through this Myriad Sea/ spirits cling and refrain/ asking in some ageless open sea/ fish dangle on taught lines wet/ Where to be/ where to go?" Gingi Grind is in a meditative state.

"Look at your prosperity and realize behind you should never be torched earth, use your prosperity to lift those who afforded you the wealth you obtained from them. Virtue is not ideal, it is an expression of love for your fellow human beings, the quality of being morally good."

"Sponti, I'm an Epicurean. I am committed to the pursuit of happiness as a never-ending pursuit! It's best when we bond together, one may bond one way, another may bond another way, in the old United States of America, they bonded for 'the better of together.' Together we survive our timid daily adversities to agree to a larger scope of idealism in space expansion and financial benefit correlated to real estate and investment, uplifting all people by supporting the 'wellbeing' of the human condition, rooted in the ETHW."

"I have an older sister," states Spontaneous Instant, "She was born seventy-five years before me. We are close emotionally, and our relationship from our unique upbringing enhances our mutual existential curiosity. Our parents are only two-hundred-eighteen-years old. They were young to have children. Now that I am less than four years away from receiving the Condorcet procedure there's no hope, they will not stay committed."

"No?"

"No, they are involved in free-roaming and openly intimate with others. It's as though they are teenagers themselves again."

"Maybe, but you're close with them?"

"Close, no. They are supportive of my upbringing and no doubt love me. There's just an adjustment they go off on their separate ways leaving me alone."

"Alone with me, is where to be, in our Myriad Sea," smiles Gingi Grind suggestively.

Spontaneous Instant says it straight, "Yes, it is better! To be with you, there is no other worthy!"

Gingi surmises, "You are hung on me."

"I absorb your love; our bond is five years in the making. With you, I can be all of me, so, yes, I am hung on you."

They touch lips sensually with a little mutual playful nibbling then the tongues come out.

Jürgen finds his tongue, "The possibilities are endless when we act instead of react."

Gingi ceases distracted by the quotation. "George Bernard Shaw," smiles Gingi.

"I know who that is, some old white British playwright."

"He's been dead nearly four hundred years Sponti."

"I didn't say he was alive, I said he was old."

"Old implies he is alive!"

"Did I get it right?" Jürgen asks, "I feel that I am off?"

"Are you serious? Jürgen, you shall think it."

"Oh, little thrown off under the circumstances." Jürgen confesses as he shows his sheer amazement with his wild-eyed expression, "Gingi Grind, pretty awesome!"

Spontaneous Instant and Gingi share laughter at the naivete of the old-world objector stumbling, questioning his staple of certainty, the quotes of G.B. Shaw.

"Greed is measured by how many intergalactic cruisers one needs to own. For instance, if you own nine cruisers and spend time on only one of them, or even all nine with one visit each in a 'work in orbit' season, the exorbitant expense of maintaining nine cruisers each year has a detrimental impact on overall population due to fiat tied up in extraneous maintenance fees, docking fees, tax write-offs. These extravagances are all offenses against the 'wellbeing' of the human condition."

"Not to mention nine cruisers is a boatload of cash," Gingi interrupts with great enthusiasm, "Pun intended. Looks like the drinks are on you guys, Jürgen, and Catherine."

"We don't have any currency."

"We don't have any jobs!" I point out, "How do you figure the drinks are on us?"

"Catherine, you, and Jürgen accumulated in the form of 'wellbeing' popularity, celebrity, and first-class lifestyle access when you were authenticated for the GPPJ. Congratulations, you now have a fresh start of two-million-five-hundred-thousand units!"

"I guess we can retire Catherine, what do you think?"

Spontaneous Instant puts a hand up, "Retire? If you spent the units with rigorous frugality, you both could live off it for three years at most."

"Then what?" I ask thinking this is going nowhere, "We're broke so we find more work, or shake our money maker and no worries?"

"Ha-ha," Spontaneous Instant quips, "Money doesn't grow on trees. You need to plug into The Glass Planet and learn disciplines, acquire skills, and continue to be a positive influence by giving back to the 'wellbeing' of the human condition and you should do fine."

"Make sure you give back! Gratitude is better than greed. Lack of reciprocation will lead to misfortune." Gingi transforms into a cosmic cocktail dress and blue hair color, "When attending a glamorous elegant reception in honor of your authentication, plans are always perfect as they possess influence with their newfound populations. The monetary units are not as important as what you do to be solvent, for little is ever given without some sacrifice of blood, sweat, or tears."

"Or any combination of the three," something of my experience in life bubbled up to allow me to make this assessment.

"'The desire for gold is not for the gold, but for the freedom and benefit,' Ralph Waldo Emerson," Jürgen states with great composure recovering from his recent episode of deviance.

"Hey guys," Gingi interrupts, "Sponti tends to experience hyper-energy levels coiled up in his body, a harmless neurosis, but energy requiring a constant release."

"Nothing is one-hundred-percent," he blurts out, "The only thing one hundred percent is absolutely nothing! When you have something in otherwise nothingness, then you no longer have one hundred percent of nothing, there are multiple fractions of existence and non-existence."

Jürgen replies, "So when the something becomes into existence, no matter how infinitesimally small, it is in existence a percentage of the whole, cutting into nothingness!"

"Correctly stated. If the something came into existence, however, and grew to expand, what-you-may-call-it, to occupy one hundred percent of nothingness, then that something becomes the uniform constant."

"Uniform constant?"

"Nothingness! The 'new' nothingness of existence and the refreshed expectations of something to be introduced into existence."

"Does it stand to reason that extinction of species is related to reaching its one-hundred-percent threshold of knowledge in how to survive in existence?"

"I believe it to be true with the already extinct. The Dodo bird had an insatiable curiosity to investigate the danger instead of running from it. Human species, I am certain our adaptability to adversities is reliant on our mutually inclusive diversity," concludes Spontaneous Instant.

"Yeah, diversity," Jürgen pointedly notes, "some of us run away from the burning building while others run into it!"

"With that said," retorts Gingi Grind, "if it delights you any, we have VIP access to Paradise. Come with?"

"Oh no, would it be safe to jettison in the orbital in our condition? I'm inebriated."

"Catherine, we can take a space shuttle over to the Calypso SS, if you don't mind paying the tab," Spontaneous Instant requests.

"No, I don't mind. How much is it?" My voice is in distress fretting to hear his answer.

"It's only forty-five thousand units, Catherine."

"Oh, that is a pittance! Forty-five thousand monetary units, for all four of us? What a bargain!" Jürgen displays his sarcastic nature in a friendly way.

"Both ways?"

"No worries," Spontaneous Instant raises his hand, "I'm teasing, my orbiter can navigate itself!"

"Nice one Sponti! TCD~" Gingi giggles. Her eyes roll wild embarrassment at Jürgen and me before she speaks her glee, "What twentieth-century dinosaurs!"

The orbiter on autopilot takes two minutes at eighteen-thousand miles per hour. Upon approach, the Calypso SS is one of the Vegas class space stations designed with party fever in mind.

Bright, colorful lighting flashes like the old desert casinos in the heyday of the Vegas strip, playful signage blinking each letter rattles in three dimensions.

The contours of the vessel are designed to elicit a warm and fuzzy sense of hospitality once inside the lobby, the gravity-free elevator is a tubular shaft with multiple off-shoots allowing patrons to travel by their device, gliding to any section of the space station.

Gingi Grind leads us to the Paradise room with her VIP access pass.

"The Paradise room is the most prized VIP experience at the Starry Rose Casino and Resort on the Calypso Space Station," Gingi explains smiling in the delight of hosting us in this opulent place.

The architectural design allows for the Paradise room to take on a panoramic view of the Milky Way while immersed in the luxurious furnishings within the confines of the diamond particle clear wall panels.

"I wonder if we would become sick from inebriation in this weightlessness?" I asked aloud.

"Sick of what?" Spontaneous Instant replies, "Chillaxin'?"

"Let's Dance!" Gingi shrills grabbing me by the hand and towing me to the low gravity dome where hundreds of revelers maneuver about with spirited carelessness reminiscent of a New Year's Eve celebration. "It's always New Year's Eve somewhere in the universe."

Spontaneous Instant follows us close behind and as we introduce ourselves to the crowd many take notice of our arrival.

My heart races with the immediate approach of a crowd towards us, getting their groove on, in the process overwhelming me with inspiring joyfulness!

Jürgen, a sour puss, as he is, sits at the VIP banquet table while groping his drink container cozy. I'm with the crowd levitating in the low gravity room intermingling within a swarm of bodies having no inhibitions from sharing.

I have the feeling of being the life of the party, as so many people are interested in meeting me and seeking me out for reasons as simple as singing to the lyrics of music entirely foreign to me.

Someone says, "Tune into the PAC mode," this instruction went 'over my head' so Gingi reaches over and adjusts my GPI.

"Public Access Channel," she shows me how to adjust channels.

Instantly the voices of everyone around me bring a sensation of adulation and positive vibes of emotional pleasures with a rush of dopamine, then the release of serotonin calms me to focus on the collective consciousness. Strangers flatter me with offers to spend time with me and their families for recreational activities to participate in as a way of 'getting to know you' gatherings. My calendar is rapidly filling up!

Others are searching for me to say how thrilled they are to be alive in the same space-time continuum as Jürgen and me. I react with excited laughter so as not to reveal my apprehension to such bold assumptive comments.

While others are on an even more nefarious path, or for the sake of politeness, looking to join our party to spend the night with us, grinding our bodies grooving to the music, at times twenty to thirty barely dressed twenty-five-year-old find it hot getting it on with a rare 'cougar' body like mine. Impossible to read all messages, forget about responding ~ although most of the messages are rude or disgusting, can use a good tongue lashing in response, there are just too many to take seriously.

Nonetheless, my concern grew stronger for Jürgen's apparent dismay.

"Why the long face Jürgen? What is keeping you alone at this table?"

Jürgen has his chin resting on his propped-up fist, ruminating as he feels out of his element.

"You sure get along with a lot of highly aggressive people." He expresses with a hint of jealousy.

This is a laughable statement by him, "Yeah, it's called socializing. You should try it Jürgen."

"No one is showing as much interest in me as they do for you. You're just more attractive or appealing to them. I heard the crowd's thoughts just as you did, cougar."

"You have a strange sense of humor Jürgen. You do have many people coming up to you, and you are turning a cold shoulder on them." I can see he is not himself. "I'll be right back Jürgen."

I call in Spontaneous Instant through the GPI. In a few seconds, he barrels out of the low gravity rooms.

"How can I be of service Catherine?"

I smile at him and pull him further away from Jürgen. "Jürgen is not quite himself right now," I explain with a calm demeanor. "Is it possible that you and he may have taken a little privilege with some pharmaceuticals?"

"What, pharmaceuticals, we don't use 'pharmaceuticals.'"

"What a relief!" I am briefly satisfied with his assurance, "What about the green flurry you consumed earlier?"

"He's had the designer brand of this awesome lab enriched botanical."

"I see. What do I not see is where one draws the line between a 'pharmaceutical' and a 'lab enriched botanical?'"

"It's as though he had multiple servings of indigo edibles. He said he wanted to take the edge off."

"Like anxiety?"

"No, he doesn't seem the anxious type, I tried to tell him tonight is when you want to keep your edge on!"

I look over to Jürgen and his posture is sloped, "Is there any antidote?"

"Give him one of these energy pills and get him on his feet," Spontaneous Instant advised, "If you like, Gingi and I can have a few of our friends cheer him up and with little effort get his spine ready for action."

"Thanks, we can try the energy pill remedy first. The pink pill resembles an antacid, rather inviting."

He turns to leave, and I hear him speaking through the GPI, "The fastest way is to connect his channel to the PAC."

"The Public Access Channel, the variety of transmissions will arouse his thoughts and bring his level of interest into the moment."

I demonstrate to Jürgen how to adjust to the PAC on his GPI.

Empty cocktail glasses are beginning to pile up.

Jürgen is improving as he holds his liquor well, "We are of the impression this society here is under ultimate climate control."

"I don't even know what that means. How do you mean, ultimate climate control, like room temperature?"

"The transparency of expression is controlling," Jürgen is not completing his thoughts.

"How so?"

"What you conjure in your brain is shared with everyone," I insisted finishing Jürgen's thought.

Spontaneous Instant is not impressed, "So, what is it you are driving at?"

"The Glass Planet! It has intertwined the human experience so intimately that the human condition is uniformly censored!"

Spontaneous Instant squints at Jürgen taking in what he offered as though it were mental candy on a stick. Delighted, he suggestively smiles, "I see you have been hanging with Marcel and Qyxzorina for quite some time!"

"You already said that. What's that supposed to mean?"

"How do you know we even know them?" I ask curiously.

"We work for them. They sent us to bring you back from the Zealot Sentinel training facility," remarks Gingi entering from the low gravity room.

Spontaneous Instant continues, "They're so conservative. They are 'self-censored' as you say, in uniformity. They tend to bend reality to fit their truth."

"What is their truth?" I ask beginning to feel gossipy.

"The 'for each other' is dangerous to the overall 'wellbeing' of the human condition. When people start picking sides based on identity it is simply tribal," he snakes his way over to a floating platform spinning around on it to face me, "Tribal means barbarism, if you know what I mean?"

I am bemused by this young insightful man, "You mean Loyalty!"

"No. Did you notice how often they speak in sync? It is a blatant illustration of the uniformity of their beliefs," Spontaneous Instant uses his coiled-up energy with body language to point to a spot on the floor to which he takes a standing jump, "They are devout, not autonomous to each other!"

"Is that not a large meaning of living life?" I wax philosophical, "To share the love with your soulmate?"

"Or mates," Gingi suggests.

That quip made me do a double take gauging her intent in her eyes.

"Coming off as swingers, are we?" Gingi flares her eyes as she tilts her head teasingly releasing a salacious smile.

"So narrow-minded," Spontaneous Instant says in disgust. "It's naive to think they represent all modern society. You both need to get out and explore a little bit more open to the world beyond Qyxzorina and Marcel!"

Gingi has another round of cocktails served in the private quarters where the party music from the club plays at a tolerable volume in the Paradise Room. She waits until everyone has a drink then raises her glass, "Cheers everybody!" Everyone stands raising their glasses as Gingi dedicates, "To loyalty and friendship!"

We tap the thin edges of our martini glasses together with a clink and then we drink.

"This is so amazing. Here we are celebrating the fact the two of you are now authentic," Gingi directs her attention to her boyfriend, "How many years has it been Sponti?"

"Five at least, maybe six or seven."

"Five, six, or seven years for what?" Jürgen asks as if he didn't hear correctly.

"It has been at least five years since you began Zealot Sentinel training," Gingi says admiringly, "You must kick ass in a bang-up?"

"Whoa now, I am so damned confused with all of this bizarre information!" I'm feeling a growing sense of agitation, "Where are Qyxzorina and Marcel?"

"We barely see them anymore, and we work for them!" Gingi smirks at the thought, "Since they forged a partnership with Patrick Riverstrike on the development of the Star Gazer Sun Tours, they are all-in getting manufacturing on the tour ships completed."

"Then they have to manage the whole operation!" Spontaneous Instant elaborates.

Jürgen is not fully persuaded, "Then how come we were in the Zealot Training program for five years? It did not seem that long."

"Keeping time is not nearly as important as how the time was spent."

"Exactly! The time was spent like shite might! Raw waste too."

"Jürgen, it is a matter of time and space. You are going to live so long that if you think five years goes by twice as fast as you would expect now, then in one hundred years, five years will seem like eight months."

"I think we have to close the tab now, I'm exhausted, and tired, and I suggest, that if time is going to speed up then we better catch our sleep."

"No worries. See if this puts things into perspective," Gingi maintains aloofness in her demeanor but is always prepared with sharp witticisms for those she feels disrespect her. "There are a little over twenty-two-billion other forms of humans with a kaleidoscope of interest, experience, knowledge and, most human of all is something we all share, our mutual ignorance."

"Life is all but a never-ending flow of adversity to overcome constantly to make our lives better." Spontaneous Instant is flying-off-the-wheel, "Greed-fascism is adversity against the 'wellbeing' of the human condition and is a high crime."

"High crime. Why does a term like 'high crime' exist? Isn't

any crime bad enough?" I said standing up as a hint 'it's time to go everybody.'

"The last thing a subservient-based society wants to see is the poor populations become economically solvent. The overall structure of the economy allows for the subservient masses to remain debt slaves if not outright impoverishment."

Jürgen moves away from the table indicating he's ready to leave, "What I value is loyalty can come from any one relationship."

Gingi follows by standing and reaching for Sponti's hand, "No matter the length of the intimacy of, the distance of, as loyalty is an idea made into a concept realized through practicing life for the 'wellbeing' of the human condition."

She throws her right arm around Sponti's waist, "It's one of the underpinnings of democracy." Gingi quotes, "'Give me your tired, your poor, your huddled masses yearning to breathe free.'"

"So, in that way Qyxzorina and Marcel check out good with us," Spontaneous Instant somehow forms the thought, "but for your benefit, let Gingi Grind and I take you on a bit less of a 'guided' tour."

Jürgen smiles toward me, and I share the strength in our informed loyalty to each other with an inviting smile. "Catherine, I know what you're thinking about!"

"You do?" My nose tickles at the tip, "Jürgen, it must be tied to our history together."

"Or some computer program simulation," Jürgen flexes his hand over his mouth to speak sarcasm privately to me. "This is no simulation Jürgen!"

"Yeah Jürgen," interjects Spontaneous Instant, "get your head out of your ass and feel your heart."

"Spontaneous Instant, do you feel emotions let alone understand them?"

Equally amused by this comment he replies sharply, "Do you know the feeling of pain and what sprouts from it? Do you know the feeling of ignorance by understanding your ignorance?"

Jürgen relents, "Who was responsible for this 'awakening?'"

"Responsible?"

"Yes, responsible." I put forth the question, "Was he a handsome devil like you?"

Spontaneous Instant laughs heartily.

"Then how did this shift in cultural views occur?" I am not amused.

Spontaneous Instant and Gingi respond in unison, "Common

sense for the 'wellbeing' of the human condition."

Jürgen's sarcasm is poignant, "You both spoke in unison, what a blatant illustration of the uniformity of your beliefs."

"You overlook a critical difference, uniformity in the beliefs mutually exclusive from others, as in personal preference is in opposition to one of the pillars of a thriving democracy."

"Of the many mantras embraced by the modern age sums up the matter best: 'Religion is as necessary to reason as reason is to religion. The one cannot exist without the other–George Washington."

"Sponti, the one about truth and pains I think applies too."

"Another George Washington quote?" I ask.

Gingi smiles in affirmation, "'Truth will ultimately prevail where there are pains to bring it to light.' I like to think in terms of nature's rules as the ultimate truth. When we speak of 'wellbeing,' we speak of truth."

We make our way through the spacious lounge in this hotel resort space station on our way to the orbiter hanger. The carpeted floor changes color with every step. A rainbow of colors as if walking on clouds with tied-dyed patterns illicit the stimulation of dopamine boosting a natural euphoric high. Pleated wall dressings are a mural, constructed from plant-based materials and possessing the natural essence to propagate an organic awakening.

Images of deep space systems transition fluidly, and breath-taking spacescapes are uplifting, spiritually touching, and warming my heart with inspiration.

People in the spacious lounge are going strong in their celebrations. Gingi and Spontaneous Instant are leading the way as we linger behind mindful of not losing them while our attention is drawn to the wild scene of happy, joyous revelers against the sprawling background of the Milky Way in the distance, another example of awe-inspiring feats of space station architectural design and engineering.

"Hey, yons!" Gingi is approaching us, "The hangar entrance is right around the corner."

We step up our pace following Gingi to the orbiter where, auspiciously, Spontaneous Instant has it hovering a foot off the spaceport floor.

As we pile into the two-seater, it became evident Jürgen has recovered quickly from the haziness he exhibited earlier as Gingi and I can settle into something like a rumble seat of this economized high school graduation present, the Clipper.

We can fold our bodies to sit with our knees to our chin.

"How long of a ride to the Sea Foam condos?"

"About thirty minutes. You're going love it there."

We share the Sea Foam condominiums marketing imagery on our GPI screens.

"I cannot deny it looks like a unique experience. They look like huge bubbles along the south Florida coast."

"I know, you have some beach to enjoy when needed and the place of solitude inside the condo under the ocean's depth of one hundred feet."

"Truly private and serene, in between the hurricanes, which there seems to be one every other week?"

"It's the hurricane season! You're a silly person sometimes. Miami is perfect for you!"

"Here we go! Hold on everyone!" Spontaneous Instant terrifies me with his bombastic outburst.

The orbiter glides out of the spaceport and into open space where the orbiter accelerates to seventeen-thousand-five-hundred miles-per-hour in thirty seconds.

"Look ma, no hands!" Spontaneous Instant says holding his hands forward toward the bow of the orbiter to frame a display with his hands cropping Mother Earth.

I presume he has autopilot on.

"Gingi, how do you spell your last name?"

Gingi's face illuminates an expression of playfulness.

"It's pronounced 'grin,' right ~ with a silent 'd.'" She points to the expression on her face. "I spell it G-R-I-N-D."

Jürgen comments from the passenger seat, "A silent 'd' as in 'Gadget?'"

Gingi breaks her grin to respond, but Spontaneous Instant couldn't resist, "As in 'adjust,' 'wedge,' or 'grudge' and 'knowledge.'"

I ask with a polite, curious intent, "Why the silent 'd' in your name?"

"My parents, duh," Gingi remarks reflect her emotional immaturity, "Are you dumb? With a silent 'b?'"

"No offense intended. I assure you."

Spontaneous Instant raises his voice to defend Gingi, "Good one Gingi! With a silent 'j' in your name Jürgen, I think you would be wiser than that!"

Jürgen rolls his eyes as I notice the reticence in his face, as he shoots me a glance, he's had to explain many times before, "The 'j' is not silent, it is a soft consonant," he remarks. "Though it would be nice small talk is why I asked. A little get to know you?"

Gingi whispers into Jürgen's ear, "Sponti's giving you a tough time because he likes you, and so do I." She leans forward over his shoulder and with a lustrous puckering of her lips she pecks at his cheek.

Spontaneous Instant intervenes moving rapidly he places his right hand on Jürgen's interface, "I'm glad you bought the issue up. Let me make one adjustment, that's with a silent 'd.'" He places his pinky finger adjusting a setting, "Now you are up to speed."

"Yes, I do feel the stimulation."

I clear my throat, "I'm sure you do!"

The amazing view of the approach to Earth is breathtaking. It is craziness to me to be hurtling toward the surface at thousands of miles-per-hours in what amounts to be the equivalent of a rumble seat!

The Clipper punches into the cloud layer and in a matter of seconds, we emerge to view the Atlantic Ocean and enter a streamlined shuttle and orbiter traffic heading west to Miami.

"Have you abandoned all sense of responsibility?" Jürgen frames the question succinctly.

"Responsibility ~?" Gingi brushes off the notion. "Confide to me. How old are you?"

Spontaneous Instant overhears me as I see him turn an ear toward us, he is all too thrilled to respond, "How old do you think we are?"

"I guess, in my opinion, cemented in my mind, based on your knowledge . . ."

"Knowledge?" Exclaims Gingi, "We haven't even begun our master's studies!"

"Gingi! You gave the answer away!"

I impart to her, "You have to be at least twenty-one based on what you had to consume tonight."

Jürgen presses on insistently asking, "How old are you when you are preparing for master's studies, twenty-three?"

"What? Seriously Jürgen, I expect to complete my masters by twenty-two!" Gingi reveals, "I am twenty, okay?"

"I am confused considerably by your assertion," I struggle to comprehend as my mind grows wearier with every thought expended, "Are you saying twenty Earth years around the Sun?"

Gingi appears disappointed by my inquiry, "You know, for elders you are extraordinarily ignorant."

"Excuse me, what's with the discourteous slight? The two of you are more knowledgeable than us if you think about it!"

"How so?" Gingi asks.

"Although we were born a long time before you, the fact you are 'fresh' to life, immersed in modern times gives you an understanding of human life Jürgen and I are oblivious to. Remember, our experiences in life ceased sometime three hundred plus years ago. You both have an immense wealth of knowledge we missed."

"Okay then, granted we are more knowledgeable about many things you may be ignorant to, but you have firsthand experiences in a place in time we can only simulate," Gingi articulates concisely, "You guys are so 'TCD,' twentieth-century dinosaurs!"

Gingi and Spontaneous Instant enjoy their sense of humor sharing a laugh at the expense of humility for Jürgen and me.

"There it is," I state pointing for no effective purpose other than to change the subject, "The Sea Foam condominiums. Do you see it Spontaneous Instant?"

"Catherine!" Gingi is quick to remark, "We referred you here, duh!"

I feel the blood rushing to my cheeks as Jürgen's face blushes as well as feeling my embarrassment from this regaling preposterous rude teenager.

As he descends the orbiter to the Sea Foam landing port Spontaneous Instant is nibbling at the bit, "There's an old saying, 'Humility and humor put ~"

Jürgen and I interject in unison, "put the 'Hu' in human! We know all too well."

"Ah, so you know you are both knuckleheads?" He lands the orbiter with gentle ease.

"Thank you, Spontaneous Instant, for your kind words and the ride home." I deliver this projecting sarcasm.

"Hey, that was very good," Jürgen states unexpectedly.

"Well then," Gingi asks wearing a dunce cap, "how old are you?"

Jürgen exits the orbiter to stand on the port tarmac extending his hand to assist me out of the orbiter.

Sensing Jürgen's disdain for their attitudes is equal to mine once our eyes meet as I exit, I bounce off his shirking glance, "We have been in this present age half the time you have!"

"Catherine, preposterous!" Spontaneous Instant wields his arms to his hips offering a look of suspicious derision as he exits the pilot seat providing room for Gingi to move into the passenger seat.

"That is weird," Spontaneous Instant frets. "Guilty are you of such ignorance about your age?"

"Bile spews from liars' mouths!"

"Though about our age in physical years we are closing in on fifty years old."

"You are closing in on fifty Jürgen, not me," this discrepancy compels me to clarify.

"Just as I thought Sponti, 'gray heads.' Jürgen, how can you be so ignorant, less informed than us, in our twentieth year?"

"Gingi, some people just can't handle our marathon excursions."

"They are so delusional!"

"I think it is a distinct possibility they are tripping balls!" Spontaneous Instant muses. "Yeah, our kind of people."

Gingi portrays astonishment, "Bizarre you mean?"

"Have you heard murder is a direct product of ignorance no matter the motivation? Criminals, who scheme it believe they can't be caught?"

"Go on."

"Whether a murderer claims jealousy, humility, anger out of rage, as rage itself is a core pillar of barbarism, and equally a direct by-product of ignorance, pain, frustration, fervor for violence or processing a penchant to harm innocence and peacefulness are all rooted in the ignorance."

"The ignorance of what?" Jürgen inquires.

"Ignorance of the truth," states Spontaneous Instant before adding, "And ignorance is nine-tenths of the law; always has been and always will be."

"Nice reference, very relatable," I said with good intent.

"Save me your nostalgia Catherine, tell us why you and your cute friend Jürgen are so 'mysterious.'"

"Mysterious? Do you mean as in our 'ignorance' we are mysterious?"

"Cute Jürgen do not play me for a fool. You guys know a whole lot more than you are letting on."

It is obvious to me who is the ignorant two of the four of us, "To answer your question Gingi Grind, it is the measure of your access to information, this I can say from firsthand experience, using the GPI as though an encyclopedia of known existence is strapped to your brain. In our day, we had to read page to page, and information, we'll say was harder to obtain."

"Sounds to me as though you two could be from the dawn of the printing press!"

Spontaneous Instant joins Gingi seated in the Clipper.

"No worries, there must be some reason for your existence," he ignites the orbiter engine as the hatch secures, he offers me searing eyes of suspicion, tilting his jaw the orbiter lifts off vertically into the jet stream joining the traffic accelerating as if racing in aerial Grand Prix.

15

Keeping Pace In Space Travel

Once Jürgen and I situate ourselves taking up accommodations at the Sea Foam condos we decide we need to invest in a spacecraft of our own.

The advice we receive from most patrons is to visit a commercial dealer in upstate New York outside of Syracuse.

"The dealer is a large investor of interplanetary cruisers suitable for a flight to Mars," I explain to Jürgen who is in the bedroom not feeling any better three days after the onset of his discomfort. "As well the spacecraft will require mobility into Earth's atmosphere."

"I think it best to purchase one with a sizable cargo hold. It may be necessary as an opportunity for employment often involve transporting materials for Earth-landers who conduct business in a free-lance manner with the GPPJ." He muffles a growl he cannot conceal.

"What are you doing in there?"

"I'm dealing with a 'boulder' of constipation."

"What could you be eating that causes constipation?"

"I don't know, but it isn't doing me no favors right now."

Anticipating the opportunity to enter varied professions, the interior must have multiple facilities capable of alternating equipment specific to the disciplines we engage.

With the probability of using a spacecraft intricately in one specific livelihood as an exceptionally low prospect, we found it advisable to also have room for up to fifty guests for business meetings to private functions like an art Exhibit.

This is where persons who may be in employment as support staff such as cargo handlers for 'white-glove' delivery, or to entertain savvy dealers of various items for sale or barter, like artwork, will come into profitable use."

Jürgen is precipitously groaning louder and louder.

"What is going on in there?"

He responds with a wavering voice, "About got her done, yeah! Whoa, that was some shiny shite might!"

"What are you talking about?" As I ask this, he emerges from the bedroom using a tissue to wipe the surface of something in his hand.

"It looks like to me," he says with giddy enthusiasm, "We have our cruiser paid for in full."

"Okay, enough already. What is the deal with you?"

He smiles at me and raises his right hand holding a rather large shiny diamond the size of a ping-pong ball.

"Is that what I think it is from where I believe it came from?"

"Exactly correct if you mean I must have swallowed this at the Diamond Bar! No doubt, I was polluted by a green flurry."

"That explains your recent sour mood, too. What do you think it's worth? Is it worth an interplanetary cruiser?"

"I should think so, about six-hundred-million units, maybe more. Let's go find out."

"It is most important, the financing, as not to relinquish a tidy sum on the purchase price without understanding certain trends of the economy that will gravely restrict purchasing power."

"We're not going to need financing with this rock."

"I recall several people advising us to get a vehicle sensible to our current means and not to rely on expectations of a consistent, reliable wealth of income from our popularity ratings."

"Sounds like sensible advice, let's get a muscle cruiser. We may have peaked with our novelty as time refugees, but an eye-catching cruiser will keep us relevant."

"After a few centuries pass on, most people would not have such excitement to offer digital fiat to gain our favor. In this vein, fuel economy and renewable energy sources offer the best value. Not a 'muscle cruiser.'"

However, once we tour this lot of all types of makes and models, our temptation to purchase a sleek body style with transforming shape and color alteration capabilities, along with a slight muscle car attitude, guides us to the Nebula Drifter series.

This is preferable as Jürgen found the interchangeable color palette of earth tones green, brown, yellow, and blue embellishes our true Earth-lander roots.

We ended up with an interplanetary class cruiser Nebula Drifter, with a spacious flight cabin for up to eight passengers and a cargo hold that doubles as a hospitality cabin for up to fifty travelers.

Each traveler will enjoy their hygiene station and a communal area for entertainment and socializing. A value priced at six hundred eighty-nine million monetary units. The huge uncut diamond is appraised for seven hundred sixty million monetary units. We made a profit of seventy-one million monetary units.

This purchase is our anniversary gift to ourselves as we will be one year residing as GPPJ citizens. We decided to mark the occasion by orbiting the planet at a below space horizon distance to view the Northern hemisphere in the height of winter at a time in December when citizens around the world observed various holidays both religious and secular.

Snowfall was widespread across the Continents and the GPPJ population has created many activities and events foreign to our experience.

The cultures within the vivariums offered ancient and traditional decorum and celebrations with decorative light and the familiar symbols associated with the season greetings, and of all religious fervor on a larger scale having use of modern technologies creating temporary structures for intricate colorful seasonal lighting displays and monuments.

Our Nebula Drifter cruiser is a magical ride, with incredible acceleration, a clear three-hundred-sixty-degree view from the flight cabin, and as quiet as a spaceship can be. The interplanetary class craft is the modern equivalent of an oversized RV or Winnebago, with autopilot navigation, despite its impressive design, it is a flying house is what it is.

16

Refugees Like Us

Something struck me as familiar, "What did you mean specifically when you said you suspect an ancient culture is responsible for us?"

Marcel furrows his brow, his eyes to look directly into mine, "Denisovans. Human lineage culturally like a human; They appeared shortly after Homosapiens."

"I know of the Denisovans."

"The refugees, like yourself, we suspect are genetically connected to the Denisovans. There's a genealogical influence that informs the descendants of a genus unique to homosapiens with a two or more percentage of Denisovans DNA."

"You believe Jürgen, and I share Denisovans genes?"

"All human ancestry does, as well as a bit of Neanderthal ancestry and other off-shoots too."

Marcel holds his cup close to his lips before taking a sip of warm java he slips in, "The analysis of your complete genome reveals a near ten percent DNA makeup."

"What does it mean Marcel?"

"You have a higher concentration of Denisovan genes than the general population. Catherine, you know the human condition is complex. Its influence is diverse, its purposes multifaceted, yet genes are random." Marcel observes, "This subservience, in contrast, is tribalism in the name of Barbarism. The result is a society's citizenry's willingness to acquiesce to power."

"Give up liberties to gain a little security?"

"Often the perceived security is a false sense of security, already compromises your safety from the start."

Jürgen starts in with another quote, "If you compromise liberties to gain security, you deserve neither liberty nor security."

"Paraphrase Ben Franklin," I quip, "Too bad a founding Father couldn't be time refugees like us."

"That would be too easy ~ Jürgen replies ~ Considering this time and place, they'd crap their pants."

"Not so," I reply to fretting hearing this as I sensed a modicum of truth in his remark, "It would be a fascination for them in this place, in space! It would be gratifying to see their fundamental constructs and principles evolve to persist through time and become the global standard of governance."

Marcel shines an optimistic smile but asserts a serious tone, "It is fine to make light of ending fascism on Earth. Tyrants, dictators, monarchies, totalitarians, and socialist communism, as enforced by a despot, are financial elitists, and oligarchs detrimental to the 'wellbeing' of the human condition. Not unlike RAKLAV ZS creating debt slaves."

"Where the masses give power to the corporate manipulation in the marketplace to optimize the consumer spending and therefore creating generation after generation of debt slaves, is the most subtle and obscenely grotesque example of economic oppression."

Qyxzorina breaks her silence to advise, "The vast human existence has been long exploited over generations by strains of greed, consolidation of power, control of hearts and minds with every new crop of human generations."

"Crop of human generations?"

Qyxzorina lets out a sigh, "These are dreadful expressions. The generations, every new passing generation, as a freshly grown crop to be seeded, weeded, and harvested, are for the sole purpose of subservience and consumerism."

"And it was these very same hearts and minds who were shackled by unceasing debt on the road to impoverishment. As was the old economic code exploiting the masses for the benefit of the few."

"Marginalized as debt slaves more or less."

Marcel appears invigorated by Jürgen's insights of the mother generation, "Yes. Until it dawned upon the masses humanity as a society, is a system, able to provide for all and not mainly for ownership. As it is everyone's natural right to help each other survive. Promoting diversity with equality will help each other secure 'wellbeing' for all."

"Greed was associated with the same characteristics as consolidators of power, fascism is the consolidator of hearts and minds by leveraging division and fear for subservience."

"Not for the 'wellbeing' of the human condition, but for their dereliction of responsibility, unethical lack of integrity, immoral contradictions in beliefs and motives to wedge the masses apart, asking for prayers from the subservient, one way of distraction from the true intentions providing cover for their egregious exploitations in self-interest against the 'wellbeing' of the human condition. Do I make myself abundantly clear to you?"

"Respectively so, but not coherently as we lack ~"

"Yes Catherine, the concept is clear, but we don't have any context to fully ~"

"Appreciate the developments over the last several hundred years."

"Catherine, you're starting to complete Jürgen's sentences." Marcel is resolute, "That is not my problem. I dumbed it down as much as possible. It's on you guys!"

We break out into uproarious laughter.

Jürgen comes to terms with my point of view on the Founding Fathers, "Political interest seems to have changed for the better of the people, to serve the people. Heck, it's a certainty given the fact the Earth is alive and well!"

Qyxzorina delights in our sympathetic tone, "Yes, politics is now management, as is every aspect of the economy, no more monopoly ownership, no more variable interest rates."

Our shared laughter intensifies with every sentence.

"What was the catalyst for this change?" I ask in a roundabout way using the levity of the moment to delve deeper.

"The awakening to the Economic Theory of the Human Will," Marcel turns gravely serious, "results in the banishment of greed-fascism."

My understanding of this topic is merely from word of mouth, as this history of events I did not experience, "How is this banishment enforced though?"

"Any endeavors to pursue crimes against the 'wellbeing' of the human condition is punishable by banishment to RAKLAV detention complex on Mars," Qyxzorina's sentiments take on a deeper meaning for her as consequences of severe neglect are the staples of human oppression and inequality. "Now those who stand against unity in diversity are in no way taken seriously. If causing provocation, then off to one of the vivariums to dwell in the ignorance shared by like-minded people."

"Awesome," starting in with sarcasm Jürgen comments, "It

sounds like a modern incarceration system."

"Sadly, it is by choice for many." She laments, "It is loyalty and friendship amongst vivarium populations fueling their ignorance, their hatred, prejudices, superstitions, and discrimination against diversity."

"And they're always ready to proselytize their prejudices," Marcel insists, "As if by merely preaching fear of adversities is worthy of embracing."

"It is a necessary evil to contain someone's belief system if it is a threat to the 'wellbeing' of the human condition," I postulate in suspicion of what the true intent of these isolated populations may be.

"It's not a belief system as much as it is an ignorance system," Marcel interprets his meaning, "The righteously ignorant are safe in their vivariums. They enjoy the benefits of the ETHW. Whether they are safe from themselves is another question, but safe from harming us with their systemic hatred in their self-interest, and to deter the 'survival of the fittest' greed-fascism perspective popular to those practitioners of barbarism. This reason alone suffices as the primary intent of the vivarium's purpose."

"Survival of the fittest. What does that mean, exactly?" I ask sensing I have pondered this question repetitively in my past. "Elitists from the era of barbarism embrace survival by all means necessary to suppress the masses?"

"You could say that three hundred years ago, as you can say that three thousand years ago. What is meant by 'fittest' would include liars, thieves, cheaters, psychopaths obsessed with obtaining the physical manifestation of the human will, fiat to afford exuberance, and wield power over the will of all others."

"There is much motivation to escape the confines of history. To become refugees like us, seeking opportunities to grow by expanding our knowledge beyond our learned wisdom. Open to all possibilities of experience."

17

Setting the Stage

As an introductory of the Star Gazer Sun Tour ship voyager line for the GPPJ, Marcel has a presentation video he plays exploring the standard private cabin and the amenities included on board an SGST ship:

Inner cabins are alike with some variations in color scheme and elegant columns with acanthus plasterwork of Corinthian ornamentation accentuating the corners of the rooms.

Every room provides sleeping capsules for up to four travelers, two bathrooms, a common room, two separate private rooms, and a common kitchen with amenities of cutlery, a food dispenser, and a refrigerator.

Bots are assigned to enter the room for maintenance service every three days or more frequently if requested.

The rooms are designed for the ultimate in privacy and quietness. Observatory monitors are available to get the real-time activity of celestial events.

There are forty bowling alleys, two-thousand earth-class and Solar-system-class restaurants, and a hologram-virtual reality lounge in every cabin quarters. Essentials including laundry service, grooming, and hygiene products are delivered to your door for your convenience.

In place of water, hydration cells offer a daily recommended amount of H2O consumption. Soluble chemical products clean plate ware, bedding, and clothing throughout the tour ships with "white glove" handling performed by human staff with the assistance of state-of-the-art robotic technology.

Want to earn extra monetary units? Even with twelve-thousand-five-hundred employees, and an infrastructure of robotic assigned services, many industries are offering part-time positions to tourists in retail or service roles for generous compensation to boost your spending power during your tour to and around the Sun.

Every accommodation possible to provide in space travel is present on SGST ships. For ten hours out of every twenty-four, the ship maintains zero gravity to increase the traveling speed and allow for replenishment of solar-supported energy reserves.

Aboard the 'Dark Eaglet,' Riverstrike's cruiser, are his top officers, thirteen governors of the SSN, and seventy-six support staff members on their way to the celebration at Fra Mauro crater Lunar City performing arts center.

In the lounge room enjoying cocktails Riverstrike sits next to and leans over to Junior and Simon to share an image of Catherine on a private device, "Want to keep an eye on that one. She's got something immensely powerful deep inside her."

"What could that be Minister?" Simon covered his mouth with his hand, "More powerful than our lovely Janalake?"

"Yes," Riverstrike concurs, "there is a truth or truths for that matter, no one can refute. If she is who I think she is, this home planet is infested with hidden foreign enemies who are a threat to our way of life. I believe she knows of this subterranean race, which may have erased her memory or at least brainwashed her to deny exposure to them."

"The whole enterprise is belly up?"

"Not belly up yet. We'll have to perform an exhumation."

Simon gives pause to consider what he said, "Don't you mean 'exterminate?'"

"Yes, ultimately that is exactly what I mean," Riverstrike clarifies, "but by exhumation of the home planet, I'm referring to unearthing the whole embedded sub-species. Give it *time*, and we return to this planet to save it from itself. Without the technical means to administer the Condorcet procedure, the average life expectancy could fall below one-hundred years."

Simon goes a little further, "Then come back in a couple hundred of years as saviors of the human race."

The Minister stifles a reflexive burst of laughter.

"Sad to say, but humans are short-sighted and a good deal of an amnesiac as a whole. If this sub-species has somehow surpassed humans in evolutionary development, then once the present technology maintaining human dominance is eliminated by us . . ."

It is a wonder the Minister and Simon do not care if Janalake overhears their every word. Why is Simon discussing such obscene scenarios with Minister Riverstrike?

"Janalake, you have held your position with great honor and are respected by the nine-hundred million who have and do serve in the Zealot Sentinels. The time has come to proactively recruit the youth from ACRES for leadership training. I would like to designate you as the Secretary of Leadership development coordinating and designing the training programs. Your new position will have you based on Earth and working with officials from ACRES and WOCH as well as esteemed academics and universities from across the globe to create an effective elite Zealot Sentinel training program."

"It would be my privilege to serve you in any way you find necessary, Minister."

"This endowment will begin no later than five years from this date, twenty-three-fifty-two. In the time leading up to this reassignment, prepare for the transition and set the table for your successor, while developing your ways and means to honor your legacy."

"Understood, Minister. I embrace the opportunity and will look forward to discussing details with you in due time."

"As you were Commander. Spend time with the governors, get to know them a little better, and see if you can elicit any recommendations for your successor."

Janalake moves on to mingle with the governors and their support staff members in the capacious lounge.

Riverstrike continues with his treasonous rhetoric, "My goal is to create a solar light system of synthesis hybrid planets, a furnace of a Sun and have dozens of scientists who specialize in fertilization, anti-aging science, sustain life technology and form a population of descendants. Initial women will be organic- synthetic-blend robots that are equipped with lab-created human tissue uterus, eggs, ready-to-fertilize ovum, and progesterone from histology scratch. That's right, the offspring are of your seed exclusively, no previous lineage than that of your own, and the genetic design you select for the embryo. They are designed to carry and support an embryo for a natural nine-month term, before giving birth in a medical facility, subject to a systemic process to procure a programmed emotional intelligence ensuring every citizen's appreciation for being created by savior Riverstrike."

Simon points out, "Why not remedy the Earth?"

"Remedy the planet?" Riverstrike squints his eyes, "There's

no economic gain anymore. Society is life in an empty fishbowl, life in The Glass Planet. There are too many earth-landers. They're stubbornly ignorant of space travel and you can only lead a horse to water, but the horse must have the will to drink it. They'll be sorry for their rigid stubbornness once they come face to face with a hell-bent subterranean savage."

"You're going to let them perish?" Junior breaks his silence, "And you're not bringing real women?"

"We'll come back to pick them up if they're still around." He states flippantly, "There are tens of millions of real women on the~"

"I want 'elite' woman access!"

"They have guns down there and hope is fractured," Simon states factually.

"Exactly why we take them with us!" Junior incurs displeasure from this absurdity.

"We don't even know if they will go! No, no, we will come back later when they're least suspecting, experiencing subhuman oppression, prime for rescue, we'll herd them up and transport them like the cattle they are to be used at our will for pleasure, entertainment." Riverstrike's chauvinistic demeanor hints at a maniacal obsession. "There is time to review and consider alterations to preparations and monitor progress with supplies and cargo before launch. Junior, you're better off with a synthetic reproductive system simulator."

Junior displays an agreeable twinkle in his eye as if his father has 'gifted' him. His eyes lose their twinkle once considering the inorganic nature of a simulator.

The Chair of the SSN Governors committee and Chief of Staff Rilke von Steyer overhears the conversation as he approaches Riverstrike.

"What timeline have you coordinated?" Asks von Steyer.

"I anticipate by twenty-three-fifty-two we will need to arrange appropriate personnel in line for the proper execution of the separation."

"I'm not entirely clear on one minor detail. The Zealot Sentinels will be conscious for the flight to the Dark Eagle?"

"Yes, but not the ZS. By then we will have an elite ZS force. Once the plan is executed, they will be immobilized for the trip to Spark Creation Genesis system," he is frank, at first, in his response. "However, I plan to evacuate a majority of the EZS via Star Gazer Mars Tour ships to make the journey. Any expectation is to create a diversion and incapacitate as many of the SGST ships. Then I will utilize all Star Gazer Mars Tour ships under my supervision, given I financed them in the first place to transport the EZS troops.

"We will have retrained the most superior physical specimens to suit them with the advanced gear. They will be selected to train at the Mars facility as all other ZS recruitment will discontinue.

"This elite force will consist of seven-million-five-hundred-thousand individuals derived in part from the most loyal ZS and the remainder I expect to be much of the elite force, comprised from the ACRES youth cadets training program over the next few years. Exceptionally talented, gifted youth recruits trained by Commander, I mean General Janalake, EZS Recruitment, and Training Corps. The initiative program of extending the human footprint beyond our Solar system will occur if we maintain secrecy Governor Rilke von Steyer."

He follows deductively, "I see, to offer opportunities to serve in the interest of furthering the colonial expansion to intergalactic destinations. What of Janalake?"

"Janalake has already been informed that she is to be re-assigned her duties to head the recruitment-training program in collaboration with ACRES."

"Then who will take command of the ZS?"

"Our lovely Catherine will rise to take that position and she will ultimately be the mother to my heirs."

Simon inserts curiosity, "And what of her present mate Jürgen?"

"That is where you come in Simon. I have wonderful plans for you too. The new system will be superior to the present models, and you will be entrusted as my number two next to Catherine, who believes in your persuasion and will come to embrace the path along the way."

Simon asks with a tone of finality, "And the rest who are extraneous?"

"Leaving behind a formidable force, under crisis, the ZS garrisons are to lock down the population for their perceived security by extending control over the planets."

"As an outpost?"

"They will be critical in doing the dirty work. The asteroid belt population will individually take cruisers from their asteroids to rendezvous with the Dark Nest as it navigates along the asteroid belt toward Mars and then onto the rendezvous coordinates."

"Minus the nine dedicated space stations of the SCG system," Rilke von Steyer states pointedly. "Most important for the success of the SCG solar light system to adapt into manufactured planets orbiting the SCG sun."

"The idea behind the frequent mobilization of the Zealot Sentinels," Riverstrike cavalier with his attitude, "As managed by me, will prevent them from having idle hands and minds from conspiring rebellion.

"I have designed an emulation of nature in replicating the power of the Sun. Human genius has engineered processes of nature for the expediency of use, from manufactured solar systems to the creation of artificial materials to withstand and overcome nature's worst threat, its' extreme randomness. Engineering of science to expedite replication Terraforming, the substitution of nature's origins of life with processes in concert with nature as created by human existence, stewards we are, inheritors of an original creator's vision or not. I am to re-envision what is and I hold the authority appointed to steward humanity to its unrealized potential, exempting artificial intelligence from achieving human experience. There is nothing closer to the truth than human experience, as it is of nature, something a conspiring artificial intelligence is unable to conceive. Either artificial intelligence effortlessly works for us, or it becomes maligned and easily disabled.

"Those who value and embrace artificial intelligence more than themselves have forfeited their humanity and shall be subject to their extinction.

"My station of eminence, my powers of perception, my sacrifices for to improve the 'wellbeing' of the human condition are examples for all conscious living beings to learn proper respect and deference to my supreme authority, to my will, for me to retain, maintain and entertain all the inferior rest, the infrastructure within.

"The cyclical mechanism of existence is what, once embraced and mastered, provides the evolution of metaphysical existential transcendentalism, ensuring the conquering of the intolerance that is of extinction. All those who have intolerance against the 'wellbeing' of the human condition shall be subject to their extinction," Riverstrike concludes his comments to the nine Governors of space stations who are co-conspirators to the Spark Creation Genesis plot. "We just need to destroy The Glass Planet and we will embark on the epoch of our making."

"Epoch?" Asks the young Admiral Barcarui.

"We will have consolidated all power technology capability. Some call it a God-complex, I am chosen as all of you are. Our beliefs are superior and relevant to my financial success, continue to make the rules to secure our privilege. We are infallible and shall continue to marginalize the standard of living of the non-chosen poor. The ETHW is outdated, passe, and no need as the GPPJ is entirely self-sustainable.

"Past this Solar system, the GPPJ is ineffective due to travel logistics. Venturing out to develop new solar light systems is now my ultimate ambition, like God, I will engineer a medium Sun. The proper order of hierarchy will be mandated as all women will look up to me as their divine inspiration. I will lead you to victory," he claims. "With the formation of the EZS, acronym for the Elite Zealot Sentinels, capable of lethality with their hands, and their hands interchangeable with firearms. I have established Elite Zealot Sentinel forces with the intent to arm them."

He has said enough to provoke the one question no one asks: How will the presence of nearly eight million EZS, half cyborg and equipped with outlawed armaments be possible?

"If anyone is curious 'how' this will be done ~"

"We all know Minister, whatever you conceive will come to fruition."

"For the record, von Steyer, I expect to enlist the assistance of one Captain Shane Colston, the world's leading ballistics specialist."

"Is he aware of this profound opportunity if not enlisted as of yet?"

"No, he is not informed about any aspect of the mission. We have a history together going back to our years in military service. We're like brothers."

There is a round of vigorous applause led by Simon Noir.

A hologram imaging of the EZS in modified uniforms and training with firearms appears on a secured brain screen exclusive for the conspirators to view.

"What you have viewed is preliminary but is an accurate portrayal."

"All information on pass card, no entrance otherwise." Admiral Barcarui instructs to secure the information files of the visual presentation under top secret vault access.

Riverstrike addresses the nine Governors and two dozen women of specific DNA markers and ideological form standing in a circle around him on the flight deck of the Dark Eaglet.

"Gentlemen, these fine women we have designed ~ twenty- four select women who possess traits representative of the genetic qualities superior to all other women who will inhabit the Spark Creation Genesis solar light system."

"Thank you, sir!" Captain Junior responds with unabashed eagerness, an expression Riverstrike allows his most senior officers to enjoy.

"As a reminder for you Junior, we have celluloid robots stored in cargo." Riverstrike mocks his son provoking laughter from the governors in deference to the Minister, their Supreme leader, who shares in the laughter.

As the meeting ends in the Dark Eaglet, the course is set to attend the inaugural launch of the SGST flagship the Soley Leve. The launch will be followed by the Fra Mauro crater Lunar City celebration, Chief of staff Rilke von Steyer quips while the panoramic view of the Earth complex is projected before them, "Since we're breaking all ties with our business partners, what kind of severance package can I get?" He abruptly stifles his reaction to his lame attempt at humor.

"The nine middle-aged three-hundred-fifty-year-old conspirators," Riverstrike has his military uniform from three-hundred years ago, the Brigadier General, "Without the possibility of war and the relative insignificance of guns, this planet and population have proven to surpass its profitability margin. Our influence will only diminish from here on out. The equality of wealth when achieved will result in stifling mediocrity. Besides, the planet Earth is beyond its peak form, well on its way to unsustainable to cataclysmic death. It is our time to seek eminent domain in our Galaxy, the Milky Way, and leave the past behind us."

18

Two Paths Taken

Journalists traipse around the SGST flag ship's command deck dutiful in securing their reserved seats where the launch ceremony will begin as Qyxzorina steps to the podium facing the attendees, "Welcome SGST ship executive officers, SSN dignitaries, honored guest, the entire GPPJ tuning in from across the colonized Moon and Mars, welcome everyone to our commencement launch ceremony. It is an honor bestowed upon me to introduce the Sun Gazer Star Tour ship founder and CEO Marcel Etrion. He is a man with a distinguished series of careers spanning nearly three- hundred fifty years. Born from immigrants to America, to a Haitian father, and his mother from Jamaica, Marcel worked hard on his education and excelled at the top of his high school class in Fort Wayne, Indiana.

"Always willing to pursue his passions in life, Marcel is never one to conform to others' expectations of him or societal pressures for the traveling the path most trodden. Marcel is a trailblazer, and when the time came, he had the choice to attend any university around the world, he made a choice from his heart. Instead, he chose to move to Colombia and join the Colombian army where he trained how to defuse land mines and detect and disable improvised explosive devices. Once he learned of the brutal oppression of the indigenous and poor peoples terrorized by the devastating impact of the reckless random placement of millions of these 'hidden' explosives, he chose his path. In this path, he became entwined with the struggle, caught up in the crosshairs of para-military groups fighting for or in opposition to the ruling government. All para-military groups jeopardized the 'wellbeing' of every economically disadvantaged population while fighting over control of the prolific cocaine trafficking operations. So profitable to para-military groups, even the well-intentioned became corrupt, as in the Revolutionary Armed Forces of Colombia, also known as the FARC, who, ironically, organized originally in the nineteen-sixties to favor poor people subject to abusive neglect from the Colombian government.

"By the conclusion of this conflict by treatise in Two-Thousand-Seventeen, Marcel chose to attend MIT where he studied in the Aerospace Engineering program, learning also structural design, rocket engine propulsion, and related engineering disciplines.

"After receiving the Condorcet procedure, he branched out into other industries making his way into space hospitality, managing The Glass Planet hotel services, then several decades as a space-ferry programmer for the iconic Immaculate Air and Space tourism program. It was during his years in these disciplines he first envisioned creating a tourism company that would provide affordable tours across the terrestrial solar system and offer sustained space flight around the Sun and returns to Earth.

"This was all the inspiration he needed to garner the financial investment to research and develop the technology enabling proximity to the Sun with advancements in extreme heat resilience, protection from hazardous radiation levels, and the filters needed to safely view the Sun without suffering any vision impairments.

"With the encouraging breakthroughs, including his successful proposal of marriage to yours truly, we joined forces to create Star Gazer Tours and with the indispensable support of Minister Patrick Riverstrike, whose fundraising and promotional efforts afforded the ability to manufacture the fleet of sixty-four SGT ships, has led us to this momentous day. Half of the fleet are SGST, or Sun Tour ships, thirty Mars Tour, and two Venus Tour ships. Without further ado, please welcome to the podium my husband, founder, and CEO of Star Gazer Tours, Marcel Etrion."

Resounding applause ensues from the thousands of attendees as Marcel takes to the stage waving to the crowd and embracing his wife in gratitude before standing at the podium.

"The Star Gazer Sun Tours, on the commission of the people of Earth, prepares its inaugural launch into the inner Solar system for a rendezvous with the Sun.

"Carrying two-hundred-fifty-thousand sightseers, tourists, some celebrity, and other distinguished members of the GPPJ, some ninety-three-million miles from home in peak orbit around the Sun and back again in twenty-five days.

"Every other day a Star Gazer Sun Tour ship will launch and will maintain an average speed of three-hundred-fifty-thousand-five-hundred-thirty-six miles per hour.

"These tour ships are the first step to mass population transitions from solar system travels to interstellar travel, then eventually some year intergalactic travel to primarily colonize suitable host planets, if not bring discovery of the dawn of an existence sharing levels of intelligence equal to or greater than human intelligence. I will open the floor for questions."

JLL continues to narrate over what he records privately along with the live procession of events:

"The crowd begins moving in various directions, to either move to the middle area of the command deck for an intimate 'Q and A' with a pool of fifty licensed journalists, entertainment lawyers, and major donors funding the Frau Mauro performing arts center, or in support of ACRES, WOCH or sponsors developing the SGST ship fleet.

"All honored guests, friends, and donors can peruse the interior features including an arena seating twenty-five thousand and enjoy a comfortable seat to tune the briefing in on the mind's eye of the GPI.

"Nobody leaves the ship; the excitement is tantamount to experiencing a historic new era of human space travel firsthand. Everyone has an interest when growth is involved, and as more people arrive at the command deck, a striking blonde male stands out, clad in platinum leather boots glistening as he walks across the command deck to stand off to the stage's right side, coming to a standstill in a position to provide security to the high-profile podium speakers.

"He wears a clear distortion mask reflecting the image of a man living with constant mental illness. It is a tortured soul that is the origin of the terrifying facade the public views. It is as though an identity conflict grips him to the point of separation from his autonomous self of free thought, from the self that is absent of simple freedoms; his actions, and therefore decisions are determined for him, by his master. It is noteworthy that he walks with a hint of the Goose Step often associated with past fascist regimes showing strength in physical force.

"We will tune in now to the press conference."

"Marcel Etrion, as the chair of the recently established Department of deep space exploration, are you planning to travel on the first tour ship launch?"

"I wish I could, however, the Lunar Hall celebration is attended by many angel donors who without their participation in economic support, none of this would have been possible."

There is a commiserate reaction of a gentle buzz from the

onlooking crowd standing along the perimeter of the command deck.

"Come on Marcel, you realize everyone would respond favorably if you exemplified the confidence and courage to command the inaugural voyage?"

"After the accolades and celebrations in observance of this human historic and momentous milestone will time permit, by the third or fourth launch for sure. The courage and confidence are inherent in the work of a collaborative effort of hundreds of thousands of employees."

"I will be waiting on that," replies the inquiring JO.

"Star Gazer Tours CEO Marcel Etrion and Minister Patrick Riverstrike, the mega-monetary harvester who is revered by hundreds of millions of influencer's, stand at the head of the flagship Soley Leve of this maiden voyage, with a group of dignitaries including nine of the thirteen Governors of the SSN, for the taking of an OG group picture.

"On the observation deck of the first voyage SGST flagship Soley Leve, most of the tourists are waving their arms, hands spread open, as they dance celebrating in euphoria. From the outside tourist enter the cargo deck orbiter and emergency escape craft launch pad area. As the Soley Leve is preparing for launch many tourists are visible from standing by observatory corridors that are located on either the starboard or port side.

"They offer short speeches, Marcel Etrion having gone first yields the podium to the Minister, each expressing their gratitude that The Glass Planet family can reach a great expanse of exploration.

"In the coming twelve days, once the first tour ship is in orbit a distance less than two-million miles on approach to Mercury, the massive cannon-like structures mounted at the front will perform the critical function of precision guidance in the swing maneuver around the Sun, or often referred to as a 'slingshot maneuver.'

"You heard me correctly, those enormous tubular apparatus are designed to maintain a safe distance, so as not to be taken in by the Sun's gravitational pull beyond the point of no return into combustion.

"With a day-long 'slingshot' orbit of the Sun, the gravity of the sun, along with solar power, accelerates the SGST ship providing a boost on the return trip. The uncertainty in the back of the minds of a majority, nine out of ten adults recognize the potential for unexpected adversity. It is vitally important to overcome unforeseen adversity with preparedness and readiness.

"This is an automated navigation system mounted on the front of each cruiser with 'tentacles' of sensors engineered to provide comprehensive threat detection protection from being pulled in any direction.

"Internal training before the launch and after fourteen days, the two-hundred-fifty-thousand passengers execute a series of steps to safely insulate within their quarters. The twelve-thousand-five-hundred crew conducts drills in the event of catastrophic radiation exposure due to compromised hull integrity, sealing off the cabins in sections to maintain oxygen density and gravity. Areas exposed to space through compromised hull integrity will endure a vacuum force capable of sucking out all oxygen and anything not bolted to the fuselage.

"All passengers must be in safety gear twenty-four hours a day for at least three days continuous, exempting maintenance of personal hygiene on approach to the Sun. In any event, the approach and brief orbit of the Sun is bar-none the 'star' of the show!

"I've been asked, 'What about Venus? Isn't it as much of an attraction, if not even more so due to the breakthroughs resulting in the complete transition of its acidic atmosphere into a healthy fresh-water planet?

"The view of Venus is about as popular, even though passengers require to register for the in-flight viewing, immersing in related interactive tasks from which all can learn as they enjoy the entertainment value. The second planet from the Sun is only six million miles in the distance from our flight path, appearing as a light blue marble, its' moons are perceptible through high imaging telescopes. There is a full reference guide in our publicity files. Once uninhabitable, Venus held a yellowish-orange hue when viewed through Earth-based telescopes. The planet's infamously harsh conditions included an atmosphere composed of sulfur oxide, acidic enough to obliterate an unmanned probe in seconds. Carbon monoxide levels made breathing impossible, the average temperatures exceeding seven-hundred-degree Fahrenheit. Passengers will get to experience its' image projected through the GPI configured monitor fields so those who wish to can view it in privacy in their cabin as easily as the same visual experience is shared amongst the crowds from the observation decks.

"The entire program is worth over five-hundred-quadrillion dollars to construct all the sixty-four tour ships, thirty-four of them are presently commissioned. The good news is these tour ships will be accessible for travel for the next seven-hundred-fifty-thousand years, give or take twenty-five-thousand years!"

He becomes distracted, his eyes are drawn to Simon who breaks his death stare on the crowd to attend to a woman who approaches him wearing a hijab and an ornate Afghan nomad dress. It is rare to see any traditional hijab on stage at events like this.

"The post-launch event Marcel Etrion mentioned, is a celebration of the unprecedented human milestone service and, as well, the celebration ceremonies will award the 'Solar Sensation' of the Star Gazer Tours distinguished medal of honor to mark the program's positive impact on the 'wellbeing' of the human condition. I thank everyone here for attending in person. Enjoy the festivities"

JJL observes Minister Riverstrike as he concludes his comments and has left the podium to approach the masked man who has shoved off the woman wearing the hijab.

JJL continues his reporting, "The highlight of the evening will be the recognition of the feat accomplished by the mysterious Catherine and according to my contacts, her very daring and handsome golden-boy partner Jürgen.

"Amazingly they survived nearly three-hundred-fifty years without the Condorcet procedure, without aging. They made it through the indoctrination process and have complete approval for citizenship into the GPPJ. The celebration ceremony will continue with a concert for the ages, with a light show designed by Hartar Reingling, a light show that the departing tourist will be able to view in the first seconds after launch as the tour ship gradually accelerates to over three-hundred-fifty-thousand miles per hour.

"The Space Cadet dancers from the Lunar City Fra Mauro crater performing arts center will perform classical music hits from the mid- to late-twentieth century; more specifically, to commemorate the first ever moon landing in human history, there will be a program from the year nineteen-sixty-nine, including inspired works from other years of the era.

"Then, after a synchronized anti-gravity intricate dance choreography of five thousand dancers above the Moon's surface, accompanied with an amazing art design inspired by our long evolution over time to overcome barbarism, greed-fascism and in turn, commemorating the greatness of innovation and the spirit of citizens resulting from a free and equal opportunity society.

"This is JJL, your lunar eyes and ears, and 'Earth JO' of all things social and entertainment of progressive choice; May all in existence embrace the joy of this milestone achievement! You have hundreds of millions of GPI casts to choose from and I thank you for tuning in, you can count on me for the facts as they pertain to reality. This is the GPPJ's journalist to the solar system, JJL JO, signing off."

By the year twenty-ninety-eight, she learned of this "Kariana," a prodigy of civil engineering with an emphasis on 'civil,' as she, through her innovations stabilized Earth's environment by nursing it and understanding how the qualities of Earth can be interacted to heal itself from human pollution.

This tidbit on Kariana she came across in her research of many more countless historical figures profiled on record. She remembers a documentary on Kariana and felt an instant connection to the genius adolescent who lost her life in a tragic accident in space at age thirty-three.

Strange how there are no images of her existence other than recordings during her 'break-out years' in her adolescence. It was an avoidable accident as experimenting with the pressurized oxygen systems to help develop the interplanetary orbiters which are in common use today, a highly improbable explosion occurred, jettisoning her body beyond the point of no return. Irretrievable by the rescue capabilities of the time, her remains may never be seen again.

Janalake frequently commutes between Earth and the developing space station network. Her primary function includes weekly reports on her construction progress to meet design and when there was a substantial development in research, she planned the presentations to the World Aeronautics and Space Project (WASP) officials to provide the update and projection expectations, as well the project expected completion dates and in expenditure, budget, and efficiency of work schedule.

With this statistical information, the workforce can always replace under performing employees with new hire candidates to prove themselves by boosting productivity rates and increasing efficiency.

Janalake is a proletariat, a concise professional who exerts little individuality beyond her smile and simple charming attitude. She bonds especially well with the common Zealot Sentinel working class, both as a colleague and as Commander.

Janalake is fitted with the Zealot Sentinel interface, is victim to mind and emotional control, subject to constant physical defense training, and molded intellectually into a recruiter before she received a promotion as the commander of the Zealot Sentinels.

The ZSI stifles her personality, aligning her to be responsive foremost to following orders and executing directed or even programmed itineraries, otherwise less independent and more like a human chattel under Riverstrike's command.

Those under her command will beg to differ, as there are no examples of high emotions related to empathy, sympathy, or individual emotions identified as traumatic or traumatizing to another ZS or GPPJ. Riverstrike figured it easier to have control through the device rather than exclusively through brainwashing.

Riverstrike began the construction of the space station network after world organizations had overcome greed-fascism by implementing needed philanthropic standards to uplift most of the human population to become solvent, educated, and aspiring in multiple disciplines in the prospect of the two-hundred-fifty-year life span afforded by the Condorcet procedure at the time.

Riverstrike was so grateful for her influence as an ambassador for RAKLAV, but more so from the engineering design, he stole from her allowing for his popularity to soar when he first advocated the principle of the human will should always act in favor of the 'wellbeing' of the human condition.

If she benefited from the ingenuity of children to change the course of world history for the better with their intuitive observation of what is, from the misery innate to human awareness of our collective ignorance, it is in learning how to see the world from an adolescent perspective; She compares herself to the Minister, "Would I, if born forty years earlier in the beginnings of the information age, a guide for others to succeed by example, instead of having to guide the chosen few by the nose? To guide with freedom of will is my choice. His is of greed-fascism promoting self-interest of a privileged super minority. As a child, these choices are informed by an instinct to do good for acceptance."

The lounge doors open in time for Simon to overhear Janalake's statement, "Excuse me, Commander? Reminiscing about your childhood?"

She views the major filtration and arrogation complex of human-made waterways conducting the overflow of the Mediterranean Sea southward onto the North African continent, and into the Sahara Rain forest from the Dark Eaglet observation lounge.

She is pleasant, "I am in admiration of the revolutionary technology invented by prodigal daughters. It makes me wonder as a little girl if I could have found the inspiration to design infrastructure to impact the 'wellbeing' of the natural world from building sandcastles at the beach."

"She was an eight-year-old savant guiding the planet away from apocalyptic destruction, for the time being, by incorporating technology she conceived playing on beach sand," Simon states factually. "Her innovative design kept the ocean waves from her sandcastles by diverting water flow from the foundation and into reservoirs."

"There is some aspect too familiar," Janalake hugs herself, "It is a perpetual itch to me."

"All great works of humanity strike most humans with a resonance of the familiar, genius is often derived from the most common denominator. Certainly, the nostalgia for a once healthy functioning living natural environment would provide such inspiration."

"Simon, a healthy functioning living natural environment?" Janalake stares into Simon's eyes, "I don't remember a time before the Earth depending on the mechanics of water and land preservation. What would it look like?"

"I wish we could venture back in time to see it first-hand."

"Venture back in time; what does that mean?"

"It means there are visual records in existence of an independently naturally sustaining Earth. It is more myth I suppose these days, but the theory is to be able to go against known laws of nature and reverse time."

"Why not use the hologram configurations?"

"Holograms are a close take on living things as in an ecosystem. The reality of it is dead artifice."

"Everything in this solar system is dead but real. Single-celled organisms can sustain themselves in underground crevices on Mars without relying on sunlight, but they die eventually from some event. Holograms simulate life without being alive. The Sun stimulates life, we can feel its distinct qualities, but it also will die."

"It will die though, won't it?"

"Everything dies Simon. For all recorded history of Earth's vital signs, the current day is evidence enough that the Earth is dying. The Sun may live ten million years more. Humankind has irresponsibly short-changed themselves by exploiting our home in greed-fascism for its perceived riches at the sacrifice of the 'wellbeing' of the human condition."

19

Sponti Goes Viral

Gingi pleads, "Sponti, let's just call the taxi tow. It is too dangerous!" Spontaneous Instant sounds off with modest confidence in his assessment, "I can do this; besides it probably is a dirty receptor," or a clogged something or another."

"There's nothing you can do to help this!"

"Yes, I can."

"No, you can't, your diagnosis is 'a clogged something or another!' Anyway, you don't have any tools."

Gingi Grind makes a call when the orbiter that is Sponti's graduation gift from high school breaks down, "Ugh, the taxi-tow is busy. I must leave a message. 'We are in transit to the Moon on our way to the Fra Mauro crater Lunar City performing arts center. My friend's orbiter has stalled, and we need a taxi tow, please locate us on beacon four-hundred-eighty-two-zero-zero-zero. Please hurry as we are attending the achievement ceremony recognizing Marcel Etrion and Minister Riverstrike's Star Gazer Tour ship first voyage launch happening today.'"

"Who needs tools?" Spontaneous Instant says as he unseals the pressurized cabin door lock, "I thought you said you had mechanical training on orbiters, shuttles, and cruisers?"

"Only for land-based repairs, not as an astronaut technician for external space repairs while in orbit."

"Make sure you have your exoskeleton system sealed."

With that, he releases the hatch lock to lift the door open and jumps outside of the orbiter.

Immediately something goes wrong as the clasp hook to the Pad Eye plate ring is not secure and the tether line it is attached to pulls the clasp from the Pad Eye plate ring once the tether extends fully, releasing Spontaneous Instant to sail off into space.

"Sponti No!" Gingi Grind is helpless as she can do little harnessed into her seat and without any options to rescue him.

"Damn fool," she is annoyed as she sends the message out touching a button on the GPI to summon in a rushed panic the Space Station Network Emergency Response Team (SSNERT) as her boyfriend is rapidly floating away beyond her sight.

"Yes, he slips, and then he was gone! Will you recover the stray distress signal first? He is my date."

"He's having too much fun without me." She surmises thinking as the GPI translates emotions evoking a sensation within connected GPIs, providing enough information to know joy from pain, it is not yet possible to feel their emotion just as they do.

"I measure his excitement exceeding mine, and that makes me jealous, yet happy for him. We all feel the same emotions at some time or another; never exactly alike, fingerprints and snowflakes are not the same.

"Sponti enjoys the thrill of the moment, no greater thrill than the invitation of the unknown, and wrap your arms around it, embrace that moment, it is fleeting the feeling of adrenaline from experiencing something never known, or for the first time. It is impossible for me to truly experience the feelings the same way he does, I sense he is sliding on thin ice, at any moment frightened by an inkling of a compromising tear in the fabric of his flight suit, which epitomizes the sinking through thin ice creating an inescapable water swath, these are the emotions of Sponti as translated to my GPI."

She records an image of her boyfriend floating off into space and posts it to the GPI for her millions of GPPJ friends to pity her, Sponti outdoes himself once again!

For Spontaneous Instant, the rapid floating into open space is an exhilarating experience not so much for the weightlessness as weightlessness is provided in controlled arenas for recreation across the Earth where it is yet restricting in range of movement. The thrill of the danger of unlimited open space as his body speeds unrestrained by any measure, with no option to be capable to change his course to a place of safety, being completely at the mercy of others to save him, has him howling in ecstasy!

The only drawback he has is the immediate rescue response from the SSNERT units alerted by Gingi to intercept him and safely retrieve him to return to The Clipper.

The rescue craft circles around the person in distress, deploying four robotic boosters harnessing a safety net to gently secure and tow from eminent danger onto the rescue craft.

"What happened out there?" asks an SSNERT rescuer, "Are you all right?"

"I'm fine. I slipped trying to repair my orbiter!"

"That is not advisable soaring at seventeen-thousand miles per hour. If your suit gets a tear, you could suffer an embolism, don't you know that? Also, a tow would have cost you less!"

"What do you mean?"

"There's a hefty fine to pay for our services, and you are in jeopardy of having your orbiter license suspended."

"Please, please do not tell my girlfriend!"

"She probably knows since she made the distress call!"

Upon return to The Clipper, an SSNERT tow craft is already connected by a robotic arm clasping onto its bow. Spontaneous Instant takes his place next to Gingi in the pilot seat.

The tow craft will escort them to the Fra Mauro crater Lunar City performing arts center to attend the celebration ceremony and the mechanic will quickly repair the orbiter.

Gingi Grind will remain silent until the entrance to the cordial cocktail party reception before the main show.

20

First Impressions

The celebration ceremony for Jürgen and me is at the Lunar City Music Hall performance arts center, Fra Mauro Crater, Moon 42007-6932.

I inquired about the zip code, and it does allow for mail to be sent to the Moon! It is a popular activity for children and earth-bound dreamers younger than the nineteen-year-old minimum age for low- and no-gravity travel to write letters of inquiry or commentary from the most benign opinions.

Eventually, at this event, we are to be celebrated for our successful indoctrination into the Glass Planet Population Journal.

Qyxzorina joins Marcel in the process of recognition for the imminent launching of the entire sixty-four Star Gazer Tour ship fleet.

The Lunar City Music Hall performance art center hosts a reception in the expansive three-hundred-square-foot gala hall featuring panoramic views of Earth and lunar perspectives through the diamond granulated window ceiling. The architecture of this building is a plain design engineered in a harsh, wild environment to grandiose effect.

Fountains of intoxicating beverages flow for free consumption among the event's variety of fashionable and elegantly dressed guests and audience members. Approximately sixty thousand attendees make this the second most high-fashion celebrity event observed behind the Red-Carpet entertainment awards show series.

Jürgen and I are handed a modern high fashion wardrobe loaned from top clothing designers I've never heard of.

At first look, I would describe the dress offered to me as quality fabrics overlaying a synthetic mesh. The mesh material-based technology allows for color scheme and design changes at the whims of my fancy.

This is the first time I have ever received an instruction manual for a dress! The manual describes having an alternating fabric factor of seven, allowing for three different alternate fabrics and four-color palette scheme combinations. The manual does not indicate it removes wine stains or the like.

"I won't apologize for saying this," Jürgen is pleasant in admitting, "You are stunning in that apparel. I love your hair braided, is it a French curl?"

"It is called the 'Cosmic Twist,'" I am thrilled he noticed. "This dress is equipped with the same capabilities that Gingi Grind uses on her outfits. It doesn't offer hairstyle changes, it's her private trick."

Jürgen is enamored by my dress, openly delighting in all its' splendor, "I doubt if it's affordable."

"It is. With the current level of monetary influence, we have on the 'wellbeing' of the human condition," I reveal a good deal of fascination toward achieving the status without even working and the lack of understanding of our contribution to the 'wellbeing' of the human condition.

"That's where you are mistaken," Riverstrike approaches with a cocktail glass attendant in hand, "As you are lacking this elegant glass of wine."

"Hello?" I respond with a curious inflection, "Do I know you?"

"Yes, do we know you?" Jürgen sounds unsure if he has met this man previously.

"You should. Allow me to introduce myself," he said handing out glasses of wine, "Patrick Riverstrike, renown philanthropist, space network engineer, interplanetary land developer, and architect of a dozen space stations in the network."

"Thank you. Nice to meet you Governor Riverstrike," I greet him courteously receiving a glass of red wine. "An honor, I'm sure."

"Yes, I'm also the co-developer of the Star Gazer Tours enterprise with Marcel Etrion and Qyxzorina Astraea."

"Quite the honor Governor Riverstrike," Jürgen extended both of his hands one to receive the wine, the other to shake hands, "We are friends with them."

"I know, after all, you two have made quite a stir among the GPPJ."

"Yes, we have. What was it you were about to say?" To my delight, the wine hit me like a soft pillow, a comfort to my weary head and a soothing elixir to my nerves.

"It is not every decade we see humans unaccounted for in the GPPJ who have emerged from an unknown origin. The fact you were cleared by the RAKLAV with full integration into the Glass Planet is a testament to your willpower, self-determination, and personal cognitive skills. You both are bereft of only one of nine categories the brain utilizes to effectively interpret and use information," Riverstrike says with veiled insinuation. "To be of an open mind, accepting adverse circumstances, and adjusting to meet the challenge is a strong suit you share. What is your time were considered extreme progressive concepts is now considered everyday routine."

"Let's not get too far ahead of ourselves Governor Riverstrike," I suggest asking, "What category are we bereft in?"

"It's 'Minister' Riverstrike actually, but call me Patrick, I prefer not to be ostentatious with official titles in casual settings, private or public. The one cognitive skill you lack is long-term memory."

"Very magnanimous of you, Patrick," Jürgen's sarcastic response borders on parody.

"We are abundantly aware of our lack of long-term memory. You can be of assistance but for now, Patrick, if you can excuse us," I hear the prompt alert for 'call to positions backstage,' "We are being called to take our positions backstage as the ceremony is about to begin."

"By all means. You two are the real prize this evening. I will join Marcel and Qyxzorina in the theater," Riverstrike graciously offers, "I hope we will have a sit-down after the show to get better acquainted."

"As do we, I'm sure Patrick," Jürgen replies reaching his hand out to Patrick, who in turn offers a hand gesture in the form of a casual 'As you were' military salute.

We watch the man of mature physical age saunter towards the Lunar Hall's entrance.

"He left me hanging!" Jürgen displays his open hand toward me, "What a mucous membrane!"

"What a weirdo, to say the least," I assure Jürgen as we turn to head backstage. "The man who guards over him wearing the clear distortion mask, I can only begin to wonder what his story is."

21

Making Acquaintances

It is a pleasure to make your acquaintance," Camilla Rosa-Laurel, acclaimed entertainer, and host of the evening's celebration greets Jürgen and me behind the curtain backstage. "It is such a rarity to encounter humans who are from an earlier century without having received the Condorcet procedure. Amazing I tell you!"

"It is amazing," I counter unsure of what to say to this gorgeous woman in body and spirit. "I assure you we are appreciative of the response and acknowledgment of the GPPJ's dedication to us."

"Can you tell me how you did it?"

"Did what ma'am?" Jürgen underhandedly delivers his innate sarcasm. I gently nudge him in the ribs with my left elbow.

"Sustained your lives for over three centuries without any therapeutics? It is unheard of, outside the tales of fiction of the likes of Rumpelstiltskin or the great Messiahs."

"I am taken by the comparison to the Messianic beings of eternal grace Camilla, but make no mistake, we are certainly more in line with Rumpelstiltskin," I boast my modesty.

"We slept a long time, but we don't remember who we were," Jürgen refrains amiable. "Other than our first names."

"And or birthplaces."

Music begins to play on the audio system signaling the commencement of the ceremonies.

"There's my cue to take the stage. Best of everything to both of you and make sure to connect with me at the post-show cocktail party."

"Thank you, Camilla, we will look forward to it," I sincerely express my intentions not necessarily knowing what would come of us after this public introduction.

Camilla waves a hand in her departure to the stage, amidst an uproar of rolling thunderous applause that sends a chill down my spine. How many people are in the audience?

We listen intently as she begins her monologue on center stage.

"Celebrity is always to be celebrated therefore we convene now in this great hall. Too many of us take technological advancements for granted in our era. With life spans lasting centuries and well on our way to achieving millennial ages, the human condition has never been so poised to venture into deep interstellar space travel.

"The tricky thing is a thousand-year life span won't go far when it comes to traveling in parsecs. Through the brilliant engineering mind of Minister Patrick Riverstrike and the groundbreaking design of Marcel Etrion's fleet of massive and power regeneration technologies of Intergalactic SGST ships ~ that's right, you did not hear me wrong, IN-TER-GA-LAC-TIC; You will see a change in your regulations and permits Minister ~ there is laughter and firm applause from the audience ~ . . .intergalactic travel to destinations scouted by probes will now be accessible to us in our lifetimes. Thus, enabling humans to begin plans on exploring the Alpha Centauri system with cost efficiency to allow for regularity in travel. What is the gross vehicle weight rating for one SGST ship, Marcel, didn't you say sixty-three-million pounds?"

Marcel reacts to the audience shrugging his shoulders with palms open facing up, he gestures on the GPI channel, "I wouldn't know right now, maybe one-hundred-sixty-three million pounds, but we can talk about docking fees, okay?"

There's an outbreak of laughter in response to the alluding to plausible criminal intent.

"With a remarkable projected service capability of seven-hundred-fifty-thousand years per tour ship, on behalf of the Glass Planet population journal, I would like to honor Minister Patrick Riverstrike and SGST CEO Marcel Etrion with the Lunar Hall award for excellence in furthering the 'wellbeing' of the human condition."

Patrick and Etrion emerge from the audience amid gracious applause to join the host on stage in acceptance of their awards. Backstage Jürgen and I are viewing the acceptance speech of Riverstrike.

"I'd like to thank the present leaders of innovation in advancing their support to sponsor the development of this ambitious enterprise conceived and developed by my colleague and friend Marcel Etrion."

Audience applause is rabid with cheers and exclamations in a show of respect. Riverstrike meets him on stage left to welcome him onto the stage with a handshake, then he takes a seat on the dais.

Marcel steps to the center stage and acknowledges the audience by delivering his acceptance response, "My appreciation for this honor is indescribable through words, but I will try!"

The adoring audience laughs kindheartedly at Marcel's opening comments.

Observing from the backstage monitor, I see the Lunar Hall is the size of a football stadium! I feel my body trembling, "Why am I so nervous?" My body quivers in stating this, "There are only sixty thousand people in the audience!"

Jürgen shakes his arms vigorously to relieve his anxiety, "Oh yes, but this is exciting because this is a big deal and we're nervous because we care about it." His legs swing from hip to his jittery knees, "And there are sixty thousand people in the audience!"

We receive our prompts to the wings of the stage in preparation for our introduction as Marcel closes his remarks, "My sincere and humble thanks for making this dream come true. Speaking of a dream, none of this would have been possible without the incredible encouragement and support from my soon-to-be wife and always my best friend, Qyxzorina Astraea."

Audience applause is immediate as Qyxzorina is projected upon the GPI as she stands for all to congratulate her.

The host Camilla Rosa-Laurel takes to the dais, where Marcel and Patrick are to take to their seats, she leads the applause, "Thank you everybody for sharing your love with our first honorees. Before we move on with the celebration, I have one question for Minister Riverstrike. I know how ambitious you are, and there are always rumors about what are you going to do next. What do you have planned next for your endeavors, Minister?"

Minister Riverstrike steps into the center stage, "Thank you for your interest, Camilla. The obvious progression is a given as we have commercial infrastructure procurement of water from Venus, and earlier designs of technology to create an atmosphere on other planets have now become a major challenge to our generation. We are to be atmosphere builders and nurture healthy outcomes, not destroyers of atmospheres in general.

"Direct air capture requires substantial heat and power inputs with the solar panel complexes orbiting Venus's reverse revolutions and taking in solar energy capture carbon monoxide by skimming the Venus atmosphere over centuries has reduced to concentration by millions of gigatons. The air today is of a tolerable temperature and with carbon mineralization or enhanced weathering, biophysics has devised the ability to create the right mineral composition structures on the already rocky surfaces.

"Remote robotic land rovers helped to discover mineral-rich rocks layered under the topography of Venus's surface.

"Electric currents through the H_2O extracted from H_2SO_4 help extract CO_2 and bio-physics help infuse phytoplankton and seaweed. Soon in another few centuries, Venus will be terrestrially inhabitable.

"The Martian Metropolis has the potential for massive population expansion, especially for a tourism-based economy. It makes perfect sense to extend the Star Gazer Mars Tour ship experiences for the masses moving forward."

"Minister, neither Venus nor Mars are stars, they are planets."

"In keeping with the realm of entertainment, Venus, and Mars are the 'stars' of the show!"

Rousing applause with smatterings of laughter ensue.

"Minister, that is good enough a reason for me! I offer you a big congratulations on your engagement," Camilla graciously acknowledges, "Thank you for the pleasant surprise, Minister."

Resounding applause from the audience inspires the Minister to wave with both arms extended over his head relaying excitement to the crowd as he steps across the dais to have a seat next to Marcel.

"Speaking about 'pleasant surprises' our other honorees' for this evening are two of the newest members of the Glass Planet Population Journal who are mysterious without any history or background on record."

A surge and crescendo of laughter from the audience as the host is an expert in patiently waiting for the correct timing, taking in the pace of and predicting the stamina of laughter before rolling up her eyes quickly before launching her punch line, "If they can't be traced to one of the vivarium communities, then they can be from outer space for all I know . . .just don't forget to follow safety regulations and make sure your vehicle is under compliance!"

An outburst of laughter ensues.

"That's right, now on a more serious point, they never existed in the twenty-first century from the administering of the Condorcet procedure. If you think that is odd, our honorees don't even know fully who they are, except that they lived in the twentieth-century United States of America, the great Fatherland of Independence of the people, by the people, for the people. Now they have come through indoctrination well prepared for success in contributing to the 'wellbeing' of the human condition. Please forgive me if I don't know their surnames, but neither do they!"

The audience roars in laughter and the host relishes the wave of laughter like a surfer riding the pipe, she waits for the crescendo crashing down to a trickling crawl of white ocean foam bubbling out quickly in the sand, "Welcome Catherine and Jürgen!"

The audience of sixty thousand guests rises to their feet with another round of spirited applause as many 'whoops' and 'cheers' are heard echoing throughout the Lunar Hall.

Jürgen follows me onto the stage holding hands, my knees are weak and rubbery as we emerge from the stage left wing.

We acknowledge the prolonged applause from the audience with numerous hands waiving in salutation, torso bows in deference in honor of us.

"This is surreal for both of us as one might imagine," I open my comments, my voice trembling, "Even though we don't know who we are, we have ascertained some basic information."

A gasp from the audience filled the Lunar Hall as Jürgen speaks on cue, "Such as our names and I believe I hail from Denver, Colorado."

"And I'm committing to Dallas, Texas for me!" I play to the audience's amusement feigning preference with an inference to my birth town over Jürgen's.

"After all, who knows for sure, we for sure do not!" Jürgen's sarcasm is infectious, "Seriously though, does anybody here vaguely recognize us?"

The audience laughs.

"We continue to work on scouring the digital libraries of files in hopes of procuring information," I state in anguish. "We're nowhere."

The conscience of the matter weighs heavily in everyone's heart as a complete silence projects the solemn mood of the crowd.

"In summation, Jürgen and I will be forever grateful for the outpouring of love and respect bestowed on us," my chest is pounding in passion. "In recognition of how beautiful it is, it feels to be alive, I quote my favorite all-time poet Emily Dickinson, the most prolific poet of all time ~ at least up to my time ~ she is perhaps the most reclusive of any major poet: 'To live is so startling it leaves little time for anything else.' And if you have any time, please don't hesitate to let us know if you remember us! Thank you all!"

A peal of gentle laughter in appreciation for us confirms there is little hope that the few million who have received the Condorcet procedure from our generation are unlikely to have a passing memory of us. They would have reached eighty years old at the earliest possible point of the procedure's availability to the public.

Anyone at an elderly age receiving the Condorcet procedure would benefit from an additional thirty to fifty years of extended life span to one-hundred-twenty-five years old when their brains deteriorated too far along to survive. Brain nutrition and advancements in the Condorcet procedure post-twenty-first century eventually sustained what the remaining Mother generation survived to receive the benefits once introduced for public application.

Jürgen and I bow repeatedly, waving to the audience appreciatively as we step to take our seats on the dais.

Camilla takes to the podium, "Once again, let's show our appreciation for the recipients."

The audience stands abruptly in applause including many calling out 'Welcome to the GPPJ' and chants of 'SGST! SGST!"

"Thank you. This marks the end of our recognition ceremony. It is time to convene in the gala hall for the post-show reception. Please follow the guides for an orderly procession from here to there!"

Camilla greets us stage left, "Okay you two, take a few minutes to gather yourselves before we convene to the post-party in the gala hall. Adjust your GPI to the local setting with a six-square foot radius signal to filter out the tens of thousands of voices communicating through the GPI channels.

"Do not use the public setting or your brains will be paralyzed by the simultaneous conglomerate of unintelligible voices."

"Understood. Exactly how many audience members are there, sixty thousand?"

"Yes Catherine, as advertised!" Camilla exerts positive sympathetic energy, "I know you must be overwhelmed in these environs, but not to worry, you will get used to the GPI settings and know better when and how to use them intuitively."

The post-show reception is hosted in the Fra Mauro crater gala reception hall, a namesake for the actual crater named after Monk Mauro, a fifteenth-century cartologist known for being the first to create the most accurate map of the planet Earth up to his time. The three-hundred-sixty-thousand-square-foot gala hall foundation is built into the surface of the Moon.

A spectacular light and laser design fill the arced ceiling

complimenting the celestial atmospheric qualities of being on the Moon, providing for the magical backdrop on an evening of drink, merriment, and making courteous relations.

Riverstrike speaks of the vivarium zones where the people societies that are incapable of evolving to the level of human intelligence to achieve world peace, some of the requirements are the 'ability to love any singularity' of a human being, "Virtuous in their words, intent and actions, from any person and reason love for the human condition and life expressed in ways allowable by law, through any choice of worship or non-worship, and genuinely reciprocate one's vice demeanor.

"These are 'Innovations with, of, in-love,' with the worship for appreciation of the persons on the opposite side of the planet, who is possible, in every way different from you, but know through your worship of your choice, that independent human being, who has human-driven needs as you do, will have a dream of their own.

"Others due to misshapen brains, genetically lacking the capability to grow physically the mass of the brains, or the 'synoptic nerve' integration, or both, is restricted to allow for one to reconcile for themselves the import of love for all, violence against none.

"Need one say more to illustrate the vicious predator carnivore with their teeth jutting out to express their fury in mind. A mind that lacks the physical and synoptic nerve integration to have empathy, sympathy, leniency, acceptance, mutual appreciation, like, love, to cry joy for people who are happy and successful?

"This is why we have laws, religions, and government. The vivarium is just an extension of the political exchange we must conduct to survive.

"There are no greater rights than the rights to equality, opportunity, and an economy that reciprocates to the most successful of every generation, as the economy also serves the needs of the law-abiding peoples of society who are productive and dedicated to the mutual interest of the preservation of humanity through the belief of serving the 'wellbeing' of the human condition.

"They serve the connotative purpose to study animals and the cultures, there's a second function as a cage to separate themselves from themselves and all of the GPPJ to achieve an optimum level of world peace, also known by critics as," Riverstrike manifests a crude Italian accent, "the world is in apiece!" He offers again, this time with more commitment to the accent, "The world a gone in a pizza!"

His remarks are heard by tens of millions across the GPPJ, as well as received by the two dozen guests forming a circle around him, with stunned silence ~ Frau Mauro is spinning in his grave.

"My statement is a reference to the 'subhuman' nature of my critics, who at this point several in the crowd begin gesticulating and renounce my remarks. The critics call me an 'elitist of a bourgeois arrogance, my comments are daggers to the back of society.' Can you believe it?"

"Yes, as harsh of terms you may cast me in, nothing matters more than achieving world peace. If evolution and survival of the fittest are not your cups of tea, then prayer and hopes will only bring you to a phrase I will quote from the English politician Algernon Sidney in his Discourse Concerning Government and popularized by Benjamin Franklin, 'God helps them that help themselves.'

"I contend our vivarium policies and the infrastructure programming is beyond the effectiveness of survival of the fittest.

Even if it's God's Will, because all are provided for through the ETHW, right, and all are considered in the 'wellbeing' of the human condition, right, and the demonstrations of philanthropic influence to create exemplary conditions to live under . . .as the 'Welfare for the wealthy' demonstrates as we have a balance in the whole scale of the human experience, this is World Peace."

"The Condorcet Procedure and genetic engineering have developed robust health and longevity carrying on the peak health until the brain fails.

"The two greatest challenges we face today are the exploration of two infinite spaces, given the modest level of acquired knowledge and understanding, of what may be a vast ignorance for all humankind.

"First, the science of the human brain and to continue to evolve by developing knowledge through rigorous study, to obtain the evidence required for greater understanding of Nature's Truth.

"Second, to continue exploration and development gathering empirical evidence to progress human civilization on to an intergalactic level with a mature understanding of the nature of the known universe, and the possibilities of what exists beyond.

"In closing, governors, civil executives, corporate executives, and to those on screen, the GPPJ, to you all, Gaudium Et Spes. Does anyone have questions?"

A young woman on screen asks, "Why are the animals in the Sahara Vivarium so much friendlier to humans than humans are to humans in any other vivarium?"

"The animals are trained!"

"So, the humans less evolved can't be trained?"

"Trained in many ways, we have the indoctrination and conditioning programs for the very purpose of vetting refugees and preparing them for a safe and successful transition into the GPPJ."

"Excuse me Minister," a tall man dressed in a sleek tuxedo, "My name is Rex Hurtz from 'Our Solar System Media Network.' Why did it require five plus years to see the two-time refugees through the program especially since they exhibit the qualities of modern collective conscience?"

"They may have the wonderful qualities of those who want to expand their knowledge and increase their understanding . . .keep in mind, they are over three-hundred-years behind in accelerated human advancement. They required much time and scrutiny and patience for them to understand two things."

"And those are?"

"The ability to accept population growth in segments and the other, how they utilize information, learn from their mistakes, accept responsibility by apologizing to all necessary parties. That is key to emotional growth, and early on they would pose a hazard to the GPPJ."

"Is EQ essential for the 'politic mind?'"

"Those without a 'politic mind' are savages. Those with a political mind who do not value debate and the free marketplace of ideas to lead the populace by informing, with verifying information, to decide for themselves are heretics to freedom. When political minds lean toward slighting the people by not serving them and are simply there, holding their posts for their self-interest are not only less than subhuman, but they are also abusers of blind faith betraying the 'wellbeing' of the human condition.

"The most deviant of betrayals, a wolf in the lamb suit are complicit among these, or a sheep to be eaten by wolves, having the knowledge of deception deployed against the innocent and part-taking in the evil by saying nothing, doing nothing, to cease the wave of moral belligerence."

He gazes into the crowd viewing Catherine, "Please excuse me, I have some business to attend to."

"The gala reception hall is bedazzling, to say the least. What an inspiring presentation from Hartar Reingling." My eyes are fixed on the wonderful cloud of Moon dust effect billowing high above across the gala hall, chameleon-like, a psychedelic mirage emitting pastel tone colors; someone hands me a glass. I look to it, a low-ball glass with whiskey and sweet vermouth. A stemmed maraschino cherry plays dead at the bottom of the drink.

"The Manhattan you gave me may pickle my liver, but it looks deceptively palatable," I hold the glass by the base while sniffing the bouquet of its cherry-oak liquor contents.

"Oh, connoisseur of libations, where did you learn to smell the bouquet?" Jürgen asks in jest via GPI private channel.

"We both share an affinity for intoxicating influences," I lift my glass high to toast, "Here's to the finer things in life!"

"And here's to the debauchery of life!" Jürgen offers his toast with a smile of maniacal intentions, "Cheers!"

At this moment I am reminded Jürgen has a juvenile stripe about him, "That's cute, cheers!"

"Yes, cheers to the both of you," Riverstrike approaches with stealth to add import to the toast as he hoists his goblet in the air to touch glasses then takes a finishing swig of an ounce of Wild Turkey.

"Yes, I would like to introduce you both to associates of mine, they would love to meet the two of you. Would you take a moment?" Riverstrike offers as he places his goblet on a service table before selecting from an assortment of cordials.

Jürgen and I exchange a look of mutual consent, "Certainly, we would be honored." We respond in synchronization.

Riverstrike points the way holding his glass of absinthe, "Thank you, will you follow me right over here?"

Jürgen relents, "Okay, you lead the way."

We navigate shuffling with our arms tight to our ribs, using our elbows as bumpers against the reception guests offering random 'congratulations.' We become diverted shaking hands while walking.

I view Riverstrike waiting by a door with a Zealot Sentinel on either side of the door. As soon as he determines we can make our way through the crowd, he continues into the room.

"Hey, you two big shots!" A euphoric voice rings out on the local GPI channel. I look past the guests presently shaking my hand to see Gingi and Spontaneous Instant wedging their way through the crowd approaching me.

"You guys were great on stage, the audience loved you! We're so psyched for you!"

My face lights up seeing the two young fun-loving friends, "Thanks Gingi, I'm happy you guys made it."

"We almost didn't, but that's another story! Have you talked to Qyxzorina yet?"

"No. Why?"

"They want to pick you up tomorrow morning around eleven to celebrate with you."

"Okay, where are they now?"

"They were invited last minute by Camilla to a private party. They asked us to confirm with you."

"Count me in Gingi!" The crowd around us begins to turn dense, "Thanks Gingi, we have to meet with Patrick Riverstrike, he's waiting for us, and the crowd is closing in!"

"By the way, Camilla asks for you to attend her after 'the post-party.'"

"Sounds like a late night. I will check in with you?"

"No worries, we'll see you soon!"

Jürgen and I make our way to the room where Riverstrike has entered twenty minutes earlier.

Once inside the room we find it is a spacious seven hundred square feet, with lofty ceilings, no doubt providing for a quiet sit down. Four well-cushioned chairs and a floating tabletop trio are ample accommodations.

Riverstrike stands waiting for us, "Let's talk. Have a seat."

Jürgen sits beside me after I take my seat.

Riverstrike, I notice now, adorns what is formal wear in a sleek black-tie tuxedo with a relaxed fit material, and takes a seat opposite us.

"Let's speak naturally through voice speech," I request Patrick. "It is something sentimental to our twenty-first-century experience."

"My sentiments entirely," Jürgen concurs with veiled sarcasm causing me to widen my eyes with caution toward his demeanor.

Riverstrike welcomes the request to adjust his GPI comms setting, "Congratulations on making it into the GPPJ!"

"I thank you again, Patrick. Jürgen and I are greatly appreciative of the considerable kindness and first-class treatment we have received."

"Strangely, you have no recollection of indoctrination, or at least I am surprised you don't have a bone to pick with me. Are you certain you feel that appreciative without objection?"

"What do you mean," inquired Jürgen, "Objection towards what exactly?"

Riverstrike holds his thought.

"Nothing in particular," Riverstrike deflects the question, "Having a positive transition is what we strive for. You know I am originally from the twentieth century too!"

"You are?" I feign surprise.

"I was born in Nineteen-Seventy-Six, on July Fourth."

"The bicentennial of the Declaration of Independence? Wow!"

My reaction was overblown, but if you're going to feign excitement you must go big!

Jürgen offers admiringly, "You are nearing the 'quarto' centennial in twenty-three-seventy-six?"

Riverstrike offers a gentle smile, "The fourth centennial is the appropriate phraseology. Also, I believe I know what year you may have . . . disappeared."

I am stunned by his claim, "When Patrick?"

"Two-thousand-five, but I admit it is a semi-informed guess."

"Why do you think two-thousand-five?" I put forward breathlessly.

"Well, before I get into details of my suspicions," Riverstrike places his hand's thumb to thumb, index finger to index finger before his nose and mouth, "how do you, or how did you survive? I don't know why the two of you survived. Yes, based on your physical age Jürgen you are forty-nine, and Catherine you are thirty-eight years old. I was thinking this could be critical to determining your past identities. Somehow you managed to live in stasis for nearly three-hundred-fifty years. And without ever receiving the Condorcet procedure? I am physical age of sixty-eight years old, received the Condorcet procedure in twenty-forty-four."

"Well, yes, we suppose, until Qyxzorina and Marcel provided it for us. Should they have not?"

"It is of no concern now, but before your emergence is the question."

"We thought Qyxzorina, and Marcel were abducting us for money," Jürgen exclaims.

"Why?"

"You know, to hold us for ransom."

Riverstrike face turns from an inquisitive expression to a relaxed humorous reaction, "Ransom," he breaks into laughter, "There is no need for ransom in the GPPJ, everyone has all they need to excel in life." Riverstrike stands to walk a few steps, "There is something about what you say that piques my interest."

"Oh?" Why do I feel like we're about to be blindsided? What's he thinking behind what he's saying is what I'm thinking.

"If you suspect they will hold you for ransom," Riverstrike pauses for an indication he has our undivided attention.

"Yes," replies Jürgen truncating the awkwardly ponderous pause.

"For what reason are you worth any ransom to anybody?"

Jürgen and I express a sigh of relief at the pedestrian question.

I blush to look toward Jürgen whose expression transitions to flabbergast. My first instinct is to reassert for financial gain, but then the nakedness of humility overcame me, once again realizing my ignorance, or in this case, my arrogance in response to the question posed.

The self-centered vanity under a pretense, a delusion of grandeur, is what I think Riverstrike must think of our self-perception, "The reason is why would they have helped us escape and then treat us with reserved patience knowing we are not in the GPPJ?"

"Yeah, we figure they must have a hidden agenda based on their abundance of generosity and respect toward us," Jürgen adds further confusion to my excuse for an answer.

"I find your confused naivete charming in an 'old world' way. It should be possible to cooperate in determining your true identities, as you seem naturally trusting and eager to reveal yourselves to yourselves and everyone else for that matter."

"Most definitely Patrick," I lean forward to stress my point. "We don't know where we are going until we know where we came from."

Jürgen adds with newly found focus, "Otherwise we are a rudderless ship in stormy waters."

"If it puts you at ease," Riverstrike reasons, "They were assuming you are refugees from one of the planetary Vivarium."

"Planetary vivariums," I place the term at the fore of my thoughts, "What would be the use of studying, observing humans in confined environments?"

"You are a scientist indeed, anthropology? More likely your discipline is archaeology, perhaps biological or a historical archaeologist could be possible."

"What are you inferring?" I ask as I stand up now sensing Riverstrike's powers of perception working a jigsaw puzzle. He knows what the puzzle looks like, and he's trying to find out how the individual puzzle pieces, including Jürgen, and I, fit into it.

"As you are possibly aware, I will make certain it is clear that neither of you exists."

"Don't exist?" Jürgen asks as he raises his head toward me, who like a tortoise extending its neck to reach for low-hanging bush leaves opens his mouth to say, "I told you we're in some alternate reality!"

"Jürgen, funny," I gently reprimand his use of sarcasm as I cross over to face Riverstrike, "There is no data available, census records, declassified secret federal files to support our existence?"

"No census listing, financial statement, or any childhood from descendants or relatives present today. Not even a birth certificate. It's like you never existed, but here you are. There's a chance your genes may find a match, but no matches made after fifteen billion tests."

The pit of my stomach aches in humble contemplation of what absurdity we now face.

"It's not so bad Catherine," Jürgen stands and approaches me, "We may not know who we are, but we don't need to if you think about it."

Riverstrike stands into a doting posture, "I'm ready to unleash my Earth-shattering connection to your unknown past."

"What's this?" Jürgen is confused, "Catherine, do you know what he's talking about?"

My reaction to Jürgen is to shake my head 'no.'

"I would like to introduce you to my most senior leadership of RAKLAV."

From beyond the entrance door, a woman of an athletic physique walks gracefully with fluid steps into the cavernous banquet room.

"Janalake, my senior Zealot Sentinel commander, the finest Zealot Sentinel there ever was, and Simon Noir," Riverstrike fixes his eyes on Jürgen as Simon Noir steps in, "My trusted advisor and organizer of my public business affairs."

Of course, we recognize Commander Janalake who oversaw our training and indoctrination into the ZS, and, to a lesser degree, the man with the mask obscuring his facial features. His name now revealed to us, Simon Noir proceeds to remove the mask from his face.

Our mouths open effortlessly as if our lower jaw bones will hit the floor.

Simon takes his place on the left side of Minister Riverstrike eerily peering into Jürgen's eyes.

"Where the hell are, we?" Jürgen pleadingly expresses, "What is this?"

Do my eyes deceive me? I do a double take.

"Jürgen, there are two of you? You have an identical twin?" I utter, "Oh my god, who are you?"

Riverstrike's voice rings out in laughter, "Not exactly a twin, are you, Simon?"

Simon fixes a snarky crescent on his face as he delightfully swivels his cranium left to right, then right to left, and again.

"No, Simon is more than an identical twin, more than a near

mirror image. He is a clone of you, Jürgen."

"When did you do this?" I am astounded by this bizarre possibility, "When do we go through indoctrination?"

The Minister pauses to reflect on my statement before stating, "Oh, by no means would I have been inspired to clone Jürgen if I had known what would come of it ~ No offense."

"None was taken," assured Jürgen.

"I am talking to Simon," Riverstrike elevates his official demeanor by clasping his hands behind the small of his back, "I almost named him Semen, based on the genetic sample my forensics people discovered in a sleeping bag at an abandoned campsite."

"In an abandoned campsite?" Jürgen points out.

"Where is this abandoned campsite?"

"Are you saying Simon is cloned from a semen sample you found in a sleeping bag?"

"Yeah, and when did this happen?" Jürgen firmly demands.

"Two-thousand-five. I was hoping you would ask," Riverstrike has a holograph map display of South America, "Have you ever been to Colombia?"

"Colombia?" I turn my head to look at Jürgen standing over my shoulder, he responds vacantly mouthing no words.

"No matter," interjects Janalake, "We have more to determine presently Patrick."

"Yes, of course. Simon, please take center stage."

"And don't forget to bring your prop with you," Janalake eggs him on smiling devilishly in anticipation of doing an act of injustice.

Simon holds a juvenile gleam on his face as he walks up to Jürgen before grabbing him by the collar, tightly gripping enough to yank Jürgen with him to the center of the expansive bare Moon rock-tile floor.

He shoves Jürgen away a few feet and assumes a martial arts stance.

"Do you have to be so rough?" Jürgen complains agitated by the violent physical treatment.

"You have to put up with 'rougher' than that," Simon delivers cryptically as he kicks off his shoes, "How does this feel?"

Simon commits a forceful lunge kick with his right leg to Jürgen's abdomen, with a force nearly collapsing him to the floor.

"Hey!" My shriek in protest is not ignored.

"Hey what?" Simon retorts launching into a roundhouse spin, pivoting on his left leg, and swatting his right leg upon Jürgen's chin knocking him down.

I move to assist but Janalake blocks me with a body flip in front of me, then a stiff two-hand-shiver to my chest angers me.

"Invade my personal space?"

I swing a backhand in fury landing squarely on Janalake's cheek, shocking her to falter back.

Jürgen gains his footing but is immediately assaulted by Simon with a flurry of jabs pummeling Jürgen sending him back to the floor.

Janalake retaliates with a double-hand claw around my eye sockets. I grasp each of Janalake's forearms in a weak effort to dislodge her double claw grip. I release my grip to vigorously perform an inverted forearm to-forearm slap, breaking Janalake's tight grip I follow up with a straight left leg high kick to Janalake's chin, but Janalake intercepts my kick with a double hand downward vaulting maneuver deflecting my kick while leaping in the air and perching on my shoulders she uses her muscular firm thighs to place a sleeper hold around my neck, her shins press on my rib cage shrinking my lung capacity to breathe.

Simon is hoofing Jürgen across the floor stringing sweeper kicks to knock Jürgen down repeatedly.

Riverstrike shows disgust, "Jürgen, you better fight back!"

Jürgen looks at Riverstrike with confusion before taking a leaping karate kick from Simon to his chest knocking him ten feet back and onto his ass.

Jürgen is infuriated by the cheap shot and embarks on a series of body flips leaping over Simon landing directly behind him back-to-back and reaching over his right side to clamp a grip on Simon's right arm by his shoulder and in one move hoisting Simon in the air tossing him clear across the room."

Jürgen is amazed by his physical achievement.

Janalake has me feeling blue in the face, so I resort to a collapsed move falling backward to hammer Janalake onto the floor, where her body smacks the surface like a belly flop into a pool of water from a diving board.

Janalake regains her composure as do I, we raise ourselves from the floor.

"Nicely done by all of you," Riverstrike is truly cordial if not entirely sincere.

"Nicely done?" I am reeling from the trauma of hand-to-hand combat, "How are we, skilled martial artists?"

Jürgen is exhilarated by the experience, "What have you done, placed some brain chip or something?"

Riverstrike is amused, "Jürgen's lazy thinking. Nice try, but no shortcuts, cyborgs are not permitted. You have trained for five years in mastering the most lethal moves from all the top lethal martial arts known. Brazilian Ju-Jitsu, Silat, Muay Thai, Sambo, and Krav Maga. These are the tools of a Zealot Sentinel, in defense and protection of the 'wellbeing' of the human condition."

Simon and Janalake take their place on either side of Minister Riverstrike, "I would like to arrange a picnic with the two of you."

"Oh, not the five of us?" Jürgen and I respond in unison.

I continue, "Where do you suggest, the campsite?"

Riverstrike appears to sense our anticipation for searching for our origins, as was he, "There is no rush, but we can do that."

Jürgen is caught off guard, "No rush? How is that?"

"Jürgen what do you expect to see?" Riverstrike inquiries fishing for a surfacing memory.

I jump in, "We will wait. You are busy, this matter is not pressing, in due time!"

"Very well. I will send notice to you soon," Riverstrike gestures to Janalake to follow Simon and himself to exit.

Janalake hesitates at the door, "Hey," she commands our attention, "Congratulations on joining the GPPJ!"

"Thanks. What's the rush? We were getting to know each other."

"Nothing pressing. I will be seeing plenty of you." She *hisses,* searingly, before exiting the room.

"Not pressing?" Jürgen displays his vexation in his response, "He found my sperm and cloned my DNA!"

"Are you nuts?" I kneel on one knee to pick up a quarter-sized piece of 'moon rock tile' from where I body-slammed Janalake.

"How can you believe any of this?"

"What do you mean?"

"Your sperm would be collected about three hundred years ago! They probably took a sample in the five-plus years we spent for indoctrination."

Jürgen asks,"Why would he clone me and not you?"

"Great point, it would seem odd that Simon Noir is the only clone in the entire GPPJ."

"Is it? With the population growth from natural birth, there is no need to clone a human." Jürgen looks at the piece of 'moon rock' tile I twirl between my fingers, "What's with the piece of the floor?"

"This would make a nice trinket for a necklace." I explain flatly,

"Our 'Patrick' possibly has much up his sleeves."

"Perhaps more than a possibility."

"There is an apparent connection to our shared past and for whatever reason, I sense we have occupied his thoughts for several centuries."

I wonder when our paths first crossed; was it two-thousand-five and, more importantly, what happened?

II

Part Two

EXISTENTIAL

22

Debrief Belief

Last night at the Lunar Hall celebration Qyxzorina and Marcel invited me to their offices.

The next morning, they pick me up in the Blister cruiser outside the Sea Foam Condos.

My thoughts are a little beyond being in the present moment as I weigh the significance of informing my friends about the strange, violent incursion orchestrated by their business partner last night as if it's a red flag of abuse.

The brutal nature of his methods to operate, or bully his way, combined with his wealth, mostly from innovations he stole the patents for, snatching the engineering and design rights from the recently departed does not fare well for Qyxzorina and Marcel.

It will have to wait as the ascent into the SSN is moving along happily and I do not care to upset the present constant spontaneous instant by mentioning difficult unpleasantness.

Our destination is on the Entrepreneur SS and upon approach, the illuminated signage of businesses operating within including 'Blister Star Tours,' is stunning in presence with earth tone colors of green, brown, and blue forming the company name, as the physical properties transform to represent different points of interest available for booking, or advertising locations soon available from the Asteroid belt. Possible tours to the solar system's outer gaseous planets, Jupiter, Saturn, Uranus, and Neptune, perhaps Pluto is a scenic attraction from afar, will require the placement of a series of remote advanced space stations for rest and recharging. My constant research is paying dividends in understanding current issues and plans and proposals leading human existence into a prosperous outlook.

"The signage is eye-popping to me!" I am more enthused by the quality of the sign than the name inscribed on it. "The name is in English, while other names of companies are in various languages.

How can one person translate all the languages?"

"Just as the GPI allows for you to hear every word translated to English. This technology has been available for centuries," Qyxzorina informs me. "Thank you for your kind words, but the sign needs to change as Marcel has agreed to 'Star Gazer Tours' moving forward."

There is a detectable increase of speed in motion and direction as Marcel maneuvers smoothly to land on the hangar landing deck. Once on the deck, Marcel taxis the Blister on a transport platform that will carry the cruiser into the hangar dock where we can safely enter the Entrepreneur interior offices, walking through polished utility desk space and cushioned high-back oak wood armchairs, up a mirrored elevator, then step onto the marble floor imitation on level eight, only two doors down to suite number seventy-two-zero-one: Star Gazer Tours, INC.

In little time we enter an office conference room with a capacity of twenty-thousand seats in the round. They sit about ten rows in from where they ask me to stand downstage center.

They explain to me they "see something in me" and asked me to, "gather my thoughts regarding the essence of 'faith and fire.'"

I'm not consciously aware of what they want, as they informed me, "I will know when the time comes." This statement, I decide, will be my premise.

"Time will tell as it can reveal the truths of the human will. I believe in the sentiments of Nineteenth-century transcendentalist anti-slavery orator Theodore Parker, 'The arc of the moral universe is long, but it bends towards justice.' Martin Luther King Jr. also expressed this theme heroically when leading a civil rights movement one hundred years later, an affirmation of the struggle for equality of rights as freedom permits.

"MLK is a hero to me, in the perseverance, the commitment in the face of hatred to overcome with his devotion to equal rights. I don't know how I remember this other than it means faith and fire to me.

"We are the engines of ourselves and like the cyclical nature of existence, where muscle may breakdown in exercise, soreness from, then rest and heal with nutrients and grow stronger; the rain falls, providing nutrients to the Earth, after cleansing the air, evaporates and reconstitutes as clouds in the very same atmosphere. I'm speaking of war and peace, death, sacrifice, victors and losers, the mitigation of treaties to form a new peace, a foundation to grow stronger societies into the future!

"It is the 'wellbeing' of the human condition, and the physical manifestation of the human will once to be known as fiat, currency, yes money for what will you do to get it, what will you do when you have it, and what will you do without it?

"This doctrine of the Economic Theory of the Human Will is in evidence with potential, action, and realization of, continuously improving the 'wellbeing' of the human condition."

Qyxzorina and Marcel share pleased expressions in one voice, "Tremendous progress."

I reveal a sliver of a smile happy my mentors are impressed, but I am not finished.

"The one final fascism is nature, in its domination of truth, what is the highest aspiration to seek other than the truth? All, including everlasting life or fortunes beyond lifetimes, have no greater measure than truth."

The sensibility of my statements is rhetorical at best . . . "The 'human will' requires no explanation. It determines what the ultimate truth is in the end. It is our collective 'wellbeing' determined by our collective consciousness to bring about the wealth of loving peace."

Qyxzorina and Marcel are without words.

"What do you think?" I ask with my right hand shielding my eyes from the bright stage lights.

There is only silence.

"Qyxzorina? Marcel? Hello?"

The stage lights fade out and the house lights go up as they are approaching the stage.

Marcel is first to the stage, "Catherine thanks, you did a-,"

"Wonderful presentation Catherine," Qyxzorina is beyond pleased, uncontrollably joyous.

"Thank you. Did I speak my thoughts well? I tried all morning to figure a premise and it came to me that you handed me the-,"

Marcel interrupts, "Yes Catherine?"

I stop speaking to listen.

"We want to hear all about it," Marcel says.

"We can go somewhere more intimate to speak. Come over here," Qyxzorina reached out with her arms, and I came shuffling my feet to the apron of the stage to sit and hop into her hug-loving arms.

The brief walk to the administrative office level is eye-opening due to the natural organic styling of the interior design.

We approach a door where they pause to show me in.

There is a circular table with four chairs and kitchen appliances from a refrigerator to the kitchen sink.

On the table is an artisan cheese and crackers tray with red grapes, juicy sliced kiwi, and stemless wine glasses.

"Wonderful little spread here." I didn't know how hungry I was until seeing food, "Say, is that stage a performance hall? There must be twenty-thousand seats in there?"

"No, it is not for performance art." Marcel intimates, "It is for company meetings and training; the twelve-thousand-five-hundred crew members per Blister, excuse me, strike that ~ Star Gazer Tours ship requires unilateral training in person. It's by regulation in safety compliance to administer 'in person' training."

"Twenty thousand seats?"

"I know it is a tiny, intimate space, but we are a startup."

"Have a seat and help yourselves to some treats," Qyxzorina offers Marcel and me to dig in while she retrieves a bottle of Sauvignon Blanc from the refrigerator.

"This is thoughtful, thank you for this. These are high-quality cheeses."

"How can you tell?"

"Do you smell the Epoisses, the Affine au Chablis, the Ardrahan? This blue cheese is sweet and creamy, there are few pockets of blue mold," I stop when I sense they are observing me. "What?"

Marcel and Qyxzorina look at each other and simultaneously respond, "How do you know so much about cheese?"

I hear them loud and clear, and as I press for memories all I can say is, "I probably ate a lot of cheese?" They were not looking for that answer. "Sorry."

Qyxzorina lightens up, "Do not concern yourself, Catherine."

Qyxzorina said as she fills the wine glasses. "What do you think of our facility?"

"What can I say? Stand-alone lamps and cloth embroidered chairs in space. The plants are synthetic though, why not keep live plants?"

"We have a space travel agency, we are not a plant Nursery," Marcel is polite in his response, "The floors are magnetized also."

"I got it," I said feeling foolish.

"You hardly look like a fool," Qyxzorina smiles hearing my thoughts.

"Should I dial in on your channel?"

"So, if you want to," Marcel is sampling the cheeses and wine fervently.

"I prefer to talk directly; it is more personal to me."

"There are enough photos displaying spacecraft in various phases of construction to fill a museum!"

"There are more spacecraft photos than plants in this office," Marcel said poking fun at me.

Qyxzorina joins us at the table, "You will notice time goes by faster and faster with the information endless and education perpetually continuous as all of us are forever ignorant."

"And the seven-hundred-year lifespan!" Marcel said unexpectedly.

"What do you mean seven-hundred-years Marcel? I thought you said the average life span is five-hundred-fifty-nine years of age?"

Qyxzorina answers for Marcel who is piling in the cheese and wine, not so much of the crackers, "Like I made you aware; Time moves quickly, as does scientific discovery and technological advances. Life spans have increased by thirty-five percent in the past six years."

"Six years? It's the year twenty-three-forty-five?"

"Twenty-three-forty-six," Marcel states.

"Well six years total with less than two years since you resumed adorning GPI," explains Qyxzorina.

My head is spinning, dumbfounded, dazed by this revelation of six years passing by and it seems like six months have passed!

Qyxzorina is compassionate, "The ceiling of learning, the ceiling on empirical innovation, evidence-driven over instinct based on the amending of past flaws to achieve a better present day; failing systems to be replaced by modern technologies, and finally empirical knowledge, hypothesis, theories sprouting from continuously new data on nature will come down to you Catherine."

Marcel wipes his face with a cloth napkin, "So tell us, Catherine, what information have you learned of your past?"

"We are nature revealing ourselves to ourselves. As a bioarcheologist, this was my adopted mantra." I reflect on a deeper memory of a vision I had upon viewing remains, "There was a visage of murdered bodies piled high. They were military men."

Marcel is suddenly taken aback and flashes a look towards Qyxzorina who expresses concern but encouraging reaction saying, "Tell her Marcel."

Marcel speaks with empathy towards me, "I was once a military man. What were the circumstances? War?"

"The circumstances are unclear to me currently. Wait a second.

It was in a jungle or rain forest I'm almost sure of it." "What can you be so sure of?"

"I'm not too sure there was a massacre, I remember a pile of bodies, I was terrified!"

"It's okay Catherine. You are describing military operations involving an anti-narcotics terrorist campaign," Marcel is actively researching through his GPI, "Classified missions, according to obituary records there were multiple casualties of covert special forces; they were deceased from the period while serving in South America. The paramilitaries terrorized the citizenry; namely, the poor farmers and villagers exploited for whatever commodities they produced in scarcity."

"Maybe Jürgen can offer insights too?"

"Okay," Marcel agrees, "we can try it."

Marcel sits back as he establishes a connection to Jürgen's GPI.

"Hello, this is Jürgen."

"Marcel here Jürgen, with Qyxzorina and Catherine."

"Hi Jürgen!"

"Hey Catherine, where are you? I came back from my run, and you were nowhere to be found!"

"I'm sorry Jürgen, but I told you this morning they invited me to their space office. Didn't you sleep in?"

"Oh, yeah. After last night into the early morning, I'm surprised you made it out of bed!" Jürgen speaks jovially, "I do not believe I ever heard of a ten-hour happy hour!"

"Okay, deceased military. Machine guns. Lethal weapons, Marcel poses with the firm suggestion, "Jürgen, have you any thoughts that speak to these terms?"

"There are no recollections for me."

"No," I broke in, "The use of guns or any lethal weapons do not exist in space."

"Why is it Marcel, there are no laser guns, not even the Zealot Sentinels are armed."

"Why? The reason is simple," Marcel refrains from his research to talk freely, "Unlike science fiction, the laser gun technology never proved useful, let alone effective. If you want to microwave a frozen burrito with laser gun technology, okay, as microwaves have been weaponized for centuries."

"What about guns?"

"What about them?" Marcel disdainfully attempts to evade the question.

"What happened to them?" I persisted, "Have guns been eradicated for the 'wellbeing' of the human condition?"

"There are guns. The Earth landers who use them are in a

vivarium. Guns in space are unsafe, period; so, there are no firearms, nothing more dangerous than our hands and feet."

Jürgen is starting to press the issue, "What about robot potential? There are few robots above my waist?"

"The best example is the robot warfare era of the mid-to late-twenty-second century. A handful of the world's potent industrial economic wealthy countries became obsessed with the proposition of manufacturing and coordinating military service dependent upon robotic combatants. The prevailing conceptualization of effective robot combatants would destroy the enemies' robotic forces to the point of the surrender of national sovereignty proved to be a false assertion.

"Each alliance of countries deploys their robotic combatants; they are mostly automated for human use through cyborg technology. The conclusion after calculating their investments of wealth, time, and labor led only to conflicts resulting in mutual destruction, a war of attrition.

"As the resupply of robotic combatants is not feasible to keep up with the battlefield losses, the dream of robotic conquest ended hastily, yielding to consumerism keeping robotics as a marketable sporting event with a long history of enjoyment.

"After sixty years, lingering global economic depression for millions of disciplined humans and with no remaining elite countries participating, as there were no 'victors' in this concept of war do not result in a clear upper hand of leadership, the result of any society without order is a dark age. With the destruction of many communities where the robotic armies fought, the price paid was equivalent to the self-sabotage of nations and hence any version of robotics became limited to service and entertainment.

"Robotics for warfare is banned, firearms banned in space, sparingly used on Earth, international commerce, and the banning of cyborg technologies development became unilaterally banned from existence."

"How about sex with robots, even robotic sex is most popular in society?"

"We have robotics to thank for enhancing sexual performance and pleasure. With the ability to incorporate the female reproductive system, women are no longer needed to create babies. Sounds good, eh?"

"Marcel! If I hear you favoring dehumanizing technology, I swear to your Maker, I will have you shopping for some new nuts."

"Now, now, Qyxzo my love, I am only being ironic."

"What are robots for? What do they do?"

"Their roles vary immensely. Their presence is kept well secluded as robotics provides the translucent technologies of our passageways, controls by automation and programming for essential tasks on the 'q micro-nano' level, as if like algae that bonds terrestrial earth together, so do the constant interactions of molecular robots.

Still, other robots have been used for sports replacing horses on ancient racetracks and adopting human team sports to a level where precision and probability statistics skills made robots navigate a world of exploration, and interaction, the stewards remain human though.

The role of the robot is to analyze, explore, document and all the while construct impenetrable designs. Humans create these robots to uncover worlds of the hidden layers of existence, macro-Humans tire from inorganic effects, as the interest wears thin without complex artificial intelligence, yet with exquisite artificial intelligence humans, most humans become annoyed with the applied perception of arrogance, spitefulness of their humor creates humiliation of humans. That dynamic can only be created by self-deprivation by human humbleness.

"And the gun technology?"

"Catherine," Qyxzorina speaks to my concerns directly, "the truth is gun use was an invention resulting from the height of the age of barbarism. The industry is obsolete, banned from space."

"It's probably not a clever idea to do this."

"Do what Marcel?" I find myself asking him more questions to peel off the layers he is hiding behind.

"We can get you to someone who specializes in the programs presently," assures Qyxzorina.

Marcel feeds a request standing in attention to receive a response, "Yes, it will be possible, to visit a vivarium escort, Roberto, in just twenty hours."

"Thank you, Marcel. Will he be able to take us to this vivarium?"

"He can take you to all of the vivariums if you like."

As the three of us depart to the Blister cruiser we pass a series of artist renderings of dinosaurs spanning the Mesozoic era's

Triassic, Jurassic, and Cretaceous periods.

Various depictions of exotic environments are mounted along the hallway walls leading to the Blister cruiser. Science is everywhere, and locations known are for tourist travel and other examples of historical scientific achievements.

"Our faith is our own, Catherine," Qyxzorina said. "You are

picking up on my thoughts."

"We know to keep business open to all, in the GPPJ each citizen repeats one another for the 'wellbeing' of the human condition, no matter what our personal religious or spiritual preferences are."

"The existential vibe these images project, knowing they share a familiarity of environment we can relate to despite the passage of time."

"Thank you, Catherine, for your generous remarks. It is another credit owed to Qyxzo for her passion in interior design."

My eyes are drawn to a six-inch by twelve-inch canvas mounted at eye level on the wall before the exit. The image strikes me to a halt.

"Qyxzorina, what is this work all about? Is this an alien figure?"

"That is a portrait found in a dig in Peru in Twenty-Sixty-Three. Do you find it a face you've seen before?"

"It seems I have, oddly, it comes to me as if it were a dream."

"Did you say, 'Comes to you?' Asks Marcel."

"As if from the past, there are memories very, blurry. Is that a portrait of a Peruvian native?"

"No," Marcel anticipates my question, "It is believed to be a thousand-year-old depiction of a Denisovans. That makes it odd."

"It would remain from the fourteenth century."

"That's right. The Denisovans perished off the face of the Earth nearly fifteen thousand years ago. This figure here probably witnessed the end of the Inca empire."

The figure's face bears the weight of daily struggle as a hunter-gatherer. You might think he spent a lot of time fist fighting or incised, becomes angry and desperate wrestling with young fellow tribesmen over the right to mate with females. His protruding brows, bulbous nose, cauliflower ears, chapped lips, and high cheekbones are blemished and unshaven, all features that reflect harsh living; then I see in his eyes a spark of common expression. And then I think about how these ancient human peoples had a hand in the extinction of the Woolly Mammoth. My mind is working overtime to recover the memories.

23

ACRES Cares

The Sea Foam Condominiums are the original "Bubble by the Sea" luxury condominiums project in the mid-twenty-first century. An engineering marvel, the first permanent daily long-term living quarters constructed on the sub-sea level off the coast of Miami, Florida.

Due to rising ocean levels, the flooding of major cosmopolitan urban areas required an infusion of structures serving the dual purpose of residential housing and levee barriers.

The levee walls are built along the edge of the city grid. The front lobby allows access from the city street level, as well as from the orbiter parking hangar where concierge and elevator banks allow access to both above and below sea-level condominiums.

I'm eating a vegetable bowl with brown rice with seasonal oils, with light balsamic vinegar splashed over spinach leaves, pea pods, and an array of garden vegetables.

I sit close to a clear surface table viewing a display projected in the middle of the table in three-dimensional form. My morning is dedicated to research topics starting with Colombia's two-thousand-five and headline topics on illegal narcotics infrastructure.

Skimming over articles about expeditionary military operations, I locate a captivating headline on a report of illegal transport of huge sums of narcotics by two government agents with military personnel aboard a military watercraft set to dock in San Diego.

This bizarre vignette is a trivial aberration of honor and loyalty. An apparent corruption of ethical patriotic duty defined by greed!

The finite timeline allows a methodical search for any records of myself or Jürgen's existence. I search how many female babies named Catherine were born in Dallas in the year of my birth.

There are no birth certificates logged or recorded by first name only. My last name may speak to me if it passes under my eyesight.

A pop-up graphic appears of a snuff box held between a pinky finger and thumb in one hand and the other hand with rings the snuff box is opened to reveal a population of a working class.

The profile of King Louis XIV, the 'Sun King,' appears with a nose large enough to 'sniff in' some of the proletariat class into his regal nose before sneezing them out, many fly off, others get a mucous excreted covering, and pinning many to this snuff box.

The graphic turns out to be an advertisement for Modern Museum of Space History: The Ages of Absolutism to Aerospace, the Modern Museum of Space History presents Alien Art Designs in Ancient Cultures and Sun Worship. Age of Impressionism series: The Comprehensive Collection of Vincent Van Gogh.

A door slides open from the bedroom as Jürgen emerges yawning waking from a nap, "What's the music?"

"I am sorry it was an advertisement. Did I wake you?"

"No, what are you eating?"

"It's a vegetable bowl. I can make one for you."

"That's okay," he waves his one hand in refusal as he clasps his hair out of his face with the other hand. "What are you up to?"

"Not much. Researching twentieth-century elementary schools in Dallas, and there were around one hundred of them in nineteen-seventy-six."

"Any specific results?"

"It's impossible without knowing our last names, especially with no photographs to go from."

"I guess it didn't make its way onto the world wide web." I take the point Jürgen is suggesting so I search when the world wide web was first in use, "Nineteen-ninety-four?"

"I was twenty-seven in nineteen-ninety-four!" Jürgen is standing beside me as he's rubbing lotion on his hands and arms, "Moisturizer, want some?"

"No, it smells refreshing, what is the scent?"

"There's a tube of it in the bedroom."

"The bedroom? Jürgen, are you sure that is a moisturizer?"

Not to say Jürgen was upset by this suggestion, but he made his alarm apparent responding with a contemplative exasperation, "What could it be, oh my god!"

"I empathize with you, but I don't think it's hair gel either."

"Holy shrinkage, I think it's a massage lube? I was about to cover my face in muscle lube! This stuff burns like hell when applied to the more sensitive areas."

"You learn from this experience?" I could not resist teasing him further, "It does have the scent of eucalyptus! Don't you think?"

"Yes, I do, but . . .these free concierge housewarming products have the worst packaging. If I got this ointment in my eyes, I'd break out in hives!"

"You're luckier you didn't get to your balls first."

Jürgen freezes at the thought of it offering the priceless expression of 'sad puppy eyes' in living the pain in his mind's eye.

"Hey, speaking of balls, what if Riverstrike claims he used a DNA sample to create Simon Noir from this campsite he is going to bring us to today? The whole thought of it is impossible to believe. It would mean you were experiencing ejaculation for some reason, eh?"

"Too funny for words." He says dismissively before offering, "You may have had a part in that!"

"Keep a lid on 'that' until we get out there on this tour." I stop to reflect, "Patrick believes we are archaeologists. If so, it explains the beige khakis we were wearing when this all started." My mind freezes with the horrifying reminder we are lost. The tears I kept from streaming are due to the anger intensifying within emotions frustrated by this unknown amnesia. "I wonder under whose oversight or grant money sponsored us?"

"Wouldn't that answer some questions? The vivarium tour we are supposed to take before our picnic with Riverstrike, how long is it before we leave?"

"Our escort, Roberto, is going to provide us transportation," I reach for a hairbrush, "He will be here within the hour."

Jürgen stands placing his right hand on his chin, "What do we wear?"

"Something light yet covering your skin head to toe."

"I'll just give the settings in the 'tailor genie' a try, this modern wonder makes it possible to wear a different wardrobe every day. What color is good for me?"

I have no idea what color looks good on Jürgen having only seen him in cream-colored khakis and the green body suits standard to The Glass Planet specifications.

"Try purple . . .or Lilac, either would go well with your eyes."

Jürgen is elated, "Wow, yeah, why not? Something more liberal."

I brush my hair rolling my eyes as Jürgen steps into the bedroom.

I place the hairbrush on a side shelf and carry my empty bowl and utensils to the kitchen where a simple insertion into a counter top dishwasher for cleaning, sterilization, and proper storage is automated.

From the dining area to the living room where the view of crashing waves from above us provides a thrilling distraction, diamond-encrusted transparent bulbous plates form the ceiling.

Looking at the ceaseless motion of the Atlantic Ocean flowing over our coastline condominium is comforting. The sound of rainfall somehow puts me at ease.

Jürgen says the waves evoke peril that could make even the most fearless sailors seasick.

For me, the energy exhibited by the bubbly, soapy waves crashing overhead is a source of strength. A feeling of security in being submerged and out of sight, of touch, or sound. Insulated by the environment provides a warmth of isolation that is unapproachable due to the hazardous conditions it provides against potential intruders.

"You are a pluviophile," Jürgen says emerging from the bedroom wearing an athletic two-piece with a lilac base color highlights of purple accents on the collar and cuffs. "What do you think?"

The mention of purple or lilac turns out to be complementary to his color palette, deep blue eyes, choppy blonde short hair, square jaw, and well-postured physique, "Definitely your colors," I compliment resolutely.

"You think so?" Jürgen gauges the style of the design, "It's not too flashy?"

"Distinguished man of the future," I imply, "Elegance, sophistication combined with under-stated self-confidence."

"I was thinking like Elvis if I had the mutton chops!"

My sense is he feels out of his element, "Maybe if you add sequins and wore those sparkling rim sunglasses."

"Add sequins?" He awkwardly voices in self-conscious ridicule.

A gentle ring tone precedes a notification: "Roberto has arrived."

"It's too late, time to head up to ground level, our escort is waiting."

Jürgen and I exit the air-conditioned levee elevator onto the rooftop shuttle strip. Sweltering hot, heavy, humid air envelopes us. Our escort Roberto is waiting outside with an executive shuttle plane idling on the levee landing strip.

I wave to him as we close distance to greet him. He returns a wave of recognition flashing a bright white toothy smile. There are several hundred orbiters that converge around us, crisscrossing above us as we emerge onto the rooftop.

"Hi, Roberto, we presume?" I thought in the last second this man may be the pilot or an impostor, though we are expecting Roberto.

"Let's see, yes, you must be the esteemed time-traveling refugees Catherine and Jürgen? I guess that would make your presumption correct," he exults in a laugh extending his hand to welcome us aboard the shuttle.

"What's with all this orbiter action?"

"Paparazzi, they are allowed to record our image, but they won't tail us, it's against the law."

Roberto is about Jürgen's age, a thick, full mane of black hair is blowing in the ocean winds as I pass by him boarding the shuttle, I detect a subtle scent of aloe.

Boarding the shuttle reminds me of the Cessna class piston-powered planes from the twentieth century. Though this shuttle has a computerized ignition system with air-breathing nuclear jet engines using turbofans with the resultant hot gases for propulsion via a propulsive nozzle discharge below the wing spans. I know this using the GPI mechanical analyzer to identify the qualities of the craft.

"Some cultures are so ancient they believe in seclusion from others, isolationism to achieve a most peaceful society," Roberto explains as we are traveling a safe twenty-eight hundred miles per hour. "Their demands are compatible with the 'wellbeing' of the human condition."

"They are locked away!" I protest.

"They prefer to stay where they are." Roberto clarifies his position.

"Not unlike the Amish communities with no interest to assimilate, refusing to use electricity and modern appliances."

"The Amish are living a mutually exclusive lifestyle at will to this day refusing usage of technology even if it would get them to live longer, healthier lives." Roberto elaborates, "Same goes for all of the cultures under the vivarium technology."

We are aghast and amazed, we protest the purpose of, "Utilizing technology to oppress portions of society whose citizenry opt not to transform into 'progressive ambitions' is questionably fascist."

"Except the oppressed parties enjoy the liberation by their guaranteed peace while living as they see fit in their controlled environs," Roberto asserts, "as the vivarium technology provides complete security at no cost, no loss of money or lives."

"Jürgen, something struck me as familiar to the vivarium technology."

Jürgen replies, "I know, it did to me too. I feel it's as if we were once in one before."

"Roberto, what happens when someone leaves a vivarium?"

"The fact people experience the natural urge for curiosity, they begin to learn. Anyone with a curious mind who wants to learn will find their way out of their respective vivarium. The law of migration from Earth lander to the GPPJ is a routine process for any age, thousands of children are raised, educated, and provided shelter and nourishment by the Adolescent Children in Rehabilitation for Educational Success (ACRES) coalition I founded.

"The focus is to instill an eagerness to contribute their honor, industry, and fortunes to the cause of the 'wellbeing' of the human condition once they reach nineteen years old."

"I am impressed how passionate you are for all the children of the world, young and old. How do you admit them?"

"They are designated as refugees; we take cognitive tests to make sure their health is sound. They begin schooling where their abilities, and skills dictate. Their skills are up to speed once they move on to adulthood. So, in effect, outside of WOCH, which stands for World Organization for Children's Health, the various vivarium societies are responsible for maintaining their own 'wellbeing.'"

"In detainment of these isolated populations?" I asked with obvious concern."

Roberto is revealing a growing frustration, "This is not hurting anyone. It was implemented when war itself transformed into a twenty-four-hour, seven days a week industry. Hostiles shooting innocent people with bullets was like serving them French fries, their blood as ketchup. All bloodshed ceases and the nightmare horrors of greed-fascism were abolished once the vivarium technology was completely in place."

"How does all of this come about?" I ask, "The vivarium's technology must be cost-prohibitive?"

"Good question. The technology's origin is classified information, but it is common knowledge computer generated vector shields create the illusion of the 'old world' atmosphere and environmental autonomy. The technology is supported by the SSN via The Glass Planet SS and operates as an inexpensive infrastructure connecting all the vivariums worldwide."

Jürgen asks, "How do people coexist peaceably?"

"Here's the rundown on how things work in our circle," Roberto states, "The super-wealthy harvesters achieve the one-hundred-million mark, then ultra-wealthy harvesters achieve the one-billion-dollar mark and continue with developing philanthropic organizations aimed at improving the 'wellbeing' of the human condition.

"In roles of leadership and job creation and profit managing with a complete delegation of resources, soft and hard assets, to the philanthropic infrastructure, the technology has continually transformed into what we know as a society," Roberto elaborates, "Especially extended life spans."

"What 'we' knew as life; Roberto, are you from the twenty-first century?" I am being polite as it is obvious due to his physical age."

"Party like it's nineteen-ninety-nine!" Roberto mused. "The people are intertwined with the ETHW, and the reality is special interest are the masses perspective of what determines legislation and taxation."

"There are government leaders, no individual President of the world though. The people are their own President and collectively the arbiters of legislation. There are formal courts with nominated Judges with term limits. There are representative legislative bodies with ten-year term limits. Banks provide security of legal actions and low-interest loans, though loans are rarely needed."

"No government, yet legislative bodies exist?"

"Sure, technology allows for each citizen to participate and represent themselves, but with mobile populations, in numbers too vast for adequate representation the process has adapted to the population growth. The representative bodies are formed for specific beliefs, ideological issues typically asserting for the common good."

"So how does a law get legislated?"

"Like all occupations in corporate positions have term limits and members frequently change disciplines, but the consensus for the 'wellbeing' of the human condition is typically an easy decision for the GPPJ to respect as law," Roberto keeps a confident smile, "The legislative bodies then work on a strategy on which the GPPJ suggests or approves amendments to the policy."

Jürgen states boastfully, "We earned two-million-five- hundred-thousand units for completing the Zealot Sentinel indoctrination program."

"You are Zealot Sentinels?"

"Only in the sense, that we underwent the training."

"It would be shocking if you were one speaking to me so openly."

"Then you never trained?"

"No, and I have a meager income. My focus is on the development of orphans and other abandoned children who require proper upbringing, education, and cultural studies from divinity to digging!"

"Digging?" Jürgen inquires, "As in archaeologist?"

"Sure, I was thinking anthropology. Some think archaeology will remain important for alien planet excavations."

"So, you are an earth lender?" I ask politely.

"Not always. I'm in the GPPJ. My passions are earthbound, with the ACRES I'm the founder of, and these kids can remain at least until they turn nineteen."

"What did you say happens at Nineteen?"

"That is the first year of eligibility for life in space."

"Amazing," I said.

"Why?" Roberto pries.

"Patrick Riverstrike said everyone in the GPPJ underwent Zealot Sentinel training?"

"Yeah, well if you believe what Patrick Riverstrike says," Roberto cautions, "then expect to give what he wants to take from you!"

"You know him personally?"

"Over three hundred years ago. He was the commanding officer for a few years in missions against the illegal cocaine cartels billed as a war against narco terrorism."

"Commanding Officer of the covert ops?" I thought to ask if he knew I was reading about these operations an hour ago.

"That's right," Roberto changes his tone from enthusiasm to concern, "He told you?"

"He told us he cloned me with some DNA sample he found in a sleeping bag."

"Where was this sleeping bag?"

"A campsite somewhere in Colombia."

"Did he mention a place called-,"

I halt his speech by interrupting, "Mosaic Caverns?"

"He told you Mosaic Caverns?" He smiles looking to the surface of Earth from the craft, "What a coincidence, look there." Roberto smiles jutting his chin to look to the surface.

An enormous rock crater below is pock-marked and enveloped in the jungle terrain surrounding in all directions.

"Mosaic Caverns?"

"Our next vivarium is my home, in Colombia. The location below us is on the outskirts. Let's take a closer look."

Once on the ground, we take positions standing along the precipice looking into the barren, rock-surface crater.

"Roberto," I ask while surveying the area for suitable campsite terrain, "What do you know about the campsite Riverstrike is talking about?"

"I don't know. We rarely bivouac, oh wait. I remember there was some issue with the American archaeology society working in this area without official clearance."

"American archaeology society?" An epiphany hit me as though Janalake kicked me in the chin. "Without official clearance. I am a bio-archaeologist. Jürgen you are with me too, but your specialty is Anthropology."

"I feel like it is a dream I may have had," Jürgen says in recall of his memories.

"That would be wonderful." I remark as I segue by asking Roberto, "Do you think we can take a sample of this soil to test ballistics?"

"What an idea. There is only one place to go to get an authentic analysis."

"One place?"

"There's no use for guns or bombs. Only missiles are administered by the World Defense Command and their primary focus is to deflect and destroy space rocks posing a threat to Earth, the Moon, the SSN, as well to Mars."

"So, we should gather a sample?"

"Yes, by all means!" Roberto encouraged, "We will be going by the ballistics specialists' vivarium. It is aptly nicknamed the 'Dome of Death.' The only place on Earth where firearms are the status quo."

We pile in the shuttle tour craft, and very quickly we ascended a few hundred feet before a rapid descent to hover over a crowd of children in a field where more children approach running from a village in which they live a few hundred yards away.

Jürgen views the growing crowd of children, "Roberto, how many kids do you administer to?"

"Millions overall, but the children are taken care of through WOCH, with the funding from commercial ventures like ACRES, of as I said I am the founding member and CEO."

One of the children first to greet us upon landing the shuttle is a young female child. She is joyously skipping along the grass field toward us as Roberto taxis' the shuttle plane to position it to use the landing strip as a runway for take-off. Watching her approach from the fuselage she transitions to a full-on sprint, as a gymnast burst of speed, she flings her body twice the height of her five-foot-two-inch sturdy and muscle-toned frame, spinning a half-dozen spirals then landing as gentle as a ballet dancer to somersault down rolling head-over-heal to a meditative cross-legged sitting position.

We rapidly exit the ACRES shuttle plane wearing ecstatic smiles as we approach her with her arms now stretched into the air, a charming smile shines brightly across her rosy-cheeked face.

"Aren't you ball-of-delightful energy! What's your name?"

"My name is for the flower painted on the basket I was born in."

Roberto explains, "As a three-year-old toddler nearly eleven years ago, she was found in a toddler capsule with lily flower prints."

The engaging adolescent asks, "Why do adults find it necessary to consolidate from others to them, wiser or richer?"

Roberto smiles at me and I return the gesture.

He moves over to pick her up, "Lily, it is because, in the brain where the adverse intentions to the 'wellbeing' of the human condition reside, it is known as psychopath or sociopath behavior."

"Why don't they just take the friendly path?"

"I don't know Lily," replies Roberto, "I wish they would. There is hope."

"Do you know why Catherine?" Lily pleads excitedly.

My god, what an adorable, beautiful little girl, "Lily, I wish I could tell you why others are mean and greedy, I do. I can say what matters is what you can control."

"Are they responsible for the ritual of forgotten sacrifices?"

"That is hard to say, Lily. The ritual of sacrifice has its origin in primitive thought and was utilized out of fear of the unknown, human suffering, and a belief of appeasement to those forces they fear to punish them with human suffering. Inca empire was the most recent of these practitioners of such sacrifice. Then there is evidence from a variety of ancient cultures that many historical leaders exhibit psychopathic or sociopath behaviors. Responsibility is a pendulum that swings between the good and the bad and the ugliest of characteristics and human qualities."

"POOPERS!" Lily's face brightens with her cheeky smile, "Profits Over Other People, Ethnicity, Race, and Sexuality!"

"Lily!" Roberto lowers her to the ground, then places his hands on her shoulders, "Where did you come up with that acronym?"

"I came up with it!"

"Could it be more appropriate?" I quip to Roberto.

A gleam of pride shines across his face, "Okay, Lily, you are very clever, to say the least!"

"Ms. Catherine?"

"Yes, Lily, what is it?"

"Are you here to visit the 'forgotten sacrifices' of Mosaic Caverns?"

What an unusual question, "I don't know that what you're referring to is possible, Lily."

"It's okay Catherine," Roberto waves his right hand between Lily and me. "Lily, Catherine, and her friend Jürgen are going to take a tour of the vivarium communities with me. Go play with the others while we are going to my office for a chat, okay?"

"Okay, nice to meet you, Ms. Catherine. Nice to meet you, Mr. Jürgen."

"It is nice to meet you as well Lily," I return the sentiment to her as Jürgen offers a smile and a wave of his hand. As Lily leaps and bounds away to join her friends I ask Roberto, "What does she mean by the 'forgotten sacrifices?'"

With a relaxed smile, he offers, "She is referring to an ancient indigenous tribal ritual with Inca roots about sacrificing young girls from the top of Mosaic Caverns during lightning storms. Very bizarre sacrifice ritual to appease their Gods by having adolescent girls wear metal headpieces contoured to their skulls to be struck by lightning bolts."

Roberto escorts us in a comfortable electric car a couple of miles along a stone-layered road leading to an office park. It is a cultured office space, decorated with a variety of paintings portraying local area landscapes, and old village scenes with depictions of Indigenous Colombians with adobe huts, furnaces, clothing, and ceremonial masks among other artifacts.

"What a collection you have here Roberto," I compliment with the true wonder of the authentic, quality items beautifully arranged throughout the office building. "This could be a museum with what is exhibited here!"

"Thank you, Catherine, that means a lot coming from you," Roberto leads us to a door and unlocks it with the press of a button. "Here is my office. I hope you find it comfortable."

Jürgen follows me into the office as we both marvel at the eye candy of the interior design consumed with the fascination of diverse artifacts on the open wall shelving. Hanging from the ceiling statuettes angled in the corners of the office accentuate an ancient motif. His office chair Is placed between his desk and centered along a wall entirely constructed of glass from floor to ceiling allowing for a flood of warm sunlight to fill the office.

Jürgen and I take plush, suede cushion armchairs within our

grasp. Roberto sits opposite us behind his large oak desk in a tall back chair with a colorful alpaca wool chair cover.

"I want to introduce you to an outstanding journalist who has made his name with his stories and reports chronicling most of the momentous events related to ETHW economics and global politics over the past two-hundred-fifty years. He goes by the initials JJL, his moniker is Lunar 'JO' for the SSN. 'JO,' is 'j' and 'o' capitalized is short for a journalist."

"Will he offer any hints about who we are?"

"Jürgen, that is very possible," Roberto conjures, "I cannot say what or when he may have reported something of relevance in the past, but I can assure you that he is conducting his research efforts to discover more about your identities."

"He is an ambitious one," I assert with a sense of hope he is prolific, "Do you think he will take an invested interest in helping us?"

"He would take an interest in pursuing the truth."

Roberto activates a three-dimensional virtual display of JJT: The Better Approach (JJT, JO 2047) – To the great escape of people from the domains of ignorance, prevailing to favor representatives who offered 'security.' Keep on solving through time we know the possibilities are endless, but the restraints are in the greed and fascism of our era!

In its place is nature and the embracing of such, a communication of wholeness, oneness. Organic instant, every passing of time in all its cycles of natural existence, to evade any path to extinction, by growing new generations many folds after, with the sagacious minds of defenders of the 'wellbeing' of the human condition. The Glass Planet was originally intended on exposing poor mental health, hateful thoughts, prejudiced thoughts, and other undisciplined mental behavior to break the enduring unhealthy habits of generational dysfunction."

Roberto disengages the display medium, "This is when I formed ACRES to provide support to children with special needs, orphaned children and provide daycare for children of parents working in orbit, or WORB, as in 'There are three WORB days in a week. I moonlight as a 'space trucker' three WORB nights a week When you have the means, then you can find the ways," boasts Roberto.

Jürgen and I exchange a curious glance before I ask, "You 'moonlight' as a space trucker?"

"Yes, I work three nights a week transporting solar cells from the charging docks to supply ports across the globe. The charged power cells are rotated around the clock to Earth for implementation as well as transporting exhausted coils back to the charging stations."

"It sounds fascinating. Do you provide energy to the SSN?"

"The space stations are self-sufficient green energy designed exteriors, soaking up the solar energy in open space is like hot air to a hot air balloon. If you need work to get you by until you find your next adventure, then I will refer you."

"We will keep it in mind," Jürgen responds.

I notice a picture on Roberto's desk, it looks like him but much younger. He is pictured with a young woman who has a familiar resemblance I cannot place.

"Ah, I see your eye is caught on the picture of me as a much younger man!"

"My apologies, I am listening to you," I excuse myself, "I thought that is you!"

"It is from the twenty-first century." Roberto sounds embarrassed in his admission and places his left hand over his smile as he speaks, "It is one of my favorites from twenty-twenty-nine. I am thirty-nine years old there, about fifteen years before I founded ACRES."

Jürgen takes a closer look leaning forward in his seat, "Who is the young lady with you?"

"That is a young lady from my home village, Kariana Yahreah. She is about twenty-four then. Incredibly special to me, she was a precocious, genius savant in engineering."

"Wow, you are about ten years younger than you look today?"

"Amazing Jürgen, that is exactly right! I did not get the Condorcet procedure until ten years after that moment."

"How is she related to you?" I ask hinting at his snug hold on her, "You 'Don Quixote!"

"Roberto let out a boisterous laugh, "Don Quixote? That is funny Catherine! I had known Kariana since she was a baby. I am sixteen years older than her. We grew up out of poverty; women faced oppression as females were discouraged to attend school and, by tradition, expected to marry by eight years old and become pregnant by fifteen years old. I am proud to say I was a mentor to her, a father figure too, though due to horrifying circumstances as her father was murdered by the narcotics traffickers who terrorized the impoverished populations."

"How tragic, shockingly terrible." A sudden heavy heart in my chest raised sorrow in my mind to the senseless lawlessness.

"Kariana eluded capture with her mother through a closet with a removable back panel leading directly to the outdoors, behind their shack. I empathized with her mother and helped set her up with living quarters with a well-to-do family, and a computer for Online schooling. This is when Kariana's drive, ambition, and focus on her passion for civil engineering for structural design and ecological power design for clean energy solutions blossomed."

"Why civil engineering?" Jürgen asks in wonder.

"In our Colombia, the wealthiest took up residence closest to a freshwater supply. The further your community or village was from the freshwater supply, the more impoverished was your population. When Kariana was six years old her mother and I would take her to the ocean beaches where she loved to build sandcastles. To prevent erosion of her sandcastle creations she implemented structural designs of rubber tubing, sand sifter, and whatever she could think of to facilitate the oncoming ocean waves from destroying her sandcastle.

"By the time she was eleven, she developed and patented an ocean water plumbing transfer system that alleviated rising coastal water levels by displacing the ocean water into the great deserts around the world. Hence, creating greater volumes of fresh water supply."

"I remember reading about her in the research I have been doing, the whole revitalizing the deserts by using the Mesopotamian method of growing barley to sow the soil after the salt was filtered out of the ocean water by the desert sand?"

"You know she was awarded Nobel Prize for her conceptual talents. I work at the solar space docks transporting the energy coils because she conceived of the technology and utilization. She further developed clean energy technologies from the twentieth century like ocean solar panels and kinetic energy-based technologies. By fifteen years old, she proposed the transporting of fossil fuel supplies for rocket fuel to the Moon and eventually Mars."

"To reduce pollution on Earth?" Jürgen lays out the question as would a child annoyed by the verbosity of his parents.

"As a residual benefit yes, but more so to offer greater efficiency in rocket fuel propulsion by launching spacecraft under low gravity conditions. And you know about the civilian orbiters?"

Jürgen and I nod our heads in affirmation.

"She created the first designs allowing for personal civilian use to orbit the Earth to travel anywhere within an hour. The orbiter's application hastened the development of the SSN by twenty-one-thirty-eight and migrations to populate the Moon began soon after. She became one of the wealthiest international celebrities, immensely generous, advocating the concept of the Economic Theory of the

Human Will by becoming the world's greatest philanthropist at the time!"

"This seems unbelievable for one person to achieve on her own. It sounds like you had an immense impact on her successes." I say this not to ingratiate or flatter Roberto, but he took it as such.

"It is a sad truth the poor and indigenous classes I grew up from were often subject to injustices and exploitation by the various factions at war in Colombia at the time. She was a great inspiration to me and the village community. So much so, I credit her for motivating me with the idea of forming the Adolescent Children in Rehabilitation for Educational Success. There were collaborators and investors to assist her, but she deserves all the credit."

Jürgen asks in fascination, "Is it possible to meet her? I mean, assuming she does work here with you?"

Roberto's face turns solemn, "Unfortunately no, as fate would have it, she died in an accident in the operational stage of the orbiter. She was lost to the universe in one of the first test flights to the Moon in twenty-thirty-eight. She was just thirty-nine years old. To make matters more painful, the Condorcet procedure became available three months after her passing."

"All Kariana thought about was the health of the planet, for all of known life the Earth proceeded our sustenance, our evolution of understanding how to nurture nature. Her mission was to seek ways to heal the environment and end the pestilence of pollution sickening our sustainer of life, our home."

"The most prominent real estate in the known universe," Jürgen states saucily.

"As a felony crime fascism in all its manifestations is to be persecuted internationally. This is how unjust autocrats were smothered from the world scene and truly allowed for the sewing of the ETHW: Money is the physical manifestation of the human will. What will you do when you don't have it, what will you do to get it, what will you do when you have it, and what will you do to lose it?"

"What will you do to lose it?" Jürgen inquires.

"Well, if you lose it," Roberto explains, "after all, like all truths in nature, proper sustenance is a model of cycles in life."

"It is a cyclical process," I say with growing appreciation.

"As is the rule of everything. It is life at various levels."

Roberto rolls up his shirt sleeves flexing his biceps, "As you break down muscle, you diet well to provide proteins, and healthy nutrients to build up to a denser muscle mass. You see the example of the most vital component of nature, water, in its various forms is cyclical. Time is cyclical, down from every moment to moment. Erosion of aesthetics and the immersion of a new aesthetic takes place."

"As was the American Declaration of Independence against the tyranny of English King George III, the Revolutionary War provided a new progressive model of government."

"A rarity when freedom flourishes from tyranny. The tables are not so easily turned, as they were to be if the opposite way. In my country growing up, all I know was greed-fascism, corruption, war, want, poverty, rape, and violent chaos." Roberto is relaxed and incisive, "The vision children possess is not only of the future but is presently the future, in other words, when children ask curiously why things are the way they are, they should not be dismissed with 'Because that's the way things are!' When they are empowered to form critical thinking from powers of observation to innovate solutions for human and world survival and ethical prosperity, their unique genius rooted in innocence is allowed to shine.

"The response should be 'therefore' and the question to be posed is: What do you think about the way things are? Typically, our youth can discern joy from pain, happiness from sorrow and injustice, discern physical abuse from physical discipline.

"The children are the spearhead of humanity as much more than senior citizens, in their knowledge and experience need to pay heed to the children for improving the fairness of human relations. Be gracious and loving toward life as existence itself is the greatest reward, the highest commission, and the grandest position anyone can afford is to be alive.

"For the enrichment of every human being born from an intellectual, emotional, creative, and cognitive understanding of the physical manifestation of the human will, life is most precious and deserves priority in its 'wellbeing,' in the health of the human condition, for the sake of the betterment of the human experience.

"Wealthy individuals are determined not by inheritance or by investments or ownership of property or business interest, they are cultivators, harvesters of money.

"Wealthy individuals in this era are solution-orientated thinkers. They are not about greed, which is illegal, but generosity is their redeeming quality as their wealth is derived from the masses. Generosity comes back exponentially when the proverbial 'invisible hand' of the free market lends itself to alleviate social ills and then elevate the worst off to a healthy standard of living. This elevation is to realize, in the form of commitment of investment to the fourth generation GPPJ citizens and older descendants, free access to all of societies means and ways to offer a leg up on an opportunity to build on their own sustainable 'wellbeing.'"

On the wall behind us is a glass encasement with a very heavy and old rock that was noticeably refurbished from being smashed into five large pieces. Upon closer look, a drawing etched on the face depicts several scenes of ancient origin.

"What is this artifact, Roberto?"

"That is a prize find of mine. It is a stone tablet dating back to eight-hundred A.D., as I have been informed, it may be a headstone commemorating warriors fallen during a violent conflict, slaughtered as indicated by the pile of corpses, by a foreign invading force.

"The Spaniards?"

"Could be, Jürgen."

"I find something very familiar about this," I say with speculative emphasis. "See the series of etchings, those are stalagmites."

"Is it something you recognize from your previous life?"

"Yes," I reply, "Mosaic Caverns is the only geographic location in the region to feature stalagmites. How do I know this?"

"Very interesting, as I found this tablet broken into five pieces within a mile of the Mosaic Caverns in two-thousand-five. Remember what I told you just now? It was when working with Riverstrike's platoon as a guide for his special operations against cocaine traffickers."

"No great or good economics can overtake the wealth provided by individual freedom. With the will of freedom of the people, by the people, for the people, anything is possible.

"She stimulates me in many infinite ways. When you know it's time and you love someone you know from life's toils, trials, and tribulations, you know who is the one for you, one existence shared, and your mind spreads open from your heart to receive all desirable love, affection, self-reflection, and honesty.

"Good is truth, and truth is nature, it is natural: right as rain, the sun is yellow, the sky is blue; erosion changes landscapes; drought makes grass paler; pollution makes the sky gray.

"The light of wisdom, knowledge shines the light of truth on the darkness of chaos, ignorance."

Roberto leads us to the recreation area where the children drop what they are doing to converge around us.

"Now, before we leave, can we get your chorus group together to perform our anthem for our guests?"

"You want us to sing for Ms. Catherine and Mr. Jürgen?"

"Would you sing a song for us?" I cheerfully plead her on.

"Okay Ms. Catherine," Lily said before turning to the crowd of children and waving to the members of her choir group.

"Ofbyfor Jefferson, Kanga Frith, Triessence Vanitha, Auloi Serlo, let us get our groups together to sing our anthem!"

Lily waves her arms toward a group of children as the other group leader children also corralled their fellow chorus members excitedly cheering to come front and center in the formation of five rows of ten children each.

They take their place on a multi-level dais with elegance suited for world-class concert performers.

Ofbyfor, wearing a dark royal blue dress suit with an orange crème color dress shirt, comes to the fore to conduct the chorus.

Roberto turns to us with glee, "They are going to sing the ACRES anthem."

"This is exciting," I tell Roberto, "What a charming young lady, how old is Lily?"

"She is fourteen this year, as are the rest of her choir members." Roberto states proudly adding, "They sing A Capella!"

The children's choir is assembled in an ensemble:

"Asleep we dream of the wonders of a world at peace/ When we awake to the joys of the world/ We find happiness/ Growing up is the time for carefree thoughts in nature's bliss/ When we arrive in our time/ We will love, we will love/ We will love with respect for each other/ as we do love ourselves/ All for one, and one for all, for the 'wellbeing"/ Our minds are with our hearts/ Entwined together our souls/ We are of the people, by the people, for all future generations/ May the glory of our common existence, persevere forever/ Onward and upward, persevere forever/ Onward and upward, persevere forever/ Onward and upward/ Till-the-goal-ye win!"

The melody of the song is a flowing rhythmical mellifluousness, each couplet ends with a harmonizing so beautiful and joyful it brought tears to my eyes!

"Fifty remarkably gifted children, Roberto," I share with him. "Bravo!"

Our clapping is drowned out by the overall cheers of thousands of adoring children all around us as far as the eye can see!"

Roberto is beaming with pride, "Wonderful Lily Violyght, Ofbyfor

Jefferson, Triessence Vanitha, Kanga Frith, Auloi Serlo, way to go! Your teams are doing impressive work, keep it up, guys!"

"Thank you all!" My spirits are soaring from the unbridled enthusiastic, sharply curious intellects beaming with contagious excitement as healthy children will, "We want to return someday soon!"

Roberto takes care to see the children and chaperons are a safe distance away from the shuttle before we board. Jürgen and I wave to the children from our seats as Roberto reaches to secure the hatch, we can see the children jumping with enthusiastic adrenaline. Roberto expresses the "stand by for ignition" with a thumbs up to the chaperons who have begun ushering the thousands of children off to a safe distance. He offers voice command, "Navigate travel program for vivarium tour."

He leans back to place his fingers in a pocket on his belt, "Here." He offers to give me a dossier chip, "This is a dossier of the vivarium destinations, including an in-depth explanation of key historical sites and chronology of notable events. It's for educational use, so feel free to upload using the public interface if you ever need to."

"Thanks, Roberto." I receive the pinky fingernail-sized memory chip, immediately securing it within my inner vest zippered pocket.

"It's very small, I hope I don't lose track of it."

Roberto laughs, "First of all that dossier chip is huge!" He reaches into his belt pocket and displays a handful of confetti-sized hardware, "These are weekly lesson plans. What I gave you includes an entire historical chronology of the cultures, the geopolitical influences, and ancient spirituality ceremony traditions. In other words, an estimated two hundred lessons with thirteen hundred hours reflecting on two-hundred-fifty-thousand years of homosapiens evolution."

Jürgen breaks in, "So what you're saying is don't lose that chip!"

"Can't we fast forward to the Mosaic Caverns segment?"

Roberto's larger-than-life laugh brings a smile to my face, "I'll listen to all of it."

THE GLASS PLANET

24

The Short and the Long of It

These days we don't bother paying attention to the years passing, other than as a point of reference in established history." Roberto says in fact, "The longer lifespan we live, the faster time goes by.

"The everlasting tidal siege of moments presented by ongoing time, pleasurable or adversity laden, is when and where we forge who we are and whom we become. These times of which require knowledge from experience, the prosperity of wealth, and health for productive, longer lives to reach generations of descendants.

"The idea of liberty, freedom, legislative rights to pursue goals, achievements contributing to the 'wellbeing' of the human condition; as children we spend hours every evening dreaming, looking to receive a hint of the meanings of life and the universe's infinite potential.

"To 'burn the stars' is to gaze into the universe to comprehend, understand, and learn to formulate a perspective to preempt generational dysfunction from being passed down through the millennium.

"No one can conceal corruption for long, and when unconcealed will not be able to live a lie. Those who defile the soul cannot conceal themselves either."

"How does the Condorcet procedure work?" Jürgen responds bewildered by the eloquence of Roberto's presentation.

"As I was saying the early successes of mapping the DNA genome spurred on countless theories of potential use like genetic engineering. The Condorcet Procedure for detoxifying the tissue cells is the breakthrough for the ages."

I can only care to hear more, "Brilliant, how does it work?"

"The cause of aging is in the buildup of toxins in the cells of the various tissues comprising our organs throughout one's life."

"Sounds very complex," noted Jürgen.

"Yes, the major complexity derives from the fact each organ has its individual, in layperson terms, unique DNA code to cleanse the cells. Research of the effective treatments to detoxify the cells took many decades to accomplish, the liver, the skin, the veins, and arteries, all major organs became resistant to decay and disease.

"Initially human life spans were reaching one-hundred-fifty years, then not too much time passed before advancements in the technology allowed for two-hundred-fifty years, three-hundred- fifty years and now we are looking at five-hundred-fifty years to seven-hundred years of life with the biological age and health of a twenty-five-year-old."

"I am having difficulty accepting the prospect of living hundreds of years while not aging past twenty-five years of age," I said looking from underneath my eyelashes, I squint to further indicate my skepticism.

"The question of 'when does death occur,' provides no absolute answer other than 'when oxygen to the brain is prevented.'"

"When does death occur?" Jürgen restates the question, "Does anyone know when life begins and if death ends life?"

"Death has slowed down these days. Exceedingly rare to have premature deaths with all the automated technology eliminating most of the human error. Corrective genetic technology has diminished the occurrence of hereditary diseases and malignancies. The rare meteor tearing through a space station has cost many lives in the rare point of no return incident. Martyr class space stations eliminate considerable risk space rocks without failure these days.

"The space rock blasting missile is a part self-guided drone to avoid friendly structures and craft; then it is part predator once locked on to its target it makes impact ninety-nine percent exploding the rock into scattered fragments."

Roberto takes a moment to speak trivially, "Do you realize before the Condorcet procedure it took one million people in a four-hundred-year span to create you? Today the consensus is to give birth to two children at least seventy-five years apart. The firstborn when the parents reach one hundred years old, maybe one- hundred-twenty-five. The greatest achievement of the Condorcet procedure is its revitalization of the female reproductive system extended for up to two hundred years!

"The study of the brain's abilities to heal itself is a tedious discipline, especially how to prevent it from a sudden shutdown like turning off a light bulb. Unexpectedly, it is the final hurdle to understating eternal life."

"Or the final roadblock in evolution to cement our extinction," Jürgen espouses an air of arrogance holding a gaudy grin while making this grand presumption.

"No, not extinction, far from it. Brain health science has made great strides in the regeneration of brain cells. We can prolong life span indefinitely, then humanity should manage well in the exploration of the galactic community," Roberto smiles at Jürgen for being so melodramatic. "The greater the expansion of population into space, the better prepared we will be to prevent an extinction event from occurring."

"What about reaching the extent of the intellectual capability to understand the vast expanses of the galactic community? If humans have a limited scope of cognitive understanding, and an inability to comprehend logistics for deep space travel, then the entire human existence is vulnerable to a race of superior intellectual life forms. An alien race capable of achieving resources enabling a more expansive jurisdiction of intergalactic presence, therefore domination, control of the will."

"Theoretically possible, but I trust in what evolution can do to expand our intellectual capability for survival. Time is increasingly on our side."

"These concepts are not easily obtainable. The sweep of impact on the human experience from living longer lives has diminished greed-fascism controlling the masses. The ETHW is a natural model as a source of health, and vitality, providing education for the growing generations and subsequently for the overall 'wellbeing' of the human condition. How is time increasingly on our side?"

"The period is six months or half of a calendar year. For Qyxzorina and Marcel's age of two-hundred-twenty-five, their six months seem like just two months and approximately seven days of every year, dwindling with each advancing year.

"While Gingi and Spontaneous Instant are twenty-two years old at the time of graduation, they are experiencing time slower as six months feels closer to eleven months out of the year.

"Their exuberance for life, hormonal activity growing at full speed in perfect health, time is open as a blank canvas ready to be drawn up with one's life in the balance of that painting.

"Unaware how many strokes it will take before the final signature is marked on, the content of the painting leaving only how it is to be remembered as they pursue the destinies of their lives.

"The atmosphere is warm in the winter's solstice for several mild winters in a row. Then, like a snow globe, the winter season becomes consistently colder for three or four years in a row.

"Then, mild again progressing to five or six years after which reverting to colder conditions for six or seven consecutive years and so on the pendulum swings until the Earth enters epic eras of extreme weather conditions spanning decades."

I am at a loss for words in reviewing the 'contracts of life.' The first response I have is the ability to manage one's desires is directly tied to their ability, say even being willing to contribute to the 'wellbeing' of the human condition:

The complexity related to one's potential for accessing genetic engineering is in direct financial ability to afford certain desired techniques, charged at variable rates, depending on what outcomes are prescribed.

The first Condorcet application is at no cost and offers a range of fifty to seventy years beyond natural life expectancy.

The next Condorcet application may extend your life between one-hundred to one-hundred-fifty years further at an expense of ten-million monetary units, to add a third application for an additional one hundred to one-hundred-fifty-years is fifty-million monetary units which may extend your life span if you reach the maximum benefit of the first three applications, beginning when you're of natural age of twenty-five, to just under five-hundred-years at the cost of sixty-million monetary units.

That is why childbirth is recommended at two hundred years of age because the couple will know what their potential income will allow for them to extend their lives, and if they will be able to assist their offspring to receive the Condorcet procedure at an early enough age for peak benefit in physical and mental health.

The female reproductive organs remain functional for over two hundred years due to the Condorcet procedure.

ACRES attends to hundreds of millions of children born to parents who invest in the longevity of their own lives but seek the safe upbringing of their offspring while placing focus on contributing to the 'wellbeing' of the human condition. They may achieve financial prosperity to sustain longevity to the final possible application.

The genetic engineering to give birth to a baby that will be modified for IQ, EQ, and CQ advantages, as well as physical health without malignancies, is very costly, yet in comparison, in the long run, more affordable. Couples who wish to be parents but are incapable of achieving sufficient monetary accumulation are left with the ethical decision of investing in themselves to afford the continuation of the Condorcet procedure or accepting a short life span. Choosing to invest in the genetic design of their offspring to enable them to better compete for a longer life span by impacting on the 'wellbeing' of the human condition to accumulate the sufficient monetary units required for investment is the unselfish benefit.

How much is the Condorcet procedure investment to extend one's life span from five hundred years to seven hundred fifty years?

The cost for one hundred to one-hundred-fifty-years above five hundred years is one-hundred-million monetary units. The total price tag for an individual to obtain a minimum of five-hundred-twenty-five years to a maximum of seven-hundred-twenty-five years is six-hundred-sixty-million monetary units.

That seems like a manageable haul, but the monetary units are not achieved or based on savings. One must give back substantial sums in philanthropy to have the opportunity to accumulate the graduated wealth, not to mention the limit of ownership is capped at twenty-five percent of your overall wealth for real estate ownership. Everyone needs to work to earn and then reciprocate the ardent appreciation of life by giving out of gratitude for the GPPJ's goodwill toward the 'wellbeing' of the human condition, as goodwill is returned.

To do their part individually in sustaining the whole. The question is, out of the twenty-two billion human lives, how many can make these investments for longevity?

To the point, how many people comprise the GPPJ, and what station do they hold over the terrestrial or Earth-landers?

If the Earth-landers and vivarium residents perceive themselves free of any bonds to their GPPJ counterparts, then they grow ignorant each passing decade as they resist engaging in economic relations, technological innovation, and the eradication of several hundreds of years of enlightenment through progress.

"Roberto, this dossier chip explains complex issues with tremendous clarity. Amazing, it will get us up to speed in no time."

"You touch on an important debate, and we will spend countless hours reviewing our insights to determine the truth, but for now, we must prepare for the next vivarium."

"Does it have a name?"

"As a matter of fact, our ballistic specialist I'm familiar with resides here in the Appalachia Vivarium."

Jürgen rushes to impress, "Ominously nicknamed 'The Death

Dome.' As you say?"

"Dome of Death is dumb death," Roberto corrects passively, "It has the largest accumulation of explosive devices, firearms, and classic long guns, excessively more than anywhere as these weapons are banned everywhere else."

"A real honest guess," Jürgen holds up his right index finger repeating a pulling motion, "There's a lot of itchy trigger fingers?"

"That's a great irony," Roberto's physical mannerisms are intuitively instructional, accentuating and clarifying in his expressions, "Firearms are obsolete as they are technological dinosaurs."

"Dinosaurs to what? Laser technology hasn't made much of a dent in any way."

"Similarly, laser guns are mere science fiction, firearms have become obsolete. There isn't any meaningful utility for them."

"Are they used in hunting?"

"No need to hunt, but hunting is the top draw and accidents occur."

"No need to hunt?"

"No. Livestock and breeding supply the modest demand for the populations. No one goes hungry."

"Even in all of the vivariums included?"

"All human populations are beneficiaries of the Economic Theory of the Human Will and the 'wellbeing' of the human condition is propositioned. If populations are loyal to the categorical imperative of the 'wellbeing' of the human condition, then peace reigns."

"I would think getting shot does not rank in the 'wellbeing' category," Jürgen asks looking for affirmation.

Roberto is smiling as Jürgen's tone of voice is sarcastic, "The silver lining? There are no more standing armies, no war. No crime from paranoia serves."

"No crime?"

"Nobody commits any crime deserving of lethal force. Within are humans of a sub-culture of Earth-landers who are immersed in many barbaric traditions. Foolish how enthusiast of private gun ownership has made second amendment right argument to defend themselves. Once the ETHW was legislated, the threat of public uprisings or government marshal law has been rendered inconceivable since the late twenty-first century."

The thought of guns 'triggers' a sudden surfacing of a memory for me. The mentioning of guns in obsolete, with no need for lethal force, an image conjures in my mind's eye, corpses piled on top of one another, military men in various uniforms, bullet-riddled bodies limp, lifeless bloodied, enemies and allies alike, rock dust filling the air as bullets ricochet off boulder formations encircling the doomed soldiers in a merciless slaughter.

"Why do you say that?" I utter my question rebounding from the sheer terror of my haunting memory. It might have been a nightmare, but I remember the nightmare's I rarely have, and this isn't one of those.

Roberto looks at me seeming suspect of my attention span, "It once seemed plausible to defend against the modern military of the time, despite the advanced armor and large weaponry. Only a smart bomb, global positioning system guided, could not be stopped by any number of guns. The missile system of The Martyr class space stations illustrates the concise precision and timing to tactically avoid fallout damage as most targets are space rocks posing a threat to the SSN extending from Earth to Moon."

Jürgen is smiling as though he enjoyed the conversation, but his anxiety is clear in the way he is grasping the arms of his flight chair with both hands clamped down, "I take a 'hypothetical' the government could send a smart bomb down a citizen's chimney stack does hold credence, but it is impossible to fully appreciate the evolving of the human will for mutual survival."

"Yes, today's technology proves a necessary use of firearms is not a necessary useful function to protect."

"As of now, I can't remember what I haven't lived through."

"Who is to say you haven't lived through it? You shouldn't remember the past."

"Why would you say that?" I ask.

"I have perspective. The world has evolved from dysfunctional barbaric behavior and greed-fascism exploitation to today's societies cherishing the 'wellbeing' of the human condition for all. Economic opportunity moving forward, without socially imposed burdens rooted in greed or bias, have beholden a healthy, robust human condition."

I was silent in my agreement as was Jürgen for a moment before he asks, "What about religions?"

Roberto smoothly replies, "What are religions?"

Jürgen is struck with confusion on his face, "You- how do you not know about religions?"

"I am playing with you; never thought you would ask." Roberto takes a glance outside, "We have arrived at our destination, but to answer your question," he pauses as he descends to make a soft landing. "Simply: Religion and reason are the basis for the moral compass to justify the sanctity of the 'wellbeing' of the human condition."

He moves toward the boarding hatch, unlatching it.

"We'll pick up this conversation a little later when we resume our tour," Roberto explains as he holds open the hatch to let us pass and he is quick to land behind us as we take our first steps onto the knee-high straw grass, a large dragonfly with vibrant neon tones of sapphire blue, ruby red and blood orange body extends its flowing wings of random patterns hovering around us greeting our arrival, "Stay with me, we're on foot for a few miles."

"A few miles? Why can't we land the shuttle close by?" I contend.

"There's no area to conduct a trajectory landing other than the airstrips miles away and all post-twenty-second century aircraft are banned from entering a vivarium society."

"Aren't there any ground vehicles for hire or rent?"

"The issue is the vivarium populations are typically uncomfortable with GPPJ, whom they view as elitist with intentions of exploitation of the locals for financial gain."

Roberto leads the way on foot, "The law is to protect orbiter's from being 'mistook' for an unidentified flying object. The citizens of Appalachia take any chance to use firearms for fun and games."

"Target practice is not my idea of fun!" Jürgen protests.

"Yeah, I agree. Especially when you are the target!"

"The locals treat unwanted visitors as if in a video game. They believe they have the authority to run life by their rules, mercenaries protecting their way of life against cultural influence from absolute strangers with alternative perspectives on livelihood."

"Self-entitlement. Whatever happened to video games?"

The distant sound of high torque engines buzzing startles me, "What are those noises?"

"The popular transportation on the forest pathways is to ride on ATVs. Use of firearms is restricted within the town center as to reduce casualties, so only one gun per citizen is allowed."

"Reasonable?" Jürgen emphasizes his sarcasm in his enunciation.

"If you hear one nearby take cover as quick as you can. There are laws for our protection, but 'prey holograms' don't stop bullets. Real prey does stop bullets, and gun toads like that reality."

"Why the term 'toads?'"

"A 'toad' sits around using its' tongue to snare prey. These people sit around all day with their long guns . . ."

"Waiting to shoot prey," Jürgen anticipates his analogy.

"Exactly, it's a fun analogy, isn't it," he expresses sardonically.

This is an interesting development. I was beginning to see what Roberto is talking about. If this little expedition works out, then it will go a long way for my understanding, we must see.

"The populations in these parts consist of a few ten-million enthusiasts and they are free to travel, but few do as lethal firearms are prohibited everywhere else outside of this vivarium."

"Hence the irony of the dome of death," my description ends with a flourish.

"Dome?" Roberto repeats as he leads us into the woods, "Take out the irony. It's not 'dome,' it becomes dumb, as in dumb death.'"

An orbiter is hovering a couple of miles away from the Appalachia vivarium. On board Gingi Grind and Spontaneous Instant lock in on the celebrity refugee couple.

"I thought so. Catherine and Jürgen are going to enter the dome of death," Gingi suspects something unusual is happening.

Spontaneous Instant is at the control of his high school graduation present, "Why are they walking? Because they used an airplane and had to land on the strip? Let's drop in and see what they're doing."

"Sponti, you know it's against the law to navigate an orbiter in that air space!"

"Those yokes will be shocked and awed, watch!" He accelerates forward at a trajectory to enter the restricted area along a tree line up and over wooded peaks gliding above the treetops and down into the open fields.

The fields are dotted with homes, farms, and silos, children stopping play to stand in place in shock and awe of the orbiter spectacle.

"See, 'shock and awe!'"

Gingi looks at him in near contempt, "Can we find them?"

Spontaneous Instant checks the tracking device. "It appears to be unresponsive, and that's strange."

"What is strange Sponti?"

"Their beacon is lost. I'm not picking up any signal."

"Sponti let's leave, we violate the law."

He surveys the landscape and views a growing number of the population standing about gazing up as his orbiter passes, "I think you may be right. Let's ascend ourselves out of here."

The orbiter begins to climb in altitude, placing a strain on acceleration at a sharp angle. A popping sound is heard before several more popping sounds.

"Sponti we're being shot at!"

Spontaneous Instant is frantically trying to maintain altitude until an explosive sound fills the cabin, sending them into a free fall! He extends his left arm to keep from rattling along with the craft his other hand he reached for Gingi's left hand.

Her face turns pale displaying a facial reaction rictus of fear.

The orbiter sways around with the bow dipping toward the ground a few hundred feet below. The free fall continues as a loud pop and then rattling sound indicates cabin instability. The emergency landing protocol activates a rescue parachute in response to free falling at five hundred feet to impact.

Spontaneous Instant gasps as a pocket of fumes fill the cabin and then the parachute swells with air to balloon out of a catastrophic event, and an unbelievably soft landing near the edge of an area of woods.

"Ha! Lucked out!" Gingi blurts out in an adrenaline rush.

Roberto moves quickly having awareness in all directions and encouraging his guests to "Keep low and move quickly through the bush."

He benefits from his experiences as a teenager growing up in war-stricken Colombia three centuries ago. He explains to me, that as peasants, he along with his younger brother, joined para-military groups as a necessity for personal survival and the safety of their family from being murdered by the paramilitary groups who used the threat to recruit unwilling youths to fight for their causes.

He says his escape from the para-military ranks and joining Riverstrike's covert operations to disrupt the illegal cocaine trade was a transforming experience. He reassures me his skill set is a product of his homeland of Colombia, the tactics and hand-to-hand battle techniques are assets to be used anytime in wooded areas.

I work to stay as low as possible as my forest green athletic suit was the fashion pick of the day, unlike Jürgen who in keeping the pace I mentioned softly, "Jürgen you stick out like a sore thumb in that lilac."

He took a double take, "You picked the color for me!" "At least you look good."

Out into a clearing, we found ourselves on the property of a large homestead.

Roberto waves for us to hold back as he extends his arms and held his palms face down to the ground, slightly bending at the knees as he began to backpedal towards the homestead.

Though this behavior is universal in its meaning, Jürgen found the need to confirm with me.

"I think he wants us to find cover," his high-pitched whisper response indicates a steep spike in his anxiety levels.

Roberto swiftly turns and made his way around to the front of the house where we lost sight of him.

As we crouch next to each other the contrast between us in the color of our clothing gives me pause, "Jürgen, I love lilac on you, it is your color."

"Thanks. It may be the death of me."

In the next moment, terror struck us as we detect the high pitch electric engine buzz of the ATVs closing in on our location.

I look over my shoulder and need to raise a little to see if any movement might inform me. The buzz steadily grew closer and more menacing as Roberto has not returned and if we don't take cover, we will be exposed!

"Okay Catherine, it's time to do something."

"Get behind a large tree," I instruct him.

There are peonies with lavender flowers! I scramble to climb into the middle of them as gently as possible. Jürgen fails to follow me.

The sound of the cracking branches can be heard in conjunction with the raging roar of the ATVs drawing nearer to us.

Looking through the branches, broad leaves, and large showy flowers of the peonies, I see Jürgen sprawling around a large tree trunk trying to locate the ATVs.

It sounds like they will be passing by, that is, until one of the gun toads can be heard, "Stay where you are fairy boy! You are dead to rights in my cross hairs!"

Jürgen is frozen in place as it appears, he can see his tormentor.

"Did you hear me?" The man's deep scratchy voice inferred an ultimatum.

It is confirmed as he slowly raises his hands. The sound of the ATVs goes from idling to rapid acceleration and four men, each with multiple firearms of varying types ranging from a sawed-off shotgun fitted with a suppressor to carbine assault machine guns, surround Jürgen who is now standing in the open.

"What do you think you're doing?"

Jürgen is visibly frightened and unable to speak.

"Maybe he doesn't speak," said a heavily tattooed gun toad, the apparent leader.

"I think you may be on to something," the husky man with a curly taupe beard mahogany brown, some graying, and a tint of yellow hairs long enough to rest on his chest persist, "Where do you think you are, pixie?"

The other three men laugh heartily each holding their guns poised on Jürgen.

"Maybe it's a spaceman?"

"Yeah, maybe," the leader says stepping up to Jürgen. "Do you know where you are, spaceman?"

The large man's breath must be hideous the way Jürgen pulls his head to the side and away for a moment.

"You got something wrong with you? Answer the question!" Jürgen was still button-lipped, come on Jürgen, say something.

At once the large man grew furious and raised his long gun over his shoulder and swung the butt of the stock towards Jürgen's head.

Jürgen demonstrates cat-like reflexes by grabbing the gun stock with his left hand amazingly holding his own against the burly strong gun toad.

I lose my focus when Jürgen is forced to the ground steadily by the overwhelming weight of his aggressor, and I grunt audibly.

"What the heck was that?" The man with the tattoos asks the large man."

My body freezes to a halt as I feel my heart pounding in my upper chest slowing my breathing, therefore sharpening my focus.

Then I sprang to attention when from behind me a fifth gun toad gains the advantage on my location, "Look what I found over here! Oh-boy!"

The tattooed man chirps out, "Caught yourself a little bunny rabbit there?"

"Why don't you come flouncing your purdy hot ass over here little rabbit?"

Reluctantly, I move once the gun toad who discovers me presses his gun to nuzzle into the small of my back.

"Keep your hands up, yeah like that, and keep walking."

"Flouncing, do you know what 'flouncing' means?"

I swing my hips back and forth to entertain him and just as I was getting close enough to kick that stinking beard into his fat mouth, a man's voice barks out, "You guys trying to piss me off?" The gregarious remark commands everyone's attention.

The large man bellows back, "We seem to have a misunderstanding here Mr. Colston!"

Roberto follows Colston across the field stopping some forty yards short of our position, "You sure do Bryce. You are harassing my guests and I am not appreciative of it. Understand?"

"My apologies Mr. Colston," Bryce turns to the other three, "C'mon you guys are getting me in hot water again. Let's get a move on."

"Hey, are you forgetting something Bryce," demands Colston, "You have to apologize for messing with my guests."

"We didn't mean no harm, Mr. Colston."

"Bryce, just because you don't know somebody doesn't mean they're not good people, no matter how different they are from you!"

"Right," Bryce is reticent in his demeanor, "I apologize to you little lady. Hey, let me help you up," he extends a hand to Jürgen to help him stand.

The other three-gun toads wave at us in humility murmuring their apologies as they begin to mount their ATVs.

Roberto continues to assist us as the aggressors drive away, "Sorry to have left you out here so long. Are you okay?"

"I'm fine thanks. I was about to shove my foot into that guy's fat mouth if you hadn't saved him."

"Oh really?" Roberto was predictably skeptical of my declaration. He moves over to check on Jürgen.

I peer out to the man named Colston. He is deceptively young in physicality for having a voice of moral character and strength.

The crew-cut reveals a stubble of red hair, fair skin, and a muscular build distinguishing himself from the four blubbery, blabbering pigs we had the misfortune of encountering.

Roberto and Jürgen pass me by luring me to follow as they continue approaching Colston across the field.

"Okay, so this wasn't so bad?" Roberto is always in a positive frame of mind despite his experiences are many chapters of conflict, loss, and tragedy marking his life. "It could be worse."

"No," I quip, "Wearing green helps!"

Roberto smiles happily looking at Jürgen in his lilac and purple-clad athletic suit.

"She picked the color!" Jürgen says accusatory.

He keeps his smile as he leads us back to Colston.

"How are your friends Roberto?" Colston asks in a relaxed and easy-going manner.

Our guide slows to a stop standing to Colston's right side and introduces us, "They are very well, isn't that right you two?"

"Nearly died a little over there," Jürgen holds a light compress to his cheek, "It looks like I need stitches!"

His injury is a mild abrasion from when he hit the ground. "No problem, I can sew that up nice and snug for you," assures Colston.

"Let me see Jürgen," Roberto has plenty of experience with the abrasions and cuts the ACRES children have endured in their rough and tumble play. "Jürgen, we'll let this one go, this time."

"What? Let it go? This needs medical attention!"

"Jürgen, it's a raspberry!" I exclaim, "Get over it." Roberto and Colston share a laugh.

"You would think refugees from the past would be 'tougher' in character," Roberto suggests to Colston.

"As we were, right? I pity you Jürgen," raising his right hand to his hip and resting on his crooked gait. His glance toward me caught my eye. Taking me in with hazel eyes, a shade was rarely seen, "You must be Catherine?"

"Yes," I am transfixed by his stare, "You are the ballistics specialist?"

"I am. Shane Colston is the name," he cordially offers his right hand to me, "Come on in."

Roberto walks alongside Colston, "Is Olivia around?"

"She went into town for supplies, groceries, and the like." Following behind him to the homestead he has received the Condorcet procedure as he carries himself like a youthful man.

The home is neoclassical in design, a colonial-era country estate.

Weeping willow trees are my favorite and center on the front lawn of the estate is the largest Willow tree with long yellowish vine branches casting shade while fluttering in the breeze.

"Beautiful willow tree!" Jürgen comments with the same sentiment of my appreciation.

"It's an old one," Colston says directing his attention to opening the heavy double doors, "It was planted in seventeen-seventy-six by the owners to symbolize the sowing of the seed of the Declaration of Independence."

"Jürgen is it me, or does this scene look like a Van Gogh?"

"You see it too?" Jürgen asks with a sense of wonder.

Those pulsating patterns, swirling forces of energy coordinate in multiple streams flowing, interwoven, and ever malleable to all forms in existence, the air that surrounds us.

Somehow it informs me, for at the moment it infiltrates me, awakens me. It is the mesmerizing perception of sub-atomic activity.

The heavy oak double doors on old-time large plate hinges are more than nostalgic, the doors are another reminder of how time is unforgiving and waits for no one. Sturdy, thick treated wood, weather-worn tarnish, not at all rotted, but lacking the original range of motion surely on those surface rusted hinges.

Gripping the doorknobs with one forceful tug the jolt rattles the doors breaking loose caked-on sediment showering us in dark wood sand dust. With a measure more exertion of strength to leverage the doors to release heavily, but open freely despite the hinges squealing in need of lubrication. I follow Jürgen inside behind Colston as Roberto courteously holds the door open in place for our safety.

Immediately I was drawn to the period architecture, hand-carved wood panels, hardwood floors beautifully maintained, and plaster walls painted white in the main foray into the living room, but I spied down the hallway and noticed shades of navy blue, emerald green, and one of my favorite colors, mauve.

White stucco ceilings and sparkling silver chandeliers above lend an aura of elegance reminiscent of the finest ballrooms anywhere four- or five hundred years ago.

In bold contrast, there are several studio lights spotlighting exhibits mounted on the walls. Various armaments including long rifles, pistols, and twentieth-century bazooka are prominently displayed.

Many photographs depicting centuries-old images of military battles mostly from the American Revolution, portraits of the Founding Fathers, Nathan Hale, John Henry, Ethan Allen, and John Paul Jones, all heroes who fought against and defeated the tyranny of King George III.

"Have a seat anywhere," invites Colston as he takes court from his desk rocking chair, "What do you have for me, Roberto?"

"Catherine, can you let him see your samples?"

"Of course," I oblige by unsealing the athletic suit from the shirt collar midway down to my abdomen, sliding my hand into the interior pocket I retrieve the metal tube container handing it to Roberto. Colston is watching my movements, gracious, and with studious patience.

Colston receives the samples from Roberto, but his attention remains on me, "Thanks, Catherine."

The comment made me blush, "Thank you for analyzing it, after all, it's only a vial of rock."

Roberto starts in uproariously, "Blast from the past, 'vial of rock,' is close Catherine, a vial of crack cocaine is as terrible as it sounds."

Jürgen begs to differ, "It's way worse, way worse."

Colston twists off the lid and digs his right forefinger into the tube and retrieves a dusting on the tip of his finger he smells before licking it to taste.

"There is carbon residue present. Where did you get this?"

"Roberto is all smiles once again, "I thought you would have guessed it."

Colston shed a steel cold look at Roberto while securing the lid on the tube, then placing it on the table.

"Why didn't you ask me out right? Huh?"

"They're archaeologists from the past. They recently achieved celebrity status as refugees with no known past. They wish to use their time to research the archives to establish their identities."

Colston appears unnerved, "Since when do refugees become celebrities in The Glass Planet?"

"These two scientists disappeared sometime before two-thousand-twenty-five and there are no records of their existence. They never became a part of the GPPJ."

"Never received the Condorcet procedure?"

Roberto swings his head subtly to indicate 'negative.'

"Only recently," I interject, "Almost seven years ago when we first gained consciousness."

Colston awakes to an unexpected truth as his eyes grow wider receiving me in astonishment.

He startles me, "Wait, why are you looking at me like you've seen a ghost?"

"Who me?" I retort feeling embarrassed I smile nervously.

His stare at me is intense until he breaks his gaze to speak to Roberto. "There's no point in going there. Big Bertha sealed it permanently and anyone unaccounted for was presumed evaporated by the blast."

"It's true," Roberto explains to us, "Mosaic Caverns is more of a volcanic dirge these days."

I didn't care what it is these days. Based on what I have seen in their relationship they know something I need to know, "Can you tell me what you know about Mosaic Caverns?"

"There's not much to say," starts Colston, "We had descended into the basin where there was a pile of corpses."

"A pile of corpses?" I pry as his 'tell' has more to 'say' than he may realize.

"We were on a routine mission to knock out a leftist FARC run cocaine factory hidden in the jungle. We had a detail led by two Sergeants to scout the disturbance. The two sergeants went missing for several days and Captain Riverstrike . . ."

"*Captain Riverstrike*," I encourage him to go on.

"Riverstrike did everything possible to locate the sergeants including using a bazooka to gain access through some force field prohibiting access."

"And no success."

"Not until one day the corpses of the sergeants suddenly appear in the basin, their bodies riddled by bullets from the right-wing paramilitary."

"What about the presence of archaeologists?"

Colston is contemplative in his response, "Not officially no. In the end, the mutual interest of all governments involved, and the American Archaeology Society decided to report their employees met their demise in a helicopter crash above Mosaic Caverns. No survivors and no remains due to the fireball."

"Yes, but they must have posted us as missing at the least by the American Archaeology Society?"

"Top secret classification for two hundred years. Presumed dead was the final determination. That is until everyone in your life cycle who knew you passed away. Then the official record changed over time enough to erase you from ever existing."

Jürgen is in dismay, "How dare they erase our existence!"

"What are you thinking Roberto?" I notice how this outspoken activist remains silent.

Roberto appears to be deep into his thoughts, "It doesn't come to me as a surprise as horrible of a circumstance as it was, back then the missions were all classified."

"Do tell, no . . . pray to tell Roberto," Jürgen is wild-eyed in anticipation, albeit in distress.

"Back then, before the Economic Theory of the Human Will was legislated into international law, the ultra-wealthy and the other players with economic interest to exploit the South American jungles, the indigenous poor, and any other angle to satisfy their opportunistic greed-fascism, go about life as if it were a board game."

"We are the 'pawns in the game of life' perspective?"

"I'm familiar with the saying, Catherine, but it is a game of greed-fascism. The winner's spoils grow each generation as opportunities grow. With investments in hard assets and earning interest on money at astronomical returns, these investments, such as stocks, clog up the market."

"Then the societal control factor is what enables the erasure of our existence," Jürgen listens to me intently shaking his head in agreement.

"Not entirely the reason though, Jürgen," Colston explains, "The game was for all the marbles, legitimatizing armed conflict when the posture in politics as 'we against them' mindset. Do you know how this constant conflict to create profits for the ultra-wealthy kept feeding itself?"

My ears perk up from listening to his line of deconstruction, "Lies, cover-ups, misinformation, and nuanced manipulations such as bribery, extortion and the like, to evoke a perception of enemies to our common 'values,' when all in all the mantra of freedom 'of the people, by the people, for the people made sacrifices through unjust, burdensome exploitative domestic legislation."

Can't you do anything from your pulpit to get the remaining thirty-million citizens of vivarium Appalachia to finally give up the use of guns? If they did and joined the GPPJ, you Mr. Colston, will be set up for five hundred years or beyond."

Colston listens with severe interest to Roberto's proposal, "If people, in general, could just wake up and get out of bed having a mutual appreciation for each other."

"No. In this world, it's not like that. When I say this world, I mean humans," Colston speaks with conviction, "A person learns what they live. There's too big a discrepancy in the life experience. Shooting sprees would be common again if you throw these folks into modernity as it is." Colston's anguish surfaces, "Anyway, Riverstrike will try to indoctrinate them into RAKLAV, if they don't kill each other in the process."

Spontaneous Instant and Gingi float down to the surface securely in the orbiter cockpit once the parachute deploys doubling in size of the circumference of the orbiter.

"Perfect landing," he checks himself for injuries before releasing the hatch.

"Wait for me Sponti don't leave me!"

"What in the world are you talking about?" Spontaneous Instant releases her from the orbiter.

"Why didn't you help me as soon as you were able?" Gingi climbs out refusing to take his hand in disgust, "Don't bother to think of me now, you blew your chance."

"I'm happy to land safely and see," he walks around the hill, "No permanent damage!"

"Yeah, so those gun toads have terrible aim!"

"You think ~ gunshots ring out as bullets whiz by ~ they'd have better aim!"

"Let's go Sponti! This way," Gingi runs in the opposite direction toward a tree line.

He looks in the opposite direction and views men riding reconditioned antique land-based vehicles speeding across the field towards him, "I'm coming Gingi, keep running!"

Gingi enters the tree line and crouches for cover. To her terror, she views Spontaneous Instant sprinting toward her, but the gun toads on ATVs are going to catch him before he can make it.

Spontaneous Instant hears the rebuilt modified electric engines closing in on him. One of the gun toads pulls in front of him and abruptly stops, Spontaneous Instant falls to the ground.

"Oh no! What have we here?"

A second gun toad with tattoo's all over his body dismounts his ATV and aims his nuzzle at Spontaneous Instants' head, "What is this thing you got here?"

"It's an orbiter!"

"A what?"

"An orbiter, they fly in the atmosphere into space . . .," He tails off his words once realizing the skies are clear.

There is no orbiter or shuttle craft activity. He felt it strange he couldn't view the Space Station Network anywhere in the natural appearing sky.

"You must be an alien. Never did I see a vehicle like this. Nobody could fly this thing," said the apparent leader of the gun toads.

"What do you think," the tattooed man asks, "should we call the authorities?"

"Huh?"

"Oh right, silly old me," he snickers, "we are the authorities!"

Spontaneous Instant attempts to stand while their attention is diverted.

The largest of gun toads takes one step and uses the butt of his gun stock to strike Spontaneous Instant to the ground, splitting open a gash along his right eye to his hairline.

Gingi looks on as she remains hiding in the tree line entirely overcome with anxiety, fear, and desperation in not knowing how to help Sponti.

One of the gun toads kicks Spontaneous Instant several times.

He curls up as the gun toads keep repositioning his body to repeatedly kick and beat him down.

Two other gun toads are busy placing explosives on the orbiter, "Come on boys she's ready to blow!"

Each gun toad surrounds and delivers a flourish of swift kicks to

Spontaneous Instant's vulnerable curled-up body.

"Just for good measure. Let's get a move on!"

Spontaneous Instant struggles to crawl on his elbows and knees trying to reach the tree line.

"Hold on one second." A gunshot rings out from the lead gun toad dropping Spontaneous Instant in his tracks.

Gingi screams out in horror.

"What the hell is that?"

"Looks like another space boy came here with another space girl."

"You don't suppose they're F.O.C., do you?"

"FOCK?"

"Friends of Colston, you dumb ass."

"That's a good question to ask the space girl. C'mon."

As the gun toads mount their ATVs revving the engines, a sonic boom rumbles commanding their attention to the sky. A RAKLAV cruiser, violating the air space, swoops down close to the tree line to intercept the ATV gang by landing between them and the two GPPJ citizens.

"What in hell is going on, an alien invasion?"

"Do you think it's more of Mr. Colston's space friends?"

"I kind of hope so."

"It sure looks like it."

Emerging from the translucent hatch are Simon Noir and Commander Janalake in full Zealot Sentinel combat gear.

"Stand down and back away from the victim," Janalake asserts, "Your neglectful conduct toward GPPJ citizens will not be tolerated."

"The four-gun toads exchange glances, the lead gun toad mocks the two RAKLAV senior officers, "Move space freaks! We didn't invite you here!"

"Yeah, another freak guy and his spaced-out broad! Watch out for laser beams."

Simon and Janalake march up to them. Janalake approaches the second gun toad as he turns to front her squarely, she splits his nose open with a right-hand jab.

Simon approaches the lead gun toad who is preparing to engage in a wrestling match.

He snarls, "Come on freak, let me tear you a second crap hole."

Simon's thrust kick into the abdomen of the unsuspecting target stuns before a follow-up roundhouse kick to the cranium knocks the large man to the ground unconscious.

"Hold it there now," warns one of the two remaining gun toads standing next to the other gun toad by the orbiter, "We don't care if we shoot you dead; so, get out of here!"

Janalake turns her back on them to face Simon.

"What shot do you have?" Simon queries excitedly.

"I feel my stars are lucky," Janalake claims as she grips two silver dollar size stainless steel throwing stars, "Have they moved?"

Simon nods his head slightly sideways indicating they have not.

The talkative gun toad speaks, "Okay, now you stand down and back away!"

Simon raises his hands momentarily distracting the gun toads; Janalake swings around to pivot on her left foot launching both stars at once.

The stars veer off towards one target each, the gun toad on the right has the star slice through his neck causing a perfectly clean cut, with near full decapitation. The fatal wound to his neck did not sever his brain stem from the spinal cord and is not emitting any bleeding.

Tracking the star to the left, she detects it veers too far left slicing off the gun toad's right ear. This slicing off his ear is equally clean in execution preventing bleeding.

He raises his gun taking aim, then presses the trigger as he remarks, "Stars not so lucky?" The gunshot blast is loud making an impact on Janalake in the middle of her back sending her to the ground face down, but not out.

The gun toad hesitates as he is uncertain of her condition.

He witnesses the flattened bullet snug in her back suddenly pop up into the air. She erects herself raising like a catapult jettisoning its payload to stand by using the leanest muscles of her legs and the strongest in the entire Zealot Sentinel ranks. The flattened bullet sails before her, she initiates a pirouette grasping the metallic piece in one move launching it back at the gun.

The jolt to the gun forces him to inadvertently pull the trigger shooting bullets into the explosive charges recently placed on the orbiter.

The ensuing explosion takes the RAKLAV officers by surprise as the gun toad incinerates by the heat of the blast. His skeletal remains are partially made of metal.

Simon looks admiringly at her, "Three is a charm!"

Janalake walks over to Simon to ascertain Spontaneous Instant's vital signs. Janalake runs a medical scan, "Simon, we need to bring him aboard to get to a hospital for life support. It would be a violation to utilize remote AI surgery hospital transmitters with a vivarium."

Simon proceeds to lift him by the upper torso and Janalake went to lift him by his feet as the buzz and hum of a line of menacing gun toads on ATVs approach from the far side of the field.

Janalake looks over her shoulder at the ten ATV vehicles approaching as if a cavalry racing into battle.

"You can get him in the cruiser."

"Sure. Where are you going?" Simon becomes whimsical, "It's becoming a busy day."

"I'm going to give these numb nuts a lesson in physics."

She sprints out to the field running to the left of the row of ATVs causing them to alter their angle of approach.

Running directly at the first ATV gun toad, she leaps above the first driver landing a fracturing blow to his forehead with her right knee.

Her left leg coils on the ATV frame to lift off to the next ATV driver and repeats the tactic consecutively to each of the next four-gun toads leaving them sprawled out unconscious on the grass.

A shotgun blast from the sixth gun toad nearly nicks her in the upper thigh, but due to her tremendous core strength, her agile legs are already set in motion around the opposite side of the gun toad's head. The contact point of her left foot's inner sole impacts the thick skull of the mindless aggressor with a knockout blow giving her the propulsion required to jettison into a leap toward the next one who dismounts his ATV and stands aiming for a good shot at the woman flipping handstands toward him.

Janalake sticks a landing facing the gun toad grabbing the shotgun. He desperately squeezes the gun with his tightest grip, only to find himself flipping into a resounding body slam rendering his body limp, lame lying unconscious.

The riderless all-terrain vehicles meander off in random directions, a few running over the helpless, and defeated gun toads, prolonging their agony, with their broken bones and torn ligaments, are now subject to the crushing weight providing unbearable pain.

Janalake shifts her focus to the distant horizon. The fading sound of revving engines is evidence of the three terrified gun toads scampering away on their ATVs.

The smell, sound, and sight of an electrical short circuit draw her attention to the creature she just body slammed. The head is severed from the base of the skull and snapped off at the spinal cord.

A stream of blue-yellow sparks flows out as a procession announcing a falsehood fizzling into a gray pillowing smoke of burning wires, resulting in the smell of the synthetic rubber connective tissue melting under high heat.

The sight of an artificial intelligence anger Janalake.

She kneels beside the head and pulls on it until the synthetic rubber connective tissue stretches to the point of snapping.

As Janalake returns to the cruiser, Simon emerges from the translucent hatch, "How did it go?"

Janalake tosses the head toward his chest and slaps her hands together indicating she wiped the slate clean, "Smashing."

"What is this?" Simon asks.

"It is what it looks like," Janalake is fuming. "It looks like corruption, cyborg for sure, where it's from is yet to be determined, but we have to get to the nearest hospital first."

Gingi Grind, in her terrified state, reveals herself by hyperventilating due to an anxiety attack. Her gasps for air diminish as she is nearing collapse.

Janalake goes to check on her, "You are hyperventilating. You're not hurt, are you?"

Gingi is distraught beyond words and shakes her head signaling she is uninjured.

"Come with us. We have your friend."

"Is he alive?"

"Barely, we have to get to the closest GPPJ hospital."

Gingi is hesitant to trust RAKLAV officers, Sponti would tell me to refuse, she confides to herself as she is in violation of the law and if Sponti doesn't survive, forget it, she will worry about jail on Mars later.

Simon re-emerges from the cruiser, "Come with us, young lady."

Janalake escorts the detainee into the RAKLAV cruiser without concern for Gingi's emotional delirium. "Have a seat in the cabin," orders Janalake.

"Where are you taking him?" Gingi barely can lift her arm, her hand shaking as she strains to articulate words.

Simon is at the control dashboard completing an analysis of the local area hospital, "It looks like Constitution City is the best available match. Hold on!"

Simon initiates a vertical launch, at a rate of acceleration to exhibit considerable G-force in the cabin, to a height of twelve-thousand feet where the cruiser hovers long enough for Gingi to ask, "How long to get there?"

Janalake sits in the co-pilot seat and catches Simon's eye before he accelerates, "Not too long now."

Simon punches the accelerator and in ten seconds flat they travel over two-hundred miles closing in on their destination.

He brings the cruiser to a rapid but controlled descent to the landing area where the medical staff of the Harmony hospital in Constitution City are waiting with a hover gurney.

Spontaneous Instant, strapped to the gurney, is skated away to the intensive care unit. Gingi remains in the cabin seat unable to unfasten the safety harness.

Janalake returns to the cabin, "Stay calm. It is futile to resist."

"Sponti! Get me out of this damn thing!" Gingi screeches writhing in physical pain from the tightening restraints.

Janalake prepares to place an audio mute to Gingi's Glass Planet interface.

"You are under arrest. Anything you say or do may be held against you in court," Janalake is courteous in reading her Miranda rights.

"I need to see my Sponti," cries Gingi, "You don't understand about caring for someone!"

"My colleague is handling your friend's security. It will be a week to ten days before he will mend. He has suffered major arterial heart damage and other major organ damage."

Gingi's eyes tear up, "He will make it okay?"

Janalake responds to all business without care, as the ZSI constrains her from feeling empathy or compassion, "We will return at the time of his release and have you face the official charges. Until then you are to relinquish your GPI and remain on Earth."

25

Old Blackmailer Picnic Party

Riverstrike receives the communique from Janalake regarding a felony trespass in the Appalachian Vivarium: We have apprehended two GPPJs in violation of 'violating vivarium air space.' There was a confrontation initiated by the domiciles resulting in fourteen domiciles being neutralized by RAKLAV intervention.

One of the two GPPJ citizens sustained life-threatening injuries in the form of a gunshot wound. The patient has multiple bruises and a severe laceration on the right forehead temple. The internal scan indicates several life-threatening internal organ injuries. We moved the patient to Constitution City Harmony hospital where he is being treated.

He closes the communique as he surveys the rocky terrain surrounding the Mosaic Caverns site. Dating back three-hundred-fifty years this whole area was marijuana and coca crops in every direction.

He saunters his way over to the precipice where the caverns were once accessible, he focuses his eyesight on the basin envisioning the layout of entrances he found now inaccessible by collapse, but then even impenetrable by conventional weapons of the time.

His thoughts are interrupted as presently the ACRES shuttle plane descends from the north. It will be a matter of minutes when the occupants will make their way to the area where Riverstrike's cruiser 'Dark Eaglet' is positioned.

Colston is fascinating to us with details on past missions over two hundred years ago with then Captain Riverstrike. Jürgen and I eagerly listen to Colston explaining platoon patrols in the jungle when Roberto appears from the cabin.

"We're descending to land on autopilot. Let's harness up."

"In less than two minutes the ACRES shuttle glides to a soft landing. I can see the minister approaching from across the field. We unharness from the seats and upon opening the cabin hatch Riverstrike stands ready to greet us.

"You made it on time!" He shakes my hand, then Roberto and Jürgen as we step out of the fuselage, "Hello all," he offers to us before noticing our fourth passenger emerging from the hatch.

"Of all the people I would never expect to see, Shane Colston,"

Riverstrike extends his right hand and maintains a firm grip on his former colleague's hand as they greet one another, "De Oppressor liber."

"Yes, sir, General, likewise."

"Never thought you would have the stomach to return to this place," Riverstrike diverts his attention to the other three. "Mind you, Colston was one hell of a courageous soldier, just goes to show you the fine men I had the honor to lead into combat."

"Yes sir," Colston acknowledges Riverstrike, "Why did you arrange for this meeting?"

"To the point?"

"Preferably, Roberto has caught me up on current events."

"Did he? Thank you, Roberto," Riverstrike nods back to Roberto's head nods. "In gratitude of sacrifice we should not be judgmental as to limit potential, but we should not forget in our indulgence for human advancement we owe something to the past, as we are responsible for the future."

Shane Colston softens up to his long-lost squad Captain, "It sounds as if you're addressing an assembly. We are of no importance, at least no influence. So, what do you say, just spit it out?"

"All right, you do remember," Riverstrike asks, "how in the basin there were several entrances to the caverns?"

"Yes, and how there was a force field of some kind."

"Right. We couldn't penetrate this force field with conventional weapons. The technology inspired top secret classified research and development, resulting in the ability to protect vivarium subcultures by securing them from engaging each other and the GPPJ."

"Short of using nuclear weapons, there was the one option left to us," Colston speaks cryptically in deference to the classified top-secret mission.

"Hence this barren result and the deformation of the entrances," Riverstrike says inferring the deployment of a secret weapon. He brings his attention to Jürgen and me, "Do either of you have any recollection of this location?"

This all sounds like 'tall tales' as I hold a suspicious expression on my face while walking over to the precipice. Jürgen follows me.

"What do you think? Does this place look familiar to you?" Jürgen whispers under his breath.

"I feel we have been here. As I felt when we became conscious. Doesn't the jungle *feel* familiar to you?"

Jürgen scratches his head as he surveys the landscape, "Where do you think the campsite is where he found my DNA?"

"That's right," I twist my body at the hips to bark over to Riverstrike, "Where was the campsite where you found Jürgen 's semen?"

"It was over on the other side of the cavern," Riverstrike takes a couple of steps, then points in the direction. "Almost directly across from us."

"On the rocky ground? I don't think so, I would remember if we had to camp on rocky ground, let alone have sex," Jürgen said with conviction. "Why do I have to be subject to such humility?"

"Whoever said we had sex?"

"Isn't it obvious?"

"No, it is not obvious!"

"So, it's not obvious, but it is possible!"

"Remember what Marcel said," I find the situation humorous, "Humility and humor put the 'Hu' in 'Humanity.'"

"Great. He must have won an award for saying it!"

"Probably got paid too!"

"There was a sub-nuclear ordinance exploded here scorching the terrain, melting the rock," Colston informs us.

"What about you Catherine, anything familiar?"

Riverstrike is convinced Jürgen was at this location, he's pressing me to come around with any memory at all.

"I don't know."

"It stands to logic you were here with Jürgen."

I am thinking about every detail looking across the basin, "It doesn't ring a bell, but the American Archaeology Society does!"

Riverstrike appears disappointed with my response. He speaks closely to Shane and Roberto.

"The one time I made it into those caverns can only be described as 'entering the gates of hell.'"

"After all, the rock became molten hot as hell!" Colston is good-humored reminiscing bonding experiences with a long-lost friend.

"Exactly my point!" Riverstrike asserts, "Nobody could have or should have survived that blast! Our two sergeants didn't make it."

"Patrick, you make the obvious point of observation, but you and I both know their bodies should have evaporated. They were discovered without so much as a 'char.' Their bodies were bullet-riddled, yet a sub-nuclear fireball doesn't do the slightest singe?"

Jürgen and I stroll over to join the three destiny-bound men. "I do not have any recollections here. As much as I hoped this place would jar my memory."

Jürgen's mind is on other things, "Excuse me, Minister?"

"Yes?"

"I do not mean to be impolite, but as I remember . . ."

"Yes," Riverstrike suddenly anticipatory of Jürgen's memory, "What is it you remember?"

"I'm under the impression we would be having a picnic?"

Riverstrike exhales demonstratively, "Right. I haven't forgotten." He reaches into his side strap burlap and retrieves a half-dozen packaged bars. "Have you tried these? They're dietary meal bars."

"Seriously?" I state mildly in settling for less than what we were expecting. After all, Minister Riverstrike is one of the GPPJ top one-million of influencer's on the 'wellbeing' of the human condition. I guess hosting a lame picnic does not register as a part of the 'influencer' criteria.

"No, not seriously," he quips. "Catering-bot deploy."

Jürgen rips the wrapping off, then quickly devours the meal bar in a few bites. "Damn, that was a picnic in my mouth! Roast beef, artisan bread, horse radish mustard, lettuce, tomato with a bit of Vidalia onion!"

"Jürgen, don't spoil your appetite." Riverstrike hears the catering-bot hover off the cruiser, "Instant picnic coming up!"

Everyone's attention is drawn to me at once as I laugh at Jürgen's eager expression while looking at a dessert bar he is about to unwrap.

"No dessert before the meal," I say to him like he is a little boy in need of discipline.

"What kind of dessert?" Jürgen asks Riverstrike. "It's peach cobbler pie."

"No wine, cheese, or grapes?" I had to ask.

"I'm sorry Catherine, no cheese, or grapes. Let's have a look at what we do have," Riverstrike suggests as the compartment bot places a Tatami seating table on a tatami flooring with comfortable cushioning.

"Looks like Japanese cuisine. I love Japanese cuisine!"

"Yes, Catherine, let's have a little rice wine," Riverstrike hits a cordial note.

He hands out Choko cups and pours the sake for everyone, "Enjoy," he says raising his cup as we proceed to have a sip.

"Deliciously sweet and chilled perfectly. This would be wonderful with cheese." I compliment. "What else is on the menu?"

"Riverstrike removes the serving tray covers on each dish, "Edamame, Morokyu, Karaage, Korokke, Rei-shabu, and Sunomono."

"I recognize the Tamagoyaki rolled omelet," I state casually. "I do not recall what the rice rolled in seaweed?"

"Onigiri rice balls," Riverstrike says, "Pairs nicely with the sake."

"It looks familiar, I seem to think of 'tuna salad' mixed in with the rice."

Riverstrike is pleased with my observation, "If you like, here it is."

The catering bot is on the ready dispensing the dish with tuna salad.

"As requested," Riverstrike takes the dish handing it to me.

"Impressive little robot, how does this cabinet-file-kitchen do it?"

Riverstrike and Shane laugh at once, "In terms, you can understand, this 'robot kitchen' is a microwave slash freezer offering variations of the programmed menu on demand. Prepared and served, made from fresh ingredients perfectly cooked."

Jürgen points to the watermelon slices, "I know what those are, but what is that lumpy white stuff?"

"I hope you're being sarcastic, for heaven's sake?" I caution him, "That's potato salad Jürgen."

"I gotcha," he says deadpan.

I furl my eyebrows at him.

"What? You asked about rice wrapped in seaweed. I know what potato salad is."

We have a seat on the cushioned flooring, very well cushioned for outdoor comfort. Riverstrike pours sake for everyone as we pass the bowls of food around.

After consuming a serving of each dish, along with a couple more servings of sake rice wine, I decided to take a moment to relax on this beautiful warm sunshine kind of day leaning back with my arms extended slightly behind me to extend my stomach. I have a question to ask, "Shane, I can call you Shane?"

"I don't mind, but my wife might."

"Can you tell us what was going on here? What are you looking to get out of us?"

Colston balks at answering my questions.

"Catherine, Jürgen," Riverstrike pauses to gain full attention.

"Do the names Augur or Martinez mean anything to you?"

Jürgen pauses as he chews on a piece of korokke. He reflects on the names for a moment. He finalizes his chewing and consumption of the treat, "Awesome, this tastes like fried mashed potato."

Shane places his hands on his hip and laughs mightily at the befuddled Minister.

"Catherine?" Riverstrike asks politely, "Nothing?"

"I'm sorry. Believe me, I'm as frustrated as you are!"

"Shane let us have a word. Will you excuse us for a moment?"

Riverstrike directs Colston to join him by the hull door of the Dark Eaglet cruiser.

"What are you laughing about?" Riverstrike's irritation reflects in his tone. "You better get back to Appalachian Vivarium." Riverstrike advises Colston, "A dozen or so of your gun enthusiast ran into some RAKLAV officers."

"What happened?"

"Whatever happened, your domiciles are hurting badly. Guns and all, they were no match for two of my officers."

"Your officers? Patrick your officer's skills in martial arts are extraordinary. The domiciles are a protected population. Why were your officers there?"

"A couple of GPPJ entered the area illegally; their orbiter was shot down by a bunch of your gun toads and a confrontation escalated to further conflict." Riverstrike explains, "Some of your good old boys took a thumping!"

"So RAKLAV officers responded to take the teenagers into custody?"

"Yes Shane, we're by the book. What is law without order?"

"Understood. If they left peaceably."

"If you call tearing your gun toads into pieces 'peaceably.'" Riverstrike asserts, "Colston, your gun toads are particular to using hostile aggression, sent a teenage boy to the hospital for critical care."

"Our populations are under vivarium protection, who knows nothing of the orbiter craft transit system? They are expected to feel threatened when they see an orbiter in broad daylight."

"I understand, but their excessive aggression invited some harsh treatment from my officers," Riverstrike displays the image file Janalake included in her incident report, "You see your man is decapitated here?"

"Sure do. How did he end up like that?"

"A Ninja Shuriken."

Colston tilts his head displaying a grin in skepticism, "Throwing stars rarely cause puncture wounds, let alone decapitate a man's head."

Riverstrike retracts the file image, "That is correct if you consider the shuriken in its traditional design." He places the file securely inside a zipped chest pocket, "Today's technology has computers instantaneously reconfiguring the size, weight, and shapes by altering properties in steel design through principles of physics combined with biological catalytic technology."

"Patrick, you are serious?"

Riverstrike shifts his body position to see the others conversing by the ACRES shuttle.

"Of course, I am. A palm-sized star can be gripped and thrown with great accuracy, and in the milliseconds, in flight, it can expand to the size of a car tire hubcap. You do have an automobile, don't you? You use hubcaps, correct?"

"Yes, I know what a hubcap is."

"It turns out your man didn't shed any blood!"

Colston's face deflates, and his complexion becomes sickly pale.

"Can you explain how that is possible?" Riverstrike's steadiness is severe as he holds for an answer. "No? I can do it for you. You can tell me if you are investing in cyborgs?"

"No, cyborgs. We don't have cyborgs in the Appalachia."

"Not yet, but it looks like you have managed to implement robotics into your populations. You know it is a treasonous act to bolster your populations with robotic synthetics. How many millions of cyborgs for humans in your last census?"

"Does it even matter?"

"Sure, for paying the fines before you go to prison for life. You will be fortunate to live thirty years without the Condorcet procedure administered to you." Riverstrike is coldly serious, "Why did you do this, is the economy that poor in Appalachia?"

"We are living more of an illusion at this point. Patrick, you would give me a chance to get things back to being legal. I mean you're not going to throw the book at me?"

"You know Shane, we go back a long time. We have seen this crazy world transform one set of rules that shaped our mutual reality, into a whole new value system. The cultural influences, rapid population growth, wealth assessment, and expansion deep into the solar system. It is all made possible due to a present time that has exposed the age of corruption and barbarism as ancient and obsolete in primitive thought and practices."

"You got that right, Patrick."

Riverstrike gives a glance around to make certain no one is within earshot. "The good news is I have something you need, and you have something I want. We understand each other so well, I think we can get some sort of old-school deal done."

Colston's face carries the look of resignation, "If we can cut a fair deal?"

"I am certain you will find yourself handsomely compensated given the circumstances, more monetary units to resuscitate this heritage you so righteously want to preserve, but there is a short timetable."

"What's your intended use, Patrick?"

"A confidential project for intergalactic travel. The Dark Eagle will require overwhelming firepower. The transformation is for the defense of a caravan of space stations embarking on interstellar travel."

"Who knows what you may run into out there?" Colston agrees, "Send me the job order and your other specifications and I will get on it."

"I'm glad we understand each other, I knew we would!"

"Can you invest in manufacturing to upgrade production?"

"If you manufacture the hardware, I can covertly transport the equipment to Mars for installation."

Riverstrike and Colston shake hands.

"Speaking of understanding, why don't you and Olivia come along with us? After all, you will be on the ground floor of an entirely 'clean slate' economy? The best devised, more so than the capitalism we have now, without the ETHW."

Colston smiles, "Olivia and I are set in our ways from a simpler time. No, we're not going to leave here. 'All this we have may not seem like much to you, Olivia will say, 'This is our home, this is our life.'"

Riverstrike is standing to leave, "And is that what you would say?"

"Hell, all I know is 'Happy wife, happy life!'"

26

Soiree

We left asking ourselves why Minister Riverstrike has an invested interest in the Mosaic Cavern. Is this Shane Colston someone who can spark a memory for us with something he may tell us?

My attention diverts to the 'harness sign' flashing upon descent to land outside the Appalachia Vivarium.

Watching him begin the landing sequence, I thought how Roberto appears to share a good deal of history with both as well.

Within seconds the shuttle plane is touching the ground and Roberto has us out getting in a stretch as he says we have barely scratched the surface of our tour.

"It was nice meeting you Shane," I ogle his eyes, "Invite us back when you have the wine and cheese."

"My pleasure, it's not too often we get celebrities down our way." Shane offers, "Come on in for a drink, I'm sure there is wine. I know I have mascarpone cheese!"

"Sounds great!" I say accepting the invitation for all of us.

"But Catherine," Roberto appeals, "You do realize there's no way we will complete the tour?"

Jürgen voices his opinion, "I think we've seen enough. Let's share a little drink and get to know each other a little. What do you say, Roberto?"

"Hey, it's not up to me, I'm on Marcel's dime for the next couple of hours to escort you."

We turned to Shane who is communicating with someone via radio channel.

"Have the gun toads, Bryce, and the rest, been picked up from repair?" Shane listens for a moment, "Good. Get us now. Love you too."

Shane stops and turns to speak to us, "Okay folks, we got a ride coming to get us." Shane starts to speak with affectation, "My wife is home and has the time!" There is an awkward pause. "No, no, just kidding, it's not like that at all! She loves unexpected company, she also confirmed we have cheese, Catherine."

"You're too much!" He is hilarious, "Now I can't wait to meet the wife!"

Jürgen follows in quickly, "Got us good with that one Colston."

Roberto reflects, "Funny guy, always has been, my man!"

"Hey thanks, but hey, don't bring it up with the wife, okay?"

Shane breaks from his train of thought hearing the buzz and whirl of an electric engine, "There she is!"

On an ATV, a young woman, she must be a Condorcet recipient, and true to the motif of the estate, she flaunts a rifle slung over her shoulder. And the ATV is pulling a small utility wagon.

Her tresses are silky black braids dangling a touch longer than shoulder length.

"Hey hon," Shane vociferates. "Thanks for coming straight out to get us!"

"High everyone! How are you all doing?"

Everyone smiles offering a hand wave in greeting.

"Who are these friends of yours, Shane?"

"Hi, Olivia!" Roberto leaps in to demonstrate his close bond.

"Hey there Roberto, it's been a little while," she said in a sing-song vocalization to him. "How are all the children doing?"

"Great! Thank you for asking. More participants now than in recent decades."

"Shane and I are very proud of you to grow from where you came from, to make a truly significant impact by giving a helping hand to wild-born children the chance to grow themselves into polished law-abiding citizens."

"It's been a dream of mine to provide the means to each child's 'wellbeing' so they can realize their potential."

"Olivia, this here is Catherine, and her mate Jürgen. This is my wife Olivia," Shane Colston is a gentle, courteous man by nature.

"Nice to meet you, Catherine."

I am struck by her confidence, charisma, and her old-fashioned style, "Nice to meet you, Olivia. I love your blouse!"

"Thank you, Catherine, it's something I wear when I have nowhere to go!"

"The fine crosswise rib effect is lustrous. Is this taffeta made from silk?"

Olivia seems smitten with our exchange, "What an eye you have for quality. It is silk, but I'll show you some of my favorites in my wardrobe later. Is this your husband?"

Jürgen clears his throat to indicate his discomfort with the objectifying comment.

"Not that we know of thank you."

I lift my left hand indicating 'no ring' by pointing with my right hand to the left ring finger.

"No, we are not married." Jürgen politely excuses the issue, "It's nice to meet you, Mrs. Colston."

"You're sweet Jürgen, you may call me Olivia," she lets out a delighted hoot, "My apologies Jürgen if I offended you in any way. I'm pleased as punch to meet you. Let me make it up to you with some homemade cooking and old-fashioned hospitality."

"I appreciate your generous offer, but we just ate."

"Okay, you can take a rain check. From the meal that is, not from the drinks!"

"All right, now we can get a move on," Shane extends both of his arms to the two points of interest, "Ladies in the front, men pile into the utility wagon."

Roberto suggests, "You two gentlemen are taller, get comfortable and I can fold in somehow."

This all-terrain vehicle is unlike any I've seen before. It is a larger modern vehicle than the vintage ATVs Bryce and his toads were riding.

It seats two with driving consoles for each seat. The bug-splattered windshield reminds me of the exotic insect life we encountered in the Sahara rainforest and jungle. As I jump into the right-side passenger seat, I view Jürgen and Roberto having difficulty fitting in around Shane's large body frame that occupies half the cargo area.

"Everybody in?" Olivia asks while revving the electric motor, she is beyond cute with her spirited, charming personality.

"Here we go!" She lets out an enthusiastic cheer as she accelerates the ATV into a left-hand 'U-turn,' to position us facing the homestead and we're on our way!

"Amazing suspension, I feel like we're floating on air in this seat!"

"We customized her a little, not much you can do with an electric motor. Shane had a nifty idea and made the motor self-recharging."

"Is that how you maintain the homestead estate?"

"No, we have a connection to the power grid," Olivia breaks into laughter, "That's very funny though."

"I'm sorry, I didn't make myself clear," I hesitate as we

approach the homestead, "I am assuming you hit the jackpot with his invention?"

"I thought so too Catherine, but the technology is in use already out there and we were unable to patent technology already in use. No one can come close to our baby though!" Olivia steers the ATV around the back of the homestead.

"Last stop! Everybody off!"

The men are behaving like they had a rough ride in the wagon.

"All right smaller guys get out and give a hand-up to this big ass, mascarpone cheese-eating tub-of-lard."

"Your husband has a robust sense of humor," I comment to Olivia as the men proceed into the rear porch entrance.

"He does, thanks. Sometimes he makes me laugh for hours on end!"

The country chateau ambiance is accentuated by an elegant arrangement of yellow-tinged Caroline wisteria draped over the porch rooftop, "This place bleeds southern charm!"

"You know, we try," Olivia looks upon the homestead, "After a while tradition is less easily obtained, or lived for that matter. As a part of nature, you find the change is the one constant."

"Is this fragrance from the wisteria a constant?" I pose this question as I sense Olivia is feeling melancholic.

"That's why you plant it by your doorways, windows, patios," there's a perceptible uptick in Olivia's mood, "but it is a beast to prune regularly!"

"It grows, it grows!"

"Don't I know it!" Olivia sparks enthusiasm now, "This variety can grow up to thirty feet. Luckily, I have the whole second story for it to expand its reach."

"You will need a ladder to get up there."

"Me? Oh no, that's why we have hired hands around. The pruning to keep the right shape and size to promote flowering is a science." Olivia steps toward the back door, "This breed better known as wisteria floribunda is deer resistant."

"That I didn't know."

"Unfortunately, there are no more deer populations in the Appalachia," Olivia says as she holds the door open, "Do you want to go inside honey?"

"Sure," I said reluctantly. "Olivia?"

"Yes, Catherine?"

"The ATVs parked in front look like the ones from those cowardly bullies we came into conflict with early today?"

"Yes, they are. Those 'cowardly bullies' are the men who work for us, they do a decent job of warding off trespassers and helping with maintenance too! My apologies for their treatment of you, they are ignorant of the GPPJ's existence. They're not used to seeing strangers at all. Come on in, everybody's waiting."

I follow her through the porch into the quaint country kitchen. The men who are scattered in the parlor having freshly poured drinks are discussing historical relics.

"What about you Catherine," Olivia asks pointing me over to the bar where the foray leads into the parlor.

The arrangement of the liquor bottles reminds me of a grand organ's pipes in an orchestra hall. "Do you have any wine perchance?"

"Yes, in the refrigerator, glad you reminded me. I'll pour us both a goblet."

She scurries away and returns as quickly as I can have a seat.

"Catherine, how about a French Bordeaux?"

"Isn't it a perfect choice?"

"It is, we communicate on the same wavelength! Be right back."

The guys have moved into the next room to discuss the historical exhibits that are displayed in the first-floor rooms throughout the house.

I made myself comfortable on the chaise lounge centered in the parlor under a beautiful crystal chandelier.

Olivia returns with two poured glasses of wine, extending one of them to me.

"Catherine, here you are. I hope you like it chilled."

In receiving the glass, I nod my head in appreciation of her goodwill, "Chilled wine is perfect for today."

"Looks like Shane is almost finished with his tour of relics," she is facing in the direction where the men are and begins waving her arms in gesturing them to reconvene, "Shane hon, bring the guys in here for a soiree!"

Olivia makes her way to a bread box near the door to the kitchen and places dehydrated sausage, wrapped rye, and a chalice of mixed nuts in serving plates using a tray to retrieve and place on the parlor table before sitting next to me on the chaise lounge.

"Here are treats to clean the palate. This wine is top-notch! What do you think Catherine?"

I lift the glass of dark ruby wine to my lips sensing the cool temperature. My nose tickles from the fruity black cherry aroma of the bouquet. Tilting the glass, I gather a teaspoon of the wine in my mouth swishing it about.

"It has a crisp licorice quality, a fresh black cherry body with a magnificent dry aftertaste. Refreshing, deliriously so!" I say noticing now everybody is watching me. "What is it?"

Jürgen stretches out on the brown leather sofa with his right hand holding up a low-ball glass, "Cheers, Catherine, to the most sublime critique of wine tasting before achieving inebriation!"

"Thank you, Jürgen, what are you drinking?"

He is holding an empty low-ball glass, "Bourbon, more bourbon!"

I place my goblet on a coaster on an end table and proceed to the makeshift bar to refresh Jürgen's drink with bourbon.

"Olivia, if there are no deer populations or game populations, then what are the guns for?"

"Security, in assuring the preservation of our way of life," Olivia answers unconvincingly.

I hand Jürgen his drink before reclaiming my seat next to Olivia.

Shane's body posture sitting on a colonial-era armchair is haggard, the weight of the world on his mind, "With the menial chores as a cover, we are using artificial intelligence robots in place of humans to deceive RAKLAV from our actual declining populations."

Olivia turns a shade pale as worry fills her eyes.

Colston explains with loose lips, "Having steadily decreased from too many gun-related deaths, and among the regular populations in the form of millions migrating into the GPPJ."

"Ahem, Shane," Olivia interrupts timidly, "I think you have explained yourself well enough honey."

"The technology used to create animatronic wildlife like deer and other game," Colston slurps an ounce of sour mash whiskey, "is now used to create artificial intelligence robots like Bryce, Tom, and the rest. They conduct the maintenance and security of the estate, but they aren't human, nope, they're cyborgs. I'm employed by the gun industry, working as a ballistics specialist and gun dealer. We need customers to survive, not just about guns, food, clothes, health care, you name it, and we continue to construct those animatronic 'people' to fill a population void. Someday this population must hold each other accountable and always be mindful of their actions. The idea of action toward the greater good of the human condition."

"I believe it is the 'wellbeing' of the human condition," I recommend, "not necessarily the 'greater good.'"

Olivia, "That's right, the 'wellbeing.'"

27

Two Ends of Population Management

Technology was created, or some say discovered, by the U. S. military after an encounter with this mysterious unknown source," Roberto claims as he navigates the ACRES shuttle plane.

"What did it turn out to be?" Jürgen asks.

"No determination was made on the nature of the force field," Roberto says, "The use of available technologies to replicate the function of a barrier has decidedly worked better than expected in creating the illusion. The Glass Planet SS is central to sustaining the computer-generated vector shields for the illusion of autonomy. Virtual reality furthers the deception and mitigates tragic knowledge.

"Ultimately those individuals within the vivarium's who understand, appreciate and value diversity finds their unique path into the GPPJ."

"Playing God by choosing people to transition to The Glass Planet is a human trafficking effort."

Jürgen states, "Doubtless practiced for profit."

"We get away with playing God because it is what they believe, have faith in," Roberto surmises, "Their societies can avoid major conflicts and in turn thrive. Why wouldn't the people love it as well?"

Jürgen and I share a glance of unease at the hum-drum forwardness Roberto assumes public acceptance of this very disturbing public announcement.

"It's as if he's talking about humans as contents in a fishbowl!" I comment quietly to Jürgen under my breath.

"The vivariums contain natural environments and sacred structures and sites."

"Those vivarium communities must be peaceful if not pacifist?"

"Quite the contrary. You would think separate communities based on drastic lifestyle contrast would have a cultural clash if they all were aware of each other. The result is the same over time, conflict arises when in societies of common beliefs conjure refined nuances creating the cracks, the fissures that fracture a cultural norm."

"The result can be as extreme as perpetual human negligence, criminality, greed in quest of power, cultural dominance, conflict, and barbarism consistent with detrimental behavior to the 'wellbeing' of the human condition. The bottom line is humans are human no matter where on earth you are from."

"The question is to what heights can be aspired to if your culture has a ceiling tied down by ancient beliefs?"

Roberto is flying the shuttle plane low above the forest trees.

"Is it safe to cruise at this low altitude, it appears risky to me."

"Don't be concerned, Catherine. We are at an altitude of two-thousand-five hundred feet."

"Is this a wildlife vivarium?" Jürgen nonchalantly interjects.

"Over here is the, is a series of three vivariums featuring many threatened life forms vulnerable to extinction. These protected zones are the only three remaining natural environments left in the North American continent."

"One zone is a thick forest; another zone is flat-windy tundra with many grazing animals with few predators; the third zone is a multi-terrain with flowing rivers, grand lakes surrounded by purple mountains forested green and three quarters surrounded by salt water.

"Though protected by the Nature Preservation Council (NPC), the land is inhabitable with a low cost of living, and plenty of urban to suburban employment opportunities. You guys could have a retreat someday."

"Well, that's a better approach on the positive side."

"Excuse me, it appears I have a private portal request."

"You see Catherine, you are already an important person in the GPPJ."

"I'm not so sure about that Roberto. Can I take this to the cabin?"

"No issues, make sure you are harnessed in a seat for your safety."

With that, I proceeded into the pre- modern cabin, not at all like the 'Blister' cabin Jürgen and I was rescued on the first day in this crazy world. I activate the signal request from Qyxzorina.

"Hello? This is Catherine."

"Hello, Catherine."

"Hello, Qyxzorina. How are you and Marcel these days?"

"I know it seems like a long time, but it isn't."

"Is there a problem?"

"No, not a problem, there are several problems."

"What do you mean?"

"Marcel and I have reviewed the recordings from your five years interned with the Zealot Sentinel indoctrination facility."

"What did you find?"

"A lot more than we expected! First off there are plenty of conversations between RAKLAV high command that you were present for."

"Me? What were the conversations?"

"Unfortunately, very ominous. They talk about a classified 'top secret' operation called 'Spark Creation Genesis' and a delivery vehicle code name 'Prometheus One' and there are plans discussed regarding a Dark Eagle evacuation."

"I have no idea what you are talking about."

"Neither do I really, except the Dark Eagle SS is Riverstrike's home base. Nonetheless, this information is disturbing. We believe Riverstrike and several governors of the Space Station Network are scheming something."

"I have no clue as to any of this. I wish I could be of more help. Can you provide some informed input to better understand?"

Qyxzorina continues, "One other thing, two of Riverstrike's rarely visible confidants, Janalake, commander of RAKLAV, and Simon Noir, his longtime personal assistant and trusted advisor, have several conversations about Riverstrike's partnership with Marcel and their involvement in developing the Star Gazer Sun Tour ships."

"Okay?"

"The main concern is the reliability of the navigation system, as though they anticipate a possible failure in the technology somehow."

"It does sound suspicious. Qyxzorina, I will keep my eyes and ears open if I can find anything out. What about recordings of the indoctrination process itself?"

Qyxzorina delays a few beats before responding, "Abusive treatment, torture, and complete domination of the heart and mind."

She speaks in a steady, serious tone, "It is a travesty of humanity, they create and maintain the living dead. Very few conversations with fellow Zealot Sentinels trainees. The basic question, simple function, directions to the bathroom, basic duties, no intimacy, no affectionate emotions only the occasional fight breaks out, no less instigated by Sergeant Gian or one of the other low-level Zealot Sentinel commands.

"Also, Parsiak is a Zealot Sentinels plant to monitor you and Jürgen to see that you remain under strict conformity.

"Then there is Sula. A Zealot Sentinel from the beginning of the organization, she was the twenty-first-century leader, political, women's advocate, and fearless leader of Afghan descent.

"She was very much a tag-a-long with you Catherine. There wasn't a day that would go by where she didn't spend at least ten hours with you."

"That sounds scary," I replied as a chill went up my spine. "How awful! This Sula, was she Prime Minister all those years?"

"No. She died in twenty-fifty-two."

"What are you saying Qyxzorina? She's a ghost?"

"We don't think so."

"No? Then can you explain?"

"She was probably abducted by RAKLAV on orders from Riverstrike."

"Abducted? Why do you think?"

"It's because of her skill as a politician. We think anyway the-"

"Wait for a second Qyxzorina," I interrupt without apology, "You make it sound like it's no big deal!"

"For Marcel and me, no, it is of no surprise. Early on RAKLAV needed top talent. In a brief period, many blossoming leaders, innovators, and creatives were dying premature deaths, even after receiving the Condorcet procedure."

"What were the causes of death?"

"All sorts of unfortunate outcomes, hundreds, though events do happen, there was one common thread. Every death resulted from an accident, but no remains of the deceased were ever recovered."

"It was accepted, no one questioned foul play?"

"Remember the population was growing with life spans extended to one-hundred-thirty to one-hundred-fifty years, there were more people. The general attitude held people will suffer accidents, commit suicide, or would be assassinated. It was the tail end of the Pisces epoch, and the space station network was in its infancy, more a dream than a reality."

"And Riverstrike was recruiting by abducting the most talented?"

"Not the most talented as much as most threatening to overshadow his skill set in specific industries with their skill sets. And Sula was training you to be a RAKLAV officer. She was posing as a Zealot Sentinel trainee. Riverstrike was recruiting more than bodies, he was recruiting knowledge and ideas to build social esteem and to consolidate power."

"Qyxzorina, is there any recourse or investigative action to be pursued?"

"There is one way we can expose hidden evils."

"Okay, you said 'we' as in you, me, Marcel, and Jürgen?"

"Yes, and a little divine providence. Marcel believes they have designs for you to become a senior officer."

"I wouldn't let that happen over my dead body!"

"You are in Riverstrike's good graces. It is the perfect cover for you to do the most productive investigating."

"It is intimidating to think of joining RAKLAV, what if I become brainwashed against my will?"

"Don't worry, you come and visit Marcel and me at our office on the Innovation space station. We have designed an assault maneuver that will give you," she pauses on her breath before releasing, "a devastating twist."

28

Then, Now, and Date Night

Lounging on the living room couch, I am capable of projecting images of the information acquired through the GPI onto a three-dimensional platform in the center of the room. I thought it would be useful to make comparisons to the quality of life in the year twenty-three-forty-seven to what it was in two-thousand-five, the estimated year of our disappearance from human civilization.

The Atlantic Ocean's waves have perked up due to a 'level two' hurricane, and I find it frightening to learn a 'level two' is a quite common event year-round. The waves crest one after the next onto the transparent domed ceiling of our shoreline Sea Foam condominium.

This condominium is truly an amazing achievement of architecture with hundreds of units, each designed as a 'bubble' made from the hardest graded industrial materials developed from modern technology, including diamond-encrusted layers with cabbage derivatives, all are constructed then adjoined one to the next in a patchwork resembling the actual 'foam bubbles' ocean waves create adrift on the shoreline of a beach.

The complex of 'bubble' structures built in close formation from the levy wall protecting the old city of Miami from flooding and extend into the Atlantic Ocean a couple of miles underwater with units constructed with a gradual spreading-out on the ocean floor to allow for utilization of amphibious craft for emergency evacuation in the event of air handler failure or potential compromised structural integrity via unforeseen disaster.

Jürgen enters the room and walks into the kitchen, "What 's going on in here?"

"Are you making a drink?"

"Who wants to know?"

"I do, I'll take one of what you are mixing."

"Coming right up." He presses some buttons before continuing, "What do you have going on?"

"I don't know, looking for some sign of our existence."

"Look no further," he says walking in and offering me a very fruity-looking tropical drink in a tall, curvy glass.

"Fruit punch?"

Jürgen laughs, "It's a classic, the 'Hurricane' in the eponymous 'hurricane glass!"

"Perfect for the occasion!"

"Drink it fast enough and it will blow you away." I chuckle, "Here's to 'three sheets to the wind!'"

"Cheers!" We say to each other, tapping our glasses before enjoying a sip.

Jürgen relaxes in a cozy sofa chair adjacent to me on the couch.

He groans looking at the turbulent, cresting waves pooling over the ceiling, then looking down into my eyes, "It feels like we're on a tall ship when you look above!"

"More like a submarine to me."

"Or a drowning victim," he said sarcastically, "What is that trinket you're twirling with your fingers on your neck?"

"Don't you remember Jürgen?"

"Remind me"

"From the pleasant post-show reception Riverstrike gave us?"

"I must have sustained a concussion from the beat down Simon gave me."

"The moon rock floor cracked from Janalake's head when I body slammed her?"

"It looks like a gemstone more than a tile of moon rock."

"Did I not get the better of her?"

"You did."

"It serves as a memento of, it seems to me, an important coming of age event."

"We should spar, I think you can teach me a thing or two."

I smile and give a little shake of my head affirmative so as not to state the obvious, "I will elaborate as to what I am doing. There are some critical changes in the geographical-political dynamics from two-thousand-five compared to today."

"I bet."

"I made a list of some."

"Sounds interesting."

My senses are freer after two sips of the Hurricane, "Okay, you're going to tap dance to this. Trivial differences from then and now?"

Always with a comedic bent, he quips, "Should I get my tap shoes on?"

"Shush," I press my forefinger to my lips, "Then: Market domination skewed for the wealthiest; Now: Free market development and expansion. Welfare is only for the wealthy while an individual maintains a gross income of over one-billion dollars. Then: Ownership Corporate. Now: Operations conducted by shareholders board who earn market salaries, have annual elections for C-level management, a twenty-five-year limit on C-level management."

"My o' my, a public trust? What has gone on in the last three hundred years?"

"Is it the people or is it circumstances that force this kind of change?"

Jürgen has a serious, thoughtful expression, "I'd like to think certainly the people, but most likely both factor in significantly."

It is a safe answer he gave me, but I can see his point of view. "A concise and levelheaded response Jürgen, it seems odd after a few sips of the 'Hurricane'."

"It's a great drink, right? You like it?"

"Yes. Let me finish my list!"

"Right, sorry, go on, I'm all ears."

"Then: Ownership middle and small business; entrepreneur and traditional capitalistic markets. Now: Same.

"Then: Mass construction building, real-estate ownership unrestricted. Now: No mass real-estate holdings over $25 million in assets. Then: Communication monopolies of broadcast and social media. Now: No monopolization of broadcast and social media programming. No ownership of any broadcast media networks for broadcasting. All networks are funded by public money and elect a chairperson and board members on ten-year terms."

"What for? The GPI is the ultimate independent platform."

"All revenue gains netted above the $100 million-mark flows to support the infrastructure of the billions of potentially impoverished Earth-landers, unlimited free access to educational resources to enable individuals to prepare for a life of many disciplines.

"Today we see the myriad of professional interests and ambitions realized, with tens of millions GPPJ made solvent every few years, the job market and expansion into the SSN will require the cessation of firearms use beyond earth-bound practices.

"There is no dignity lost in exchanging work responsibilities, especially once one is following their passions, other challenges and opportunities never considered may broaden an individual's horizons over several centuries of living to contribute to the 'wellbeing' of the human condition.

"Human actions define the human experience. Human action defines how we value the human condition. Human action defines the physical manifestation of the human will. Who does not 'will' the 'wellbeing' of the human condition?"

"That is a very insightful comparison you put together there Catherine." Jürgen's solemn tone lends authenticity to his comment.

"Thanks, but I found the research potentially endless due to the sheer volume of sources providing multiple viewpoints, I mean countless individual perspectives. It's amazing to think a consensus can be formed on any single issue!"

"Catherine," Jürgen moves to sit on the sofa with me, "What are we doing?"

"We are doing what we can to learn who we are, how did we get here, and for what reason do we exist?" I provide partially fueled by the mild intoxication from consuming the Hurricane.

"Two of those three questions are answerable. Even if we discover our past identity, there is no merit in this present reality. How we did things in the twentieth century has become mostly obsolete. Unless we can form a reenactment society of interest to the present times, our past lives have little bearing on what we make of ourselves today," Jürgen expresses valid points.

"If we find out how we got here Jürgen, would we have a viable way back from where we came?" I think this is a simple enough concept to embrace.

"Do you think you would want to go back to the twenty-first century and be faced with all of the 'barbarism' of the day? Do you think finding a way back to the twenty-first century would alter our destiny or the destiny of the GPPJ?"

"What about any family? We must have left someone behind, parents, a sibling, loved ones?"

"RAKLAV has our DNA, and they haven't found a reasonable match yet. We can't put our lives on hold indefinitely until we get notification from the Minister of possible matches. At least I'm not going to live in this shell."

"You want to move out of here too?" I said feeling the growing isolation living under the ocean waves. "Maybe we can find a sunnier place to live going forward."

"That's the spirit," Jürgen says encouragingly placing a soft kiss on my forehead.

"Excuse me, I wasn't thinking just then. I should ask to kiss you first?"

There is no question in getting to know him better, spending all this time together, that we are potential lovers.

"No, I understand. Just watch your manners next time. I accept your affection Jürgen. I take your kiss as proof of what you are feeling. You're acting on your instincts. My instincts are consistent with yours, Jürgen. Besides, what is living life without recognizing, and expressing your feelings for each other?"

He holds me gently caressing my arms. He slides his hands to my upper back. I lean back feeling his embrace, the waves crash above us as his face meets mine, his impassioned kiss brings me in. Within a few minutes, we shed our clothes on the sofa before sliding to the shaggy carpeted floor.

I convinced Jürgen to attend the Van Gogh exhibit that night at the Modern Museum of Space Exploration. The Ages of Absolutism to Aerospace; Alien Art Designs in Ancient Cultures and Sun Worship is the main exhibit, while the Age of Impressionism series: The Comprehensive Collection of Vincent Van Gogh is the temporary exhibit at the Boethius fine arts hall on the Et Consolatio Philosophiae SS.

I explained to Jürgen the Van Gogh exhibit features one-hundred-eighty-eight of the genius's best-known works all completed from Eighteen-eighty-eight to Eighteen-ninety. The work has something specific to my experience in the perceived reality expressed in most of his work. It is hard to describe, the phrase 'seeing the macro in the micro' came organically to me, without my preconceptions or expectations. Ever since emerging from the cave the resonance or better put, the reverberations is stunning to perceive. The witnessing of the activity of sub-atomic particles comprising the atmosphere the fluctuating of atoms consistent in waves of energy, light waves, sunbeams, fire and ash, and sound waves all visible in the interaction filling atmospheric space is sublime yet powerful.

Reminiscent of viewing the crashing ocean waves cresting, swirling, and dissipating above the ceiling at the Sea Foam

Condominiums, the 'macro in the micro' refers to the currents of sub-atomic flow and the imperceptible becomes dimensional.

Jürgen has expressed the same capability; I believe most resolutely together at the homestead did we encounter this spectral dimension. Looking upon 'The Starry Night' and 'Tree Roots,' 'The Red Vineyard,' 'The Night Café,' 'The Olive Trees,' 'The Sower,' 'The Sea at Les Saintes-Marie-de-la-Mer,' 'Cypresses,' and many more paintings elucidates the perception of a dimension unrecognizable by most other than a 'sense of knowing' to those with keen observation and with high emotional intelligence.

The other exhibit 'Alien Art Designs and Constructions in Ancient Cultures and Sun Worship' comes off as pseudoscience; Easter Island, The Great Pyramids, Stonehenge, the 'astronaut' geoglyph in the Nazca Desert of Peru, in terms of historical archaeology the supposition that these amazing structural and aesthetic feats are attributed to extraterrestrial is profoundly a European and American racist perspective as the vast majority of these ancient sites are in Africa, Egypt, South, and North America among indigenous populations. Prevalent racist attitudes deem these phenomena must be created by a 'higher intelligence,' hence the research racism denigrating the humanity of many ancient cultures.

As for the Sun God exhibit, little to no relevance to my interest from 'RA' to Apollo to Sol Invictus to Freyer, the topic is shallow, "I'd rather get lunch at the fast-food restaurant we passed by.

Jürgen asks, "Did you care to peruse the Sun God, or what is it, the Sun King exhibit?"

"The Star Gazer Sun Tours is more in my realm of interest," I replied.

"This old boy likes the satirical bent." Jürgen laughs aloud, "We are off to the fast-food joint."

We may be teenagers in spirit riding in our new Nebula Drifter, taking a stop at every feasible destination like the fast-food dispenser 'fly thru.' Not a very intimate experience as we place our order into the dashboard and the order is piped into the side fuselage storage compartment and delivered to the console situated between our flight deck chairs.

What drew our interest is the dual purpose of the fast-food restaurant, as the dozen or so employees are responsible for utilizing the massive telescopes fixed in various directions to capture a three-hundred-sixty-degree horizon field keeping an eye out for doomsday asteroids approaching on an impact trajectory to Earth, the Moon, Venus, and Mars.

There may be dozens of these hybrid fast food dispensers and telescope observatories throughout the SSN, set to alert any one of the Martyr SS missile class interceptors. The Martyr SS series provides an abundance of defense against the unlikely need for asteroid intercept but as the possibility of an extinction-size asteroid evading detection until it is a matter of a few days away before impact, the feasibility is enabled by the self-sustaining profits generated from the fast-food sales.

29

The Styling of Nature

Enemy of the people: Fascist, totalitarian oligarchy greed is evil and illegal to democracy. Roberto states as he cues JJL recording for the playback of The Styling of Nature.

He is preparing for takeoff in the ACRES shuttle plane to attend the live birth event on the vista south of the Moab saltwater lake. The shuttle plane will take close to two hours to reach the destination within fifteen minutes after the start of the event.

He receives the latest on the wind currents and determines the presence of tailwinds that may make up the time. Besides, he has attended dozens upon dozens of birth events, and they never start on time depending on how long the mother is in labor beforehand.

Roberto initiates the launch, harnesses into the flight chair, and takes in the musings of JJL, JO: It is love that is the economy of life. It is seen everywhere in the styling of nature. When for survival love is plentiful, there is peace, there is nourishment, and there is always love in reciprocation. And now the more bridges we cross, the more vibrant love will and shall spread.

We have money harvesters on wealthy welfare to allow them the security of financial success without the power to blindly mistreat, mentally, and physically abuse the masses as hostages to the greed of their manipulations. Money is the physical manifestation of the human will and requires its guard rails with thoughtful, thorough legislation.

The opportunity for innovation in a free democracy result in inventions to expand human potential. Economic equality illustrated by the physical manifestation of the human will have resulted in the untapped potential of those recently lifted above poverty, above survivals' uncertainty, and into the thriving pulse of opportunities realized and of those yet to be realized by the mind, soul, hearts' desire to create for the 'wellbeing' of the human condition."

"Money is not free speech," Roberto speaking out loud to himself emphasizes, "and then the madness ended."

He turns the volume up on JJL, JO: To put the foot down on felons around the world starting with dictators has eliminated fear in the hearts and minds of the masses, the crowds who convene to celebrate the best in life, is life itself to begin with.

Any villainous, nefarious acts against the 'wellbeing' of the human condition never go unnoticed! The GPPJ finds strength in their freedom, finds unity in their mutual respect for the 'wellbeing' of the human condition, and finds hope in their shared love.

The unanimous consensus among the masses, as achieved through the introduction of The Glass Planet personal configurations, allows the ability for the multitudes to connect.

To be one in the collective unconsciousness, where the center of the whole human experience exists, allows a balance of reason and religion to exempt villainous acts against this categorical imperative.

A thought crystallized becomes common knowledge, like the sun is hot, water is wet, and fragility is life. The same is true for human independence and our inalienable rights to freedom. 'The Styling of Nature' permits love as the economy of life; the physical manifestation of the human will is the currency to deliver all love.

We are indeed not capable of equal achievement in multiple disciplines. The awakening of all humankind is to understand knowledge within a common moral compass at the point of contact. It's key to build upon the collective conscience before engaging in the never-ending constant spontaneous instant where everything infinitely is experienced at once in a continuum.

Janalake is responsible for securing the GPIs of the two young detainees. The procedure mandates the GPIs to be secured in a vault located in the security control room of the centralized operations facility. The Glass Planet Interface was conceived to be a medium for intelligence quotient (IQ), emotional quotient (EQ), and creative quotient (CQ) affecting every aspect of cognitive abilities and potential to support the 'wellbeing' of the human condition. This is a concept she is sworn to defend, yet as a Zealot Sentinel, she has never adorned one before. How is it possible that Gingi's behavior or at least poor behavior occurs while utilizing a GPI?

Janalake can reason Spontaneous Instant's poor judgment is due to some deeply rooted condition in the physical brain structure, likely his brain has a misshapen frontal cortex, deficient in brain matter affecting his decision processes.

Her impression of Gingi Grind is of a misguided heart, vulnerable to having a well-developed anterior insular cortex and therefore endowed with a healthy sense of empathy and in turn, feels sympathetic toward Spontaneous Instant's penchants for unexpected behaviors.

The standard ZSI program is limited to promoting discipline to submission without experiencing a full range of EQ or CQ. Having never adorned one before, the curiosity of trading in her specially designed ZSI, enhanced to afford her inquisitiveness and initiative related to her objectives in executing orders, in exchange for Gingi's GPI is sure to provide insights into Gingi's life experience. This will be an interesting 'study' over the next five days before medical clearance will be processed for the detainees to be transferred to Mars Zealot Sentinels HQ to undergo the debriefings and evaluations.

The Commander of the ZS secures one of the GPI in the cruiser security vault while she retains Gingi's. With a few idle days on Earth, why not see what it is like to adorn a GPI? Using hers will allow the Commander to connect to The Glass Planet in search of answers she yet knows the questions to.

She finds the reconditioning an uncomplicated process of quickly downloading encyclopedias of information to her hippo campus, followed by the stimulating of cognitive awareness heightening her emotional quotient to levels not experienced by her since before her enlistment into RAKLAV, and the instinctual abilities to interpolate the stimulus of her perceptions strengthening her abilities to imagine the translation of reality with her newfound creative quotient.

A matter of minutes passes when she obtains a complete understanding of the operational function of Gingi's GPI. Janalake opens a message sent to Gingi Grind's GPI now connected to The Glass Planet.

The message plays: "It seems like forever since we last communicated, I hold you dear as a friend and would hope you would be able to attend the birth of my child. Surprise! Hoping you can make it, we know it is discouraged to start a family before receiving the Condorcet, and our parents, everyone is supportive but critical as you might imagine. Do come, there is so much to share. If you're squeamish about getting too close, no worries because the idea is to give our guests all the distance they need as it's taking place outdoors."

Janalake doesn't accept the invitation on Gingi's behalf but does set course for the place and time of the expected birth event.

She finds the GPI is simple to navigate, maps and other frequently required commands surpass the ZSI in the level of social network pinning, the elements she understands are easily processed by the GPI and uploading the image of the location to her mind's eye requires merely a thought command via the GPI. The ZSI requires a link to the RAKLAV server as all images are filtered and monitored to meet the security protocols.

The sense of control adds confidence, the readiness to obtain data about everything under the sun provides a sense of invincibility to be capable of overcoming ignorance. She learns to 'have' ignorance is a standard human quality, to 'be' ignorant about what is accepted and understood as fact by the vast majority of GPPJ is neglectful ignorance that disrupts the trust required for optimal human evolution. The harbinger of neglectful ignorance is the administer of fear, uncertainty, confusion, hatred, and greed, to name a few less desirable human qualities, legitimate in their malcontent, but a crime against the 'wellbeing' of the human condition. Her first thought is Riverstrike, her perception enhanced allows for her to connect to the collective consciousness, there is mistrust towards him by the general GPPJ.

This ritual of birth she is attending to view will take her into suburbia. It is a rare opportunity for her to explore the regions of the Earth where GPPJ live peaceably, respectful towards one another, and always expand their horizons of appreciation for their cultural, ethnic, religious, and personal identity differences.

This mutual respect and appreciation for the miracle of life are consistent when the GPPJ are hard at work. Many who enjoy four-day WORB weeks and partake in the miracle of human ingenuity and innovation to build their capital, and then indulge in the riches of Earth's natural beauty and commerce, do so to sustain the 'wellbeing' of their Earth-lander neighbors.

Janalake offers a question, "What is the average number of babies born per year within the GPPJ suburbia populations?"

"One-hundred million are born per year, equating to one-billion population growth with every passing decade."

Janalake feels her ignorance about childbirth, how it is to raise a child and why it is a highly popular activity. Equipped with the ZSI as far back as she can remember, the entirety of childbearing is lost to her.

The RAKLAV cruiser signals closing distance to the event location geographically south by southeast of the manufactured Moab salt-water lake. Another example of the innovative genius in the redistribution of the overflowing oceans reveals attribution to the child prodigy Kariana Yahreah. The manufactured saltwater lake of Moab, Utah is best known for the underwater community grids of self-sustainable full immersion water homes and businesses, mostly a vacation resort with lodgings, recreation centers, and restaurants all accessible by amphibious craft. Tubular tunnels afford express travel underwater and levees double as entertainment centers with amphibious craft docking as public parking.

The green energy communities on land thrive within breathtaking red rock cliffs, dinosaur parks, and a convergence of the Colorado River and reservoir ocean saltwater.

The childbirth event is taking place above sea level, in fact, a popular destination point for tourists where the manufactured Moab saltwater lake meets the Colorado plateau, the expanse is miles due south of Moab, UT.

The RAKLAV cruiser closes the distance in a matter of three minutes.

A crowd has convened earlier, near sunset the evening before, to commiserate and celebrate the morning's event, she views tens of thousands of revelers attending the live birth event among a colorful barrage of temporary shelters from tents to compact home trailers. Many congregate around open fires frolicking about, many wearing only their birthday suits.

After she does an aerial once-over of the location, she lands the RAKLAV cruiser a few miles away on a secluded section of the Colorado plateau.

She grabs a few energy foods from the cruiser's food supply, including fresh apple juice, to her an apple is an organic health energy boost, before pressing on for a delightful dawn trot four miles yonder on the Colorado plateau.

When we met Janalake at the live birth event, a lot of negative feedback from those who are uncomfortable with the formal wear and RAKLAV space suit made her stick out like a sore thumb. Wearing work clothes to the occasion is excusable, but when you are the Commander of the Zealot Sentinels everyone gets a little freaked out!

"Look over there," I drew everyone's attention, "Is that Janalake?"

"It is," Marcel is quick to recognize her. "Quite obvious too, isn't she?"

"I wonder what she is doing here?" Qyxzorina is quick to draw up suspicion, especially seeing the commander of the Zealot Sentinels unannounced at a public event and wearing her commander suit.

"Let me find out," I said as I stood from our informal outdoor fire-pit arrangement. It has been a cold evening stay under the stars made tolerable by the controlled hearth we reserved anticipating Gingi and Spontaneous Instant to connect with us, but who are no-shows and have yet to provide an explanation calling in.

The thought occurs to me we are about to learn why they are absent noticing Janalake is in possession and adorning Gingi Grind's bright pink GPI.

"Hello, what a surprise seeing you here dressed like that!" I called out to her gaining her attention.

Janalake is taken aback for a moment, "Catherine? Jürgen? You're here to witness the childbirth? How did you get invited?"

"That's funny," Jürgen shoots back, "We were going to ask you the same, especially since you are wearing Gingi Grinds' GPI."

Janalake has a bleak expression on her face for a couple of seconds until she recalls, "It's a long story, but Spontaneous Instant and Gingi Grind were mixed up in an escalated conflict in the Appalachia vivarium."

"What a horrible development," I state to Jürgen.

"Not too surprising though," Jürgen quipped sarcastically. "What happened?"

"Long story short they required medical attention and are now recuperating, and they were to undergo reconditioning."

This alarms me, "So they are being indoctrinated at the facility on Mars?"

"Reconditioning for a felony violation." Janalake is candid in her response, "They are to undergo debriefing and evaluation in about three weeks. Psychoanalysis is required as they broke felony trespass laws entering a restricted air space with an orbiter. They caused quite a disturbance that required intervention by Simon and me to bail them out as they put themselves in harm's way. If you like, we can coordinate to set out for Mars so you can escort their safe return to Earth."

I offer as I recognized people taking alarm to the Commander's uniform, "Let's go to our new galactic cruiser to use the 'tailor genie' on board where we can get you properly dressed for this event," I said leading Janalake and Jürgen to the Nebula Drifter cruiser to find something more appropriate to wear for the occasion. I thought to reconsider my garb too as it is rough and tumble for this intimate event.

What I requested to wear from the on board 'tailor genie' does improve my figure, a casual outfit cut to flatter, tricked out to reveal my body in a way no one has ever seen, including me.

Jürgen is beside himself, "MY, my, my. What an exceptional concept for a casual, earthy, elegant one piece. Catherine, you look stunning!"

"Do you think so? I am comfortable, almost feels like I am naked."

Jürgen's expression alters in contemplation of my revelation, "Kind of like wearing body paint for clothes?"

"No, it's not like wearing body paint."

"Have you ever-"

"No, Jürgen I haven't," I take a seat in the cabin, "and you can stop thinking about it too."

"No offense intended, I'm just curious."

"How could I remember such a thing?"

Janalake appears from one of the courtesy cabins taking over the energy of the main cabin rocking her hips like she owns the catwalk.

Her outfit is a combination of traditional Alpaca fleece of rose-gray manta shawl, with a vibrant pink sarong caressing her hips and lightly veiling her midsection to emphasize the contours of her hourglass figure. The silk under-clothing matches her vibrant rose-brown skin tone.

Janalake looks at me with her piercing green-hazel eyes, positioning herself standing over me her eyes glow reflecting a rejuvenated soul, "Do you see in me what I see in you?"

Despite having absorbed the vexing sexual energy emanating from Janalake's body, she flexes her contours to seduce me easily to desire her touch, I keep my composure, "Probably not at all."

"What do you mean?" Janalake tempts me, "Don't you think I am gorgeous?"

"Sure, absolutely gorgeous."

Janalake shines her magnetism with a steady, controlled swaying of her shoulders and tilt of her head, "And don't you find yourself gorgeous too?"

"Dressed like this," I said with slight trepidation in my tone, "but Janalake, you are always gorgeous no matter what you wear."

With that, her thinly veiled facade melts away with a polite smile, "Thank you, Catherine, for your kind words. Look at us, have you ever felt so liberated by fashion? These clothing designs are comfortable as they are beautiful."

She extends her hands for me to hold onto assisting me out of the flight seat.

"They are personalized to the sublime, a subtext to our skin, and what confidence, it elicits peoples respect for who you are, and not what others expect you to be."

At this moment Janalake informs me of the vulnerability, generosity, and intelligence awakening in her soul, "I'm very comfortable in these clothes, so soft, and nothing like wearing the uniform, yet somehow, I feel confident wearing these clothes I have known but have forgotten from long ago ~ happiness."

"Yes," I confirm, "and sharing is caring, so let us go show the world how liberated and happy we are!"

As we turn to exit the Nebula Drifter cruiser, I see Jürgen is motionless in his flight seat, he is flabbergasted, and I need to call to him like a lost kitten somehow stuck in a tree, "Hey Jürgen. Jürgen?"

"Uh?" He breaks from his fixated expression.

"Are you going with us?"

"Of course, I am, would I want to be anywhere else?"

He shakes off his stupor and smiles at me as he marches by to exit. I am comforted by the perspective he shared with me at the Sea Foam condominium: 'No, you wouldn't want to be anywhere else.'

Roberto arrives at the event landing the ACRES shuttle plane nearby the campgrounds. Walking gingerly to make up time, he locates Marcel's beacon he traverses directly to the coordinates. As he enters the perimeter of the event grounds, tens of thousands of attendees immerse him, of whom many are singing around campfires, playing musical instruments, and consuming food and beverages. There are drum circles, people dancing carefree and recklessly, constantly forcing him off his intended path, yet the sounds of laughter and merriment bring a smile to his face.

A dog trot's up to him, a mixed breed German Shepard and Greyhound raises to place its paws on Roberto's shoulders and licks his face vigorously.

"What a good boy, aw, okay, now you're slobbering," Roberto explains to the cheerful dog as soon as someone calls out the dog by name: 'Pepe! Come here, Pepe!"

Roberto pulls a handkerchief to wipe the saliva off his cheeks and neck, he looks in the direction of the coordinates and views Qyxzorina and Marcel.

They see him as he approaches and waves to him, as he does to them in return.

Marcel is first to welcome him, "Hey, mister, glad to see you made it in the flesh!"

"At long last, I get to shake hands with the next great GPPJ visionary, Marcel Etrion."

Qyxzorina stands to greet Roberto with a hug, "Roberto, so good to see you! How are you?"

"Likewise, Qyxzorina, you are radiant this morning! It is fine, golden dawn for public childbirth!"

Qyxzorina reaches her hands towards the skies, "This is the strongest relationship we have ever known! Bless the mother! Bless the baby! Bless all these beautiful people!"

Roberto spreads his arms open, "May God bless you Qyxzorina!" The two share a loving, rapturous hug.

Marcel offers a tease, "Roberto, you are here to scout out another prospect for your charity?"

"Marcel, you know I work with orphans and children of disconnected parents. By the looks of this crowd, the expecting mother must be an overwhelmingly popular person."

"Indeed, she is," Qyxzorina agrees, "she is only nineteen years old!"

"I see what you mean, fresh out of schooling." Roberto has a seat next to Marcel. "I've been meaning to ask you something, Marcel."

"Okay, I'm all ears."

"Do you trust Patrick Riverstrike enough to venture an enterprise with him?"

"Yes, I do. Why shouldn't I?"

"Nothing of recent concern, but I served as an intelligence and logistical expert when we first met. Let's just say he may tell you one thing, then do another or worse, smear your name behind your back."

"I see," Marcel reasons through his suppressed laughter, "To leverage our partnership for his financial gain in reputation, basically putting all liability on us while he can maintain a laissez faire capitalism."

"Well said Marcel," Roberto asserts, "I have experienced this behavior from him over the centuries!"

"These general accusations from other former associates of his, merely business rivals and I am aware of the tightfisted, knock them down and out nature of the real estate world."

Marcel and Qyxzorina look at one another and turn their gaze back to Roberto. They respond in tandem, "The bottom line is you survived to talk about it another day!"

"That's right," Roberto acknowledges, "But not without having put my safety, as well more importantly my family's safety, in great jeopardy."

"Hello, can everyone hear me? This is Marcel Etrion."

His message is over the public communique, "I wanted to let everyone know before I forget to mention, the first round of twenty-three Star Gazer Sun Tour ships have successfully navigated around the Sun and back. We will be conducting our second launch round in two days and will continue our tours around the Sun in perpetuity. We thought to let you know for there are thousands of vacancies that are selling out fast and to post me or Qyxzorina if anyone would like to take the most magnificent voyage of a lifetime! Thank you and God bless." Marcel is not a man of many words but is responsible for being the face of the business as CEO and part owner with his wife and Minister Riverstrike.

"Great news Marcel, already onto a second round! I will need to find the time to venture with you."

"Yes, thank you. Naturally, Star Gazer Sun Tours offer future voyages around Venus and affordable round trips to Mars!"

"Truly magnificent!" Roberto exclaims over the PAC, "The Space Carrier Truckers Union is equipping the tour ships with nuclear fusion cells for propulsion and solar cells to provide energy for internal operations."

The crowd cheers, spreading merriment in reaction to the impromptu announcements.

"Reservations are pouring in Marcel! We are near capacity already!"

"Qyxzorina, you sound surprised?" Marcel's face hints at amazement as his smile spreads ear-to-ear.

"Of course, the response is massive." Roberto lifts his right hand near to his face, limply pointing his index finger while swaying elbow to the wrist for emphasis, "Once they learn the propulsion cells are being mounted, the gravity of the opportunity lights them up."

I can see him as he stops speaking abruptly with one glance of Janalake approaching with Jürgen and me.

"Roberto, long time no see!" Says Jürgen.

"Come hither silly man!" I open my arms to greet him. "We wondered if you would make it!"

"Catherine, welcoming children into this world is my thing!" He states with enthusiasm before focusing on the beautiful woman with the amazing resemblance to one of his treasured loves and a life-long muse in his philosophical writings.

"This is Janalake, our favorite RAKLAV commander."

Roberto offers his right hand in greeting, "My pleasure Commander. You are the first RAKLAV officer I've had the good fortune to meet."

"Our friend Roberto, CEO of ACRES, and our vivarium tour guide extraordinaire!" I introduce them noticing they have a spark, a connection sharing mutual respect. Janalake reaches out her left hand to receive Roberto's greeting.

"Hi, Janalake?" Roberto smiles. "Hello?"

"Will you sit with me?"

"My pleasure," Janalake is relaxed having her guard down around Roberto.

We all make ourselves comfortable anticipating the event's beginning.

Early dawn is not the optimal time to catch a glimpse of the Milky Way through Earth's atmosphere, though it is wonderful for viewing many stars as a backdrop to the space station network. Soft hues of sunlight illuminate dozens of space stations glistening above the sky, above the dark cover of the night cast over this warm, vibrant Terra vista scene.

On the other side of the ridge leading to the event, the guests enjoy a festival of lights with morning music and cheer.

We all make ourselves comfortable anticipating the event's beginning.

The daybreak is minutes away from achieving sunrise, sounds of jubilation and celebration can be heard in sporadic outburst as the constant chattering of young tongues creates and culminate in a buzz of anticipation. Janalake too is gaining severe interest to witness what is about to transpire.

Roberto intensely watches her with a fascination with the fluency of her every movement. There's a subtle grace within her spirit, the confidence of a strong woman comfortably sitting next to him.

"How long, if I may ask you," he waits as she gently motions her head affirmatively, "have you served as a RAKLAV commander?"

"It seems as though forever." Janalake takes a moment to reflect on her response, "If only I knew what forever is, it would be that number. Why do you ask?"

Roberto slowly draws in a deep breath, "You bear an impeccable resemblance to someone once very close to my heart."

"That said, was she as gorgeous as me?"

Roberto laughs in relief at the timing of Janalake's sense of humor, "You may be a doppelganger with her, and she was close to my heart."

"No longer is she close to your heart?" Her demeanor is cordial as her voice carries a soft, caring tone.

Roberto laughs gently in kind.

"Why do you laugh?" Janalake remains lighthearted, breaking a smile as she continues, "Are you passing judgment in my favor?"

"I find you charming." This response tames Roberto's excitement. "You are as gorgeous of a woman as there is. As there ever was. My heart aches for her presence. She passed on centuries ago, tragically."

"I am sorry for your loss. She meant so much to you as you are still mourning for her after so long?"

"No, the mourning is over for me but endeared to my heart she remains. Her death is considered heroic, as her life was awe-inspiring."

"Have you been to an event like this before?"

"Yes, and I attend many other events."

"How about this 'birthing' event? Have you ever seen one?"

"Have I ever witnessed a live birth, yes, many times? How about you?"

"Not that I remember."

"Does RAKLAV prohibit procreation?"

"Not that I know of." She ponders what is this 'procreation?' The GPI provides her definitions and visual aids on her brain screen.

"Is that what it is? No, this is new to me ~ it looks painful."

"You do know what procreation is?

"I'm aware ~ she replies timidly to the concept disturbed by what she retrieved from the GPI. "It's life-giving."

"It is a miracle."

"Look at Roberto and Janalake," I say to Jürgen, "Do you notice

anything?"

"Yes, they seem to be enjoying themselves," Jürgen tempers his sarcasm forcing himself to respond in line with his actual emotions.

"They have a warmth about them triggered right from the moment I introduced them."

"Okay Catherine, I know you well enough that you are constructing a theory."

"There is a case to be made here; the anima of Roberto's soul is a natural fit with Janalake's animus."

"What do you mean?"

"I'm talking about the collective unconsciousness. C. G. Jung's theory?"

"Oh, the late nineteenth century to early twentieth-century psychoanalysis psychologist. I thought we went over this before?"

"Sometimes Jürgen you show a talent of sarcasm I'm comfortable with."

Jürgen is taken aback by the apparent slight. "We can talk to C.G. Jung anytime. Why now?"

"I hope Gingi and Spontaneous Instant are safe. I feel worried for them." I think for a moment, "We should tag along with Janalake the next few days, get to know her. We can convince her to help them, especially since they are young and so naïve, they deserve a break."

"Gingi is the one into the collective unconsciousness," Jürgen oddly slows his cadence of speech, "What do you suggest we do?"

I adjust my GPI comms to request a private link with Janalake.

She reacts with surprise before she looks over at me. I gesture with my right hand to indicate adjusting the comms control on Gingi's GPI.

"Hello?" Janalake spoke in response to my call.

"This is a private line, I wanted to ask you something."

"Okay Catherine," Janalake smiles at me.

"Jürgen and I were thinking we could tag along with you since you have idle time the next few days. This way we can voyage with you in our Nebula Drifter and return Gingi and Spontaneous Instant to Earth without taking up your time."

"Good to hear. What did you have in mind?" Janalake maintains a pleasant, fixed smile as she communicates over the GPI.

"I don't know, just about anything you would like to," I reply trying to conjure someplace in my mind I may have seen that appeals to me. "I see by your smile you are in a good mood."

"Nothing coming to mind?" Janalake asks with an enlightened

expression on her face, "This GPI private line is exhilarating to sense what you are thinking visually!"

"It is, in its way a little frightening," I offer her a gentle glare of my eyes accompanied by a smile. "Sensory projection can range from the IQ to EQ to the CQ as related to your interpretations."

"How about we set out to the orbiter racetrack, it is an adrenaline rush and I know Simon would be into joining us. Have a look!"

"This looks intense!" I lean to nudge Jürgen to join us. "Yes, ladies, what can I do for you?"

"Take a look at this Jürgen, it's an orbiter racetrack right outside of Denver!"

"Are you serious? Looks like the only way, I'm in!"

"That's the spirit Jürgen." Janalake raises an eyebrow at him, "We can see who else would like to join us as it is an open arena."

"Sounds like fun!" I look into her eyes. She is suddenly ruminating. "What are you thinking Janalake?" My intuitive control of the GPI allows me to access her thoughts formulating into words while algorithms of her facial expression reveal something of her emotional quotient. This is a sneaky way to anticipate peoples' actions.

Her thoughts are something about Simon and the consideration of their working relationship.

"I realize I cannot wear the GPI as it is forbidden for me to do so. I will need to adorn the ZSI and attend with Simon in our RAKLAV uniforms."

In my heart, I would tell her to shun expectations, but it is her life, her decision to make. As an innocent curiosity, I pose the question, "Why is it mandatory?"

"It is who I am. It would be best to not recognize me or informally address me, especially related to this event as not to raise suspicion with Simon. Be alarmed to see us to keep Simon off the scent."

Many in attendance are wearing wool knit robes, and a range of people adorn colorful bead necklaces, with silk flowing garments and tie-dyed headbands. Only the Mother generation and their immediate descendants have age-worn on their faces, and the fashion choices vary immensely, Qyxzorina's revolutionary vision for contemporary fashion over her one-hundred-twenty years in fashion design stays popular eighty years since her retirement from the industry. Her motivation comes from her faith in what binds us all together. She called the line 'Human Constellations' as the emphasis placed on the joints of the human body as the stars in a constellation would shine or glow. The individual's skeletal system personalizes her designs made from a tender sponge layer with fabric that molds to the body features of the wearer.

Most of the guests are Gingi's age, and many are undoubtedly friends of hers. Near to our location is an ambitious artistic group making handmade painting tools: Brushes, canvases, palettes, easels, and handmade crafts for sale or trade.

A quiet moment blankets the crowd at a rapid pace.

Vocal prompts over the PAC inform the main event is about to take place.

The sunrise provides a warm glow as four young ballet dancer dancers appear bounding onto the stage and perform a "Birth Dance" with a pointe technique and then plie into a pelvic drop exercise indicating the star of the show is in labor.

Then entering from the orchestra pit below on a riser platform is the young woman in full-term pregnancy about to give birth, face to face with the audience the delivery is billed as 'natural,' without an epidural.

Janalake asks, "What is the difference between a 'natural birth' and an 'epidural birth?' Qyxzorina?"

With her mouth suddenly agape, Qyxzorina is speechless to the grown woman's question.

"Qyxzorina?"

"Yes, Catherine," She answers with her eyes fixed on Janalake for the moment.

"The modern delivery techniques I assume have advanced in the past three hundred years. How have they changed?"

"I am so sorry not to have explained before."

"Please do."

"You may want to listen in too, Commander Janalake. It's a matter of preparing the baby for a rapid entry or is it a rapid exit?" She laughs at her own expense.

"It's both I believe, but what do I know?" I suggest politely remembering Qyxzorina has never had a baby or have I for that matter.

"It is an occurrence of three stages of labor: The shortening and opening of the cervix; descent and birth of the baby; and the delivery of the placenta. Labor is the longest stage lasting up to twenty hours."

"We're not being asked to stay here for hours of labor, are we?"

"Oh, heavens no," Qyxzorina reassures me, "These days an event like this is coordinated with the expected time of delivery within two hours."

"Thanks to the GPI, the thousands of invites are sent automatically, and RSVPs are secured from what I understand."

There's a request to join our conversation from Jürgen. He's right next to me. "Let's have Jürgen join the conversation, it will be edifying for him," I urge Qyxzorina.

She laughs and repositions her body to face the both of us, "Hello Jürgen?"

"Hi, thanks for letting me in. What's going on with using the 'cranium talk?' Any juicy gossip?" He has a cheesy smile as he bobbles his eyebrows.

"You will enjoy this information on the birth event. There may be broken bones in a difficult birth, especially to the clavicle or the humerus are most frequently broken. The birth is not so messy with excretion of fluids, but the delivery of the umbilical cord and the placenta will be a flash flood from the vaginal canal." Qyxzorina has a moment to reflect if she's overlooked anything important, "Oh yeah! The birth and delivery of the placenta to the cutting of the umbilical cord take approximately fifteen minutes."

Roberto speaks to our circle, "Hey everybody, she's getting close!"

Qyxzorina offers me a happy face as I do to her as Jürgen looks at us with an air of disgust about the image painted for him.

"Feeling okay Jürgen?" I touch his nose with my right forefinger arousing him.

"I'll make it through," he said with bravado, "Now that I know better what to expect."

About twelve minutes later, after the birth of a healthy baby girl, Jürgen touches my nose with his lips, my lips finding him we lock in a loving embrace. Warmth in my lower belly and a feverish feeling urging me on despite our surroundings, we hear the uproar of the crowd breaking us from our embrace and an immediate lull from the crowd in doing so. Jürgen and I look around to find Qyxzorina is transmitting our image to the entire GPPJ!

At the point of face-to-face with the GPPJ, the 'Birth Event' audience proceeds with rousing applause, tears, and cheers alike, I offer a 'thumbs up' as Jürgen crumbles a napkin and tosses it desperately at Qyxzorina who mercifully stops transmitting.

"How could you Qyxzo?" I pleaded affably with her.

"Do you realize how many monetary units Qyxzorina just

accumulated for you?"

"How many Marcel?" Jürgen's attention gains focus beyond our embrace.

"A number with more zeros to count than you have fingers on both hands!"

"Is that your first kiss?" Asks Qyxzorina.

I nod my head yes, "Publicly."

"There is no telling how much until I tag this as your first."

"Go ahead," Jürgen is delirious, "Tag it, tag it!"

Janalake may have felt like she had given birth herself. As mesmerizing of a spectacle, it is for her to witness, the profound truth of nature in the sublime urge of human existence and perseverance touches her heart deeply, shedding tears weeping openly among her jovial friends, who at first appreciate her tears of joy, but are soon to interpret tears of a distraught woman scrambling to get to her feet.

Roberto is in concern for Janalake who is troubled by the jubilant crowd as she rushes away without offering goodbyes.

"Janalake!" He is compelled to chase after her through the dense crowd. "Janalake! Wait for me!"

She runs with the strength of a triathlete ascending the ridge leading to the rim of the Grand Canyon.

Roberto needs to use his universal boot-wear hover thrust function to keep pace climbing the ridge as he finally reaches her on the ridge top after she yields to his calling out her name.

"Janalake what is it? Where are you off to in such a hurry?"

Her complexion is ablaze upon witnessing the newborn baby girl, breathing the first breath of her life, inspiration of nature's innovation she at this moment has found what was lost in her when she followed Patrick Riverstrike into the ZSI.

"I'm sorry Roberto for behaving poorly. This is the first time I have ever witnessed such an event! Let alone lacking memory of any education or knowledge of the circumstances, I am unaware and rocked to my core with the revelation of my potential to give birth."

"Yes, Jana, you would be an excellent candidate to give birth!"

Janalake is struck by his enthusiasm for a moment, then to hearing his using 'Jana' she experiences an epiphany: Her whole understanding of her identity transforms as memories stampede from her past, memories so intimately hers about her innate genius in engineering and being hailed as a child prodigy, the quick revelation of her life stolen is a confirmation of suspicions she privately held but was unable to articulate under the guise of Commander adorning a

Zealot Sentinel interface.

With the thought of betrayal, she faces up to the skies, "Truth prevails as nature is truth, it awakens me with the day itself under the slow warming beauty of a sunrise, I too stand at the precipice eager to fulfill my natural promise of potential previously stolen from me."

Roberto moves toward her to hold her warmly into his arms, "What is it Janalake?"

He wipes tears from her eyes hazel green ~ her Over Soul emerges revealing gorgeous vibrant brown iris', "Roberto, I am Kariana."

Roberto is caught off-guard repositioning his head to an angle to take in her essence, "I cannot believe it! It has been two hundred years I could sense it in my heart!"

"Roberto, please don't tell anyone."

"You are revitalized wearing the GPI, the ZSI made you seem like a different person. Your eyes . . .it is you! What happened?"

Kariana sheds tears of joy in relief, "I'm not completely certain, using the GPI has brought forward memories, emotions, and inspiration I have not felt in a long time. It's seeming like forever."

Roberto bounces on his toes thrilled to be in her loving presence. He faces the divinity of the clouds, his smile speaks of a mending heart, he clasps his hands feeling gratitude for this moment of truth.

"I'm so amazed to see you have returned!"

"You must swear to me, that you will not say a word to anyone. I need to keep my cover to investigate what is going on."

"You have my word, Kariana. Kariana!"

Roberto embraces Kariana as both relinquish tears of joy due to the reunion of their mutual natural bond.

30

Space Trucking and Racetracks

Hours later Roberto is busy hauling solar cells from the recharging space docks. The dozens of other truckers are performing emergency energy distribution exercises to include coordination and execution of hypothetical energy failures from terrestrial based to various space station shutdowns with critical scientific materials to protect.

The hazards to address by the procedure in damage control are exercised in preparation drills critical to the function of sensitive science labs, and the strategies necessary to contain the destruction of a Martyr class SS with its heavy arsenal of supersonic nuclear missiles. This is training elemental to all WORB employees.

"Hey, Roberto ~ boss man, we're in for some major workload equipping, what is it, thirty tour ships with solar energy cells?"

"It is a major development to have the SGST ships for the monetary purposes supporting industry," replies Roberto matter-of-factually.

"This is my first WORB assignment, I can attest to the 'wellbeing' of the human condition. My monetary units have never reached the 'seven-figure fancy' and I never imagined through the Space Carriers Truckers Union."

"Congratulations Jay, you make sure you give back some to the GPPJ to maintain that upward mobility."

"Excuse me Roberto, but that isn't going to happen," a vigorous voice interrupts, "first paycheck over seven figures deserves a celebration!"

"Burrooks, you are so on the money. Hey Roberto?"

"Roberto here, go ahead Jay."

"Did you see the time travelers kiss the other day?"

"Didn't everyone?"

"It's about time that dude made a move publicly, as hot as she is," Burrooks expresses disgust, "I'm surprised they haven't sprung a kid yet. What are they waiting for?"

"I'm sure they'll get around to it Burrooks," Jay says with a smile on his face. "Now that Kariana is around, Roberto, can we gain the respect of a broader audience, say the RAKLAV?"

"I'll believe it when I see it," Burrooks quips.

"She will find her way. It's good, better than belief, she has returned. What that means to RAKLAV is not what RAKLAV leaders would like it to mean."

"Too bad for them, nobody will be providing any 'wellbeing' their way."

"All right, let's get back to focus on the task at hand, and remember guys, Kariana doesn't want me to tell anyone about her current status, so forget about it and let things run their course, okay?"

"Yes sir, boss man," assures Jay, "What about you Burrooks, 'mums the word?'"

"Word ~ replies Burrooks placing his fist, knuckles facing the GPI viewfinder for emphasis ~ you have mine, my brothers."

"Good, as well as moving on, listen closely: The SGST ships use the same technology as a terrestrial city lighting grid. The solar-electric power is a supplemental system to the nuclear propulsion accelerators that run off state-of-the-art nuclear fusion reactors. These simulation exercises are taxing on the senses over time, especially when these actual exercises have never been tested in actual emergency events from hence the day of their design and implementation."

"Burrooks, this is Jay, over."

"Go ahead Jay, this is Burrooks."

"Sounds like typical SSNERT to practice something never proven to work."

"I wonder why the procedures in the first-place boss man?"

"The propulsion unit in the Tigris SS tragedy could have saved thousands of lives as the Tigris SS power outage from an early direct hit prevented the space station from taking evasive maneuvers. These procedures include extraction techniques for damaged solar energy cells, and the installation of fully charged solar cells to maintain nuclear fusion generation."

The GPPJ utilizes sporting events and recreational activities like jet sledding down the Himalayas or Mount Kilimanjaro. Jet-pack usage on ski slopes makes for an outrageous gravity-defying trek down, or up, a mountainside! These are extreme sports for Jürgen and me, we registered to participate in an indoor orbiter racetrack as we are advised of the relative safety of the competition and the simplicity of operating sports craft orbiter terrain runners around an indoor track.

We arrive in our new Nebula Drifter landing at the landing pad area some five miles outside the arena where we will ride in with the public on the shuttle escort. The shuttle is accommodating but the revelers are a bit rambunctious and outright debauchery. It is crazy to be surrounded by thousands of twenty-five-year-olds of various degrees of experience interacting jubilantly while riding each other's shoulders or moshing and body surfing atop the crowds.

I am drawn to the social side of the event as there is a festival village complete with visual arts truly mesmerizing in a variety of concepts, live music, and multi-ethnic food offerings. As we meander around engaging in the festivities, we learn it is World Peace Day, the first day of a week-long celebration of peace and love throughout the GPPJ.

The race events number near one-hundred-races involving thousands of participants sharing the use of one thousand orbiters over ten hours. The partying goes on constantly.

The GPI reveals the conversations, thoughts, and emotions of those who are fortunate to have the opportunity to adorn it. Jürgen and I are prepared to be nonchalant in the presence of the RAKLAV officers known to us as Simon Noir and Commander Janalake, as not to jeopardize Janalake's credibility having adorned the GPI as a sworn Zealot Sentinel, Jürgen and I establish a mindset not to refer to her as a 'friend' in public environments. The ZSI is designed to avoid attempts of persuasion or influence over the allegiance of the Zealot Sentinel to the 'wellbeing' of the human condition, maintaining the integrity of the Zealot Sentinels by preventing access to their assigned orders, duties, and overall operations working in the confidence of the GPPJ.

"Jürgen, don't look now but the Riverstrike's officers are here!" I said discreetly so as not to draw their attention. I held onto Jürgen's arm to prevent him from reacting out of the instinct of fear by peering around to look for them.

"What do you mean?" Jürgen tilted his head to face me.

"The clone, Simon Noir, who wears the mask on his face, and the Commander, Janalake."

"Are they following us around or what?"

"Good question," my voice reflects the growing uneasiness now brought on by Jürgen's not-so-sarcastic question.

"If they are, they're not attempting to hide their presence!"

I slide my hand down Jürgen's left arm to clasp his hand and begin to lead him away from the RAKLAV senior officers moving quickly through the crowds on the concourse level.

"Where are we going?"

"Let us move around to see if they tail us," I said as I quickly glance back to look for them.

"We continue to move through the crowds as we listen to announcers' enthusiastic fervor from inside the racing forum. The roar of the crowds cheering on the orbital drivers as they compete around various track courses ranging vertically, horizontally, and diagonally in layouts.

"Catherine, are we heading to any specific destination?" He allows his pace gradually and I with him to stand off to the side, angling to a position where we can view the orbiter's racing as well as casually scanning the crowds looking for the two officers.

"It appears they are not looking for us," I assess after a minute of observation. "What a relief."

"Good," Jürgen said changing his tone, "This is a race? It looks as though they are flying around like a swarm of bees!"

The crowd shrieks in horror as a collision occurs between two orbiters setting off a chain reaction of collisions taking out one-fifth of the racers. The disoriented racers wildly go off track in several directions; the orbiters are lodged into the protective structures designed to absorb a high impact by giving way enough to prevent any significant structural damage or from harming any spectators.

My concern enables me to distract a patron, "Excuse me, sir." My call to him verbally falls on deaf ears, so I engage him with the PAC, "Excuse me, can anyone tell me if anyone is injured in this shocking collision?"

At once my head was filled with comments of disdain for me, many were too difficult to comprehend in the deluge of snarky remarks, the gist of the overall response relates to 'the absurdity of the nature of my question!'

My astonishment, which I realize reflects on my facial expressions once I see Jürgen adjust his setting to the public as he observes my face; he too is stunned by the comments of the crowd seeing his eyebrows raise offering an expression of confusion to disbelief.

The consensus forming reveals an expectation to witnessing such catastrophic collisions, understanding the result of any injury to the pilots is minimal to highly improbable. The chaotic energy sent their way is unnerving.

The crowd feeds off this conflict between ecstasy and violence.

"The integrity of the cockpit is impenetrable due to a collapsible design of the hull and with a high-grade non-combustible fuel source," the unidentified male voice transmits, "The surrounding structures are engineered with padding capable of absorbing any high impact by equal transference of energy displaced throughout the entire structure of the forum."

The male voice cut in on the transmissions overriding all others to be heard as if through a secure, private line.

"Thank you for the explanation." I am intrigued by the lack of an identity tag on the transmission, "May I ask what authority you have to transmit privately on the PAC?"

"Certainly, you may ask. Have a look behind you."

Jürgen and I turn simultaneously uneasy to realize who it is.

Simon Noir standing calm expression with Commander Janalake standing next to him with an imposing stare on me. We dispense with the public comms link.

Simon Noir, wearing the face distortion mask reveals only the movement of facial muscles as he speaks, "What a coincidence running into the two of you in a place like this."

"Is it a coincidence?" Jürgen snaps back defiantly.

"As far as you know, it is," Simon replies.

"Have you come here to wager on the races?" Janalake asks with insinuation, "You should know whether you win or lose, you are casting shade on your character."

"No, in fact, we are registered to race," I feel a surge of confidence, "Do you plan to race too?"

Janalake remains unaffected as she posits, "It will be my pleasure to defeat you, as I owe you one."

"I don't know Commander," I lift my chin to show my skepticism, "Are you capable of rebounding from the ass-kicking I gave you?"

Her eyes flare open in furious contemplation of our Lunar Hall confrontation.

"What about you Jürgen," Simon pries, "Do you share the same misguided resolve of your companion?"

Jürgen spreads a tight-lipped smile turning to gesture with his eyes to me, "Do you believe this guy?" He revolves his face with a stern look toward Simon, "You just keep that mask on Simon, after I bust you up, I wouldn't want anyone to mistake you for me."

Simon exhales a short blast of breath out of his nose, "You are of no threat to me, you puny curmudgeon!"

"Let's get it on, it's the only way," Jürgen replies projecting severe confidence, "I'm in!"

"Jürgen," I turn to face him, "Simon is a skilled pilot as are the other ninety-eight pilots."

"I got this," Jürgen confides, "I just finished training to pilot the Nebula Drifter."

"What does that matter?"

Janalake intervenes chidingly, "Catherine has you on a short leash?"

I turn to leer at Janalake in the eye over my shoulder, then turning to face Jürgen I pin my clenched fist to his shoulders, "You got this."

By the time we exited the elevator up ten stories to the orbiter hanger where we are registered to check out our assigned orbiter racers, Jürgen and I are resolute to gaining the upper hand in relations with the senior officers to Patrick Riverstrike.

"You got this Jürgen," my encouragement is in support of his need to redeem himself after Simon humiliated him in their encounter at the Lunar Hall performing arts center. He appears confident and self-assured of himself.

"Thank you, Catherine," Jürgen fixes his deep blue eyes onto mine.

I lean into his face to engage our lips in a heavy kiss. "You're welcome."

His face lights up as a warm smile spread across his face.

"Come on Jürgen, it's our turn to board the orbiters," Simon speaks in a snarky tone.

The path to our assigned orbiters takes us by hundreds of orbiters including the ninety-six competitors in our assigned race. These machines are impressive, larger than your standard orbiter the average

GPPJ citizen would navigate into space and around and about the SSN.

These racing orbiters are sturdier in the frame design and are elongated to provide efficient aerodynamics built for speed and high-precision maneuverability.

As I watch them depart for the boarding dock, I am struck all at once by Janalake, her personality vastly affected adorning the ZSI, and I am left to our wits with all the awkward, hostile energy of rivals.

She wears her dark black hair close-cropped, her hazel eyes are piercing, and her complexion a radiant rose-hued warm brown glow on a sharp angular bone structure holds my attention speechless.

She walks toward me, her officer's uniform is worn under an insulated, winterized coat. She smiles mocking a friendly gesture before she speaks, "Catherine, did you consult a stylist, or did you coordinate that charming winter outfit?"

"My outfit is rather 'functional' more than 'stylish,' but thank you for the compliment." I am put at ease with her remark. "That is, I find it hard to wear clothes as well as you do."

"Nice try, but this outfit is my uniform," she then states coyly, "You haven't seen anything yet."

How strange I should find this statement alluring aware of our intimate interaction with the tailor genie at the birthday event a couple of days ago. After spending five years of my life seeing and being in RAKLAV training for Zealot Sentinel, albeit under the oppressive guise of the ZSI, the impact of the ZSI on her personality, the loss of recognition of our recent fashion collaboration depresses me."

"An announcement comes on the public channel: "The next pilot group 'E' must board your assigned orbiter racers; pilot group 'E' as in Echo, visual assistance activated; group 'E' must board your obiter racers at this time."

"Happy World Peace Day, Janalake," I offer in good faith.

She has an expression of pleasant surprise on her face, "You are familiar with January Eleventh, Two-thousand-one-hundred- eleven! You have been doing your homework."

"That is for sure," I match her intensity, "but the sentiment ceases while in the cockpit of the orbiter racer."

After every pilot has secured themselves in the cockpit of their assigned orbiter, each one of the hundred racers positions their orbiter craft into a mark at the opening of a funnel tube. The countdown ensues and the contest begins with a rapid jettison into the tube leading into a large vacuous cylindrical racetrack. I find myself traversing along a grooved track until reaching the opening to the main racing area, then launching off the track as it leads to a conglomerate of orbiter racers in tight formation grazing wings side-by-side.

I compose my breathing and focus as within moments the field opens as a collision takes out about twenty percent of the orbiters, twenty or so craft careening off in every direction, many disappearing from my sight lines, while others incur high impact collisions into the walls of the arena structure without explosion as the design is to absorb the high-velocity energy resulting in minimal hull damage.

Immediately I transmit to Jürgen on our private channel, "Jürgen, this is Catherine, do you read me?"

At that moment a racer to my right glides across my nose nearly clipping my orbiter with the tip of its' tail wing, and I check my position making a slight dive to a lower row of racers to avoid a collision.

"Catherine, this is Jürgen, I'm pursuing Simon through serpentine maneuvers. What is your position?"

"Jürgen, this is Catherine. I'm below three levels from where we started; I've lost track of everyone."

With that, the hull of my racer vibrates to a rising intensity, and a rumbling sound follows. There's a racer taking a position to my starboard side, it is Janalake, "Never mind, Janalake is trying to pass me now!"

As I say this she closes in on my position and attempts to rise above me. I notice an opening forward of my position, but below the racers are in front of me. A loud metallic thump occurs on my upper hull and my racer jolts down as if air turbulence in an old commercial airline jet flying through stormy weather.

That was a close one, the flight rods shake my hands off them in a moment sending me further into a downward trajectory.

I regain my grip and use my momentum to throttle past the racers on the lower level and into the open space. Punching the accelerator allows me to exploit the opening to gain significant positioning forward of Janalake.

That was a close call, but I am more at ease due to maintaining control on an aggressive move taking a turn to the left I take the lead!

"Catherine, this is Jürgen," his voice is in a higher register than normal, "Simon is creating some havoc sending racers into tailspins that are collapsing in altitude. Keep your eyes open."

A severe shock to the rear of my racer causes me to lose forward direction nearly sending my racer into a tailspin. "It is Janalake," I speak out softly as racers on both sides of me are creating collisions as they careen into the structures of the arena's sidewalls.

"The field is opening up!" Initiating a steep climb to shake off Janalake, I notice there is an open ceiling. I continue to climb above the top layer of the racer's formations, and I can see that heavy snowfall is twirling into the arena from the open retractable translucent roof.

"Jürgen, this is Catherine," my voice reflects my excitement, "Do you notice the snowfall?"

"Catherine, I'm tangling with Simon," he says in a panic. "Where are you?"

After his question his transmission becomes unintelligible. "Jürgen, I've climbed above the pack of racers! Where are you?"

He responds with an unintelligible exclamation of anxiety within a horrifying scream!

His racer appears ahead of me pirouetting, ascending in a near vertical position up and out of the open ceiling.

Close behind is Simon zooming in tight proximity, following him out of the open ceiling!

My instinct is to follow and assist Jürgen, but before I can make a move, Janalake's racer rams my orbiter racer from underneath forcing the bow of my ship downward. Any attempt at changing direction fails as I determine her racer is somehow locked into mine, sending us both into a free fall crashing into several of the competing racers.

Our entanglement sallies the other orbiters making them spiral in all directions like a handful of metal jacks being tossed gently toward the ground, bouncing, tumbling around below me, a reckless abandonment, unlike any thrill I can imagine!

The momentum of her orbiter with the leverage from her position above me has me skirting to the corner of the arena, with both of our racers at full throttle.

My position against the curve of the corner wall allows for a gradual turn and sliding along the grooved surface. The orbiter racer gains friction, the torque of my craft's engine is beyond the force on the hull causing damage to its integrity, the very steel bends forcing rivets to grind weakening the bond to the degree of near separation.

The innards of my orbiter spew heavy, gray smoke plumes, filling the cockpit with blinding, eye-searing toxins. My throat and nasal passages flare in pain to the harsh burning of membrane tissues, causing convulsive coughing and preventing the intake of oxygen. I struggle to maintain consciousness.

I don't believe I will survive this, as the air is being cut off.

I grow tired, . . .a black smoke seeps into the cockpit blinding me; am I dying? Slipping into unconsciousness a memory surfaces . . .Angel speaks . . .a long time ago I had a friend who told me the definition of what Angel speak is.

The two orbiter racers careen off the lip of the open ceiling sending each flipping 'aft' over 'bow' in rapid succession a dozen revolutions before one craft slams into the snow cover field rendering the pilot unconscious. The other orbiter racer regains control and is using the GPS on the interface to circle to proceed through low visibility due to dense snowfall over the terrain. The safest approach to land by the wreck is to hover a couple of feet above the accumulated snow, the trees are easier to identify and navigate through safely.

Operating above the treetops in windy, low visibility provides no advantage, only hazards.

The pilot moves with purpose exiting his orbiter immediately and securing it. He holds his right arm shielding his face as he pumps his feet one weighted and slippery step after the next.

The orbiter lays on its side, and the hatch is open and taking in snow. There is no way to extract him as the open hatch is damaged leaving enough space to fit only one arm long enough to retrieve the interface for system data memory retrieval, providing evidence of how the orbiter met its demise. He slid off of the side of the orbiter to land haphazardly onto his feet into thirty-six inches of accumulated snowfall. One step with open arm swinging to create momentum, nearly falling on his face he pulls himself up by grabbing onto his racer; He returns to the orbiter racetrack flight deck level three to see if she is alive.

An intergalactic class cruiser appears descending from the exosphere landing with great caution by the orbiter racer wreckage. Two humanoid figures emerge through a translucent hatch and proceed to extract the comatose pilot, retaining him incognito into the fuselage of the intergalactic class cruiser before it lifts off and then ascends into space.

Moments later Janalake pilots her orbiter racer out of the open ceiling in search of her colleague and the rival orbiter racer, where she quickly locates the wreckage and hovers to a soft landing where she exits her craft, she cannot remove her helmet in the subzero temperature, she can move graceful and quick through the now thirty-eight inches of accumulated snowfall.

She examines the wreckage up close perceiving immediately the vacancy, she looks in all directions for evidence of second wreckage with zero visibility due to blustery cold winds and heavy, blinding snowfall.

Her focus turns upward as she senses a hum of a craft ascending away indiscernible other than the blurred lights' sequential blinking in the distance marking the unique positioning of the lamps.

She urgently climbs into the orbiter racer to return to the racetrack flight deck level three. She passes emergency response units right after liftoff.

The non-responsive female pilot overcome by the toxic plumes of smoke resulting from the collision and impact to the corner wall of the arena structure is evacuated to the Emergency Resuscitation Clinic (ERC) housed within the racetrack complex. The patient is in a hyperbaric oxygen chamber for therapy detoxification of hazardous smoke inhalation, including the presence of carbon monoxide created by the forceful sustained pressure resulting in the melting of metallic components in a rare event.

Upon docking his orbiter racer on flight deck level three, the pilot descends from the cockpit tuned in to the GPI private channel unable to contact his female counterpart, "Catherine, this is Jürgen, where are you?"

He continues to rapidly make his way to the concourse seeking out an official of the racetrack, tuning in to the authorized channel, "Flight deck three concierge, my name is Jürgen, assigned to 'D' group orbiter, over."

"Jürgen of 'D' group, this is flight deck three concierge. What can I do for you?"

"I am unable to connect with my companion Catherine who is registered in the race log assigned to the 'E' group. Do you know her whereabouts?"

"Yes, she was involved in a collision disqualifying her from the race, as were you I believe. You exited the arena jettisoning through the open ceiling?"

"Yes, yes dammit," his frustration grows beyond self-discipline, "Involved in a collision? Is she in the ERC?"

"Your friend is undergoing resuscitation in a hyperbolic oxygen chamber. Proceed to the emergency room clinic waiting room on concourse two."

"Thank you," he acknowledges his gratitude for help before dashing away. He accesses the emergency personnel VIP passageway to the ERC.

Janalake makes a slow, controlled approach to racetrack flight deck three as a ZS shuttle passes her in the direction of the orbiter racer wreckage.

She docks the orbiter and then proceeds to the ERC. She is authorized to access the emergency personnel VIP passageway to the ERC. Upon entering she views Catherine as conscious and fully recovered sitting up and being consoled by Jürgen.

Roberto approaches startling her, "How are you?"

"Excuse me?"

"Oh right," Roberto reaches into his shoulder bag and takes out Gingi's GPI. "Here, put on this interface, let me help you take off your ZSI."

Janalake removes her ZSI handing it to Roberto in exchange for the GPI and slips it on. She can express herself as Kariana now that she has disengaged the ZSI.

"I'm sorry this had to go down as it has!"

"I'm sure you are Kariana," Roberto tries to console her.

"I need to look after Simon, or suspicion may arise from the Minister."

"Where is he?"

"The Minister is quick to secure any injured or wounded personnel. I suspect he will transport him to the Dark Eagle." Kariana exhales a desperate breath, "Shoot, I have to transport two detainees with me back to Mars."

"I understand what you have to do." Roberto gently states, "Kariana, please take care of yourself."

"Thanks, Roberto. For everything."

"What do you think you will find?"

"Who knows, in case there may be evidence of foul play." Her concerns are re-directed to Simon Noir.

She departs for the RAKLAV cruiser to collect Gingi Grind and obtain custody of Spontaneous Instant from the Harmony hospital Constitution City, then returns to the Dark Eagle SS one-hundred-million miles away to track down Simon.

It is a thought that first crossed my mind, but I don't believe she intended to kill me.

"The hyperbolic chamber works to cleanse your cells, you should be feeling fully recovered in a few minutes," the administrating doctor advises me. "You are lucky, not too many patients recover from dying."

"That's great. What happened?" My friend steps in as the doctors leave my medical bedside.

"As I can remember, Janalake gained an angle on me and somehow maneuvered above me, using leverage, she drove me into the arena walls and drove my orbiter into the corner."

"I'm sorry to hear that, but why or how did you inhale toxic smoke?" He is mystified, "I mean the fuel is not combustible, were there flames?"

"I didn't see any, nor do I have any burns," I am taking inventory of my body while examining the slight bruising on my thighs. "The explanation given to me was high-pressure impact sustained on metallic structures with carbon components."

"Not from the impact? The arena walls are designed to absorb and distribute the force of impact equally."

I strain to think how certain I am of the cause, "It must be from the actual force from Janalake's orbiter pinning me to the wall, perhaps the friction and sustained force compromises the integrity of the hull protective cage?"

Jürgen deduces a logical scenario, "The metallic panels on your orbiter suffered the most damage. I'm suspicious that Janalake persists with intentional destruction. What was she trying to do other than cause you harm or even kill you?"

I reaffirm my belief with complete certainty, "I don't think she intended to kill me!"

"No?" He asks seriously not to dismiss the possibility.

"No, absolutely not," I refute his insinuation, "I think she would have done so if she wanted to!"

Upon departing the racetrack in our Nebula Drifter, we witness the wreckage clean-up going on, flying low enough to rubber neck the scene.

"What happened out here? Is that wreck your orbiter?"

"No, Simon lost control after his orbiter nicked the lip of the open ceiling. The orbiter flipped 'bow' under 'aft' several times before slamming into the field."

I found this surprising, "Did he make it out?"

"I didn't see him in the wreck when I flew back to check, and he hadn't ejected, so I don't know, but I'm sure we'll find out in due time."

"How tragic," I relate as we move on.

"Riverstrike will hold me at fault for whatever happens to Simon. You know it, I know it, and everybody who witnessed it knows it."

"Since today is 'World Peace Day' I did some research on its history while waiting to be released from the ERC. It explains all the jubilation."

"What do you know about it?"

"In a nutshell, I know on January eleventh, two-thousand-one-hundred-eleven a treatise was signed at the World Convention of Liberty and Freedom (WCLF). An international agreement adopts the 'wellbeing' of the human condition as the ultimate overriding common unilateral moral truth to which all humans are expected to adhere to in all human relations. It was adopted and signed by democratically elected leaders in record time."

"Is it?" He responds pleasantly. "Yes, a revolutionary moment in time." He laughs gently.

"What is so funny?"

"That is quite a 'nutshell,'" he humors himself.

"I may be a little vague on the details," I admit humbly, "but there is a celebration of lights and music across the world this evening." With that, I activate the audio system on the Nebula Drifter, "World Peace Day celebrations."

The Nebula Drifter posts a list of cities from across the world offering a digital map displayed across the dashboard.

"That is very awesome."

"Go ahead and select a city," he instructs, "We can shuffle through and get a visual on the celebrations taking place in real-time from around the world."

I first select nearby Denver, "What a beautiful scene, the modernization is incredible! The celebrations are overflowing onto the surrounding terrain of the city's outer limits, the futuristic skyline serves as a sensational backdrop!"

He views the scene on the dashboard, "Looks as beautiful as ever." He comments. "Very contemporary skyline, nothing futuristic about it."

"You are kidding, right? Your sarcasm knows no bounds."

"What do you mean Catherine? Denver has always been a

beautiful city."

"What a strange thing to say Jürgen, you are from Denver, at least that is what you claim, but we haven't seen what it looks like these days until just now."

"Yeah, as I said, it looks as beautiful as ever."

"I've never seen it as it is today, it's freaking amazing!"

"What do you expect?" He says blandly, "It's twenty-three-forty-seven Catherine."

I let his indifferent attitude slide. Scrolling through the other cities around the globe provides a captivating spectacle one after the next, each Capitol of each country branded by national colors, highlighting their unique landmarks accompanied by music genres culturally representative of the heritage past and present!

The populations of these celebrations I find overwhelming in the sheer numbers of revelers attending enormous venues intricately designed to provide a diaspora diversity of human experience.

Our four-hour tour of the holiday events is enough to satisfy our curiosities, that is until the unified global coordinated rendition of the iconic song Silent Night is carried by the voices of the Earth in its thousands of languages, sung almost as prayer by all denominations from all religious peoples, as festive to secular populations equally.

For one, my belief in the sacred beauty of humanity embraces the unified indulgence of celebrations on World Peace Day as it is heart-warming as it is inspirational.

With a slight touch of the dashboard panel, the Nebula Drifter elevates its nose jettisoning out of Earth's atmosphere into space.

"Why the abrupt change in altitude?" I ask.

"This is where true silence is, out in the void of space. This is where sound waves cannot travel as there is no oxygen to vibrate sound; a powerful demonstration of nature's omnipotence."

Jürgen speaks with weight behind his words as if roused by the encounter with mortality this evening. He is showing signs of post traumatic stress disorder with his refocus on the impermanence of being alive.

Without the risk of upsetting him further with debate, I take a hold onto his right hand and squeeze gently, gazing into his eyes with a reassuring smile, "I love you too."

He offers a look of concern briefly, then his mind relaxes, and he releases a deeply held breath, "I do too."

We set course for the Sea Foam condominiums as I am left to believe Jürgen is not quite right in his mind.

III

Part Three

TRANSCENDENTAL

31

A Natural Progression

The Commander has a signal of Gingi's whereabouts due to the microscopic beacon she embedded in the small of Gingi's back before releasing her from custody. She has embarked on the pretense her boyfriend is being released from the hospital.

"We may have to remain on board waiting for the nurses to hover gurney him and secure him in one of the cruiser's medical observation holding units," the Commander states flatly. "It won't be long before we're setting off."

"Setting off where?" Gingi asks with derision.

"Zealot Sentinels indoctrination and training center."

Gingi paralyzes in fear, although her instincts inform her to protest, "For what? I was a passenger in the orbiter! I did nothing wrong."

"It is a felony to enter vivarium air space in an orbiter or any other spacecraft."

"I wasn't operating it," Gingi pleads, "How can I be held responsible?"

The Commander proceeds to the cockpit, "Accessory to a felony. You should have stopped your Spontaneous Instant."

Hospital personnel has Spontaneous Instant on a hover gurney securing him in the on board intensive care unit. He draws breaths from a streamlined oxygen apparatus.

"Sponti," Gingi is elated to see him, "What did they do to you?"

Kariana dutifully secures the safety harness on Gingi before entering the cockpit.

Gingi whispers to gain his attention, "Sponti, are you okay? Sponti?"

He lifts his chin from his chest and wearily peers in the general direction of Gingi's voice. "I've been better," he mutters gaining momentary cogency.

"It looks like your injuries are healing already."

"Yeah, they injected this serum, it promotes rapid cell restoration. The gunshot wound is deep and painful, but they numbed me up good."

Gingi listens noticing how well he is articulating his words, not at all slurred. As the hospital personnel exit, the Commander takes Gingi in her handcuffs to a private detention cell.

The cruiser is programmed to lift off without warning and within twenty-five minutes the RAKLAV cruiser passes by the moon at five-hundred-thousand miles per hour and accelerates.

The RAKLAV craft is at the forefront of spacecraft technology. With shape-shifting rudders and a combination of electromagnetic motors made with neodymium and nuclear fusion cells made from hafnium; this ninety-million-mile trip will normally take sixteen days one way.

The Commander throttles the RAKLAV cruiser to maximum speed utilizing all nuclear power reserves to achieve one million- miles per hour to arrive at the Dark Eagle SS in four Earth days flat. The voyage is very taxing on her health as traveling at this rate of speed puts all navigation systems to the test of functioning beyond optimal performance, to the point of demanding her constant attention.

Particularly harsh is the capacity to detect space debris, meteors, and other commuting spacecraft between Earth's moon and Mars.

One-million-miles-per-hour detection of a collision trajectory will result in diminished reaction time. She checks on the others through the cabin monitors.

Gingi Grind is isolated in a secured holding quarter with the necessary accouterments for a comfortable, hospitable experience. She is solidly asleep in a fetal position without a worry in the least.

Spontaneous Instant is placed in a medical observation station under stable life support. His wounds will heal over the four days, but she is most watchful of his ability to handle the level two g-force.

Her stamina is maintained through a rigorous daily workout regimen involving high resistance strength training and a few hours sparring with a variety of simulator bots, agility, and core strength exercises, as well as mental acuity tests.

The nuclear power sources are shut down forty-seven-million miles mark so the RAKLAV cruiser will maintain the speed and gradually reduce to a manageable speed when it comes to docking on the Dark Eagle Nest SS (DEN SS).

As she prepares to dock, she views the Dark Eaglet in its hangar undergoing mechanical reconditioning service and inspection for hull integrity.

Her RAKLAV cruiser is on auto-dock and guides itself into the service hangar.

The Commander uses simple voice commands to access security checkpoints and access points leading to the medical center. The center has thousands of patients, mostly recovering from a physical injury from Zealot Sentinel activities, then laborer injury from mining metals on asteroids such as the asteroid *Psyche*, known to have seven-hundred—quintillion monetary units in mineral and rare stones value.

The number of asteroids designated for mineral extractions, optimizing logistics as the average distance between asteroids in the belt is six-hundred-thousand miles and the belt itself spans one-hundred-forty-million miles wide. There are other health concerns derivative of accidental injury that include suit depressurize, suffocating from lack of oxygen, punctured oxygen supply, and an assortment of phobias, anxieties, and overall mental illness capable of neurological paralysis.

Despite the high occupancy of patients, the Commander can easily locate and access Simon Noir's whereabouts using the priority of medical services patient evaluator available in the executive suite.

"There are no visitors allowed at this time Commander," Doctor Amelia Padilla explains, "The patient's condition is critical with severe burns, broken bones, and a punctured lung. There may be a need for prosthetics and skin replacement."

The Commander is completely understanding of the situation including why Simon is in a comatose state. The nature of the injuries sustained will require a calculated, time-consuming approach.

"Thank you, Doctor Padilla."

The Commander exits the medical center and is approached by Minister Riverstrike waiting for her, "Commander Janalake, it is good to see you exhibiting initiative out of concern for Simon's condition."

"You didn't stick around long enough for my account of events."

"This is true," Riverstrike states understanding the Commander's point for immediate reconnaissance on the event, "I should have checked on your status, but there was no time to waste in rescuing Simon based on his critical condition."

"I am glad you did have the concern for Simon's welfare." The Commander speaks without emotion in large part mimicking the conditioning of the ZSI she is expected to wear, "but given the extraordinarily well-equipped medical facility at the racetrack, the injuries suffered by Simon are of a common expectation in the environment. It is a part of their culture."

"My intervention was necessary."

"Mobilizing him for a four-day voyage put his life in great jeopardy. The medical facility there is capable of resuscitating patients from death. I have witnessed it!"

"Yes, but in the healing process, it is imperative Simon's identity as a result of his disfigurement must be kept under a shroud of secrecy and not be made public." Riverstrike states with finality, "Most importantly is his ongoing security in his capacity as my senior advisor. Currently, you have an indoctrination and conditioning orientation to oversee. To keep up appearances, have the previous orientation recorded hologram in use until Simon recovers to resume his duties as usual."

Spontaneous Instant is back to full health and able to walk under his strength with Gingi into the Zealot Sentinel training facility after being transported from the DEN SS for twenty-four-hour monitoring of his vital statistics for medical clearance.

The bay doors of the warehouse-size indoctrination block slide open in a blink. The interned subjects are escorted through the primary entrance. They are placed there until other refugees to The Glass Planet will undergo the same brutal conditioning.

Designed to break the will of self-dignity, self-respect, and self-identity to conform to the understanding of their existence is to serve at the will of their leader minister Patrick Riverstrike.

Soon there are hundreds of other capsules placed in the warehouse size hall.

The capsules are charcoal gray and at once the capsule lids flip up on top hinges.

An electric shock is pulsated through all the capsules rudely awakening the drug-induced slumbering occupants.

Jarred into awareness by the violently throbbing sensation of low-level electrocution, Spontaneous Instant, and Gingi gasp for air before holding their breath the moment in anticipation of excruciating pain.

Gingi exhales laughing, "It kind of tickles, doesn't it Sponti?"

"I know," he giggles, "You would think it would like hurt or something."

"Move out of the capsule. Move to the diagnostic modifier."

Spontaneous Instant heads off towards the oddly luxurious contoured units.

Gingi gestures to Spontaneous Instant whose attention is taken when another refugee can be heard.

"No, I won't go!"

She looks around to see a woman being coaxed by several others to continue.

Three drones arrive taking positions around the woman. "Break up this insubordinate behavior. You are all subject to severe discipline."

As they continued to move on, so did those assisting the insubordinate other, leaving her vulnerable to further attack by the drones.

"Check it out Gingi," Spontaneous Instant is beyond the illusion attempted to be infiltrated into his mind.

There is a loud distinct cracking sound, and the body is carried out by the drones, floating the motionless cadaver out of the block.

"Damn, Humpty Dumpty fell off the wall," Gingi refers to the egg in the nursery rhyme.

"Ironically the origin story of Humpty Dumpty falling off the wall had to do with a cannon named Humpty Dumpty being hit by another cannon's cannonball, causing Humpty Dumpty to fall off the wall."

"I am familiar with that story, but that robot's head made the sound of a really big egg being cracked open!"

"You are a mindless scourge have twenty seconds to obtain a seat and secure yourselves in. Do not fail this command or else lose your life, as worthless as it is, you all should be grateful for this mercy."

Most refugees react in dire panic to obtain a seat and strap themselves in.

Spontaneous Instant and Gingi are quick to secure consecutive seats and strap themselves in.

"Let's hope this will be something to talk about," Gingi is teetering on as if she is not getting the value of the price she paid for admission.

"Probably nothing to write home about, but they are nice for trying!"

"Keep your limbs close to your body. Warning against any level of insubordination, intentional or not intentional, is to be dealt with."

"This could be fun," Gingi suspects the instruction to keep limbs close to the body is the same as the roller coaster MOON BEAM

MONSTER at the Lunar City amusement park.

There is a series of panels with a suspended platform where a man appears wearing a face disfiguring mask. Not a descriptive mask, it is a clear, transparent mask with qualities of distorting the appearance and voice of the one who wears it.

"Each of you contributes to the one, and no one of you is individual."

There are smatterings of murmurs and echoes of dissent from those being indoctrinated.

The masked man places his hands together and as he wills it sends subliminal messages of demoralizing effect via direct download to the specific areas of the cerebrum initializing the first application of brainwashing.

The other side-effect administered is the element of energy waves through the frontal lobe, cerebral, spinal, and nervous system causing intensely sharp stabbing pain throughout the body.

The screams and gargles of fluid in throats are loud and the suffering is excessively prolonged.

"To not be misunderstood by you vile, insignificant scum of the Earth, your choice is simple: Accept subordination or accept death."

The masked man surveys the refugee recruits with an air of indifference, "Ironically it is not your choice, as the pure definition of your subordination is that you have no choice. Refugees like yourselves are unwanted. Nobody wants to suspend their highly fulfilling, amazingly uplifting, fortuitous lifestyles to be burdened by less than ignorant, stupid, dumb pinheads who come to us from more primitive eras in human history. What is your worth?"

The man in the mask, motioning his arms and hands to administer another dose of mind cleansing on the refugees to quiet the few protestations, further prolongs the torture of excruciating physical pain as perceived in the brain.

"Gingi, I'm convulsing and writhing in pain from crippling electrocution. Can you tell?"

The Commander stands in observation from her DEN SS quarters keeping a close eye on the youngest recruits, Spontaneous Instant, and Gingi Grind, admiring their mental resilience, physical toughness, and their amusement in the process.

She suspends the session to have the two recruit's bodies scanned for foreign substances, "What do you two think you are doing?" She asks in hologram from her position twenty million miles away.

"Having a little bit of 'child's playtime;' No, no, rather more like 'down time' if you want to know," Spontaneous Instant complains.

"This technology is ancient, the twenty-second century kind of ancient," Gingi points out humoring, "What's next the iron maiden?"

The Commander absorbs their context, "Onto direct debriefing with the likes of the two of you."

Their harnesses are released and the two are attended by four guards who escort the lawbreakers to the incarceration holding block.

The neighbors may be oblivious to their incarceration, despite the three individuals' imitativeness and capability of having an original thought. Parsiak is native to India, Xiang Li is a form of muscular chiseled steel, and an Afghan woman named Sula.

Parsiak, "They did not make it. They were expelled from Zealot Sentinels and sentenced to permanent incarceration."

Xiang Li, "Do not ask why, as I do not know 'why,' but they moved the others for not knowing."

"Not knowing what?"

"The answer to their existence, but do not ask me 'why.'" Xiang Li warns before turning and promptly exiting.

Sula is very friendly to Gingi, "My journey was not an easy one. I was born in a vivarium population under the oppressive, misogynistic male-dominated culture. Raped at eight tears old, I was able to arrange an escape before I was to be married at ten years old. I was assisted by an organization helping to promote female equality and end the greed-fascism rule. I manage to make it to a GPPJ city as an orphan in estrangement from my society.

"I found help and a family and a home with ACRES. By my nineteenth birthday, I was able to enlist in the GPPJ as I prayed not to return to any vivarium."

"Good for you!"

"My purpose was already determined for me without me realizing it. RAKLAV agents apprehended me countless years ago."

"You look twenty-five years old!"

"I turned twenty-five in the year twenty-two-twenty-seven."

"You are one-hundred-forty-five years old!"

Sula's face broke slightly as if a deep depression set in, "I've been here for one-hundred-eighteen years?"

"No, add two years, it is twenty-three-forty-seven."

Sula dazes off into a blank one-thousand-mile stare.

"Are you okay? Sula?" Gingi jostles her arm gently nudging her shoulder. "She is in hibernation."

She moves the woman to a horizontal position on the single bed.

"Sleep well, Sula."

Spontaneous Instant stands in the doorway observing, "Did you see the look on her face? She is horrified by her age, and you go ahead correcting her that she's one-year older."

"Two years older. That wasn't a good thing to say?" Gingi considers what impact her comments may have on Sula, "She is borderline Mother Generation."

"A clinical depressive," he suggests.

"Oh well, live and learn."

"That's why I love you Gingi Grind! Always seeking the positive side of the matter."

The Commander has the two young upstarts downgraded from a six-month indoctrination to a five-week containment in the Zealot Sentinels training facilities for a debriefing of their unlawful incursion into the Appalachia vivarium, including weekly physical health scans, psychoanalysis, and emotional evaluations.

Indoctrination would be too much of a hassle, risking potential conflagration of protests, for their upbringing in the GPPJ already qualifies them as citizens and their civil rights would unquestionably be violated. What they need is disciplinary instruction due to their arrogance, profane sense of entitlement, and the fact they committed felony trespass. Also, common in the modern era of childbearing, as she is informed by physicians from the Constitution City Harmony hospital, the teens have an insatiable need for attention.

"They are unable to complete the requisite six-month indoctrination in any event due to their age. They are within five years of receiving the Condorcet procedure."

In time, the hospitable communications-hub-inspired finished product of The Glass Planet struck my eyes as a mechanically engineered moon, in its presence are five other space stations that were not hinted at in previous images.

Another interesting inclusion in the reports I've been reading is the growing frequency of Patrick Riverstrike's stories as a philanthropist, an engineer, and an investor, beginning in the Twenty-Forties, consolidating power while cultivating and harvesting monetary wealth.

Roberto explains the 'cycle of willpower' as a water wheel of wealth connecting humanity to its most natural, potent, viable, and peacefully productive formulation. The concept is the foundation of The Economic Theory of the Human Will.

When the Condorcet procedure was first utilized on the human population Roberto had to wait, as the poorest, non-white majority citizen of the country, he was to wait for the procedure to be made affordable, via mass production facilitation and at the time in the old economy, fossil fuel-based was beginning the massive transition to Eco-friendly technologies.

Energy centers and specialized labor did help to build this new infrastructure establishing the greater distribution of opportunity and wealth. The application of natural energy innovations engineered into the SSN continues to this day. The design of the fuselage is radioactive insulated and transfers through absorption into energy utilized for illumination. A popular design contains solar panels along the exterior of a space station riveted to scaffolding or cage-like steel structures, the effect is that of a sailboat in the wind. A space station generates enough expendable energy to maintain orbiting speeds or rotating motion to assist in the gravity generators maintain livable conditions.

32

Sling Shot

As the SGST flagship approaches Mercury the engine propulsion ceases, set to maintain 'momentum speed' for an approach to the edge of the Sun's gravitational pull. The conventional slingshot maneuver around the Sun will result in acceleration of the cruise ship as it navigates around the Sun, the thrust is set on a return course to Earth.

Marcel and Qyxzorina mingle with some notable tourists, Dr. Ariel-Li jun Song, an astrophysicist who transforms her work into inspirational conceptual art, mega-influencer Herbert Mueller, who is the Chair of the Technological Space Travel Internal Surgery innovations foundation; other dignitaries including a handful of space station group governors, the entertainer of the galaxy, Rock Thrillion$, and Camilla Rosa-Laurel, the Artistic Director of the Frau Mauro Performing Arts Center.

"Welcome all, you are some of the luminaries on board the SGST flagship Soley Leve, to enjoy the historic journey around the Sun," Qyxzorina graciously states.

"Your achievements in this participation of evolutionary progress ~ Camilla Rosa-Laurel endorses ~ will be this year's honorees of the Frau Mauro Performance Arts Centers achievement awards."

Everyone delightedly applauds, and the reaction launches a smile on Camilla's face.

"For Marcel's Etrion this will be your second award in the past six years."

Marcel suggests, "Madam Camilla, with all due respect as fine of a presentation you offer at Frau Mauro, it would be my tremendous honor to host the ceremonies aboard our SGST flagship. Our performance stage has seventy-five thousand seats. Each SGST ship has an amphitheater with acoustics for mixed performing arts, magical choreography of dance, sublime musical performances, fine arts presentations, and hologram arts; the Soley Leve is the perfect destination for a festival of ingenuity."

"This voyage could be the Titanic of Space Travel," sneers Rock Thrillion$. "If we crash straight into the sun."

Camilla laughs flirtatiously, "Good thing there are no icebergs in space!"

"There are asteroids," Dr. Ariel-Li jun Song infers, "many may be composed of ice, as icebergs are, but an iceberg hidden underwater is more predictable than uncharted space rocks can be."

"At least not in our Solar system at the moment," chides Thrillion$. "It's the excitement of anticipation of our greatest fear occurring that is of equal magnitude."

"You don't realize the added value of traveling on a city-class tour ship. I'm so sick and tired of the humdrum of personal mass trekking, don't get me wrong, I find Martian Metropolis to be a charming location, but as for an extended vacation I'd much rather spend a month on this exquisite ship."

Rock Thrillion$ clasps his hands, "Agreed Camilla, have we ever known what we would encounter traveling to the center of the Solar system? Careless hours playing low gravity baccarat, while having a wonderful cabin view of Venus while dining on Chinese takeout with Savory sake."

"I'm happy for your excitement, it is delicious Chinese takeout, you have an opulence about your imagination," Qyxzorina offers cheerfully. "Are you attending the concert this evening?"

"We secured the passes when we booked the trip." Camilla relishes, "We wouldn't miss it for the annual performance of the holidays is one of my life-long favorites."

Rock Thrillion$ comments, "It's nice to know the philharmonic space orchestra is still participating since the inaugural launch of the fleet."

Qyxzorina acknowledges the popular Symphony, "We are into our third year of launches. From the start, we wanted to contract with them as they're a perfect match having classical and Avant Garde compositions and they have thirty orchestras' ensembles to perform in rotation of thirty consecutive launches!"

"Indeed," Camilla has become deliriously eccentric in her speech,

"We are having a most wonderful time!"

Everyone laughs in jest toward her flailing arms shaking her torso in ecstasy while doing a two-step jig like a tightrope walker wielding a balance pole recovering from a slight slip of the foot.

"Will we see you there with Marcel?" Asks Camilla.

"Yes, it is a part of our work and pleasure. We hope to see you tonight."

The guests offer reassurances as they exit toward their cabin and Qyxzorina proceeds to the quadrangle and views the event calendar to check the availability of the concert attendance; only a few passes are remaining in the seventy-five thousand seating capacity.

Standing a few feet away from her are two vacationers having a spirited conversation, an esteemed influencer, Dr. Murgatroyd Chromia is a debonair man of note. He is a developer of open fund investments.

The woman is dressed in a traditional cloth of Middle Eastern cultural influence, a shroud of burnt orange with dark yellow trimmings. She wears her hood covering her face only to be seen from in front of her.

"Are you looking forward to viewing Mercury and shortly after the gravitational slingshot, gravity assist maneuver, or 'swing by' around the Sun?" The woman asks with a delightful buoyant curiosity.

Dr. Chromia turns his shoulders focusing his shamus eyes to look into her eyes for any signs of inebriation.

"It will be both a nerve-racking few days leading up to the maneuver as it is an extraordinary adventure, I assure you, madam." He sounds off smiling as he sways heel to toe with his hands in his pants pockets.

"When I was Prime Minister of Afghanistan, I learned of the diabolical conspiracy at the time when, proven as a reliable intelligence report, the efficient enterprise ~"

"Excuse me, Madam," Dr. Chromia politely interrupts, "Did you say you were Prime Minister of Afghanistan?"

"Yes, oh, nearly two hundred years ago, but I understand if you are not aware." The woman states confidingly, "We intend to provide similar services for observance; back when there was a fight for The Glass Planet between the privileged wealthy who plotted to conceal the Condorcet procedure from the proletariat, to gain an advantage over generations accumulating wealth and power uncontested by those denied longevity."

Dr. Chromia is beguiled, "The Condorcet procedure has been available to everyone for the past two-hundred-fifty-years."

Marcel walks over to Qyxzorina, "Qyxzo, are you eavesdropping on our guests?"

"If you heard what this woman is saying, listen." They communicate on a private line.

"It was Dr. Chromia who is a genetic scientist who defected from the ethics commission of the Condorcet procedure to ring the alarm!"

"May I ask what your name is?"

"I am Sula, from Afghanistan." She reaches her hand out to greet the gentleman, "And you are . . .?"

"My apologies madam Sula, I am Dr. Murgatroyd Chromia. I am unaware of who you are as you're not listed on the GPPJ. You must excuse me as I must attend to my wife and family at this time."

"Typical response from a 'Money harvester!'"

"What do you mean regarding me as a "Money harvester?" Sula turns away from him demonstrating her annoyance, "No, you are a capitalist economy harvester!"

The man contemplates a response but decides to brush her off with a hand wave as he departs.

Marcel and Qyxzorina approach Sula to introduce themselves. "Hello, my name is Qyxzorina, and this is Marcel. You are a welcomed guest to Star Gazer Sun Tours."

Sula has a pleasant expression as she smiles at Marcel and Qyxzorina taking them in, "You are the entrepreneurs of this tourist operation. My name is Sula, and the pleasure is all mine!"

Qyxzorina is unnerved by Sula's tone in her voice, and the ringing familiarity of her name, "Where do you come from Sula?"

"It is of no concern the capitalist economy cultivators are those citizens who possess a parlance, a vernacular, jargon, or lingo with the ability of a contractor, in the sense of power and finance, used to speak between the lines."

"We want to encourage you to meet us for a meal sometime along the way." Marcel hesitates for her response. "Enjoy the time for the thirty-day round trip aboard the Star Gazer Sun Tour ship voyage. The accommodations orientate for recreation and relaxation."

Sula snaps at him, "It's funny how the wealthy preach to address national issues by telling the government how to allocate tax-paying citizens' money, but the tax-paying citizens are unable to tell the wealthy how to spend their money, especially since the wealthy make their fortunes off the tax-paying masses. Education is tantamount to changing the way the world works, knowledge is power."

"I can tell you are from the Twenty-first-century," Qyxzorina surmises, "Mother generation?"

Sula pulls her hijab tighter around her head. She does so to stare at Qyxzorina as she feels paranoid about her aging and is dogged in questioning the fact. "Do I know who you are?"

"You might, I'm Qyxzorina Astraea, former fashion model, and high-end clothing designer. It's nice to have you aboard the Soley Leve."

Sula offers the squint in her eyes of a cynic before she turns and walks away to exit, her posture is noticeably bent at her lower back.

Marcel places a hand on Qyxzorina's shoulder to help her center her emotions stewing from Sula's rude behavior.

33

Three Engagements

An engagement to remember, "I appreciate your adulation Jürgen, you know what, I'll take you up on your offer."

"Is that a 'yes?'"

"I say yes, it is a yes."

"Wonderful." He holds me closer, hugging me, but strangely avoiding kissing me.

"What's the matter?"

"How do you mean? Nothing is the matter. I'm the happiest man alive!"

"Wouldn't you want to express that with a kiss?"

"If it pleases you."

I cannot believe how awkward Jürgen is behaving as he delivers a peck of a kiss to my lips. I let out restrained laughter.

Jürgen seems irked, "Does my kiss tickle you?"

Wow! What a disappointment!

"It does tickle me Jürgen, it does."

He is pleased by this revealing a satisfying smile. What instincts? He smirks at me.

"Me too. I love you beyond measure. We should find out how to go about arranging the ceremony. Can you imagine the monetary increase we will get in return?"

"Oh, sure it would be immense. I wonder what reciprocation he would be justified to offer in their generosity to support us."

"I think a baby would be a great expression of our appreciation of the masses."

What is up with him, 'baby?' This is from the guy of adventure, who has no time for fatherhood.

"I thought you would rather make a significant transfer to ACRES; remember you said it would be nice to help the development of refugee children of vivarium societies?"

"I see, you make a great point, very pragmatic of you."

This is news to me, Jürgen, on May twenty-fifth, two-thousand-fifty has taken the initiative after asking for me to Marry him, I thought it was a dream, but it is real, he has gone ahead and decided for us to move into a mansion on a remote mountainside near the Grand Canyon in Arizona. We move in there and it wasn't long before he is expressing an interest in training as a neurosurgeon for practice in the SSN.

My interest in pursuing life beyond a domicile waned once all my attempts to discover our past entities arrived at dead ends. Once we found the American Archaeology Society ceased to exist in the mid-twenty-first century due to advancements in satellite sonar imagery penetrating the Earth's crust and mapping out every buried artifact existing across the globe, the need for independent study by archaeologists became unnecessary, outmoded in the face of commercialized expeditions.

The prospect of interplanetary archaeology will have its day, but the feasibility is undefined and will be for centuries to come. In time the robotics of exploration will certainly prove far more cost-efficient and expeditious than sending humans. A poetic evolution in the cultural fascination to weaponize machines. Our ancestors from the mid-to-late twenty-second century proved robotics in warfare leads to attrition and that's not good, to be in a war of attrition. A failure at the apocalypse is a suitable final 'death nail' to the epoch of Pisces and all it stood from martyrdom to progressive imagination.

My pursuits in life are a combination of academic, artistic, and working in community groups organizing social events of all kinds, as every day there is a festival, celebration, memorial, or competition for local regions. The larger regions spanning the Earth, Venus, Mars, the Moons, the SSN, and the asteroid belt can be described as 'the Solar System that never sleeps!'

The home we live in is built into the mountainside and features an epic view of the Grand Canyon facing west to northwest. The days are typically dry and warm, and the orbiter commuter traffic is routed away from residential areas and nature park reservations have no presence audibly but provide a spectacle distantly above the altitude of fifteen- to twenty-thousand feet. After the daily glorious sunsets, the air traffic lights mingle below the lights of the SSN and the dense sky scape of the Milky Way with a backdrop of stars further into deep space. The layers of lights with propulsion activity so often mesmerizing, never replicate a pattern from one evening to the next.

Working in from the viewing deck, the contours of our mansion include spacious rooms with elegantly designed furnishings. The dining rooms, cozy thick walls framed by oak banisters, and columns accentuating broad corners provide a casual stately feel around a sleekly designed dinner table. From the automated kitchen, there are open walls and wood flooring throughout the living and eating spaces. Hardwood floors accentuate the spiral staircase and the floors leading into the bedrooms, including the master bedroom with the exposed mountain as a wall, and it has gorgeous en suite facilities.

A courtyard garden with cacti and fern bush highlights the landscapes of smooth rock formations and beautiful marble fountains; circulating wading pools with soothing warmth with cushion interiors, the scent from the saltwater Jacuzzi reminds me of the ocean. Under the shade of Joshua trees planted along the backyard perimeter during the day are glamorous deck chairs, and an outdoor kitchen overlooking a mesa formation thirty yards below provides an overall feeling of privacy.

It seems years since that fateful day when Janalake discovered she was the legendary prodigy, Kariana Yahreah.

To me, it is a terrible irony the way Patrick is revered by society and is held in high esteem for 'visionary leadership' in planning out and developing the Space Station Network by managing 'human capital.' In generating livable accommodations for eight billion consumer debt slaves in the GPPJ, he adds to his legend and the lie.

For her part, Kariana has since joined forces with Roberto to assist in ACRE's ongoing efforts to raise neglected and abandoned children to well-adjusted adulthood. She is Commander Janalake until she works out the entanglement of her passions with her allegiances.

Jürgen and I meet up with them only twice a year and I must remind myself how their perception of time is altered from ours. They have lived for several hundred years, while Jürgen and I have only lived about fifty years give or take five years, as we were mysteriously unconscious in suspended hibernation for over three hundred years.

For Kariana and Roberto, a year is like a week, yet for Jürgen and me a year is around ten months.

In the past few years, my network of friends has grown into so many people I can only guess I have tens of thousands whom I may have experienced a dialogue with, and yet who knows how many more people will claim friendship with me in their networks to their advantage, vanity, or avarice. Regardless, in Jürgen's absence, I began training with Kariana at ACRES alongside the five young cadets under her advanced tutelage, honing my Marshal arts self-defense skills, and working secretly with her on the 'Twister' Qyxzorina trained me with.

Marcel and Qyxzorina have found immeasurable success with the continuation of the Star Gazer Sun Tours. There is little question they will enjoy maximum life spans with the fortune of their endeavors, as many monetary units are accumulated by franchising their ships as they gain from the mere operation of the core of their business providing tours around the Sun, Mercury, Venus, Mars sometimes at charitable rates, then one day the plan is to extend trips to the gaseous planets beyond the asteroid belt. A plan of great undertaking as an outpost for refueling and relaxation will be necessary for the longest trips to Uranus and Neptune.

We have only communicated through the GPI platform and have not sat together for a meal since the morning after the Fra Mauro Lunar City ceremony. I remind myself that time passing is only a matter of weeks to them in comparison to my experience.

Spontaneous Instant and Gingi Grind are in over their heads enrolled to earn their Master's degree for studies in quantum physics and biophysics. They are twenty-three years of age, and their days, weeks, and years are longer by their perception than us, as we are over twice as old as them.

We haven't heard from them as they enjoy the privileges of youth with their classmates before receiving the Condorcet procedure for the first time when they reach twenty-five.

Instead of prolonged separation, Jürgen and I are getting along well enough. There is truly little drama in life outside of marriage. The tragedy is a myth it seems, death is a rarity except for those who are either not able to afford the continuation of the Condorcet procedure short of the maximum life expectancy, or they have reached the last hour of their brain's ability to function. The final stage occurs sometime between their seven-hundred-twenty-fifth year to seven-hundred-seventy-fifth year of life expectancy. Brain science about illnesses has accomplished the elimination of Alzheimer's, Parkinson's, and every malignancy afflicting previous generations, yet research continues behind the learning curve, the more knowledge grows, the more unique challenges reveal themselves to us.

It all does matter to me, the circumstances and outcomes further define my existence, my being. Will my positive ethical efforts impact the cosmic fabric with how I inform it?

One friend whom I have maintained a constant dialogue with is Olivia Colston. It is no wonder we naturally maintain correspondence.

I often visit the homestead to delight in the country prairie surroundings, the stunning beauty inherent to the quaint daintiness of the environment in vibrant health. The one thing we have most in common is the time we spend alone, without disruption from others, especially the frequent absence of our significant others.

Olivia moves throughout her home in the comfort of the familiar and in the conceit of the collage of memories embodied in photographs, videos of family in celebration, and memories represented in cherished objects decorating the rooms. She tells me of memories of her past emanate strong emotional stirrings, her toughest demons of past times, and spirits generating feelings from the ever-changing times imposing a sense of loss, hopelessness to the final fascism of Nature's truth in the experience of death, her fear above all other of her fears.

In the three years since we became acquainted our relationship grew into a friendship where our bond strengthens from her reminiscence of her early life three-hundred-thirty-five years ago and my severe eagerness to identify with any part, any modicum of a morsel of any memory I can muster from my personal experience.

These conversations are the happiest exchanges I shared with anyone in this life. Olivia's buoyancy of spirit of attitude generated a memory of someone whom we mutually admired as young women, and we laugh as we announce simultaneously 'Dolley Madison,' with delightful relief!

It has become clear to both of us how we provide fulfillment for an emotional yearning, something we once found possible with our male counterparts. Jürgen is distant more often emotionally than I ever could have anticipated. Shane is absent while dutifully working on an assignment with a contract Patrick Riverstrike has negotiated for material manufacturing for a Mars project. Together we find solace in our concern for their 'wellbeing.'

The contract is immensely lucrative as hundreds of millions of monetary funds have secured them the privilege of obtaining the maximum Condorcet procedure while exceeding one billion dollars annual income affording them the dual benefit of directly improving the 'wellbeing' of the human condition and enjoying the freedoms of being on 'welfare for the wealthy.'

We sip the finest wines while swinging on the Willow tree bench, accompanied by trays of the richest cheeses.

"I find it difficult to go on day to day without sharing our lives," Olivia confides to me as we bask in the bright, warm sunlight, a gentle breeze cools my scalp while my hair is pleasantly caressed and tossed by the swirling air.

"Shane expresses the same to me. He is required to travel to Mars on a quarterly schedule to fulfill the obligations of his contract with Minister Riverstrike."

"It has taken three years so far. Has Shane given any timetable for completion of his obligations?"

"As I believe him when he says, 'Not much longer,' I recognize he says that every three months when he returns to oversee the manufacturing of parts and equipment, only to depart over and over again." She says with an apologetic tone, "What makes the situation difficult is the enormous compensation that not only benefits our security but as well benefits the entire populations of the Appalachia from the Southern regions to the Northern."

"My heart goes out to you Olivia, I can relate. Jürgen has pursued a Ph.D. in neurosurgery and since he took the initiative to move us into the mountainside mansion, he has left me to endure a sort of social isolation. If it weren't for work as a local event planner, I would have zero human contact most days except in the hotels ~"

"They're called 'Spatels' in the SSN; you didn't know that, as an event planner?"

"Spatels?"

We share a moment of reflection before she exclaims, "At least we got each other babe!"

I laugh amused by the sentiment and how true it is being creatures from a less complicated time, we are not of the prevailing modern practice of unexcused infidelity.

"When will I get to meet your children?"

"That's right, you haven't been introduced to JoJo and Gary. They do stop in from time to time. They bring the darling children with them, of course, they're all twenty-five years old, isn't that something? I'll tell you what, let me see if I can coordinate with the four of them and their spouses can have a meet, greet with you, and see if Jürgen can find the time to visit, okay?"

There is the question, to find a time Jürgen must visit. Not so much will he have the time, no, if you were to ask him to spend it with you, he would make the effort no problem.

The issue these days is the lack of interest in meeting with anyone socially. Other people are relatively social butterflies compared to Jürgen. "He has absorbed himself into his studies to the point of all work and no play has made Jürgen a dullard. Olivia, what do you suggest I do?"

"It's obvious to me. He needs to go out with you to reveal your popularity, the allure you hold over others," Olivia offers with sagacity, "Once he is reminded how the two of you are revered in person together, he'll rethink his current isolation from you. Invite him over and we can take him to the upcoming jamboree!"

"It may become painfully obvious how anti-social he is." I respond rhetorically, "For better or for worse, if he does not acquiesce, then I have to move on my way."

"Jamboree!" Jürgen is emphatic in response to the idea of attending the mundane activity sponsored by the population of Appalachia, "It seems to me you are conforming to the mindset of the uninspired Earth-landers. It might be I am at fault for your demise into mediocrity. What happened to the adventurous inquisitive erudite woman I knew and loved for over the past few years?"

"I don't know Jürgen, it might be if you found yourself spending more time around here and not off into the SSN engaging in the medical academy, or whatever you do to occupy your time, maybe we both would be happier together."

"Do you mean that? Is it what you want?"

"Of course! We are better off together, at least we share an experience no one else can attest to and it is an opportunity for us to inspire the populations of the world to unite further, by being the example of human transcendence between time and first-hand accounts of place."

"What do you mean by that? Do you imagine you can influence the meager minds of the barbaric populations within the vivarium societies to make peace or to make money?"

My optimism for exhibiting a common purpose with Jürgen suffers a setback, "What do you think was the reason for our instant celebrity once enduring the indoctrination and conditioning into the GPPJ? The mystery of our existence off the grid of the GPPJ and without any record of our story as Earth-landers is what made us of interest, iconic!"

He takes me in stonily, "Is that what you believe?"

"Isn't it obvious? You know there is a continual division in the human populace. Earth-landers are deprived of certain medical care to promote longevity, the benefits of the GPI in promoting mental health, emotional positivism, and creative inspiration. The vivarium societies are containment apparatus, the citizens are subjects of observation, living specimens of the final fascism of nature, imperfect as any human is by nature, the citizens of the GPPJ are evidence of an evolution of the human condition expedited by scientific advancements intended to adjust the imperfections imposed upon us by nature.

Jürgen is tight-lipped in contemplation of my postulation.

"Everything is, and forever will be, imperfect?"

He grapples with my cogency, leaving me disappointed he is not up to speed with the rationale having we both admit to sharing our vision, "To understand the nature of why will lead to the new absolute nothingness as Marcel has insightfully pointed out if you remember from our earlier conversations."

"Catherine, you have a mental illness. Your brain was damaged in the orbiter collision."

"All right, to what extent am I suddenly mentally ill?"

"Enough that it motivated me to pursue neurology as my discipline, to better understand how one's brain structure can change after a traumatic injury and how to cope with it."

"I experience anxiety and I have fits of depression, but who wouldn't, living a far more isolated life than an extrovert like me can endure?"

"Your condition hinders your focus, and your brain's ability to retain memories."

"What is this? The Condorcet procedure should counter the damage?"

"Not for the brain, the healing process is a prescription of abstinence from artificial light, loud noise, even rigorous movement is to be avoided. You can have that and fresh air living here on the mountainside."

"How long must I be 'detained?'"

"You are resting, is all. For your safety and 'wellbeing.'"

"Here you are persuading, cajoling me into domestic living."

Jürgen gives me a look of concern, "I am empathetic for you suffering a traumatic head injury, I am. You should use the hologram and virtual reality life zones to keep yourself in practice."

"Now you sound like the one with head trauma? Why don't you use virtual reality for your neuroscience? Is it because of how ineffectual the use is, the technology is impressive, but it is not real Jürgen, a connection may be possible, but long-lasting bonds are not made with an artificial intelligence leading to a happy life enriched by mutual affection under mutual frailties and imperfections? It would be helpful for you to conduct studies from our home using GPI integrated remote controls. I could care a less about who is dependent on simulated realities, or in toilets that analyze feces as it examines our colons, or how food is engineered for fast food joints orbiting the Earth, or the idea of surrounding myself with monitors and taking part in voyeurism. This quarantine is not justified, why am I living like an Earth-lander?"

"You make a valid point ~"

"It doesn't matter, anything without an organic connection does not cut it. Your practice is a simulation, even if you are working virtually twenty feet away from the patient.

"How do you know this?"

"I'm researching Online up to sixteen hours some days. The feature and benefits are nominal at best. Can you please commute more often?"

"You know the current stage of my training involves emergency scenarios at any degree of severity, at any location across the SSN, under various predetermined circumstances. It is a clock responsibility, impossible for me to physically break from my training."

"How much longer is this training?"

"I don't know for sure; it depends how long before I experience the complete set of ~"

"They don't tell you when the training period concludes?" I find it implausible, "I can see the macro in the micro, the composition of the hologram illusion is to me as if interacting with a mannequin. The molecules of human replication cannot resonate as the substance of the cosmic fabric, nature's canvas of origin. And you know that too."

Are we insane? Have we lost our minds? Are we mad? Or is it just me? To what is what, we see in the cosmic fabric, the patterns of persuasion, molecules, atoms, all more like rivers, streaming about rambunctious in filling space, the constant spontaneous instant.

Olivia leans on her positive attitude as a matter of obvious beauty and strength of character with her determined persistence. "I do say, Catherine, you would think scheduling six-twenty-five-year-old for the inter-solar cocktail party wouldn't be too much of an inconvenience or distraction to attend."

"Especially amongst family," I state consoling her, "Living a longer life span comes with its' cruelties wrapped inside the benefits.

"Thanks, Catherine, sometimes the intangible forces constantly sway our emotions, and feelings to the point of ad nauseam."

"I know, it's not unlike traveling to Mars at the two planets' closest orbit of ninety-three-million-miles in fifteen days, all extremely exciting the first time, although most of the journey you can choose to be sedated. There are many distractions to engage in while conscious during the time, as two weeks is nothing to get upset about."

"I don't think of such travel, I don't know what it is, it has no meaning for me."

"When do you think you'll hear from your family about arranging the cocktail party?"

"I already have, and we will not be able to see them for six months!"

"Say, Olivia, would you like to go with me on this trip to Mars?"

"With you and Jürgen?"

"With me, you can take Jürgen's place. This mission is too routine to take him away from his training."

"If his training is hands-on, I suppose it's not unreasonable for him to engage in surgery or whatever ~ skills he's training for."

"His curriculum is mainly conducted on The Wishing Well SS, some one-hundred-thirty-thousand-miles from Earth in the middle of the SSN halfway between Earth and the Moon."

"I have some wonderful news Catherine," he offers with exciting undertones, "Minister Riverstrike wants to extend an offer for us to enlist into RAKLAV as executive officers."

It is confounding that Jürgen would change the subject, "This is certainly proving my point Jürgen," I state to emphasize the relevance of what my meaning is, which is not to be ignored. "All due respect Jürgen, Minister Riverstrike does not epitomize my idea of virtue. Haven't you claimed to notice changes in your sense perception? In your processing of events, information?"

"Surely you recognize what it would mean for us to be involved with RAKLAV at an executive officer level? Yes, in the man's methodology he has committed ethical and morally questionable practices, in achieving his station in the GPPJ. Don't you think I have my doubts placing my trust in him? Is the legacy of creating a platform to further the 'wellbeing' of the human condition by facilitating the infrastructure to allow the sustaining of the GPPJ his vision, to materialize with precision in execution, gaining reverence as legendary?

My opinion of Jürgen is changing as he is no longer the

inquisitive, light-hearted, gentle caring respectful soul. A definite change in his personality concerns me and is a result of his newly found initiative to assimilate to the modern culture, as in the result of distancing himself since acquiring the mountainside mansion and his commitment to pursuing a discipline in neurosurgery over spending real-time with me are hints it may be time to separate.

I believe this opportunity to work closely together may be the redeeming feature of our relationship, as I admit to myself having a wandering eye affecting me. Anyway, if we do drift apart, the executive officer position with RAKLAV will provide me substantial monetary gain, enough to enable me to purchase the full extent of the Condorcet procedure life span!

"Do you know when he will be available to meet?"

"Probably this week." Jürgen checks his private screen, "I'm receiving a response from the message I just forwarded about your interest, and he says he would like to come to visit us here at the mansion in two days!"

Jürgen is working closely to Riverstrike.

"Let him know the afternoon is best. I have a pottery class in the morning."

"He says, 'no problem as long as you are there,'" Jürgen smiles at me.

"Okay, sounds like a plan. I'm in!" I say to humor him, but my reference using his custom response goes unnoticed.

"Very good!" He says in relief holding me long enough to plant an obligatory kiss on my lips. "After the minister's visit, I must take off for a few weeks for work. I promise when I finish my business, we will spend many hours and days together."

A few days later Jürgen and I meet with Riverstrike where the Grand Canyon Dam held the freshwater reservoir, the filtration facility is one mile north of the dam, and another five or so miles north from there are the docks where recreational watercraft are available for rental, as well as leasing dock space for the privately owned craft.

We land the Nebula Drifter at the expansive parking port mesa where we are to meet with the Minister about taking on high command positions with RAKLAV.

Riverstrike greets us with a surprise in tow, "It is wonderful to see you, Catherine. I can't express my excitement to know you have accepted the position of Commander of the Zealot Sentinels."

"My! Yes, I can't wonder what you think my qualifications are?"

"Oh, it is easy, more like repetition, the longer you're at it, then the more you shine!"

"Is that all it takes? Repetition? I suspect there is some 'passion' involved perhaps dedication too?"

Riverstrike pauses to look into my eyes, then his face eases into a smile, "I see you have powers of perception, rather strong senses indeed. I don't expect to find a lack of passionate dedication from you."

"Unity through diversity is my belief," I state with firm resolve.

"Yes, well if you are half as adored by the ZS as Janalake is, then you should stand a chance of succeeding!" Riverstrike muses.

Riverstrike is holding a sturdily designed metallic vest with contour design padding for comfort.

"Hello minister," Jürgen offers as I smile feeling discomforted by the thought of what surprise Riverstrike has in store for us.

"Hello, Jürgen." Riverstrike smiles in return saying, "What's the matter, Catherine, does the cat all of a sudden have your tongue?"

What a strange thing to imply. Holding my focus on the vest in his grasp I notice the back is a solid compartment with an apparent propulsion system, "Is that what I think it is?"

Riverstrike raises the vest and displays it by rotating it around, "I don't know, what do you think it is?"

"A flight propulsion backpack?"

Jürgen and Riverstrike share a laugh at my expense.

"Yes, it is of the kind," Jürgen remarks candidly, "Isn't it, Minister?"

"Very good indeed. Although unlike fossil fuel jet packs of yesteryear, the propulsion system is powered by ionized air and solar-charged electronic propellers. Let me demonstrate for you." He lifts the vest over his head and fits his arms through well cushion insulated straps, snugly fitting the harness over his shoulders.

"It appears deceivingly lightweight," I comment as Riverstrike fastens the support straps across his chest, abdomen, and hips.

"It is. Try one on for yourselves," he gestures with an extended arm toward two other vests laid before him. Jürgen picks them up one in each hand offering for me to take one.

The vest pack is as lightweight as a chilly weather overcoat and comfortably contours to my shoulders, back, and rib cage as I firmly secure the fasteners strapping the vest to my body.

"This flight vest is easy to navigate after ascending to fifty feet altitude, you merely visualize your intended direction for travel or flight path. Your GPI controls all of the operations including the deployment of the mobility propeller and, in the unlikely event of a mid-air malfunction, the personal parachute will automatically deploy."

Riverstrike illustrates with his hands as though to aid in providing the imagery of said applications.

"Let me show you like this."

In the blink of an eye Riverstrike lifts off directly above us to fifty feet altitude, then a slight rotation and he maneuvers one hundred feet to hover over a landing pad.

He transmits between our GPIs, "Effortlessly I envision my course and on my way!"

Riverstrike continues to maneuver in various directions up, down, and side to side.

"To add centrifugal force, you deploy nano propeller!"

At once a structure materializes in the form of a rotary blade propeller twice the size of Riverstrike's six-foot-two-inch frame. His movements become increasingly vigorous as the propeller enhances directional movement and his legs are dangling behind swinging freely in the opposite direction the propeller takes to.

"Where did that propeller come from?" My voice projects my amazement.

"Nanobot technology generates the deployment of molecular bonds of the program synthetic material comprising the propeller." Riverstrike states calmly and clearly as he begins his descent, "It is particularly useful for soft landings."

He times his words with the touching down onto the flight port pad. The propeller apparatus rescinds rapaciously as soon as he is safely on the ground. "Now you give it a try!"

At the mere thought of a vertical lift-off, I find myself using well above fifty feet altitude.

"Make sure you envision your path of flight!" Jürgen exclaims as he remains some twenty feet hovering below me.

With that in mind, I visualize descending at a forty-five-degree angle even in height with Jürgen thirty feet apart from him. He looks at me and approaches with caution to about ten feet before proceeding to circle me maintaining his distance.

Riverstrike has joined us hovering in the air forty or so feet from our position, "Looks like you got a handle on it."

"Very intuitive, more like we have a 'thought' on it!" I express feeling a little anxious about where all this is leading. "So now what?"

"There is an incredibly special place we are going to visit. It is time to extend propellers and have a 'look-see' in the Grand Canyon!"

With that Riverstrike rotates west toward the Grand Canyon extending his propeller to accelerate quickly.

"Think 'activate propeller,' Riverstrike advises, "If I haven't instructed you to do so already."

Jürgen looks at me and smiles, "I'll race you to the precipice!"

We simultaneously deploy the propellers as I remark, "You're on!"

Riverstrike hovers over the precipice until we arrive to hover beside him.

"My god the view is utterly magnificent!" I proclaim as the beautifully immense diverse rock formations are breathtaking from beneath us to far off on the horizon.

"Okay, time to focus on maintaining altitude while you two follow my lead," Riverstrike orders as though commanding troops embarking on a mission.

"Copy," I respond short and sweet.

"Lead the way Minister," Jürgen states dutifully as a subordinate employee would.

Riverstrike pushes onward and upward. We accelerate and gain height remaining parallel to each other. It is at first terrifying once, beyond the precipice, the canyon floor goes from thirty feet to three hundred feet like a safety net is suddenly withdrawn. It is too imposing to look down knowing my survival is dependent on my focus and concentration; it's best to block out the peril I would face should the propulsion-pack fail, or worse should I become dizzy and disorientated.

We traverse for ten minutes at an average speed of eighty miles per hour before Riverstrike breaks radio silence, "What do you say, Catherine, did you ever go para-sailing before?"

"No, if it was anywhere as exhilarating as this, there's no way I could not remember!"

"Agreed," acknowledges Jürgen.

"We are near our destination so we will begin a gradual descent," Riverstrike instructs us as he remains thirty yards ahead of us. "Down we go!"

As we descend to about one thousand feet above the canyon floor, where the voluminous Colorado River sparkles under the sunlight. I'm overcome with thoughts, dreams, a sense of flying over a coastline rock formation, a shadow image of varying shades of gray. The outlines of the topography are distinct and clear as a fog allows. The coastline and the distant horizon shine through, only now in full color, with the added perception of molecules varying in density between objects, cactus, rock formations, and the enhanced water volume of the river.

The sunlight sheds its particles shimmering with the swirling flows of atmosphere molecules.

I look toward Jürgen and perceive artificial tendons and portions of his musculature and his skull are inorganic. This mystical sensation is troubling to me as it is wonderful.

Looking forward the organic form of Patrick Riverstrike is leading us directly into the face of a canyon wall. As he navigates smoothly to an opening of a cave, he hovers at the mouth and gently lowers himself onto the ledge before the cave. Upon his feet making secure contact his propeller rescinds.

"You go first," Jürgen offers to me. "I will hover in behind you."

"Copy Jürgen, ten four," I instinctively use radio jargon feeling like a commander myself as I will be employed with RAKLAV, qualified Commander of the Zealot Sentinels.

It's a proud moment for me as I made an effortless landing, regaining my senses and focusing on the approach to the mouth of the cave, I see the lip of it has several steps chiseled out of the canyon wall.

"Are those steps at the mouth of this cave?"

"Yes." Riverstrike replied further explaining, "Thousands of years ago this cave was ground level. The Colorado River has eroded the terrain over hundreds of millennium."

Riverstrike leads us into the cave, surprisingly vast in space from the cave floor to the ceiling easily ten to fifteen feet in height. The cave walls are even a further expanse from side to side. I wonder if Jürgen shares the experience of the mystical perception we had in previous times. The fact we are on a guided tour with our new boss makes me hesitate from mentioning it to Jürgen as he seems unaffected. I dismiss the urge to mention the episode for the time being, allowing for a brief consideration it may be due to neurological issues. It seems to me highly unlikely both of us would share correlated neurological idiosyncrasies.

We traverse the dark tunnel illuminating the curiously leveled pathway with our GPI sourced led lamps. The walk takes twenty minutes until Riverstrike stops to wait for us.

"Be careful with your steps down this staircase, they are very short steps." Riverstrike points downward in front of him as we approach. I stand beside him and look down at a properly constructed staircase chiseled out of the rock, "Why is there a staircase in this remote cave?"

"That Catherine is as good of a segue as any for what I am about to show you."

"What do you mean?" His statement has piqued my interest.

"Nearly four-hundred-fifty years ago an explorer, G. E. Kincaid along with one Professor S. A. Jordan accompanied by a team from the Smithsonian, reportedly found in this cave an abundance of artifacts. They discovered relics in the chambers beyond this staircase extending nearly a mile underground."

"Relics?" Jürgen breaks his silence, "What kind of relics?"

"Egyptian relics." Riverstrike announces with dramatic effect, "Thousands of copper tools, hunting traps, vases, urns, jewelry, and hieroglyphic etchings all associated with the age of the Pharaohs five to six millennium ago, before the Aries epoch. There were even mummified males entombed with spears and other weapons."

"How can that be possible? There's never been any evidence in the genetic makeup of the Indigenous peoples of the Western Hemisphere to suggest any such migration of Egyptians from that late of a stage throughout human evolution."

"Very interesting to hear your confidence. How knowledgeable are you Catherine, about human history?" Riverstrike pries further, "How do you think you know such things?"

His question took me by surprise. It dawns on me like the first sunrise ever known to homosapiens, my recollections have afforded me a path to remembering my identity.

"I am an archaeologist, a biological archaeologist and my last known place on earth was Mosaic Caverns before I died in two-thousand-five! Do you remember Jürgen, do you recall our assignment outside of Medellin and how we were drawn there by something?"

Jürgen is unmoved by my revelations, "No Catherine. Honestly, I am at a complete loss!"

I look into his eyes and for the second time, I notice there is something not right about him.

"You were presumed dead Catherine." Riverstrike speaks with intense authority, "You and Jürgen's remains were never retrieved."

"No. Is it real? I'm not an apparition, am I?"

"You are very much real and alive Catherine. Jürgen and you encountered some form of species that for some unknown reason, could preserve you in hibernation, or some variety of stasis to prevent you from aging and dying. All I can tell you is at the time I encountered a technology emanating from Mosaic Caverns that was nearly impenetrable. In the end, I came across residual shadow markings on the cave wall created by immediate evaporation due to a sub-nuclear explosion. It most certainly was not the outline of a human." Riverstrike shines the light of his GPI onto the staircase before us. "Go down those stairs and be prepared to meet your destiny."

"Jürgen?" I look up to his face, he is holding a stonily cold expression, "What do you think?"

"I think we need to take a look-see." He takes the first step down of twelve steps, "Hold onto my hand."

The stone steps are a challenge to walk down, it is necessary to place one foot at a time sideways on each narrow step.

There is a buildup of heavy metallic ore minerals, rock dust and shale filings making each step treacherous.

We make our way into the cave opening at the bottom of the stairs and a massive chamber. There are stairways chiseled into the stone leading to higher elevations as well as to lower chambers as if constructed into a city-state. Most compelling of all, as we ventured into the various divisions were then hollowed-out spaces throughout the stone walls having the earmarks of individual living or sleeping quarters.

I stop to peer inside many to see etchings on the walls depicting vignettes of everyday life, hunters, kayakers, horses, birds, bison, reptiles, and hieroglyphics that I am unable to translate. This location may have served as a temple.

Jürgen reminds me the GPI will facilitate translations by capturing the images digitally for evaluation. Most of what is written are of daily life, the rest is human misology among the general population, and, to a smaller percentile, of great planning and organizing from the military leaders, the people of wisdom, and philosophers.

After hours of examination and venturing through endless passageways, the flight vest made the process less arduous where we never felt to lose our bearings, I estimate up to fifty-thousand occupants were living everyday life here.

Riverstrike makes it down to meet us after an hour and spent a couple of hours exploring with us.

"Why is it such a unique and impressive find that has never surfaced to the public record?" I ask as this find wasn't in any of the

Online files I researched.

"The cave was first known to be discovered in Nineteen-hundred-nine and I said, there were thousands of artifacts, including mummification, jewelry, and statues, some of known Pharaohs, others of cats, sphinx idolatry chiseled from the rock walls. All of it was confiscated by the government under William Howard Taft in nineteen-ten."

"The relevance of migration from around the world five thousand years ago indicates a transitive tendency of knowledge of the entire human race, and that genetic human physical variances are within a mere three percent or less of RNA coding." I formulate, "The spread of the human seed is not a hierarchal one, and our differences are due to the environments human tribes survived in over two-hundred-fifty-thousand years.

"What matters above all is your talent to contribute, support, and innovate for the 'wellbeing' of the human condition."

Riverstrike replies quickly, "Culture's span eras Catherine, an epoch if they possess an inspiration of knowledge, and ambition for exploration, expansion of their civilizations to prove dominant by making an impact so indelible it leaves their cumulative imprint on the universe. The Romans had it, the Greeks, Chinese, and the Egyptians to name civilizations of immense import to the human condition in every genre of life; here, this cave exemplifies Egyptian conquest encircling the world. And now I, along with the GPPJ, the EZS, represent human's conquest of the universe."

34

Graduation

For some say the fascism of Nature is the final fascism. The laws of nature in creation can be emulated. The constructs, nature, the building blocks. The forces of power, catalyst, osmosis, the altering of aesthetics through erosion, the transformation of matter into various states, liquid, gaseous, solids, electromagnetic, nuclear, pressurized gases, and combustible and non-combustible are examples of nature's identity.

"The human is nature, as with all emotional, physical, creative imagery and all specific sub-sets of these states are representative of nature. The fascism of nature is what it is."

"Only where, but Mother Earth, do icebergs exist finally melting into the oceans empty of fish, or any sea life? As the heightened temperatures of the thinning atmosphere are destroying all plant life, wildfires taking down the huge Amazon, are not as rapid compared to the mining of gold and other valuable minerals. The access to a huge fortune of precious rock and minerals extracted from the asteroid belt has helped offset the practice of mining in the forested areas on Earth.

"It's all made mostly of what humans are made of . . . And what humans take too! Anyway, my name is Kariana."

Her mother stands proudly behind her precocious daughter, "Tell them how old you are Kariana."

"And I am eight years old!"

The applause from the graduating class of twenty-three-fifty-two Adolescent Children Rehabilitation for Educational Success is as appreciatively loud and heart-warming as any of the two-million classmates. Kariana's retelling of her youth in development brings tears to her eyes as the ability to recall precious long-lost memories of how she overcame momentous adversities is as freshly heard from her mouth to her ears as anyone in attendance.

"Emboldened emotions from courage to fear, the disparities of vanquished by the victorious, the perception of hope exceeds the consenting fury of storms, of wind, water, heat, of Sun erode the aesthetic of what is created, through passing time all aesthetics achieve their demise, whether living animate or inanimate, everything that exists must perish, but, only where, but Mother Earth, and all its inhabitants to compose of it, is there the omnipresent truth of Nature's truths in conflict with Nature's self-perception through human senses.

"For that, Mother Earth, I offer you my invention, my creation of an aesthetic as beautiful as it is meaningful for sustaining all known Nature you possess, with replenishment of what existence has lost due to the inventions from the tail end of the age of barbarism, the end of the epoch Pisces, relenting to the birth of united humankind in concert with glorious promise of the epoch Aquarius.

"And I know now in my heart, my brain and through every part of me, all of you may see we are, each human life lived, a part of the overall aesthetic of our existence, and we may recognize the importance of 'wellbeing' of the human condition, experience life to inform younger generations for epochs beyond to the edge of existence within. Congratulations to the graduating class of twenty-three-fifty-two! You have the ability and opportunity to enhance the 'wellbeing' of the human condition for your generation, and all descendant generations to follow you."

She receives outstanding applause as she yields the GPI screen to the 'second in class,' Ofbyfor Jefferson who approaches wearing an orange gown and cap.

"Greed is 'bad,' and 'fascism' is 'bad,' and greed and fascism are one. The greed for more power, influence, money, self-adulation, and delusions of grandeur overtakes one's senses and perpetuates a maniacal infatuation to subordinate others and disregard for intimate one-on-one or of the masses. To maximize exposure of profitability by complete control of power and influence over news dissemination reeks of the foul breath of falsehoods.

"Yet in the context of a fleeting time of no more than one-hundred-twenty-five-years of age, we are pressed into achieving or not achieving in the context of our destinies, but in the deep pockets of the consolidation of money and power. The expense of receiving the Condorcet procedure should not be a question of 'deep pockets,' but a reflection of spiritual wealth within a human's heart and mind to assert in achieving the 'wellbeing' of the human condition.

"What do free people look like? There is no limit to what free people look like: The desire for freedom, democracy, and economy for all is caring for others, giving equal respect to anyone in need, or to anyone you see with the genetic variations determined by Nature's truth. To hold an appreciation for our differences as beauty because our variety is intended, we must hold trust in each other to pursue growth by investing our efforts for the 'wellbeing' of the human condition.

"You're rotting the grave with your greed. The advice for all the people," Ofbyfor says, "We shall unite to meet our ancestral mutual commitment for survival with the extended wholehearted focus on exploring space, protecting planetary and space station inhabitants.

"You think you're smart? With your hatred in your heart. Wasting your mind through time trying to find what? That you're a part of the problem against the 'wellbeing' of the human condition to exist in your presence? Then guess what? You exclude yourself with your thoughts from being a part of the 'not willing' to have basic, common respect for other human beings, homosapiens. Do you call yourselves superior to anyone within the GPPJ? If you are so superior to a race, then why do you work so hard to oppress others?

"Should your self-perceived superiority suffice in securing your place in a just society? Diversity is the lesson of, by and for all living beings as set in place by Nature's truth."

Immense applause erupts as he yields the screen to the first-in-class Lily Violyght who is wearing a purple gown and cap as she takes to the podium. Ofbyfor descends from the speakers' podium to take his seat on the dais.

"Mind control, emotional abuse, and megalomaniac tendencies are characteristic of the 'avarice' kind who subvert all for building up one's self-esteem — they are mean sociopaths and psychopaths.

"And . . .I follow the stars in the night sky to see what inspiration for possibilities is unfounded, and I see it is endless when the matter of the mind is in tune with love over greed-fascism. The former is the truth of the law, the truth of nature; the latter is corrupt, dishonest, and diseased minds as I termed as a fourteen-year-old: 'POOPERS': Profits Over Other People's Ethnicity, Race, Sexuality. Whoever tells lies murders a piece of the world.

"The poor, impoverished, interned for all people shall be considered as plant life, flowers and the suffering are to be attended to. When the fruition of financial solvency creates a healthier garden, then we achieve honor to Nature's example of cycle and rebirth.

"There is no greater accomplishment in human relations than overcoming one's own internal hatred and prejudices.

"We are amazed to think fruit flies often die on the same day they are born, and in comparison, to the life span of humans to some alien race's length of life spans, the human appears as a fruit fly to the aliens who possess life spans of tens of thousands of years.

"Everyone tries, vows, and participates to support the 'wellbeing' without malcontent. Everyone wants to expand the human race; we all have our warrants over our endeavors. It makes overwhelming sense to each of our eras to invest their common sense with all ideologies, where it is the same to benefit the human condition overall."

Lily yields the screen to Roberto as the classmates and guests express a strong applause for her, and a towering show of respect for the founder of ACRES, and the Director of WOCH, as the two exchange places.

Roberto is considered an Earth-lander citizen and the GPPJ citizen as his existence is mutually inclusive on Earth and WORB.

Good thing too as it is necessary for someone who is raised from the Earth who has actualized the dream of all dreams and his contributions to The Glass Planet and the overall 'wellbeing' of the human condition for underprivileged populations, a desire first developed midst the struggle of his peasantry upbringing in his formative years of youth.

"I can see now and know the pain, though we are born of different centuries, even of the different millennium, through our trust we share an unbreakable bond.

"Appeal to the genius of love and not to the ignorance of fear. The old generations are dying, and the young generations need hope, teach the genius by expressing it with everyone including enemies.

"Respect everyone for their differences and live together in our common humanity. There is nothing more valuable than that, looking after the common people.

"Adorning the GPI does not mean you are a cyborg or are you becoming one. You are merely adorning an apparatus like you wear any device, these are so readily accessible they do become a part of you, metaphysical as well as existentially by connecting intimately with the forces of nature.

"The meaning of life can be discovered in one individual's lifetime. The imprint you leave on nature's fascism whether or not overall it is positive will result in your truth. It must not be selfish, greedy, or achieved by force alone. In the lifetimes of people, some say the meaning of life is love, to have love, to give love, to be loved. I contend love is the catalyst for humans' persistence in existence.

"Love is the glue that bonds us all for overcoming the adversities, the challenges facing, confronting human survival in the existence of life. The ultimate bonding of present and future generations for the love of the miracle of life itself is evidenced by the dedication of the living to both the dead and the future living generations. To the dead not to be forgotten for their sacrifices made toward creating a more perfect union for future generations. The same dedication is for the present generations to achieve the intuitive 'wellbeing' of the human condition and pass it on to the younger yons.

"Liberty is worth more than the money you make, Liberty is what allows you to make your money, and all populations embracing liberty should be recognized, cherished, and heralded as the true source of wealth in the world. The full cycle is to return and keep in full participation all living humans.

"'Liberty without order is a mess. Order without liberty is a menace.' – President Theodore Roosevelt, the twenty-seventh President of the United States of America, the Fatherland of Liberty and Freedom for all."

"There's an arousing flourish of applause Roberto accepts with a smile and the placing of his hands overlapping on his chest, acknowledging the praise with great humility. He maintains a gracious smile, quieting the audience before continuing to speak.

"It Is in general terms and conditions of the standard of living, if maintained by everyone, forms a heightened level of positive awareness and influence in society.

"Human nature, it's who we are, whom we want to become compelled by the force of nature, good as bad, to know the truth is nature's reality, truth is good in human nature.

"The one final fascism is nature, in its domination of truth, what is the highest aspiration to seek other than the truth? All, including everlasting life or acquisitions of fortunes beyond lifetimes, have no greater measure than truth.

"It is our collective 'wellbeing' determined by our collective will to create the legislated philanthropy to secure the 'wellbeing' of the human condition in the pursuit of continued prosperity for all to earn.

"About revolution and the way of life, with the eliminations of humans' most rudimentary evil element, the spirits of people must realign themselves beyond previous beliefs, to effectively implement the best practices toward a more perfect union.

"By the rule of our moral compass go forth emboldened by a spirit strengthened by the creativity unleashed. To bring about new beginnings and continuously so with the constant evolving of technologies in efforts to unlocking the secrets of nature near and from afar."

Roberto does have his moments of robust eloquence.

"Love is an expression once understood between people, even animals in many examples will affect the growth of bonds in trust. Trust is required for building the blocks, the connectivity between us all which inspires action of goodwill. Goodwill is in the faith of people being compassionate about people who are experiencing similar and diverse adversities to the pursuit of happiness, and virtually every moment in our lives.

"May I ask you who are you enthralled about? This Earth is hardly ours, as humans in general, never mind the nutcases who believe they inherit the Earth ~"

The crowd of forty-two million observing from the grounds on ACRES to the thousands of monitoring platforms hovering twenty feet to two hundred feet above in a gradation to the slightest margin encircling the seated graduating class of two million students receiving certifications this day for occupational work, shower him with laughter understanding the context of his joke.

"As of today, this remark elicits laughter. The topic was always of grave concern and a constant ignition of human conflict. What did we learn after the perpetual war? We can agree as we are all born on this planet, then we are all 'stewards' of the Earth.

"The participation of the entire world community to join into a concentrated effort to begin human ventures into deep space but also the need to sustain exponentially growing generations must be addressed to ensure their prosperity.

"The Earth, therefore, as all of existence is unanimous in the presence of 'being alive.' Although the fact if we die off in generations, the Earth will persist, substantiating itself to fend off the ailments of extinction.

"We, as a race of humans must hold on for dear life. To go forth, graduating class of twenty-three-fifty-one, take the world into your loving arms, give back your appreciation for those who in loving sacrifice has made the present possible for your 'wellbeing.' By making the necessary sacrifices, in the quest of building the plans for providing human preservation, go out of here to pursue your dreams and fulfill your promise to your ancestors to broaden horizons in pursuit of perseverance of the human existence."

Roberto's comments are met with appreciative applause, long-lasting after demonstrating his grand eloquence as a mindful champion of peace, love, and respect for the 'wellbeing' of the human condition.

After the founder of ACRES gives final comments, the graduates receive their Occupational Work Certificates. Half of the graduating class will be, if not already are, employees of disciplines of their choosing.

Most of the remaining graduates will be reporting for duty as Elite Zealot Sentinels between RAKLAV HQ on Mars and the rest on the DEN SS.

The five newest Cadet recruits are born leaders, a cut above the other ACRES recruits, and are a team for special operations designated under my command.

As liaison to ACRES as a trainer in Martial arts and the ethical standards to abide by in GPPJ moral conduct codes, and as a RAKLAV Commander of the ZS, alongside Kariana designated Senior recruiting coordinator, we trained these five trailblazers to excel in defense of the 'wellbeing' of the human condition, and how proud we are as they're the top five graduates in the entire class.

35

Same Truths

Jürgen has been away many hours of the many days he promised to be with me, as many weeks have passed turning into several months.

I was finally able to catch up with Kariana and Roberto after graduation. ACRES began an early training program for children who, at fourteen years of age, begin the indoctrination and physical conditioning to become members of the Elite Zealot Sentinels by their graduation at nineteen years of age. Their training includes learning the five deadliest Marshal Arts within five years, then finishing a Doctorate in biophysics engineering by the age of eighteen.

The final year of the extensive training is focused on the operation of navigation systems including voice and EZS interface controls for orbiters, RAKLAV shuttles, and interplanetary cruisers.

In terms of the last six months of training for the likes of Ofbyfor, Lily, Triessence, Kanga, and Auloi, who are now nineteen years of age in twenty-three-fifty-one and are eligible for assignment in the SSN, their advanced training for use of the Elite Zealot Sentinel Interface, a.k.a. EZSI, is complete.

Their first space assignment is the training for the usage of advanced systems being fitted to the Dark Eagle Nest SS in its preparation for interstellar travel.

Here is something to note: The Dark Eagle Nest SS is closer to Mars now than it has ever been since the initial launch from orbiting Earth in twenty-two-sixteen, having traveled within ten million miles of Mars.

The time has come for the overall servicing of the space station's nuts and bolts while offering the crew of two million staff their first terrestrial time in ten years. A long-awaited extended rest on planet Earth. Tourism councils expect the influx of vacationers to provide a major economic boost across all of society to the tune of Forty-three-trillion-five hundred billion monetary units during the Dark Eagle Nest space station's twelve-month terrestrial leave on Earth.

The mission includes the mobilization of a caravan of space stations voyaging jointly with half of the Star Gazer Tour ship fleet comprising thirty Star Gazer Mars Tour ships. Riverstrike intends to transport seven-million-five-hundred thousand EZS troops to the Spark Creation Genesis solar light system, the soon-to-be neighbor to our solar system.

My firsthand account I witnessed while as a trusted confidant in direct conversation with Minister Riverstrike and his advisor Simon Noir. They often share uncensored thoughts with me and gave me insights on highly classified missions.

I am presently the lead liaison and Headmaster overseeing the enlistment program at ACRES representing RAKLAV. As a ZS General, I coordinate the training program while personally interviewing the program's instructors and the enlistees themselves.

I find the GPI informs my reasoning by enhancing my cognitive abilities to enable deducing my memories previously limited by oppression while under the control of ZSI.

As I sense greater awareness, I acclimate to my past amazed and frightened by thoughts of what happened to me. All refugees from the vivariums are subject to centuries-old systematic deceit in abducting then brainwashing hundreds of millions, like me, our right to live in freedom denied.

I instruct my recruits that no one person is above another abiding by the economic theory of the human will and the ETHW is no longer a theory, it is a truth with monetary units representing the physical manifestation of the human will.

I make it clear as a sunny day, a choice one makes to declare their moral values living within the GPPJ.

I intend to use the wealth of information I have from my experience to weigh down on the Minister, as well as the man Patrick Riverstrike, into a slow, humiliating decline in the ranks of the GPPJ.

At all costs, I must remain dignified, and honor myself in the here and now by unveiling his scheme to the GPPJ. The uproar from exposing the plotting of the hijacking of SGMT ships will cost him his station in life, his title, and the pure greed-fascism he harbors within will sentence him to the banishment of the Condorcet procedure.

It all began in the twenty-twenty's when the major data-research and security associate RAKLAV would alert the power structure of my intuitive abilities to innovate new technologies. Patrick Riverstrike had his eye on me from my earliest days of accomplishment.

He put me under a highly classified designation as a revolutionary against the fossil fuel industry. RAKLAV was interested in controlling my genius to exploit it, not to nurture it for public consumption. My identity as Kariana Yahreah was methodically erased from the GPPJ soon after my feigned death.

By now he had developed programs controlling data points to identify every single human in the world's population. Another aspect of his plot is to control the development of human relationships to confiscate top talent like me as if a human chattel.

It was Riverstrike who interned me to contain and maintain me as a cooperative. At first, I made it difficult as I was indignant and resolute in my convictions and passions for engineering.

Riverstrike needed to draw me closer with the plan to 'hire' me to help engineer the space station network. I espoused vitally needed strategies to reallocate fossil fuel production to colonize the Moon, Mars, and the asteroid belt.

Once he quarantined me from the general population, I became consumed by the work and was afforded special trips around the world for designation in secrecy, but I was surveilled to catch any relations that may jeopardize my secrecy or worse, cause me to be recognized for my identity in public.

My cover name Janalake was designated by Riverstrike. And that was the time he created Simon from the DNA frozen growth technologies. Not an exact clone of Jürgen, but a strong resemblance.

It wasn't long before I began to question the changing responsibilities as explained to me as a national and world security expert. My assignments diminished my social connection with anyone. The prime directive of my responsibilities kept me at RAKLAV headquarters on the DN SS and amended to the DEN SS when the two behemoths unite as one gargantuan space station. Most of my command over many more decades included reconditioning and training refugees at the Zealot Sentinel headquarters on Mars and vetting out those qualified for integration into the GPPJ. It was only a matter of three years before he developed the prototype of what would become the Zealot Sentinel interface.

Once administered, the credit for engineering designs for space stations and the orbiter craft and the outlines of a solar coil recharging station for large output cells in solar recharging lots facing the Sun twenty-four hours, seven-days-a-week, were all transferred to Riverstrike to his benefit in monetary units per the ETHW.

With inventions, he never contributed input, but he found a way to take credit for the inspiration of the concepts, by having the capital needed to invest in proper research and development to bring the concept to market. If the desires in my heart and mind were not stifled by the ZSI, he never would be able to keep up with me.

His control prevented any separation from my identification as Janalake to the point of not to even thinking of the possibilities.

This initiated a meteoric rise in his influence, logistical control, and stewardship as Minister of the Interplanetary Space Station Network (MISSN); he stole the keys to the car having the foresight of his greed-fascist ambitions.

Kariana's firsthand account supports the information I have discovered in my research on Patrick Riverstrike. He also maintained his position as CEO of RAKLAV, despite public outcry jeopardizing his popular influence. To absolve criticism of his apparent monopoly he adopted the space station network of Governors as a board of directors of the RAKLAV as oversight to the powerful position he created for himself.

By the year two-thousand-eighteen, he retired from military life to join the new personal data collecting organization RAKLAV. The transformation of the organization's activities has transpired entirely under his guidance to the dark space, literally and figuratively, that permeates all human activity.

"There came a time by twenty-two hundred," Kariana said, "Riverstrike relocates the RAKLAV HQ beyond the asteroid belt in a massive, top secret, a nearly undetectable dual space station called 'The DEN SS.' This name alludes to the function of the space station as a beacon of communication into the universe. A colossus in information gathering, as RAKLAV is headquartered there, mostly keeping me removed from the GPPJ and to always have me nearby until I proved my loyalty, indoctrinated, and conditioned to become commander of the Zealot Sentinels."

The ZS operations HQ is stationed on Mars and is home to the top-secret indoctrination and conditioning methods to vet out refugees who defect from the Earth-lander vivarium communities.

When these people defect, they become refugees who are indoctrinated by the RAKLAV forces upon being detected by various probing devices placed to monitor the appearance of humans not in the GPPJ. Their personal information is recorded by RAKLAV who watches over the population with face and voice recognition as they are considered human capital stock. The division of the world's societies for a hierarchical order never occurred to anyone to be unethical, the classes, especially the ruling class, are considered ordained by God.

Kariana presents a content chip, "No matter how you represent yourself to faith, we all answer to the same truths, we all are a part of what makes each of us."

She has downloaded her memories on a digital 'cerebral recording' chip allowing for Roberto, the five cadets, and myself to review.

"Riverstrike uses the vivarium societies to study for marketing purposes, initially described as a tool to maintain peace. The nefarious intent for each society is to condition each 'human capital' by identifying, and if necessary, creating new businesses or products to appeal to the masses for consumption, to shepherd the flock of 'human capital' into unbridled expenses encouraging each person, each citizen to become 'debt slaves.'

"The vivarium refugee, before admission into the GPPJ, goes through indoctrination in part for analyses of who we are individually from DNA and RNA genetic engineering purposes.

"What those purposes might be are classified as top-secret information, beyond my security clearance. The other part is the downloading of the memories utilizing the digital 'cerebral recording' technology to confirm the preference data by aligning it with the researched data, and then to erase the memory of the 'debt slave' formatting system in use to prevent any suspicion of aberrations, or inconsistencies that may be detected by the GPI formatting, therefore, revealing the meddling of Riverstrike's treasonous, exploitative programs."

"This is a striking revelation." I say in disrespect and with anger, "To overtake your emotions and deduction of reasoning to do the bidding of one man."

"Except for you Catherine, he is looking for something more from you than being human capital. No one is conditioned for five years."

"How long is the indoctrination and conditioning program usually take?"

"Only six months." Kariana stops speaking to fix her oversoul eyes directly into mine, "He envisions you in a significant role involving the Spark Creation Genesis project."

"He will not need to abduct me, or fake my death," I can state firmly, "My lackluster lifestyle, and my reduced ability to contribute to the 'wellbeing' of the human condition, it has already become clear to me what my next calling in life will be: Employee of RAKLAV, Commander of the Zealot Sentinels, the sworn conscripted defenders of the 'wellbeing' of the human condition," I say in a way mocking the idea to get a response from Kariana. She breaks a smile, as she squints her eyes in contemplation. "The maintaining of the leadership position will ensure my safety, restore my capability to contribute to the 'wellbeing' of the human condition ~ at the expense of leaving my present state of mediocrity."

"Oh, I get it, Catherine, that is funny!" Her genuine laugh reveals a sensitive, mindful thinker of refined acuity. I smile to share in this moment of levity.

"As soon as I consented, Jürgen submitted the proposal to accept Riverstrike's offer post haste. Though I thought the opportunity is nefarious, it is as Qyxzorina explained to me, that I am in a special position while in the good graces of Riverstrike to hold influence over him.

"This is not to be underrated given the Minister's reputation celebrated for popular designs conducive to a futuristic motif, a discipline I will benefit from learning from him."

"Do not believe the LIES!" Kariana offers casually with sincerity, "If there is anything you have a question about, I'm here for you Catherine."

"Thank you, Kariana. He is a major philanthropist and one of the top influencer's to many SSN employees, entrepreneurs, industry leaders, and established financiers, all giving of themselves to support the 'wellbeing' of the human condition under his leadership. It would be an interesting place to be, in the middle of it all ~ the GPPJ and SSN, ETHW markets, and where does Patrick Riverstrike fit into it all?

36

JJL JO ETHW SSN TRAGEDY

The two-week voyage to Mars allows for time to review the data Roberto offered me on the vivarium settlements. I listen to the narrative by JJL JO as the corresponding images are reflected on the brain screen:

"Capitalism operates often beyond democracy, in tunnel vision pursuit of monetary profits, yet capitalism can only flourish and persist in a democratic society.

"The issue is democracy needs to have its legislative hand guiding the moral, ethical, and fairness of the invisible hand of the free market, by which the 'wellbeing' of the human condition is secondary to the exploits of individual economic interests, feeding oligarchy greed and breeding the fascism of inequality.

"For example, the democratic society given the oversight of private industry regulates and administers penalties to corrupt corporations by liquidating assets and ownership, therefore, rescinding the sole rights to the products and services and redistributing the patents for technology to businesses less developed in the same discipline of the corrupt corporation.

"Capitalism, in the era of modern barbarism, was prevented from growing broadly to equate for success for all, due to the maniacal greed of those who acted as a blood clot to the brain on the notion of 'reasonable fairness' towards all. Claiming money is free speech, special interest lined the pockets of politicians as the vehicle of persuasion, in substitution for a reason and balanced manifestation toward the 'wellbeing' of the human condition.

"The self-entitlement by individuals as well as corporations, excuse me, as major corporations were deemed by the Supreme Court as being people too, revoking the ban of corporations and unions limitations on expenditures and electioneering communications.

"It is against federal law to own a person and when contested in the highest court of the law at the time, the 'Organizations of Perforation,' in other words loophole exploiters, were struck down and all ownership of major corporations rescinded and turned over to the oversight of Public Trusts. The maintaining of the accumulation of wealth in the form of hard assets and interest on investments were deemed as being hoarded 'never to be spent in a lifetime' kind of wealth. The ruling opened the door to the Economic Theory of the Human Will for the 'wellbeing' of the human condition through the opportunity for all with equal basic modernization of the varying world economic systems, all rooted in capitalism, then adapting to specific needs and quirks unique to a region's geographical makeup.

"In the economic theory of the human will, wealth is defined to replenish the basic needs of the hundreds of millions living below the poverty line, to lift above deprivation of basic survival needs including health care, education, and employment.

"Otherwise, this capital is at a point of immobilization for any practical involvement or improvement on this categorical imperative.

"Capitalism in the post barbarism era moving forward into the Age of Aquarius epoch meets its intended promise to the free market system. The systemically impoverished masses are now afforded a leg up, as fourth-generation citizens and older generations are. By having the basic needs of survival met with the expectation of marked upward mobility from each generation onward.

"Rigorous education, training, and opportunity to be as self-sufficient to shop on one's own and able to obtain other upward mobility identifiers such as a home on the market for sale. It is a simple process in theory but complicated by outside sources.

"The other essentials for a 'leg-up' including basic solar, wind, electricity, water powered housing, and housing amenities, include one reliable natural energy sourced mode of personal transportation, nutritional allowance for sufficient healthy dietary intake, one stipend for commercial or business attire, one stipend allocated for everyone from the fourth generation of citizenship on for general clothing purchase, and to receive one GPI for all educational, communication and healthcare needs.

"This is capitalism when it meets its intended promise to lift everyone in a 'free market' and capitalism is not to be a breeding ground for what is officially known as 'Greed-Fascism.'

"Countries around the world who have deemed it illegal for people to be owned, therefore ownership of any corporation, deemed as people by the same court, above the financial median line of one-hundred-million dollars is illegal and will be deemed public trusts and operated by an ongoing succession of C-level executives who may serve up to ten to twenty-five years upon annual term elections involving the GPPJ voting for candidates. The scrutiny of the masses reveals the most qualified of the candidates."

The playback is silent for a moment, then resumes, "A meteorite shower bombards two space stations, the Tigris SS and The Glass Planet SS. Tens of thousands of crew members of each space station are impaled by space rocks ranging in size from shard-like balls to three-inch pellets. Emergency rescue units from the SSN Emergency Response Team based on the Wishing Well SS allowed saving many more from deadly exposure to extremely harsh space conditions. Initial reports by SSNERT confirm catastrophic damage impacting various independent system operations equipment considered critical to maintaining suitable conditions for basic survival activities are either beyond repair or have been obliterated.

"The death toll of twenty-four thousand is expected to rise dramatically for those impaled by the meteors who are accounted for were mostly contained within the fuselage and independent work areas located in the interior sections of the space stations. There are at least two thousand GPPJ fatalities unaccounted for whose workstations are along the perimeter of the fuselage. These crew members are believed to have been propelled into space, without any of them in protective space suits exposing them directly into the void of space. Their bodies dehydrate as all fluids are boiled down and vacuumed from their mortal coils.

"These images aboard The Glass Planet SS show where the dozens of pallet-sized meteorites perforated the fuselage traveling at speeds up to one-hundred-thirty-five-thousand miles-per-hour. The Tigris SS suffers critical damage drenched in the impact blood and smeared guts from remnant pieces, crew members' bodies sliced into shreds of flesh and bone within whole sections of the fuselage workstations before shattering into obliteration. –JJL, JO Lunar news reporting."

Gosh, those pour souls were gone in a blink of an eye. One-hundred-thirty-five-thousand miles-per-hour!

It was the most horrific tragedy I found in all my research in the modern era, Dateline: August eighteenth, twenty-one-eighty-three, only one-hundred-sixty-two-years ago. Not everything went smoothly in the development and construction over two hundred years of the making of the SSN and with no end in sight. Why should there be any end in sight? Another JJL segment to listen to: "The core investment was a biblical effort as the world came together on each subsequent project. The necessary resources provided by high-yield monetary harvester companies and governments from around the world assist in the ETHW combined with legislating specific laws to encourage the super- and ultra-wealthy money harvesters for their investment was all that was needed.

"Better yet I discover the investors of the very first permanent recreational space station to become known as the cornerstone of economic prosperity spurring a construction boom that has continued up to today. Once the first one became operational and self-sustaining, the subsequent space stations were constructed with greater efficiency, worker safety measures, and advancements in engineering for structural design, energy resourcefulness, propulsion, and the continual alterations to spacesuit ergonomics, communication systems integration, and joint, musculature, nervous system, and circulatory support made marked advancements in technology.

"With the prior enterprise of 'ferry rides' into the exosphere to experience mere seconds of weightlessness, wealthy tourists, some exceptions for others on charitable sponsorship, increased confidence in the needed investment to modernize commercial sponsored flights to the most anticipated weekend or two days excursion for two adults for fifty-million-dollars per.

"Reconstruction of The Glass Planet SS features luxurious lodging cabins with breathtaking views of Earth and the star-scape, even a performing arts center, technology center, museum of space exploration history and two five-star restaurants make it a popular destination point.

"The wealthy tourist is unanimous in seeing the potential of a long-term investment, if managed properly, The Glass Planet SS will be the number one tourist destination in annual revenue.

"The reality is the investors considering involvement must factor in their generational wealth, as The Glass Planet SS, built in twenty-three years, is a make-or-break proposition.

"The return on investment with only super and ultra-monetary harvester individuals does not make sound business sense. Either the life spans of humans will need to be increased, or most importantly the super- and ultra-monetary harvester lifespans.

"The volume of the masses with modest income production from the middle and upper-class living healthy one-hundred-fifty years can invest incrementally to make a fee of fifty-million dollars per adult.

"The hypothetical expectation of the age-defying treatments did not elicit favorable market activity. Until a procedure is proven safe and effective, the prospect of middle and upper-class citizens contributing to offer a significant impact on profitability was unlikely.

"Although when there is a will, there will always be a way. The Tigris SS was irreparable for active commercial use but was restored to be established as a site in memorial of the victims of the worst natural disaster inflicted upon the space station network.

"The popular success of Nativa City, South Dakota, the first city to be powered exclusively by natural energy sources, features environment-friendly corporations, and municipalities emphasizing pedestrian, bicycling and electric train transportation roads and parks. Implementation of new reusable technologies allowing for kinetic energy to be created from walking on stairs, floors, and carpets within all public buildings to be stored in lithium battery cells for off-peak energy usage. The year-round utilization of moisture, snow, ice, and rain converters purifying public drinking water stored in manufactured underground reservoirs is used in tandem with bottled water. No gas stations within the city limits, yet electric car charging stations in every parking space within the city limits."

"The major factor of Nativa City's success is the awarding of all retail, service, construction-related, and development contracts to Nativa citizenry and newly established firms, with young talented leadership, and a work history long enough to establish proof of competency.

"The influx of burgeoning companies with blossoming creative and innovative talent help to distribute wealth in the overall economy to multiply the high- and super-wealthy ranks, providing volumes of The Glass Planet SS tourist.

"It was still the Pisces epoch, and the era of barbarism was holding fast until greed-fascist persuaded themselves to consider the viability of the long-term profitability of a space station network. The shrewdest decision to be made was to, for the first time in world history, invest major capital into the procurement and eradication of the impoverished, destitute, neglected, uneducated human populations.

"The scope of which included the reform of a prison system always seeking for perceived criminals to maintain profitability in tandem with unreasonably harsh legislation written into the criminal justice system. The reform of the prison system would result in the elimination of what will become an obsolete, antiquated system.

"In this way, the 'Economic Theory of the Human Will' came to be known. 'The physical manifestation of the human will' is economy, hence money: What will you do without it? What will you do to get it? What will you do when you have it? Providing the training and tools necessary to earn a solvent livelihood will transform the self-perception of a nation's populace into a level of measurable equality based on participation, performance, and respect for being essential to one another.

"For purposes of speculative profits, the world's population, with the United States of America, the world's most industrious citizens to all have environmental energy technology skills and to receive continual training learning skill sets for at least three different job disciplines as so desired by the employee, establishes a malleable workforce ready for continued expansion into the solar system.

"With the diverse multi-cultural, multi-ethnic, and the greatest free loving religious diversity is ever known since the start of the modern era of Enlightenment, the wave of progressive advancements is embraced by all who are involved, and said progressive advancements are here to stay!

"Early images of The Glass Planet SS exterior are a majestic conception of an architectural facade and functionality. Solar energy panels cover the entirety of the fuselage providing the benefit of protection from passing space debris, even a shield deflector designed inspired by the hardest insect shells, composed of diamond-infused steel, to handle meteors traveling minimum speeds of fifty- or sixty-thousand-miles-per-hour.

"According to the American Meteor Society, meteorites usually hit the Earth's atmosphere going around one-hundred-sixty-thousand-miles- per-hour. Meteors enter the atmosphere at speeds ranging from twenty-five-thousand-miles-per-hour to one-hundred-sixty-thousand-miles-per-hour!

"The compact structures built from inside the protection panels are the twenty courtesy cabins for two-night benefactor guests. In later images proceeding every ten years or so, intended additions constructed on Earth, are transported to be 'attached' to The Glass Planet Space Station. –JJL, JO Lunar news reporting."

37

Hidden Money, Terrible Horror

On the Dark Nest SS, a city-state exists. The vertical length of the space station is equivalent to the height of two Empire State buildings, a height of minuscule stature in open space between Mars and the perimeter of the asteroid belt, its assigned position is usually thirty-five-million-miles from Mars. Presently it is ten million miles within the nearside of the Moon, maneuvering toward Earth.

Its' operational purposes are multifaceted, the DN SS occupations include two million scientists, ZS support staff, and security. The average age to be first assigned to work there is one-hundred-twenty-five years of age and the average age of retirement is three-hundred-twenty-five years of age. This career plan allows for financing the maximum Condorcet procedure benefit affording one-hundred-twenty-five years average retirement before natural death.

The professional facilities include office space, chemical labs, biological labs, nuclear radiation labs, propulsion labs, and deep space exploratory scientific experimental labs.

The city-state offers Terra forming parks with organic plant growth, healthy green grass is everywhere on recreation fields from team sports to golf courses, rock climbing to sporting events, and hills and tundra enhanced by virtual encapsulation.

The variety of transportation modes include shuttle carts, monorail trains, and trolleys for mass transit; Bicycles, skateboards, and hover-boards are popular for physical fitness; Hover taxis and orbiters allow travel to ports around the exterior of the space station for rapid mobility.

Most of the lower third of the DN SS consists of cargo docks where Cargo Carrier Craft (CCC) transports the yield of gems, minerals, silver, zinc, and gold from mining belt asteroids. These one-hundred-ton loads are delivered by hundreds of thousands of CCCs arriving and departing on an hourly schedule. The cargo dock bay doors are constantly opening and closing with the flow of the transports; from a distance, they create an effect of shimmering lights, tens-of-thousands-of-blinks glowing like the abdomens of a colony of fireflies hovering thousands of miles in the breadth of width.

The returns in the mining of asteroids' dense metals include platinum, as popular as gold, there are other metals to be valued higher than platinum, and gold as belt asteroids contain a plethora of riches. The wealth generated strengthens the ETHW, as more wealth is attainable across the entire population of the Earth.

The other commodity of great import is the operation of rover probes exploring thousands of planets across the Milky Way for potential Earth-like qualities to serve as host planets. Many target planets have been identified by deep space probes that were capable to execute diagnostic imaging from great distances in qualifying each target planet's habitability.

The disqualifying factor is the human technological inability to travel to these unfathomable distances. Riverstrike, ever the innovator of real estate development filling the void of space, has achieved an 'end game' strategy taking the first bold step of human colonization beyond the Solar system.

The primary operational mission is the Spark Creation Genesis via the Prometheus One probe, to replicate 'the God Particle' and create a medium red Sun. Orbiting around this sun will be three individual synthetically constructed planets teeming with life and water. They will be on non-collision orbit trajectories all at the same distance from the medium red sun for environmental conditions optimal for photosynthesis.

The nine regional governors who have sworn loyalty to Riverstrike have initiated conditioning and reprogramming of the hundreds of millions of employees in the preparation for the intergalactic voyage to embark on with their space station fleets.

These space station fleets serve as the bearers of resources ranging from nuclear energy components needed to construct operational nuclear fusion cores to the storage of commuter vehicles and the volumes of fresh water extracted from Venus to maintain human life on the long voyage, and secondly, until the atmospheres of the three planets develop a water cycle forming clouds, releasing showers, and achieving evaporation of water into clouds again.

Medical apparatus, land-based infrastructure, and food cultivation are manifested from biophysics and biochemistry across the three planets like the predecessor to three-dimensional fabricators creating objects in slices from these science disciplines coordinated with artificial intelligence encoded within the 'glue.'

In the luxurious chief executive and VIP office suites equipped to inform and entertain with subdivisions of restaurants, music halls, and dance floors, integrated into conference rooms, banquet gallery halls, and inter-media virtual studios, Minister Riverstrike summons Admiral Barcarui and Captain Junior to review the progress of Prometheus One probe and Spark Creation Genesis mission.

Admiral Barcarui is Captain Riverstrike Junior's commander on the Spark Creation Genesis staff.

Admiral Barcarui prompts the Minister's son, "What is your prepared update, Captain Junior?"

"In summary, the mission is on course for reaching ground zero point of destination on the date April twentieth, twenty-three-fifty-two. The propulsion systems are performing as expected, the vital statistics are intact. The navigating system is impressive as it avoids the smallest of micro-meteorites. The graduated speed is currently three-hundred-twenty-million miles-per-hour, traveling at half the speed of light."

"Will the Prometheus One probe," Riverstrike asks suddenly aware of the possibility, "reach light speed before detonation?"

"It will not only reach light speed, sir," he speaks with a rush of adrenaline in anticipating his father's approval, "after detonation it will become light speed."

Minister Riverstrike receives his son's percolating enthusiasm as a garish display, "Settle down junior, we can pat ourselves on the back on April twentieth, twenty-three-fifty-two. Admiral Barcarui, how are the space station infrastructure and Terraforming support caravan holding up?"

"As expected, my lord. There have been no complications thus far. The nine governors are leveraging resources for ample sustenance of eight-hundred-million essential staff, including scientists. Captain Riverstrike Junior has executed his duties on point," Barcarui offers the Minister reassurance displaying spread arms with open hands facing up.

"Good. Junior, see it through and you will make me proud!"

"Admiral Barcarui will take command of the third Battalion

EZS and continue the training preparations of the troops for the commandeering of the SGMT ships based outside of Mars. These troops are to take a forward position on SCG securing infrastructure by overseeing the technologies installations created by the biophysics probes introduced about five years before our arrival."

"Will there be significant plant overgrowth covering the facility infrastructure?"

"There should be considerable overgrowth."

"Bring a Weed Wacker, Junior."

"I will depart for Mars," states Admiral Barcarui. "Where the troops are presently preparing plans to take over the SGMT ships for the journey. Each of the three battalion leaders will take command of ten SGMT ships."

The infiltration by saboteurs who were formerly decent citizens, now brainwashed and indoctrinated by Riverstrike's order to sabotage the SGST ships. The ZS personnel who are not going to afford a second Condorcet procedure and are vulnerable to die before age one hundred fifty years represent the ideal candidate for the grim handiwork.

If they succeed with their sabotage in destroying an SGST ship and live to talk about it, then their lives will be afforded an extension of the Condorcet procedure; compliments from the reserves of hidden fortune stored from the excesses of abundance contributed by the asteroid mines. We do not know exactly who the herders are. We see them, the institutions with the seed money. The investors of business get their wealth from mining the asteroid belt and it serves the population.

The communique was relayed from the SGST flagship Soley Leve from those reaching the Sun first, on this tour number ninety, servicing twenty-two-million-five-hundred-thousands of GPPJ in one year, to perform the slingshot maneuvers. All thirty Sun tour ships of the fleet are past the fifty percent mark of no return without any control over immediate propulsion, nor the ability to navigate due to major operations failures from possible sabotage.

Distress signals are received to indicate the tour ship's gravity systems' capabilities are disabled as well.

"This may benefit the capability of the ship's safe return, but the travel course may run adrift, leading any number of SGST ships into perilous wandering away. There are no specifications of the safety of passengers and crew."

"It can be some unforeseen deficiency in the shield against electromagnetic radiation field emitted by the Sun."

"Could be. Are there any information feeds relaying recent diagnostics?"

"No, nothing has been received in the last transmission window, by any of the ships!"

Admiral Barcarui shows increasing interest, "Where is the location of the flagship at last tracing?"

The SSNERT official Admiral J. P. Jones has the up-to-the-minute report, "The flagship Soley Leve completed the slingshot maneuver, as did four consecutive ships after the flagship."

Admiral Barcarui appears annoyed by this information. He paces precisely to the center of the homing map built into the floor recessed like half of a hollowed-out marble ball. The surface projects a three-dimensional outlay of the SGST ships stranded across the void of space from Mercury to half-million miles from destination Earth, "When does the fifth ship tracer location expect to register?"

"It already should have, as well as the sixth, seventh, and with ships in line. Their absence indicates they may have each veered off of course."

Admiral Barcarui responds with incredulity, "Do you mean they were taken In by the Sun's gravitational pull?"

Admiral Jones responds, "This is possible, but there is no way to verify their present location."

Admiral Barcarui takes a moment to ponder the realization of a cataclysmic disaster taking place some ninety million miles around the Sun.

Admiral Jones continues, "We are working on contacting the ships within two-thirds of the distance to the Sun using rocket probes and system diagnostics analyzers for possible rescue."

"How many ships?"

"Up to seven or eight tour ships may have completed their slingshot maneuvers, and there are possibly ten tour ships unimpeded."

The rapid communication exchange is possible by a network of satellite transmission buoys based on the Wishing Well SS and is dispersed every quarter-million of miles to reach Mars' complexes. The Glass Planet can boost the signal for the transmission to travel between buoys at a heightened level of speed.

"Unimpeded?" Admiral Barcarui asks.

"We have an initial headcount, and the second half of the convoy seems to have averted the danger."

"Terrible devastation," he says under his breath though clearly audible.

"Admiral Barcarui, this is Captain Junior, over."

"Captain Junior, this is Admiral Barcarui, over."

"Admiral, the SGST fleet had fourteen tour ships damaged or lost from saboteurs we suspect detonation of planted mines, but no confirmation yet. The first eight in the caravan have passed the Sun, but each is crippled without propulsion capabilities. The fourteen lost were the closest to the Sun making their orbit slingshot with the saboteur's damage exposing to g-forces greater than nine times the pull-on Earth, impossible for anyone to survive."

"The Sun's g-force is twenty-eight times that of Earth's pull, breaking the fourteen into shreds instantly drawn in by the Sun's gravitational pull. The remaining ten were on approach to the Sun but appear to have taken evasive measures aborting propulsion to enter sling-shot maneuver. Half of the two-million passengers on those first eight tour ships should be boarded on a Noah's Arc class evacuation ship by now. The SGST ships with the most efficient deploying of the evacuation procedures achieved one-hundred percent success rates."

"There is no excuse for any inefficiency in emergency evacuation procedures," Admiral Jones states to Admiral Barcarui.

"It is most untenable Admiral Jones. By my count, we can confirm eight tour ships, including the Soley Leve, to survive the sabotage and clear the wrath of the Sun. What are your recommendations?"

"Have the evacuation cruisers with less than eighty percent capacity return to the boarding docks of their assigned tour ships to evacuate remaining tourists. Send SSNERT commanders orders to assist the fledgling eight tour ships in need of evacuation and tow assist. And we need to establish contact with the SGST ships diverting their trajectory to evade the looming danger. They will get a hand with the assistance of remote probes providing guidance propulsion boosters to help taxi the stranded inbound ships. Request deployment of solar energy cells by the Space Truckers Union. They're to be designated for towing capabilities, to limit exposure time to deteriorating conditions structurally, and to limit the exposure to potential exterior hazards, such as radiation fields to further cause chaos."

The quandary of Marcel and Qyxzorina with the sabotage of the Star Gazer Sun Tour flagship is what caused the ship's propulsion and navigation operations suddenly to fail and leave the immense tour ship in a reckless end-to-end rotating trajectory. The impotent Soley Leve's circling to its' starboard side has a trivial effect on the occupants other than sheer panic. The gradual motion is imperceptible from inside the tour ship, but the knowledge of the loss of propulsion and navigation control has many pondering their fate.

Marcel is patched into the operations officer channel, "Is there any diagnosis on what happened?"

"No sir, Captain, the only indication is of possible sabotage. It's not an incendiary device either, it's a cyber attack and it was downloaded manually aboard the ship within the last week."

"Loud and clear, see what you can do to locate the point of infiltration."

Qyxzorina is checking with the chain of tour ships following their lead. Her sour face reflects the grim statistics on the stranded fleet, "SGST ships two through eight have cleared the Sun's gravitational pull in completing the slingshot maneuver."

"Each of the tour ships is similarly crippled by a cyber attack. SGST ships twenty-three through thirty-four diverted courses well before the approach to the acceleration point and report no damage whatsoever."

"And what about nine through twenty-two?"

"The whereabouts of their location are unknown at this time."

"They had no possible chance of escaping the Sun's gravitational pull without nuclear fusion propulsion, and to compromise the navigation system marks certain catastrophe."

"The tour ships' resilience to the Sun's volatility could have prolonged the suffering with steadily rising temperatures in their final minutes until absolute combustion occurred vaporizing each innocent life."

"It was more of a direct course into the Sun causing instant death, no suffering on the SGST ship. What can we do about emergency evacuation?"

"Emergency evacuation is initiated, and all twenty-six Noah's Arc class evacuation ships are being boarded."

"Let us hope only the propulsion and navigation systems are targeted."

38

A Fly in the Ointment

She launches the RAKLAV cruiser from the DN SS main hangar to cruise the short distance to dock on the DE SS on her way to confront Riverstrike.

A way to steer clear of a mind with vain tendencies is to understand empathy for the human condition, love for human existence, and think of others before you think of yourself.

She remembers an awkward disclosure involving Simon in a curious exchange they shared once.

"Simon, you were conceived in a test tube."

"More like petri dish but go on."

"And I had a previous life of promise; it was stolen from me."

"I never knew about that side of you."

"No, nobody would, because the record is over three hundred years ago when I died, and she was born."

Tilting his head toward the floor, "I do not understand what you are inferring."

She takes in a deep breath. Drawing from memory with her mother who would tell her to start in with a deep breath steadily inhaling then silently exhaling until her head is clear of the toxic emotions polluting her thoughts before speaking another word.

"Simon, you are easily confused as you cannot comprehend emotions, therefore unable to appreciate the emotional quotient. I know of your limitations wearing the ZSI, and I am without the worry of repercussions, though if I were to make a direct appeal to you to exact revenge on Riverstrike, I would ask your duty in loyalty to report me for incarceration."

"I am more aware as suspicion arises from rumors of you wearing the Glass Planet interface a direct violation of Zealot Sentinel Oath. And the incomprehensible words and behavior of the renowned Zealot Sentinel commander were informal, losing the discipline of her professionalism."

Her recovered memories are the fountainhead of her bond with Catherine. The insights unveil the hidden truth of crimes against the 'wellbeing' of her human condition, as well as of the hundreds of millions of Zealot Sentinels in her command.

At her peril in a blind rage, she disregards to conceal her pain and fury incited by these insights. She blazes the cruiser's propulsion upon docking on the Dark Eagle SS causing a fireball to flare entrails, as if dragon's breath, once oxygenated within the hangar air. The aggressive approach to the landing dock ignoring safety protocols gave a harsh throttling of security alarms.

She disembarks the cruiser and is greeted by Captain Junior, attended by a dozen Zealot Sentinels.

She easily could outmaneuver Junior and 'walk on the heads' of the other twelve ZS, knocking them down or taking them 'out' if required. The burden of unwieldy emotions will not get the better of her as she chooses to surrender without a fight.

At this moment she has the clarity to see not to harm any of the Zealot Sentinels as their support will be needed, once she is captured, to free themselves. By surrendering she expects to be on the fast track to confronting Riverstrike from a position of deference when he will least suspect a source of revolt.

"Looking well rested Junior."

Junior laughs a grizzled musing and signals for two Zealot Sentinels to bound her.

Junior steps up to her reach up and detach the GPI off her body.

"You're looking rather pathetic," he retorts staring directly into her lush brown eyes.

The hallways of the Dark Nest are steel panels with air ducts close to the ceiling every twenty feet. The design concept promotes cleanliness as disinfecting bots continuously traverse the hallways from floor to ceilings throughout the space station. The steel wall panels are to reinforce the integrity of the fuselage in the event of a meteor, or worse, a meteor shower from penetrating any critical mass.

He turns to lead the platoon with her as a prisoner marching expectantly to the detention block as she notices the route Junior was leading her on is not to Riverstrike. They were waiting for her all along, prepared with maximum security measures to ensure her detainment.

"Big guy," Kariana begs for his attention repeatedly, "Hey big guy ~ I'm talking to you ~ doing your father's bidding to gain his favor?"

He continues to ignore her.

"I hate to tell you this, but you're not even on his radar ~ reconsider now before I have to further humiliate you."

They enter a freight elevator, made a tight fit with the presence of Junior and each of the dozen Zealot Sentinel's bodies touching hers, boxing her in the middle between them. They will guard her to the point of physical obfuscation, not allowing her the freedom of movement to attempt an escape.

The elevator door opening is a great relief to her from being buried by seven-foot-tall, long-limbed males with groping hands. Two steps into the hallway her destination dawned on her recognizing the grimness of the cell block level robbing her of any sense of comfort.

They march her around a turn in the hallway and proceed to pass through the double bolster security doors leading into the cell block. A security robot is a sentry monitoring the activity of the facility while wired into the operating all surveillance systems, and to function as a physical deterrent to anyone entertaining ideas of an uprising.

Two ZS pull her by her wrists with her binds forcing her into an internment conditioner, securing the hatch where she is removed of her possessions, disrobed, thoroughly decontaminated, and ushered through to the inside of the detention cell where Junior and the platoon await her re-emergence.

"You can keep this hat on," he quips as he places a prisoner detainment cap on top of her head utilizing biophysics technology built into the cap to secure comfortably tight on the prisoners' contours of their head ensuring non-removal and capable of paralyzing a disobedient brain.

The platoon marches Kariana to a maximum-security cell where a Zealot Sentinel waits with a body cloth that he hands to her; with the other hand, the waiting guard held the force field door activation button to the cell. A violent shove by order Junior, she lands on the cell floor, her body smacks the surface cushioned only by positioning the folded body cloth gripped tightly by her bound hands to protect her head from contacting the steel floor.

They exit and Kariana lays face down, hands flat on the floor, in a manner of releasing tension and the continuous pressing toxicity of the betrayal of her abduction by Riverstrike.

She thinks of Roberto, and how she was so appreciative of his efforts and allowing her to speak and mentor the children.

A few deep breaths, exhale slowly.

Admiral Barcarui folds the GPI apprehended from Kariana before throwing it onto the table of the executive office conference room.

"Where did she get her hands on the Glass Planet interface?"

"It appears to be from one of the juveniles by the name of Gingi Grind."

"Weren't those apparatuses to be sealed away with all the rest?"

"Yes, minister. Janalake was assigned to secure the Glass Planet interfaces."

Riverstrike bites his lip, "What a disappointing oversight."

"How so?"

"She may become enlightened to the point of experiencing memories that would compromise her loyalty to the life she now lives."

He speaks his command, "Detainee block forty, image in cell eighteen-D."

A visual inside the cell with the Commander now meditating, legs folded with her hands on her knees palms facing up wearing wrist and ankle constraints.

"Breathing exercises." Riverstrike analyzes the situation, "Meditation to clear her mind of chaos."

Admiral Barcarui remarks, "You gave her everything she could ever want Minister?"

"It's all forgotten unless we can persuade her to go under indoctrination reconditioning, soon. She's going to be missed if she is unable to reconcile her past with her present."

"Then what?"

Riverstrike voices indifference, "We will be forced to leave her behind unless she changes her mind in the final hours."

Red and white lights begin flashing and a high pitch buzz signals alarm to a breakout.

"Someone is trying to escape," Barcarui is stone-face as he states the obvious to the Minister.

"Is that why those lights are flashing? I wonder who it could be?"

Barcarui takes the bait, "Commander Janalake?"

The image in cell eighteen-D is empty. Security tracking a display of the blueprint plans immediately illuminates her location.

"Of course, the air conditioning ducts, are obvious," Riverstrike forwards the link to Barcarui. "Did you receive it?"

"Yes, the security tracker is synced, and the Zealot Sentinels have received their orders."

Riverstrike is inconvenienced by this disruption, "Good work

Admiral Barcarui, not challenging work, but well done enough."

"Thank you, Minister. Should I lead detail to the flight deck?"

"No Admiral Barcarui, her leaving is the least of my concerns."

"Why?"

"Uncharacteristic lack of insight from you ~ Riverstrike offers a look in disdain toward Barcarui ~ If she's not leaving it's because she's coming for me, that's why."

"Make it certain minister?"

"Yes. Have a company of the Zealot Sentinels fall back on this position's perimeter. Give the order to monitor activity to the air conditioning ducts." He pauses to articulate his greatest fear, "I suspect she will find a way to avoid electronic surveillance as she makes her way through to me."

The holograph diagram of the mechanical infrastructure of the space station indicates the location of Kariana as she moves. The Zealot Sentinels are reconfiguring their positioning within the hallways of the Dark Nest mirroring her movement through the air ducts and the mechanical engineering nodes.

The Commander has a vantage point from above two Zealot Sentinels who are standing guard on the air condition duct vent she presently occupies. On a closer look as she peers through the mesh vent, she determines each Zealot Sentinel is brandishing a weapon. She recognizes one device as a stun gun with a 'snake tongue,' a discharging cord with a reach of one hundred yards, even in jagged or multi-corner passageways.

The other weapon she recognizes as a 'Suppressor,' the name describes its purpose. The handheld launcher does have a 'silencer muzzle' on the barrel. It is a pump action barrel that discharges a leather pouch filled with steel ball bearings delivering a bone-breaking knockout impact.

She speaks softly to herself as she plants her feet on the corner edges of the air conditioning duct, "You got this Kariana." She coils her body preparing to maximize her propulsion out of the air duct onto the unsuspecting Zealot Sentinel visible below.

From the Zealot Sentinel's position, all he can view is the mesh vent exploding into dust, then the smash of a heavy heel upon his forehead.

The Commander uses the solid heel to the one's forehead to launch a scissor kick, in a complete change of direction, mid-air, inverted as her legs extend above the other Zealot Sentinels' head to land harshly on each of his shoulders, forcing the release of the suppressor with a popping sound discharging a heavy canvas bag filled with steel ball bearings.

The force of impact from the projectile causes a dimple in the sleek steel wall plate revealing a glimpse of the bright pink insulation wall padding underneath.

"Local suppressor, a knockout punch, potentially lethal at close range," She whispers securing both weapons to carry with her, placing one in each sleeve snug to her biceps. She is aware to confront Riverstrike and retrieving The Glass Planet interface is the easy part; it's the ZS security contingent of one-hundred-thousand devotees who are the pivotal factor; there's no telling how many will support her cause.

The executive office is self-contained eliminating the possibility of gaining access to the inside, a stun gun cord will be useless without an access point.

The hordes of Zealot Sentinels attempting to prevent her from reaching Riverstrike never materializes. She stands before the entrance way of her unimpeded ease of movement.

"Janalake," she whispers firmly.

The barrier dissipates allowing her to proceed carefully with each cool, quiet barefoot step arriving at the corner edge of the open walkway to the conference room. Her neck fully extends enabling her to peer in where he is seated in the ministers' chair situated on a raised platform with a fifteen-step grand stairway.

There are wall-mounted screens feeding images to his brain screen monitoring the progress of the intergalactic deep space exploration missions.

She approaches the figure under a shadow cast from the grand stairway, she is up to the base of the platform, "Patrick, you fiend, face me! Damn you!"

"The Prometheus probes offer a variety of distinct and unique environs on extraterrestrial landscapes performing techniques searching for any form of life, as drilling into a rock for fossilized evidence or discovering microbes in deep thin crevices."

The figure remains seated as a light source dims the eye, "Have you lost the loyalty of the Zealot Sentinels?"

"To the contrary, Minister, they remain as loyal as ever."

"Janalake, my dear, why have you forsaken the Zealot Sentinels sworn allegiance?"

"Don't give me any of your lip service Patrick. My name is not Janalake, it is Kariana." He is as sincere and transparent in his slippery fork-tongue devious, scum manner.

"Kariana Yahreah," Riverstrike surmises, "Child prodigy if you want to know."

"Yes, do tell me all about it," she holds her cloth garment close to her body to conceal she is handling two guns though she is otherwise naked.

Riverstrike hums his vocal cords inhaling gently into a deep diaphragm, "For your talents, the powers that be, put you under a highly classified designation as a 'revolutionary' against the fossil fuel industry and the RAKLAV. The fossil fuel industry wanted you wiped out of existence. We, at RAKLAV, were interested in controlling your genius with an emphasis on not exploiting it.

"It wasn't long before you began to question the changing responsibilities as explained to you as a national and world security figure of interest, as Commander of the Zealot Sentinels. This made extraneous or casual relationships a risk and therefore you were deprived of social presence or connection to anyone.

"I approved and administered the Condorcet procedure for you. It was nearly the same time as my 'clone project' of DNA found in a sleeping bag. A clone of Jürgen as it turns out, in the form of Simon."

"Simon?" Kariana is not convinced, "Only one clone?"

"One illegal clone is enough to be condemned for," Riverstrike airs his modesty, "as well it is easier to conceal the fact with only one clone. There are only two creatures of value on the face of the Earth: Those with the commitment, and those who require the commitment of others."

"You dare quote John Adams?" Kariana condemns his show of arrogance.

"A few years before I developed the prototype of what would become the Zealot Sentinel interface, I needed to secure my senior officer staff to help recruit refugees into the ZSI. And like Adams and the Continental Congress, I merely teamed with you to recruit and lead the masses to an inspirational vision, a common goal for the greater good."

"The lesser good, no doubt about it. You are a conniving manipulator." Her development, power of innovation, and general popularity for contributing significantly to the 'wellbeing' of the human condition could easily have her claiming her rightful place as Minister of the Interplanetary Space Station Network. "You are not the 'wellbeing' of the human condition."

Riverstrike attempts to obtain her remittance, "It was a

prosperous move for the both of us, and I think many people agree, with my leadership, connections, combined with your talents, our collaboration has paid dividends for the both of us."

"I'm not having any of this manipulative talk, you stole my life. And for what? Your greed-fascism is for 'what?'"

Patrick smacks the tip of his tongue against the back of his front two upper teeth, "I'm sorry you see it that way."

Kariana is infuriated by the arrogance and megalomania God-complex exhibited by Patrick, "You abducted me, faked my death, and then brainwashed me!"

She is incensed to hear herself speak these words. Equally liberating to her as it feels unnerving, she trembles to a chill goose-stepping up her spine, revealing the true horror of the psychological pain suffered from the burdens of autocracy.

Having adorned the ZSI for two hundred years, after receiving indoctrination to disable recognition of emotions, unable to have moral judgment, passions, or feelings under the oppressive influence of the ZSI has made a desert of her soul.

Her jaw muscles flex as her teeth clench bringing her cheeks to a pucker, as her fists are limber, her eyes stare filled with deadly resolve; she takes two steps toward Patrick, then she abruptly stops.

Taking in breaths, she can hear her mother tell her as a child ~ Relax your heart, get oxygen to the brain, meditate, and visualize the goal ~ putting her mind at ease.

Kariana is worlds away as she held in her mind's eye the location of the GPI. Her eyes see through their lids expanding her mental reach to locate the GPI beyond the confining walls. She turns to complete a three-hundred-sixty-degree turn.

"Have you decided to do the right thing yet?" Patrick gently says, "Not to imply I hold your destiny in my hands."

"I will take your question as a quid pro quo, trying to leverage my ambitions against me? You hold no quarter over me."

She fixes her eyes on Patrick's eyes projecting strength and determination so infallible ~ Patrick is suddenly withdrawn, his eyes appear sullen, his upper lip quivers in response, as his resting expression reveals fear of her betrayal to his commands.

"No more," replies Kariana with the firmness of finality. She sprints up the platform stairs drawing her weapons from the sleeves of her cloth covering as it flails like a cape. The arousal she provides him is enough to distract him from the weapons once she leaps in the air; her movements further distract him in these split seconds when she uses the suppressor gun on him knocking him back to his chair. With her right hand, she hoists the stun gun to aim it at the fallen Patrick.

She fires the stun gun; the probes pass through Patrick's abdomen puncturing the back of the chair. Kariana lands on her feet next to the chair where the hologram of Patrick fades away. She steps to the minister's chair to extract the probes.

Focusing her attention directly opposite her position, she locks in on a secured gate that leads to the holding area.

Before taking one step down from the platform, the accelerated thumping from hundreds of Zealot Sentinel's march in rank and file fills the executive office in elbow-to-elbow formation.

The Zealot Sentinels come to attention and salute her as their Commander Janalake. Her most cherished proletariat still genuflect on her, and a core group within the ZS ranks reflexively venerates her.

With a deep breath release, she walks quickly through the formation to gain the holding area access door where she gives the drill command, "At ease!"

She jaunts down the access hallway to the holding area's secured door. The security code for the door is set to be simply 'River Lake' for easy memory for her as well as Patrick. She locates Gingi's GPI and takes the only spare GPI with her by fitting it on. She finds a proper service uniform to wear and retains the body cloth to conceal the GPI she wears and the weapons she carries on her.

39

Uniquely Zealot Sentinels

It's amazing the ergonomics of the cockpit as we accelerate to thirteen hundred miles per hour in fifteen seconds. "We're mere minutes away if you do as I tell you we will be in 'snug as a bug.' And no problems."

We love our private craft the Nebula Drifter, designed with all the amenities for interplanetary travel, but its speed will help our efforts become trans-formative. The sleek design on the outside is an illusion of the expansive interior accompanying fifty travelers.

"Catherine, Jürgen, this is Kariana over."

"You're on live, go-ahead Kariana."

"I know Patrick is intent on bringing the Dark Nest to the rendezvous point, over."

"Kariana, this is Olivia, over."

"You're on Olivia, over."

"Kariana, Catherine, and I will proceed to Martian City to search for our MIAs, copy?"

"Copy Olivia, our paths will diverge only a million miles from Mars. Then I will set a course for the Dark Nest to retrieve Patrick's strategic plans blueprint, and to record an update of the Spark Creation Genesis mission control room. We will rendezvous in Martian Metropolis, over."

"What condition are they in, indoctrinated ZS?" I ask wondering what to expect, "Did they go through the same deconstruction program as Jürgen and me?"

"Yes, but they did something unprecedented. They completely saw through the technology used to create the facade of indoctrination. After ten minutes I had to send them to a holding block before they made a mockery of the entire process in front of other, older recruits who are not predisposed to the dated technology programs."

"I never once thought we were plugged into a simulation." I marveled thinking how 'real' the experience is.

"Most refugees emerging from the vivariums are from cultures, societies that predate the twenty-third-century, but your friends are born in the twenty-fourth century and are not impressed with the technology, they can see right through it."

"How far out is the DEN SS?" I ask abruptly out of concern. "It is repositioning towards the inner solar system. It's a chance for the crew and scientists to have a reprieve, a homecoming of sorts. It is now passing Mars from thirty million miles out but heading toward Earth."

"That's interesting, they don't alternate time off and transporting by interplanetary cruiser?" I ask only as I am curious why such a space station of critical function is traveling out of position for rest and recreation when the DEN SS could transport thousands of employees on a regular schedule.

"I know we haven't met before, but Catherine told me about the racetrack accident; I want to tell you I am sorry for Simon's critical condition," Olivia states remorsefully. "Terrible accident, as was yours."

"Jürgen and I should never have entered the race," I admit regretfully.

Kariana is receptive to their condolences, "Do not blame yourselves. It was a 'freak accident.' It is good to see you recovered Catherine, I was worried I went too far in defeating you!"

"Thank you, but they had to resuscitate me from death!"

"I am dreadfully sorry having put you through that," Kariana expresses sincerely, "It is a result I did not intend on but wearing the ZSI compels me to disregard my true feelings."

"I didn't think you intended on killing me."

The next day she arrives and settles the RAKLAV cruiser on the landing pad by the main entrance to the Zealot Sentinel training and indoctrination facility on Mars.

She exits wearing a climate control helmet and light suit to protect her from the extreme sub-zero temperatures and radiation emitted from Mars' core. In three graceful leaps, she reaches the hangar door and enters.

There are two guards distracted by their preoccupation with

martial arts sparring.

As Kariana hustles by them, to their alarm, they stand to attention to the commanding officer's unexpected, sudden appearance.

"At ease," she states passing by them.

She focuses mentally on tapping into the open communications link to bring all levels of the chain of command into the main twenty-thousand-seat amphitheater.

She reaches the security node where a communications link is accessible to summon the elite chain of command to the amphitheater.

The corridors quickly fill with Zealot Sentinels in their SIUs, short for 'standard issued uniforms,' silver chest stripe and trimmings with a blue quality athletic cloth, or a gold stripe on black cloth, bronze on red maroon, racing to claim their seat on their way to the impromptu meeting called by 'Commander Janalake' to introduce Commander Catherine via hologram presentation.

Kariana makes it to the amphitheater in time to spy from backstage as the chain of command assembles into the twenty-thousand seat arena, she thinks of them:

They are all beautiful people I have known for decades, in some cases centuries. It is humorous how playful they are as they assemble, as their comrade I felt I must lighten their experiences day to day to allow them to make the most of their time with each other. Bonding is the most fulfilling emotional growth possible wearing the ZSI.

It is time to mobilize this bond, so unique to their development as adults in passionate to defend the 'wellbeing' of the human condition. As humans, they offer a rare perspective. They pride in themselves to secure longevity in this dystopic age of interned discipline in the name of serving the GPPJ.

She creates a visual 'brand' to reinforce her message, the one symbol to embody all that stands for liberty and freedom: The Statue of Liberty encircled by the thirteen stars representing the national flag of a burgeoning United States of America, combining both the Revolution for Independence and the Centennial celebration of Liberty and Independence as gifted from the outstanding country of France for the Centennial Eighteen-Seventy-Six.

Once the auditorium is filled, she emerges from backstage and is greeted by a cheer of confidence from her respectful colleagues. She raises her arms with palms open toward the loyal officers as to command their silent attention.

"Human life must be free, each respected, independent, if not independent then assured assistance to achieve independence.

"And the final aspect essential to the creation of human spirit, the development of the soul: The cultivation of a constant emphasis on the encouragement of expression of one's uniqueness. Therefore, I announce an official disbanding of the ZS and the banishment of the ZSI."

The sprouting up of murmurs across the room favors enthusiasm as the audience transitions to riveted attention.

Kariana continues, "The promotion of myself to General of Recruitment and Training at ACRES will mean that Catherine has received the promotion to Commander of the Zealot Sentinels. She is qualified for the position, I should know I have been training her for the past seven years for the job, without her even knowing it. Catherine, will you address the ZS command?"

"Thank you, General." I am unable to view the entire room through the hologram portal, but I feel very connected to their presence, "Without uniqueness, a society can become uniform in relations and work. It deadens the senses, and cuts us off from our emotional lives, reducing creativity to confusing dreams of utter futility.

"With unique individuality humanity breathes deep breaths of its strength in diversity, nurturing young minds and old alike to venture out to create and grow, with innovations for the 'wellbeing' of the human condition strengthening the visceral fabric bonding us all, every living human as well as every human that has previously lived.

"Uniqueness from others gives inspiration and proof we are very much the same, but in every individual, there is a uniqueness rising to ask questions about our nature, about everything known within our realm of experience, and individual uniqueness has the effect of creating new perspectives transcending progress in step with continuous changing times.

"Uniqueness also inherits questions with its development. It brings out the kind of innovations only the genius of individuality can awe us, inform us, unsettles us, make us think, promote the creative urge and it is us feeling our emotions, interpret them in the context of mutual respect as the reward of innovation, to be for all to experience."

There is a divide in the reaction within the audience.

Lower rank personnel are dumbfounded. The senior officers are delighted buzzing with the excitement of the possibilities of emotional growth.

"There is no reason to go through this world without the

opportunity to realize your passions." My words do not intend to incite agitation or anger among themselves, "An informed confidence in realizing an ideal, innovated for the 'wellbeing' of the human condition, attainable in your own unique skill set and ambitions. The concept of domination is marginalized as a practice from the 'age of barbarism,' is archaic, outdated, and obscene."

A gentle applause flutters like feathers of a flock of pigeons evacuating a New York City Street corner. One time ago they were no more as obtrusive as the squirrels moving along their way. With the advent of the popular Regional Patrol Light Cycle Assist (RPLCA), most occupants in certain parts of the city, like the shoreline, find they are the go-to commute option above the reservoirs that disrupt the activity of regular land craft.

Amphibious crafts are for commercial use and city transit.

In ancient NYC, the owners of an RPLCA tend to live on the second floor or above structures; most city dwellers use them and rarely choose to walk unless there is daylight. It is then when they step foot onto the pavement, they become engulfed, entrenched along the sidewalks and atop storefronts, worn from the years of not misuse, but of decades-long human absence and disuse. Pigeons galore, and their smelly pigeon shit is everywhere, along the walls where high tides wash up against them, to float the pigeon uric acid white yum-yum to the fish, and the bottom dwellers that remain find blind nourishment, unlike the eggs from waterbirds.

"What is most necessary going forward as we emerge from isolation is our mutual understanding of the 'wellbeing' of the human condition, our empathy for all who are in agony. We will heal through the support we provide each other. And all will abstain from further ignorance, indignities, and injurious contempt of human life," says Kariana.

The audience stands in ovation, some senior officers are moved by the animation of whistling. Like a handkerchief dropped to the ground, they settle down unevenly returning to their seats.

"At this time the DEN SS is closer to Earth for the first time in over one hundred years." I must do as when an angel speaks, with the clarity you can understand between the lines, "The explanation is the dire need for rest for the crew members by visiting Earth for a year."

Sgt. Gian raises his hand out of respect for his commander, "Why are you doing this General Janalake? Disbanding the Zealot Sentinels?"

"We are not disbanding; we are re-branding who we are to redefine ourselves uniquely in a changing society.

"The Zealot Sentinels are a creation of the greed fascist-minded Patrick Riverstrike, to serve as his guard." I need to speak demonstratively, "All of you, by the inherent rights given to us by nature, are being unjustly oppressed."

"My name is not 'Janalake.' My name is 'Kariana,' and like you Sgt. Gian, I was abducted, brainwashed through indoctrination, and suited with the oppressive Zealot Sentinel interface."

"The propulsion system is operated through GPI and utilizes 'ion imbalance' to combine with the body heat to generate energy. The exoskeleton is malleable once worn and contoured to the wearer's body so musculature can import its synopsis, therefore, receiving near-perfect synchronization in force and form of the user. This feature allows for combat readiness in any scenario: Gravity free; low gravity on the moon and Mars; underwater to sandstorm conditions; to open space physical engagement, impenetrable to present day technology."

Xiang Li heads over to a platform where he can demonstrate the final key features, enhanced strength, and force. The audience watches mesmerized by the diagnostic physicality of his warm-up movements. With great confidence does his glow shine.

He stands before an oak block five feet thick weighing one ton before performing a lunge kick to the exact center point of the oak block splitting it in half.

"This is an example of the space suit power." He follows with a high roundhouse kick landing on the top block severing it from the lower half of the oak block to land several feet away. "What do we do now?" Xiang Li asks as many others echo his concern in a flourish of rampant whispers.

"We take the RAKLAV initiative and as refugees, we must join the Glass Planet Population Journal." I am beginning to get the hang of this 'Commander business,' "Once fitted with the GPI, trust me, your lives will be liberated. Xiang Li, will you present the exoskeleton space suit demonstration?"

Xiang Li stands exiting his row and bounds onto the stage. "One moment," he says passing by Kariana backstage.

Moments later he wheels out a large block of wood and has one exoskeleton space suit.

"Everyone, Xiang Li takes the stage," Kariana steps away from the stage.

Gentle applause out of professional courtesy and respect for the Second Lieutenant revered for his honed skills and dominance in hand-to-hand melee.

The physically fit man of five feet ten inches is built with muscular density and an agile, thin body.

"I will demonstrate techniques in martial arts while wearing this advanced extreme exposure exoskeleton that will be useful in various space environments such as low gravity, zero gravity, exterior space station encounters, and underwater conditions.

"The space suit exoskeleton is innovation to the next level of human reconciliation between art and technology. It is the year Twenty-three-fifty-one, and we have a propulsion system to maneuver like an average flight pack while protecting a human from exposure to harsh space conditions. This design would protect us from the negative four-hundred-fifty-five degrees temperature of the 'cosmic microwave background' left over from the Big Bang that permeates the universe.

"We wear these and they will give us an advantage of mobility. We will be able to swarm like bees without a clutter of spacecraft with nowhere to go. I peel the exoskeleton's securing clasps on each side open and stand onto the foot contours where the feet are conforming for maximum comfort and support. I press the front of this exoskeleton to my face for the ability to pull the rear exoskeleton half to engage with the front in place, securing the clasps and allowing for the nano computer technology to provide a seal-tight bond. Oxygen is dispensed from micro compressors allowing for six hours of sustainable breathing."

The audience is not amused, but they laugh anyway, appreciative voices reassure one another.

"The strength and force are the highest graded in performance of any pugilistic exoskeleton made available to the GPPJ."

"Thank you, Xiang Li for your demonstration."

Applause for the Second Lieutenant from the ZS officers as he bows courteously leaving the stage.

"I specifically selected everyone due to your Regional Command Responsibilities within the SSN. There is an urgent need to equip about three-hundred-fifty-million troops spanning from the Earth to the Moon within the rotation of their mutual orbit."

"Where do we find enough of these GPIs? There are hundreds of millions of us," Sergeant Gian pleads in anguish due to the uncertainty of the proposal.

Kariana is charmed by the bombastic and mindfulness of Sgt. Gian's true personality. She is reminded of a classified project to re-engineer the ZSI to be closer to the GPI. This was not a RAKLAV project, it was an attempt by The Glass Planet and the commissioners of the SSN to modify ZSI covertly reassigning the enhanced ZSI to the Elite Zealot Sentinels, when after they became aware, enlightened, and more than capable of basic reasoning, achieving an ability to deduce outcomes based on a series of events, making them more efficient with their destruction.

"There are only nine-hundred-millions of us, about half are stationed on the Dark Nest or throughout the asteroid belt. We will retrieve what inventory is on the DN SS for those stationed there.

"With twenty-two billion in the Glass Planet Population Journal, it will take a little over a week to amass enough of the GPIs to equip all who will convert with us.

"The Dark Eagle SS is nefarious in its intent positioned between the Earth and the moon. Communications are conducted between nine space stations out of thirteen where governors are stationed throughout the SSN. They have initiated mobilization en route to depart the Solar system, all but one.

"Aboard the Dark Eagle measures are being taken to attack the core establishment of the SSN, along with The Glass Planet. The destruction of the GPPJ and the SSN infrastructure will set back progress on Earth for hundreds if not thousands of years.

"Riverstrike is in the grand position of slaughtering hundreds of millions of GPPJ and destroying The Glass Planet will leave six billion of the Moon residents without a sufficient chain of supply. The debris fallout from obliterated space stations will turn the moon's surface and its' residents into mincemeat.

"The Dark Eagle SS has lift-off from the Dark Nest SS and is passing by the caravan of space stations headed by the treasonous leadership of nine space station groups. Operations carried out by the recently sworn Elite Zealot Sentinel troops indoctrinated and conditioned for the preservation of secret covert separatist colonists known as the Spark Creation Genesis population journal (SCGPJ.)

"We have agents who are embedded in these ranks providing this reconnaissance. The Dark Eagle and Dark Nest space stations' Zealot Sentinel personnel have been subject to the reconditioning and scaled indoctrination process over the past five years and are now dedicated members of the SCGPJ."

With that Kariana is faced with hard silence from the audience of the ZS chain of command.

She holds strong as murmurs turn into utterances whispering into vocalization's espousing enthusiasm for the revolution for independence against the oppressive tyrannical forces covertly conspiring to inflict harm upon them, and arousing cheer emanates from a unified chain of command in support for her efforts:

"We are with you . . .We are with you . . .We are with you!"

There is a murmur in hesitation as the oath turns into cheers.

A sudden chant of "We unite" and "All for Liberty" breaks out distinctive at first before morphing into, "Protect our rights, protect all our rights, protect all *of* our rights!"

40

A Toast to Goodbye

It is an insult to treat a GPPJ citizen with this overreach of incarceration and the attempt to brainwash us," Spontaneous Instant sits in the cell block in a stylish sofa chair opposite Gingi Grind with a teapot cart between them equipped with amenities and crumpets.

"I say, old chap, it is the sheer rudeness in their handling of unintended guests that has me . . .pissed off," she remarks as she takes another sip of her tea. "I must say, all is forgiven with the quality of this delicious tea."

They are interrupted from enjoying a relaxing tea together when, taking the moment to soak each other in, admiring each other for their God-given physical gifts they sense a slight disturbance in their beatitude, the doorbell rings.

"Who would ring the doorbell?"

"I don't know," he is bland in his response. "Who is it?"

The cell door opens, and two Zealot Sentinels appear before them in the hall.

"We are to transport the two of you to Earth. Please, come with us."

"The two ZS's are our age?" Gingi whispers to Spontaneous Instant while gesturing to the two ZS's.

"Two ZS twenty-year-old's who carry auras of hopeless discontents," he speaks in a conversational volume. "What are you here for?"

Slack shoulders, untidiness in their gait as they walk, and a dreariness from the dominant male, "This life sucks, but we are ordered and honored to make your transport."

"Wait, you are Zealot Sentinels?" Gingi is irked by the

lackadaisical nature of the young men's approach.

"We are not officially graduated into the Zealot Sentinels, we are interns," claims the other young Hons, "If we knew how lame this job is, we would never have wasted our time volunteering."

"Wait, you guys volunteered for this clown work? What were you thinking?" Spontaneous Instant grills them in a tone parody to Gingi, bringing into question the young recruit's 'states of sanity.'

"We don't know, we thought maybe we would benefit from a life of enforced discipline and a regimen of healthy food and exercise."

"What are your names?" Gingi asks.

"My name is Tomas ~ he extends his left arm placing his hand on the other man's shoulder ~ this is my lover-boy-toy."

"And my name is Lonnie. Nice to meet you."

"Nice to meet you, too, I'm sure," Spontaneous Instant replies, "My name is- "

"We know who you are Spontaneous Instant." Tomas states with modesty, "You too, Gingi Grind, how could we not?"

Gingi is startled and looks at Sponti as he does to her.

"The both of you are legends to us after you disrupt the indoctrination and the conditioning brainwashing process," Tomas lets loose in a hullabaloo, "ZS recruits are no longer required to endure the 'fear-dome' of the indoctrination cycle after you exposed its fallacy. I think it's the reason why we enlisted!"

"Why couldn't you have said 'delusion' or 'myth'?" Lonnie asks with mild disgust.

"What do you mean? What is wrong with 'fallacy'?"

"It's your play on words Tomas, 'fallacy' as if you are alluding to the 'phallus'?"

"Now you are being ridiculous, Lonnie, let's just stop there."

"Hey, thanks guys, you are sweet," Gingi offers.

"We are thinking maybe we can stop in for a few drinks at 'Romulus and Remus rhythm and blues bar?" Spontaneous Instant suggests, "We know the bartender, Larry!"

Gingi adds, "Come with?"

The crew members of the Soley Leve are the best trained as evidenced by their perfect execution of evacuation protocol. Of the twenty-six Noah's Arc class evac ships, twenty-five were loaded to a capacity of ten thousand passengers and launched successfully on their way toward Earth. The propulsion capability is less than an interplanetary cruiser by far as the Noah's Arc class evac ships will expand the nuclear fusion reserves after five days at twenty-five million miles and cruise the remaining seventy-million miles on solar sails resulting in sixty-days of travel time. It will require strict adherence to the rationing of food and water to ensure a one-hundred-percent survival rate.

"Qyxzo, we need to make sure the evac ships are at capacity, if not, have them return to their tour ship to escort all tourists to safety."

"Understood. Marcel, what do we do about the tour ships?"

"Issue the order for the undamaged ships to set course for Earth. They should get about seventy-five million miles in the next ten days before expending the nuclear fusion coils. Admiral J.P. Jones must have received our distress beacon by now and hopefully, SSNERT will be out here to tow the Soley Leve and the other seven tour ships within two weeks."

"I have to say the composure of the tourist under these circumstances is remarkable, order was kept. It is time for us to join the rest of the crew on the final evac ship."

Marcel carries a stern look, "Near three-million people just died in the past eighteen hours. That is a little more than one-hundredth of a percent of one percent of the human population in existence."

He is overwrought with emotion as he hits his forehead with a clenched fist from his right hand. He starts sobbing uncontrollably, tears flow across his cheeks, and he is paralyzed by his anxiety.

"I know Marcel, you had no way of knowing this would happen," Qyxzorina says as she comforts him with a gentle, firm hug also crying. "It was Patrick who did this to us ~ he had to ~ who else is motivated by such greed-fascism?"

The mood could not have felt more copacetic to the smooth rhythmic strumming of the stand-up string bass, accompanied by the blues slide guitar and the soft brush sticks of the snare drum percussion, and the wispy hi-hat cusping.

The Happy Protocol Trio began their first set of the evening to a modest crowd of ten people, give or take the stragglers as the evening will wear on.

Larry felt every right to calm his constant anxieties by taking his prescription muscle relaxers and often melodic music causes him to think more about what his worries are than serving to help him escape his routine. The routine does not offer enough kick in his moment-to-moment experience, without any investment in anticipation of a promising future he is bound to mental illness, namely chronic depression.

The front door opens, Gingi Grind, Spontaneous Instant, and the two young ZS escorts make their way to claim the four bar seats together in the center of the bar.

"Hey, Larry, my man, how's the Mars crowd these days?" Spontaneous Instant approaches with his right hand extended to shake with Larry's.

"I thought you guys said you were visiting from Earth. Did you decide to move here or something?" He notices the two ZS escorts as he spoke his final word.

"You remember Gingi."

"How could I forget you Gingi, you are the brightest light in these parts in a while!"

"Thanks, Larry, for remembering me, I feel it in the heart coming from you," She stands on the foot rail to reach over the bar to hug Larry.

"How're things?"

"I'm making my way; every day presents new challenges. Had a little radioactive sand in my boot, no biggie."

"Isn't that the way with life, constant adversity every day from getting out of bed to making it back into it again!"

Spontaneous Instant smiles humoring himself, "Especially when you're trying to get someone in the bed with you at the end of the day."

"Except for these guys." Larry alludes to their company, "No offense, but if you don't mind me asking, do you always bring Zealot Sentinels wherever you go?"

"These guys? They're with us," Spontaneous Instant explains, "This handsome fella is Tomas, and his boyfriend Lonnie, right, Lonnie that is your name?"

"Yes," Lonnie responds taking Larry's hand in greeting. "Lonnie's with me. Don't try anything funny Larry ~"

"Nice meeting you. Are you stationed at the facility?"

"Yes."

"I've never seen either of you here before?"

"Lonnie and I arrived six months ago, we had to go through reconditioning to get suited with a ZSI."

"Tomas, invite some of your friends over to join us," Gingi

suggested, “I have something special in mind for all the boys tonight!”

“That sounds interesting,” Tomas places his arm around Lonnie.

“Here,” she extends her hands out, “One raspberry-purplish flurry gel for each. Take one, you’ll blast off in a matter of minutes.”

They reach to take the edibles for immediate consumption.

Spontaneous Instant taps Gingi on the shoulder, “They’re into men Gingi, what did you have in mind?”

She remarks coyly, “Sponti, what I have every man wants, namely flurry-gels, and I can carry a show-tune!”

“Gingi, you just earned a free round with that response,” Larry places shot glasses upside down in front of each of the four guests.

“Now we’re talking Larry,” Spontaneous Instant responds, “Put the first round on, four Martian Comets!”

“You got it,” Larry responds and looks over to the slide guitarist as the band is between numbers, indicating with a nod of his head for them to pick up the pace.

“Take an edible, the party must go on!”

“Indeed, dame?”

A person wearing a head mantra approaches Spontaneous Instant and Gingi, “What are you earthlings doing here?”

“Excuse me?”

“Escorted by ZS troops?” The stranger asks, “Are you some special disturbance we need to worry about? Before you wreak some havoc and cause undeniable pain?”

“To you, we are no threat. What is your meaning casting aspersions upon us?”

“You are a darling teenager, have you ever thought of shutting your unruly mouth, even for a moment of self-reflection?”

Gingi breaks in, “Hey you serpent, foulest of all inconsiderate people, why don’t you mind your own business?”

Tomas has overheard these comments and interrupts the stranger before he can respond, “Let me handle this Gingi,”

Tomas shows his palms to her, “You beguiled, infested creation of horrors, you know you are not allowed to be inebriated by decree of local jurisdiction of the Martian Metropolis.”

“My point exactly, Zealot Sentinel,” replied the belligerent drunkard, “I will relent my perversions.”

Tomas shakes his head as the offender retreats into the crowd. Turning to Spontaneous Instant, “There you go. He’s a well-known drunkard leach in these parts. Make sure you’re not missing any possessions.”

They look at each other communicating privately through their GPI, he starts, “Not too concerned about the ‘wellbeing’ of the human condition here on Mars?”

Gingi agrees too ~ at least there is an honor for the respect of others ~ then back to Tomas. “We’re fine,” they respond simultaneously.

Larry notices the looks of astonishment on their four faces, “Don’t let that careless drunkard get to you. He is an original settler and the last survivor of the first colony on Mars. He tends to show xenophobia around strangers when he gets drunk.”

“Is he the only crass and cross person on this whole planet?”

“Unfortunately, there’s a whole nest of them at the ZS headquarters. It can get harried in here sometimes and arrests are often made.” He looks casually about the bar making sure there are no on-lookers, “I want to share something with the two of you.”

He waves his hand for Gingi and Spontaneous Instant to follow him behind the bar well. The two get off their stools and carry their drinks with them.

“What are you hiding Larry?” Gingi asks.

Larry has his right hand on a panel door he slides open, “Join me in here.” He holds the door retracted turning his head to address Tomas and Lonnie, “Can you guys tend to the bar for a few minutes?”

The two ZS react with the attention of two sloths cuddling after emerging slowly out of their hibernation gaze and into each other’s eyes confirming they are up to the task by tapping foreheads before taking positions behind the bar.

“Thanks, we’ll only be a moment.” Larry looks to the band on break, “Carry on ‘trio!’ What do you think I pay you guys for?”

Larry enters the stairwell leading to a stockroom basement where Gingi and Spontaneous Instant are wandering around examining the metal crates of bar supplies, and a living space designed with a complete communication center, oxygen reserves, and sleeper beds.

“What a cool underground space Larry. What’s it for?”

“It is part storage room young lady, and part living space and part oxygenation cabin.”

“Do you spend much time down here?”

“I don’t, but you can.”

“What do you think Sponti?”

“What would you charge us for rent?”

“That impressed, are you? If you are planning to stick around, you can work here with me. The tourist season will be picking up as Earth and Mars approach their closest orbiting distance in three months."

"How busy is the tourist season?"

"I checked the launch schedules for economy tours on an older interplanetary spacecraft that use the less expedient 'slingshot' maneuvers around Venus, and they are sold out. Then the wealthier tourists arrive a couple of months later traveling in their high-speed interplanetary cruisers. That is once the economy class clears out and accommodations open on the Medusa class space stations."

"What are the living space capacities on a Medusa SS?"

"Seventy-five-thousand per vessel, times five vessels."

"That's it, Larry, we can rent a place on a space station and find work in hospitality."

"Not so fast Spontaneous Instant, you can work a menial job on the space stations, but you wouldn't be able to afford a rental on that pay. You will need to save some fiat, and what better way than to work in a bar receiving tourist tips while living rent-free?"

"You make a solid case Larry, definitely something for us to consider, right Gingi?"

"Most righteous, thank you, Larry. Now can we go upstairs and celebrate?"

The musical trio picks up the Caribbean rhythm to a version of the song 'Dindi,' as sung by a jazz legend, a robust mature woman's voice, with a side of 'scat' sprinkled in with the Maracas shaking dried beans, and Gingi breaks into a dance raising her arms, swaying them above her head while holding her beverage she scoots around Spontaneous Instant-on her toes as a jazz ballet dancer would.

Spontaneous Instant sets free alongside her, hip bumping to the bass, shoulder tugging to the saxophone, the horns are nose to nose in playful celebration of their youth and regained freedom.

Tomas and Lonnie join in disarming themselves at the bar as Larry secures their batons. The crowd's merriment escalates, their enthusiasm for happiness in this evening's happy hour to the rocking free form pannists creating the festive sounds of the steelpans. The music is piping hot, the jiving to lusty regions, the singing of the trumpet chants of old fashion Boogie Woogie blends in well with the swell of knees buckles, hard bass string spreads, and the blind-eyed beauty of jazz as the recreational edibles begin to kick in.

Olivia and I approach the Martian Metropolis in awe of the stylish designs of this most modern city, and with an eye on landing near the center of the popular mall zone. There are no vehicles parked where we did, and that is our intention. 'Romulus and Remus Rhythm and Blues Bar' is slightly off the central part of the mall and we would like to locate Gingi and Spontaneous Instant for rapid extraction.

The noise is isolated to areas, where there is air, in oxygen sound waves travel, and all is silent. This is the first time for us to explore the Martian Metropolis on our terms. The atmosphere is thin, and sand is often stirring up, walking the steps is bouncy. Our exoskeleton space suits with helmets protect us from the extremely cold temperatures and the radiation emitted from the planet's core. Olivia and I enter the hallway complex and remove our helmets as we trot toward the swing of live jazz music.

The entrance doors are ajar for better ventilation in a low oxygen environment, the music is thriving with infectious unbridled happiness shared by everyone fortunate to be in attendance into the evening, approaching early morning.

"This joint is jumping!" Olivia exclaims into my ear.

"Let's grab this table over here," I point to two open seats, "they are probably from people on the dance floor."

We quickly move over.

"Doesn't look like any service going on, this place is past service!"

"We can sit a moment and see if there is service in a break from the action."

Just like clockwork a man walks over from the bar and asks the band to hold their tune.

"Okay, everybody. All right I'm sensing what an awesome crowd out here!"

A wild, inebriate-inspired clap of hands and hands slapping tabletops support cheers and jeers.

"And if you didn't know tonight, it is 'open mic' night!"

A smattering of mixed applause and the banging of tabletops with beer steins tails off to a toast, "Tonight, we have a first-time visitor to Mars, however, she's been here before, tonight is her first night of imbibing."

The crowd goes berserk with more cheers and jeers chugging down their beverages.

Kariana enters the bar and immediately spots me; I gesture with my hand for her to join us.

"Have you found them?" Kariana asks via a private channel as the room grows quiet, "Where is Gingi?"

"Take a look at who's going on stage," I said in excitement, like a proud parent at the school talent contest.

"Having said that," the man pauses briefly, "She has assured me she is sober . . ."

A single patron yells out, "Oh sure she is! Not in this room full of lushes!"

"Okay, let's settle down and give your love for the spoken word of Gingi Grind!"

Gingi walks up to the mic taking her time to set herself brushing her hair back with both hands, she checks her internal script prompter.

"This poem is entitled, and you may be familiar with it: 'The Voices Come Alive':

Anyone who loves life/ is open with their heart/ Will be open with their heart/ For it is all a miracle/ Any of us is here to experience the joys of Freedom/ To Love/ To procreate/ To build/ The aesthetic they desire/ Life is as beautiful/ As it is fragile/ Life is real/ as you can imagine/ the path to creating/ When our time comes/ when looking forward/ is broad and wide/ progress towards equality/ turns into a healthier all of us/ a 'wellbeing' of the human condition/ for all time before/ the Sun sets on your life/ Undefined, not well specified/ And lacking explanations/ we see our time shrink/ On this planet Earth, our home/ For rent, as life is just for lease/ There are no excuses when men are ruthless/ so why count the red stars from/ the white ones/ When knowing that our time/ will be simply done/ and the only/ Thing that matters/ will be how much did we care?/ How did we love?/ How much did we hate?/ Why did we die?/ How did we live?/ Be hopeful, do something/ You millions of a new age/ To change the/ Human existence/ Succeed into space/ In love and peace/ Through thoughtfulness/ Sacrifice and commitment/ To gain a better place/ Leaving all for successive/ Generations to thrive!"

Gingi brings her eyes to level with her audience. "I dedicate this reading to Kariana Yahreah, who is the Omni-visionary poet of great acclaim, an inspiration to me in my childhood, one eight-year-old to another. Today I celebrate her birthday. Thank you."

Gingi steps down from the stage and greets patrons in the crowd offering their praise for her reading of the classic poem. "You're all too kind," she repeatedly states over again as she casually makes her way to the bar seats gently quick walking by the deeply emotional crowd.

"That was a wonderful reading," I turn to Kariana, "Don't you think so?"

She is wiping tears from her eyes, "Yes it was, very much so!" Gingi walks up to the table.

Spontaneous Instant gives her praise, "Nice reading! You rock Gingi!"

"Thank you Sponti!"

I smile at her in approval, she smiles recognizing me, "Catherine, wait, where did you come from?"

"Earth, just like you!" I announce in jest.

"You're as inspiring as a songbird in the mornings of the Appalachian valleys!" Olivia states emphatically.

"What a beautiful reading," I offer anticipating her reaction to seeing Olivia and Kariana, who she is yet to know their true identities. Gingi turns her face slightly to view the woman sitting next to me.

"Hello, darling, I'm Olivia. I haven't seen or heard a reading done with such originality and emotional connection in centuries!"

"It's nice to meet you, Olivia, my name is Gingi," she offers a hand wave with rolling fingers towards Olivia. Her pleasant mood turns to a serious focus on the other unexpected face, "What? Commander Janalake? What brings you out to lounge with us?"

In her confusion she whispers to Tomas and Lonnie aside, "I said invite your friends, you guys, not your boss!"

Tomas and Lonnie raise their eyebrows and move their hands signifying their mutual bewilderment.

Kariana stands up and offers her open arms to welcome a hug with Gingi in appreciation for the reading, "Amazing Gingi, thank you for remembering my birthday, so beautiful!"

Gingi appears dumbfounded, she is careful in her embrace, "Thank you, Commander."

"Gingi," Kariana laughs lightly, "No Gingi, I am Kariana!"

"What?" The tears well up in her eyes to release in blush with her noticeably genuine expressions of gratitude for Kariana's legend.

"It is you, Kariana ~"

A round of applause interrupts with a smattering of clapping, then increases in participation sounding like popcorn popping from across the Romulus and Remus Rhythm and Blues barroom audience.

"How about a splurge of champagne for a toast to true genius among us!" Olivia boasts over the crowd stepping on top of her chair, "To Gingi and Kariana, may your natural affectionate friendship blossom, especially now how you both know who you are!"

There is great laughter ~ I raise my champagne glass hailing a toast I wish Jürgen could've been here to make for *me*.

41

Sabotage War

Sula appears on the command deck of the Soley Leve to Marcel and Qyxzorina's surprise. She is in wide-eyed appreciation of the magnificence of the aesthetic design, and strong, secure setting attendant to a sense of tremendous responsibility in conducting the ship's operations.

"Can we be of service to you, Sula?" Marcel asks glancing once to Qyxzorina to keep an eye out for this one.

"Why haven't you reported to your designated evac ship?"

"That is simple Ms. Astraea, I do not . . .plan on . . .evacuating."

"You can address her as Mrs. Etrion ~ "

"You both can address me as Qyxzorina, and don't wear it out. Tell me, Sula, why don't you want to evacuate the ship?"

"I haven't much time and I want to tell you a tale that will tell you all."

"Listen, Sula, this is going to have to wait, you can tell us later."

"I haven't any time later."

"Marcel, we can afford some time for Sula to tell her story," Qyxzorina speaks like a hostage negotiator, giving off the vibe that there is something to be learned from this gray head. "Tell me, Sula, why will you not have any time later?"

"You know, please do not mock me, I never asked for the injustices inflicted upon me over my life. My abduction was truly the end of my life, my living life, and now recently decommissioned from the Zealot Sentinels, I can no longer afford the Condorcet procedure and I grow noticeably weaker by the day."

"What is it do you want to say?"

"I once was prime minister of Afghanistan. Yes, it is true, and my rise from the dark ages of misogyny was historic and improbable, and so it was transcendence for my culture, and for the development of females around the impoverished world was achieved. I did not do it alone, for generations after generations the number of women who renounced their cultural oppression grew like wildfire, and equality of opportunity flourished in the light of the ETHW.

Thankfully, with the ostracization of those consumed with greed-fascism and the emphasis on the 'wellbeing' of the human condition, progressive efforts to enforce democracy are here to stay, burying the ambitious contempt by autocrats to practice the politics of imbalance and inequity."

"This is all very well and good what you say, and the archives confirm your existence. Why was your death faked in twenty-fifty-two, or why were you abducted?"

"For the very talents, leadership skills, knowledge of the Earth is for everyone, to my efforts in achieving equal opportunity for all."

"What does the term 'Eight tears old' mean to you?"

Sula takes a stoic posture as she looks intensely into Qyxzorina's eyes, "You seem to know a little more about me than I know of myself."

"You have quite a history, nearly three-hundred and fifty years of it," Qyxzorina reminds her, noticing the apparent depression she associates with her age. "The conditions of your era and the abuse, neglect, and misogyny against women in your culture are well documented. You were abused as a ~"

She breaks her intense gaze as her face falls sullen and her eyes widen, pupils and all, vulnerable to revealing her tortured childhood, she begins sobbing.

"Look what you've done Qyxzo; she's not going to die anytime soon. Sula, you don't plan on detonating a bomb or anything?"

"Marcel, please, be patient."

"I was raped for the first of many times at eight years old. Abused, intimidated not to speak, and brutalized whenever I read a book. Knowledge is power, and that is why I speak to you now, in the name of the 'wellbeing' of the human condition. Riverstrike has selected candidates like me whom he considers expendable due to our decreasing value in achieving his ambitions. He no longer needs my abilities for training officers, he reassigned and promoted Commander Janalake to the rank of Brigadier General overseeing the training of officers and conditioning ACRES recruits for the EZS."

"What is the EZS?"

"Elite Zealot Sentinels, as much cyborg as they are human, the ACRES recruits are considered the cream of the crop for top command, something called a homo-excelsior experiment. But it doesn't matter anyway. Riverstrike assigned one infiltrator per tour ship to download a cyber attack into the navigation and propulsion operations. He does not want to destroy you because of your innovations, but he wants as much destruction and death as a distraction to his plans of getting a sneak attack underway."

Sula looks at the vast monitors that reflect the brain screens of all evacuees, "By the time they get back to Earth, there may be no space station network remaining."

Marcel is irate, "The back-stabbing Patrick Riverstrike, to hell with you! What are we waiting for? We need to get on our way Qyxzorina."

"Come with us Sula, we will get you back safely," she says extending her hand out to Sula.

"But I must die here, this is my suicide mission."

"Suicide mission? These rigs are going to be towed back in two weeks, come with us and you will have enough units to acquire the next two rounds of the Condorcet procedure."

Sula takes her hand as Qyxzorina receives it warmly, "Marcel, order that evac ship away and hurry up along!" She escorts Sula towards the body transport bay where they are going to fast track to the Blister Cruiser docked in their private executive hangar.

"If it's worth anything, I deleted the cyber attack downloads on the remaining ten tour ships once I witness the traumatic horror of destruction they cause to the convoy in the chain of succession."

"It is worth a lot more than the reward you will get, Sula, but the lives you saved in the name of derailing this unspeakable devious action speaks to your faith in the 'wellbeing' of the human condition."

The dedication and loyalty the Zealot Sentinels demonstrate in response to her leadership takes a few words of explanation to convince them to follow her commands in achieving a takeover of the Spark Creation Genesis control room. To successfully lead a suppression against the high command insurrection it is incumbent to permanently disable the Audio Fragmentation Suppression system (AFS) capability on both the Dark Nest SS and the Dark Eagle SS. As one unit, the DEN SS has moved within Mars's orbit of the Sun and is gaining speed.

"The time is here Catherine and Olivia, to take down the AFS. Catherine, we should go in to have each other's back. Olivia?"

"Yes ma'am?"

"You should stay in the cruiser and keep an eye out. If you see anything suspicious, then let us know using this private line."

"Anything suspicious? Hell, everything is suspicious looking to me up here."

From the observation platform in the Spark Creation Genesis mission control room, we are mystified by the thousands of empty seats where engineers, flight technicians, and other specialists monitor the over fourteen hundred Prometheus missions ongoing in perpetual operations to be monitored.

We test our GPI connection with Olivia waiting in the RAKLAV cruiser.

"Catherine, Olivia, this is Kariana over," she has her brain screen on to share what she views remotely with us. I do the same.

"Kariana, this is Olivia. Where are You? Over."

"Olivia, you are loud and clear. We're in the Spark Creation Genesis mission control room on our way to disabling the Audio Fragmentation Suppression system utilized on the Dark Nest and the Dark Eagle space stations, while they are presently joined as the DEN SS. Are you receiving the video feed, over?"

"Kariana, I'm receiving both of your transmissions in high definition, over."

"Catherine, as you can see a substantial portion of the workstations are vacated. I have no understanding of why at this point, but the good fortune is that our path to the AFS is unabated. We can approach it and access its internal operations drive and permanently disable its function, at least causing enough damage to require a complete replacement of the hardware infrastructure, over."

"Kariana, this is Olivia, over."

"Olivia, go ahead, over."

"Kariana, are you certain it is worth the risk of being apprehended attempting to disable the AFS, over?"

"They couldn't hold me down for one second, plus they do not know we're here, over."

"Kariana, the GPI is translating spiked stress levels. I can feel your nervous energy~"

"It is my heightened awareness, no time for nervousness."

"I can't wait to take a ride with you Kariana," Olivia disregards protocol in her excitement. "You must have some cat-like reflexes in evading space rocks."

"I read you loud and clear Olivia, but that is a topic better explained by the technology in use." She stands in place taking herself off the comms link to speak to me directly, "Are you sure you want to stay with her? I'm beginning to think it may be better to have you bring Olivia back to Earth. You are at risk without any training or experience in mechanical environmental hazards."

"I feel quite capable of watching your back if you should be exposed to any hazardous materials. We'll have Jürgen meet to join us, then we will return Olivia safely home."

"How long will that take you from now?"

"Just about two days we will reach the space station network, then Jürgen will board, and we can drop Ms. Olivia off at the country estate."

"Darn!" Olivia exclaims under her breath.

I look at Olivia on the brain screen to see her genuine disappointment expressed by her furled lip, arms crossed at the elbows, and humor-laced frustration from understanding why her trip must be cut short.

Her eyes roll into mine, "You will make sure Shane stays out of trouble?"

There's a hopeless morbid sentiment in her awkward 'say something' moment.

"Of course, we will do the best we can to bring everyone home safely."

I see Kariana enter the Spark Creation Genesis mission control room. Kariana carries a graceful gait, along with an air of confidence, the posture of a gymnast with fluency in her step makes her one cool cat.

I watch Kariana's movements inside the mission control room as she approaches an entrance to the mechanical engineering room housing the critical hardware to be sabotaged. "Catherine, I am going to insert the prongs of the taser gun behind the console panel and with the emission of seventy-five thousand watts of electricity the circuitry board should overheat and incapacitate the system."

"Kariana, please do not risk injury." I turn around to figure out the best place to hide from an EZS response to the explosion, "I'm ready when you are."

The field of vision is limited to the console panel as she affixes the prongs and suddenly her transmission is interrupted by a blackout.

"Kariana, do you read me, over?"

There is no transmission, no signal connected, and the mind screen feed is pitch black.

"Olivia, this is Catherine, over."

"I'm sorry Catherine, this is Olivia, go ahead."

I'm not certain what she is 'sorry' about, "I lost Kariana on my end through the GPI, and there is no outlet on Kariana's end."

"Catherine, what do you think happened?"

"I don't know, obviously we lost the feed."

The situation could not be worse for us as we have no communication with her, and it seems highly improbable that she would not have anticipated disruption in our feed link and not inform us of the possibility.

Suddenly I have a bizarre thought: ~ I can't believe you took that woman with you in my place. ~ It is Jürgen. ~ Why not, Olivia and I have grown close. She's a great friend of mine. ~ His voice answers me, Great friends. ~ There's a noticeable bitterness in Jürgen's temperament, "I think the kick to your head has a lasting effect on you."

"Kariana, this is Catherine do you read me, over?"

How frustrating it is to feel so far away from noble minds.

She steps down to the control room floor and proceeds to the primary mission hub as she adjusts her GPI lock. She is going to pass me by without detecting me under the stairs, behind a sliding panel.

"Hey Catherine, come out from there, all is clear."

Before I say a word, she is sliding the panel back extending her hand and I join her in viewing the immediate surroundings.

"The empty seats can be explained, the staff personnel huddle around the massive monitors in the furthest section from us," Kariana peers around the wall corner to get a better view, "The display is the final stage of the Prometheus One probe's deployment."

A series of blinding white-light flashes is indicative of the massive explosion in succession, the catalytic transformation is something never witnessed by anyone.

The creation of a star in deep space, with space station planets in orbit, will someday serve as a refueling and relaunching base for future exploration missions to Alpha Centauri.

The monitoring hub is malfunctioning with disruption in the video feed suddenly ceases operation altogether. I follow her reactions as she looks over her shoulder to view the plumes of smoke emanating from the mechanical engineering room where the AFS is smoldering from her act of sabotage.

"You did it!" I said before being interrupted by a burst in jubilation with cheers, clapping and handshakes involving the thousands of personnel huddling around the Prometheus One control room grips her attention. On one side she beams in pride for the success of the scientist's long, difficult, patient journey to see the creation of the first human-engineered sun.

On the other side, "The AFS is destroyed, he has no defense against The Glass Planet's AFS. There is no time for delay."

We quickly make our way across the empty half of the control room floor towards the three-dimensional imagery hub centered in the Prometheus One sector, displaying on a high-resolution screen from transmissions in a deep space point of interest, is the medium size star, the result of the Spark Creation Genesis project? It's hard to believe.

The feed is of a never witnessed by human eyes event, the birth of the first human-made star captured by monitoring satellite probes designated for this assignment to relay the content to the Dark Nest. The observatory deck telescope also records the images of the overall scene from its great distance and takes the feed hours to transfer to the observation screens and logged into the micro-memory files.

This is one of those rarest human-inspired events, impacting the human experience it hearkens back to the invention of the wheel, sliced bread, the first utilization of fire, and the evolution from hunter-gatherers to an agricultural farming civilization with livestock and irrigation, at the beginning applying buckets of water directly onto crops before canals, hand-dug-trenches, dams, dikes came about.

The same irrigation techniques evolved over the millennium are deployed by the child visionary innovator Kariana Yahreah, insights resulting from the culmination of growth in knowledge passed down through the generations to her.

Techniques to enhance the growth of crops, forestation, ocean plants, and coral reef health exist as life support for the Earth's ailing environment.

Similarly, this miracle of the creation of a medium star is a moment of transcendence for the path of human achievement beyond space exploration to the point of human aesthetic design for prolonged survival amongst dark matter through deep space exploration.

42

Mars: A Fight to the Death

Spontaneous Instant and Gingi Grind stir the emotions of the population of Mars' civilians enlisting the help of the ZS to stand against a small but formidable force of EZS, stating on the public interaction forum, "The invalidity of the whole Zealot Sentinel indoctrination process is a misanthrope illusion. The duty to preserve the existence of humanity is paramount. God speed in the defense of our Martian civilization."

They shelter in place with Lonnie and Tomas at the Romulus and Remus Rhythm and Blues Bar. From this location, they expect to be safe from the pending battle while Larry keeps serving them his Martian Comets.

"The wealthiest ought to be grateful for their opportunity and subsequent successes to the country and its masses in the setting of a democratic, capitalistic society. To make so much off those who appreciate you, must be responsible to give back to create a better union. At the time so few were considered people, less given any rights to freedom. It is the marketplace of ideas with the invisible hand allowing for self-interest, freedom of production, and consumption with the First Amendment the factor of voice given to the previously silenced. Look out the window to see what evils hinder human existence from reasonable continual growth in all facets of survival.

"It is progress based on lifting the floor higher toward economic success for all by conceptualizing industry for the mass population into space. Work hardest on driving and do not deprive others.

"Look at your prosperity and realize behind you should never be scorched earth, use your prosperity to lift those who afforded you the wealth you obtained from them. Virtue is not ideal; it is an expression of love for your fellow human beings." Spontaneous Instant claims,

"I'm an Epicurean. I am committed to the pursuit of happiness as well as the desire to avoid pain. Life and liberty are now institutionalized, and happiness is the never-ending pursuit!"

"Me too," says Gingi Grind, "It's best when we bond together, one may bond one way, another may bond another way, in The Glass Planet, we bond for 'the better of together,' no matter how or whom you bond with."

"For together we survive our timid daily adversities," continues Spontaneous Instant, "For the nurturing of familial generations, Democracy is a given right by the fact of nature, every individual has a moral compass and a brain potentially harboring logical and moral principles based on reason," Spontaneous Instant slurps down the remaining cocktail extending the empty glass to Larry for a refill, "but keep in mind the most ardent rule of the GPPJ is of the collective consciousness, there is a love there in the collective consciousness anyone can connect to expecting a 'wellbeing' of the human condition."

"All you have to do is download the app!" Gingi lets out a guttural laugh crouching over the bar as she is feeling the effects of her third Martian Comet.

Spontaneous Instant asks, "What is going on here?"

"There's a battle for the tour ships." Tomas, inebriated, responds in pompous drunkenness, "Aren't they?"

"Shouldn't we be joining the fight, Tomas?"

"Two drunk bitches like us?" Tomas spreads a smile across his face, "What fight?"

"The fight outside, you know?" Lonnie, seeing the look of skepticism on Tomas' face, has let go of his sense of urgency. "Sad. Incredibly sad."

"Don't feel so bad guys," Gingi says attempting to console them. "Tomorrow will be just another day in the life for all of us."

Spontaneous Instant sips at his refreshed cocktail, "Look at it this way, in another one-hundred years you will look back and say, I'm glad I didn't get mixed up into that frivolous violence to die like millions did die meaningless deaths that day."

Larry is resting against the end of the bar listening to the four young lovers, "That's right kids, value your lives. Youth is too often wasted on sacrifice. Instead, celebrate the love you share and get blind drunk, and dance the *fight away*." He moves to pour himself a low ball of whiskey, "Here's a track of your song Gingi. This time by Frank."

He activates the song then reaches below the bar top to set the special mood lighting deep blue. 'Dindi' instrumental prelude fills the air bringing comfort to the solemn mood.

She places her arms open for Sponti to slide into her space and lock in an embrace. They begin a two step holding each other snug, and the slow dance allows for his long legs to envelope her from mid-thigh down to their ankles rubbing, legs grazing, comfort in their knees bumping, Spontaneous Instant brushes his left cheek to Gingi's left cheek.

"Let's go away, Gingi. Tomorrow if we can."

She whisper's in a warm breath, "I love you, Sponti."

Their lips press to a deep kiss, and their lip skills are dexterous, maintaining a passionate grip, and it sprouts happier spirits within.

The two pairs solemnly embrace each lover's body in a warm caress, intoxicating themselves to oblivion, into painless escapism.

The Zealot Sentinels at the proper time with their indoctrination and conditioning will attempt to prevent the hijacking without regard to their own 'wellbeing.'

Zealot Sentinels poor out of the hub to intercept the EZS from hijacking the SGMT ships. The EZS is equipped with firearms integrated into the interface technology enabling them to fire bullets at two-thousand rounds per minute per firearm.

Two-hundred-million Zealot Sentinels are led by Xiang Li, Parsiak, and tens of millions of mid-level officers to secure and defend the Martian Metropolis and the ZS headquarters.

"Xiang Li, what can we do to save the tour ships?" Parsiak asks as he is second in command to Xiang Li in the defense of the Star Gazer Mars Tour fleet.

"Against this firepower, we can only die!"

The EZS, led by Admiral Barcarui intend to displace the civilian tourist on the thirty SGMT ships by hijacking and occupying them with seven-million-five-hundred thousand troops.

"Seven-million-five-hundred thousand EZS versus two-hundred-million ZS without firearms but equipped with the martial arts weapons," Xiang Li communicates from the ZS HQ control room. "We will have to throw everything we have at them."

The landing port for the massive SGMT ships is sixty miles from the ZS HQ and currently houses the entire thirty tour ships of the Martian fleet.

The seven million-five-hundred-thousand visitors from the GPPJ are residing in luxury accommodations in Martian City as well as the five Medusa class SS surrounding the planet. The civilian population is not prepared for violent incursion by the EZS, they're no match against the technologically advanced interface, even with the exoskeleton space suits.

The massive dock for the Star Gazer Mars Tour ships spans three hundred square miles. The tour ships when docked are maintained by a minimal rotating crew of five thousand at any given time per ship.

The EZS easily swarm the dock with platoon formations of five-hundred thousand troops coming from all directions of the docks. The minimal report from a firearm would be impossible to hear where sound waves do not exist, only a few thousand ZS troops present on the outskirts of the three-hundred square mile chain of dock platforms were massacred. Boarding and taking command of the ships is a breeze as the civilian crew surrender without a fight.

Parsiak does perceive a strategic advantage, "While the ZS troops are dedicated to defending the SGMT ships, the talons of the Medusa class SS can in effect halt the launching of up to twenty-five of them. The Medusa's are ten times larger than each of the tour ships and by the sheer rigorous construction and weight by latching on to the bow of each SGMT ship, each of The Medusa class space stations twelve talons can snare most if not the entire fleet."

"Yet the death toll will be high for us against the Elite Zealot Sentinels with their unrelenting prejudice against us," Xiang Li surmises. "The Medusa class space stations are designed to deflect meteorites and small asteroids, not to harness the immense power of an intergalactic tour ship!"

Fifty million ZS troops equipped with innovative propulsion space suits form an attack force to attempt to intercept the EZS invaders. With slightly more than a seven-to-one advantage, the Zealot Sentinels hope to overwhelm the EZS despite taking heavy casualties against the outlawed firearms. The strategy is to rush the docks in overwhelming numbers and occupy as many of the SGMT ships to prevent launching, followed by gaining defensible positions from within and around the occupied SGMT ships.

The momentum is with the EZS early in the battle and, to the demise of the ZS, continues to gain as the fighting escalates.

As the ZS forces diminished precipitously, the flight crew of one of the Medusa class SS decide to descend toward and into Mars' fragile atmosphere. As the behemoth approaches the SGMT ships being hijacked the crew realizes its error in gaining too much speed.

The captain of the runaway space station barks orders at his dismayed pilots.

The talon operators target the nearest visible SGMT ship and land two talons on the mid-ship area ideal for compromising the Tour Ship launching ability. The SGMT ship is at full throttle forcing the Medusa talon to sheer in deeper, further restricting the tour ship's velocity to failure, taking it down altogether. The downward momentum takes the combined seven-hundred-twenty million tons of the most durable construction materials known under the Sun, forcing the enormous space station to collapse with the thrust assist momentum of the snarled intergalactic tour ship onto the Martian Metropolis City with a direct hit.

The impact is from a twenty-three-degree angle, wedging the Martian crust up and over the neighborhood grids and burying the center of the city with hundreds of millions of tons of debris and Mars terrain.

What little sunlight there was is gone.

No one is on the ground able to view the departing twenty-five tour ships. Ominous in their similar monolithic design, bright rear thrust that shines light reveals their 'W' flight formation. The remaining three Medusa SS are not capable of Pursuit. Dust debris clouds encircle Mars too thick to see beyond, even if someone has survived.

There is not a vibration to be heard, the quiet in the void that is space; the hijacked SGMT ships might as well be the grim reaper's hallowed gravestones floating away with the souls taken in battle unjustly wrested from their mortal coils and awash in the sacred blood of heroes in defense of the 'wellbeing' of the human condition.

There's not a jazz note to be heard; it is a desolate scene, as bare and primordial as with some endings, the erosion stings and wins the hour.

Admiral Barcarui could not have anticipated the entire mass of regular Zealot Sentinels could be swayed to loyalty for the cause of defending the Star Gazer Mars Tour ship fleet in the name of the Glass Planet Population Journal. The indoctrination and mind conditioning regimens did not stick if at all permeate the conscience of morality with their faith in humanity.

The Admiral could only be certain of the Elite Zealot Sentinels' loyalty as each of the seven-million-five-hundred thousand are cyborg capable designed and manufactured by the unwilling but compromised genius of Shane Colston to operate automatic firearms firmly in place of functioning arms on a human torso, and to have target tracking 'aim-lock' on the brain screen display.

The EZS easily massacre the unrelenting charge of the up to two-hundred-million Zealot Sentinels. It did not take more than an hour for the suppressing gunfire to obliterate the main contingent into beads of organic tissue and shards of bone filling the thin atmosphere of the untamed, undeveloped portion of the Red Planet.

He is informed the Martian civilian population remains protected under the artificial atmosphere enclosed within the electromagnetic induced force field. The eight-hundred-million live souls are to be left stranded as the armada of RAKLAV interplanetary cruisers are divided to form an escort to the nine treasonous space stations well on their way into deep space.

To enhance the survival potential, an Armada of RAKLAV vessels is amassed to escort the divided fleet of SGMT ships from Mars. The Spark Creation Genesis solar light system voyage begins by taking a path deeper towards Jupiter before the confederat convoy leaves the Solar system to travel an unfathomable distance and time ending up ultimately at the mid-way distance to the red dwarf Proxima Centauri, the closest sun of the three known suns in Alpha Centauri.

43

The Dark Eagle Strikes

Riverstrike has taken on the persona of a despot on a rampage, "Catherine, I do know your identity, but it is not enough, I need you to," Riverstrike's choice of words becomes terse, "disclose the facts, I demand you tell me what you found in the Mosaic Caverns."

I am taken aback by Riverstrike's pressuring me, "What can I say? If I honestly don't remember anything, then how can I tell you what you want from me?"

"Let me tell you, this moment in time is critical to your destiny. You are the only surviving immediate relative to yourself."

"What are you talking about?"

To protect all future generations of human existence, it was required to make you disappear, as premature death, along with Jürgen, in the beginning. After forty years when the Condorcet procedure became available to the masses, it was necessary to eliminate your entire immediate ancestor tree, as to 'nip the bud' of any recollection of you or Jürgen's existence by siblings, cousins, aunts, uncles, nephews, and nieces. Anyone that could serve as provenance supporting your ever being born."

"You're a madman, what you say is impossible to conceive, let alone execute."

He walks over to the bio-hazard container on a bio-hazard cart; opening it, he uses the protective clamps to extract an object, placing it on the sterilized alloy enhanced board surface on top of his desk.

I look at the object under protective wrapping as he unfastens the securing straps and peels back the covering to reveal a skull!

This skull is thousands of years old, and it resembles a human adolescent skull, except it isn't. The skull is slightly elongated from the crown to the chin and is of an oblique shape. It somehow seems familiar to me.

"You do recognize it? I see it in your expression Catherine. What is it you and Jürgen encountered in those Caverns? Watch out now, this is bigger than you or me, Catherine," Riverstrike warns.

"Look at yourself, Patrick. If you dig deep enough, you will find what you fear the most."

"I do think Mosaic Caverns is a portal to hell and whatever it was you did encounter has afforded you and Jürgen the demon life to let you survive in purgatory until now!"

My mind is spinning in a cloud of confusion unable to make sense of Riverstrike's claims of hell and the paranormal, "Are you insane?"

"Jürgen admits as much, he recognizes this skull," Riverstrike's demeanor is intensely offensive, he is biting his lower lip. "What evil are you harboring?"

"I'm not harboring any evil ~ Damn you, Patrick, ~ What do you mean Jürgen admitted to recognizing that skull?"

Riverstrike leans back and away from me, reaching for his lapels with both hands, he summons a command on his commander channel link as I can hear his voice echo from my ZSI, "Bring him in here now!"

In a matter of five seconds, I hear the scuffling of someone entering the door behind me. I rotate the chair around to view two Elite Zealot Sentinels dragging a ravished, beaten, and emasculated Jürgen into the office.

"Jürgen?" I don't believe my eyes, can it be, "Jürgen?"

Alarmed, my adrenaline sets me to my feet I rush over to help him from collapsing on the floor entirely.

At this point, I hold him around his back, and under his arm, I support him up as he is weakened to the point of delirium. Another man enters the room.

What I see horrifies me, sending a sense of fear and panic as if confronted by a machete-wielding psychopath, and the skull of another on a desk I could reach for if not for a listlessness overwhelming me as I lose my footing from under my crouched body.

Could it be the terror of realizing how I have been deceived, manipulated, and utterly taken advantage of?

"She is knocked out by your appearance Simon," Riverstrike takes pleasure in our reactions. "I must say job well done Simon."

"If you say so, my noble lord." Simon takes a few steps into the room before stopping in place. "It is always my pleasure your nobleness."

"Do you see Catherine? Whatever plan you had to execute on behalf of your demonic allegiance you have failed." Riverstrike expresses piousness in his tone, "I am the Savior of humans. I am the deliverance of holy righteousness on the pathetic human race, and to offer rescue from the perils of evil, unholy hell!"

Riverstrike faces Simon, "Have these heathens transported to the deck in cloaked restraints. Now, we will show them the true meaning of God."

"As you wish your nobleness."

As Riverstrike exits, Simon is slow to turn around, but in time enough to catch the heel of my left foot in his right jaw breaking several teeth in his mouth, he spits out copious amounts of blood, followed by fragments of several teeth and pulp.

My second kick could kill him had I opted to strike his second cervical disc shattering it would render him quadriplegic, a reversible condition; if I were to sever the phrenic nerve that sustains his diaphragm, controlling lung function and his ability to breathe, it is possible to repair given the patient is on a respirator. With my right foot, I deliver a roundhouse kick to his chin, knocking him down and out for the count. I retrieve his identity strip and secure it in a pocket, then seeing Jürgen struggling to rise off the floor, I help him to his feet, "You're doing fine, can you stand alright?"

"I can, I can stand," he is joyously surprised.

"Here, put these on," I hold my empty hands open to him.

"What?"

"They're supposed to be cloaked restraints, get it?"

"Oh right, he said to . . .

"You got it, what can I say? I'm in!"

Jürgen lifts his head to look me in the eyes, "Hey, that's my line."

From the flight deck, the treasonous leadership convenes digitally from their remote commands appearing on their brain screens does create a bond from the illusion as if all are physically present.

Riverstrike has the faithful leaders, governors of space stations, intergalactic cruisers, and the EZS, who are fitted with the new hybrid interface, all kneel to one knee, "You swear allegiance to the cause as your one-hundred-percent commitment is what makes you elite. One hundred percent faithful to lord Riverstrike, dedicated to your sacrifice is to be understood, you swear an oath to defend our supreme society at any cost."

Governors, commanders, and the EZS respond aloud in unison, "Hail noble lord Riverstrike, creator of our SCG system, the origin of our destinies! Sworn destinies to eliminate the savages from human existence!"

The euphoria of the treasonous confederate conspirators is not shared by the five ACRES cadets or neither by Jürgen nor me. At a complete loss in this show of fascist zealotry, Jürgen and I are to keep a distance from Patrick Riverstrike by remaining secluded within the formations of EZS standing at attention across the flight deck.

Riverstrike is filled with self-delusion, once a man of integrity and values, starting centuries ago to battle the scourge of drug dealers' ruthlessness to gain profit illegally spreading addiction and death creating epidemic overdoses.

It is reported he is targeting space stations of immense importance to the continuing development of the preservation of human existence, the Glass Planet is the top priority.

The Dark Eagle SS is modified by Colston to be fitted with an assortment of machine gun turrets, batteries of scatter fire canons, and enhancing missile silos to launch Supersonic Tactical Cluster Honing missiles (STCH.)

The EZS troops are equipped with firearm robotics integrated with the elite zealot sentinel interface synchronizing with the brain operation of cyborg technology for thought command performance; aim lock capabilities. The difference with the Mars command under Admiral Barcarui is the live ammunition usage from the EZS to slaughter the enemy. The DE SS command of EZS is regulated to using rubber bullets due to the potential high-risk outcome of mass destruction of the DE SS.

Colston's development process of the technology lacks consideration for the possibility of reckless irresponsible behavior, with the potential onset of madness from mentally imbalanced EZS malfunctions.

Once the self-proclaimed 'noble lord' gave the order to 'fire at will' the Dark Eagle's exterior mounted machine gun turrets initiate automatic fire, the canons blast eighty-eight-millimeter shells, and the STCH missiles are jettisoned numbering in the tens of thousands dispersing a swarm of destruction across the combat zone.

The horror of it all results in the obliteration of billions of human bodies with the most majestic space stations exploding into lethal projectiles in all directions, the largest fragments descending from orbit as fireballs through Earth's atmosphere, or the space stations closer to the moon having devastating crater impacts on the surface vaporizing hundreds of millions of innocent people.

Sergeant Gian leads his ZS troops in the exoskeleton propulsion space suits to perform evasive maneuvers of the lethal debris from the shattered space stations to assault against the Dark Eagle SS.

Riverstrike opens fire on the two-hundred-fifty million attacking Zealot Sentinels resulting in carnage never known before as body parts, torsos, legs, arms, decapitated heads, clumps of flesh, muscle, organ tissue, and bones float, spin, rotate randomly about in space the grandest face of barbarianism ever recorded. An ocean of human remains vacuumed in the void of space, their resemblance best described as 'sun-dried driftwood,' absent of any moisture, rapid vaporization is the cruelest fate.

Ghastly visions of billions of lives needless to perish are the ghosts to haunt every person who witnesses their sacrifices this day. The living, in shock, as they offer solemnity towards these horrific fates, have introspected the jeopardy their own lives are in.

The Glass Planet is struck by large fuselage debris and a large portion of exterior transmitters for the protective computer-generated vector shields are incapacitated. This compromises the vivarium societies' protection on Earth revealing the occurring disaster of destruction hailing down from the heavens.

The Earth-landers viewing the peacefully content environs of their homes under the threat of hell from above as fireballs descending into the atmosphere begin fracturing into many deadly razor blade-like hot rocks, are freaking out to the point of shrieks of horror.

To most Earth-landers the End of Times seems to pour down upon them; all hope is gone for what to do about circumstances foreign to their experience; ignorance prevails as the clocks of understanding have expired.

All they can do now is hide.

The ACRES cadets are technologically savvy and well prepared by Kariana and Roberto to endure and dismiss all indoctrination and conditioning procedures.

"We would like to prepare for battle by featuring our five ACRES recruits."

The five-step forward as they draw their weapons.

I introduce my Cadets to the EZS, "These are the recruits of ACRES prior to Condorcet procedure age. They are willing to lay their lives down for freedom, fairness, and the 'wellbeing' of the human condition.

"Would any of you do that? Sure, some of you bow your heads in disgrace, but I see ninety-five percent of this special EZS are gun-ho for violence and death.

"It is your choice to decide, who you are, in this place, at this moment, in the constant spontaneous instant we all experience with perpetual consequences, some in our control, others beyond our control, or as adversity is often too unexpected to respond to until it has struck its burden on you.

"Do not expect a wilting flower if you think to conspire against human liberty. Its primary disruptor 'greed-fascism' wilts away at the human soul, the truth of a person's identity where far too many cares more, and receive less, opposite to the few who care less and receive more."

Once the images of horrifying body parts, internal organs, and shattered space stations, many pulled down by Earth's gravitational pull, were seen by the cadets and by EZS troops on board the command deck, an intense sense of emotional divide arises.

The EZS troops are hard-core devotees to the treasonous conspirators and view empathy as a weakness. They see triumph.

The five cadets are appalled by the exhibited contempt of democratic civility resulting in an ensuing impulse to commence battle by the attack.

The cadets are outnumbered by the EZS troops on the Dark Eagle flight command deck thirty to one and though they are inexperienced, they have perfected their martial arts skills acquiring the stealth, the discipline, the wisdom, and the tenacity associated with the deadliest of martial arts known to humankind: Brazilian Ju-Jitsu, Silat, Muay Thai, Sambo and Krav Maga, including handling of their specialty weapons. The EZS is prohibited from using live ammunition on board the space station, a strategic disadvantage despite their overwhelming numbers.

Ofbyfor specialty is the use of two-bladed Tonfas, a steel version in the shape of a handgun with an elongated barrel. It features a diversity of usages including a hammer, a club, a blunt ax, or a baseball bat when leveraged. It is body armor using the Tonfas to support the forearm in deflecting projectiles or the blows from a staff. The strength of his core enables him to exact deadly slashes to the opponent's neck, or mid-section, even a stab in the back with an over-the-shoulder-vault maneuver drops the enemy for good.

Anybody, or bodies, within ten feet circumference of his wielding are subject to a rapid demise.

Kanga uses the Rope Dart as her preference. The Rope Dart can be made of various materials and is one hundred ten inches in length. She often prefers to place a five-pound stainless steel ball in the pouch at either end of the Rope Dart, as opposed to rope dart hooks that are an average of seven inches in length and require time-consuming manual extraction.

Nonetheless, when she gets the Rope Dart in motion, harnessing it around her body before twirling in the circles above her head, the steel balls transform the Rope Dart into an extended club a direct hit to the opponent will leverage significant bodily damage and physical pain, if not merciful death. She has ‘knockout power’ from an attack perimeter of twenty feet.

Auloi is an expert at the Ninja level in the use of the Kama. Like a pickax, the Kama are two lethal blade weapons worn with the wrist straps to achieve the motion of lodging one into someone’s back, certain to maim or to swing horizontally to slit a throat. With an attachment of a ball and chain, the Kama offers skilled control sending the ball and chain to wrap around the opponent’s ankle and therefore pulling their legs out from under them. The length of the chain may allow for intricate snaring of an opponent’s weapon and wrapping it behind the opponent while using the chain to bind the opponent against their device puncturing a vital organ before severing it via the exposed wound using the sharp pickax-like Kama.

Triessence Vanitha is a master of Nunchaku with mesmerizing quickness and speed she can hit several vulnerable parts of the body leaving the opponent at once entirely disabled. The gymnastic qualities of her physical style of fighting are unique to her design. Not only can she take down an opponent with the blunt sticks, but with the chain holding them together she will strangle them to death or mercifully snap their spinal cord for instant death. Her stamina in the battle taking down her share of EZS stands out impressing her friends . . .she loves the limelight.

Lily favors her Katana and her Wakizashi, the long and short swords of Daisho. Traditionally used one at a time featuring the long sword Katana, with the shorter sword Wakizashi worn concealed under the clothing, the opponent is caught off guard. Lily’s training as a ballet dancer before her martial arts training has her endeavoring into the realm of innovating combat movements gracefully bewildering, or enchanting, yet deadly to the hypnotized opponent’s surprise. Her expertise is using both swords, one in each hand, and sometimes juggling between the two in defensive moves as well as creative offensive attacks.

The Nitoken technique, using both swords at once does have its distinct advantages including parrying with the Katana and retaliating quickly with the Wakizashi in a thrust or slashing to the opponents' vulnerable areas the center line from the genitals to the abdomen, to the sternum, the throat, the chin, the nose, and cranium. The Wakizashi can deflect an armament while extending away from the opponent to allow a swing of the Katana to decapitate the opponent.

She flourishes with a plie when she executes an original innovative choreography leading to an impressive defeat of her opponent, typically impaling them with the Wakizashi or the usual decapitation with the Katana, in graceful, flowing motions.

Riverstrike can sustain his wits as he can place protective headgear and maintain the deck for a brief time. The cadets grind down the EZS troops. It becomes evident to the Riverstrike retreat is the only option to avoid capture.

I understand my betrayal of the 'wellbeing' of the human condition; I came to understand the hope of perseverance, the beauty of love, and the spirit of optimism. I am willing to lay my life down for redemption. I will subject myself to extreme radiation exposure to detonate explosives to tear open the nuclear fusion reactor compartments, an act debilitating the propulsion systems leaving the DE SS to stop it permanently. It is of no consequence my remains will be thrust into space if it brings down Riverstrike.

I have reconciled with my existence, after coming to understand the reason I was cloned in a petri dish to be viewed as a carbon copy of the essence of Jürgen into existence, and this fuels the revenge on my mind.

The more I accept who I am the more I loathe myself. The creation of me was spurred on by a sociopath searching for the identities of two scientists the lord minister suspects are a link to a sub-human race civilized enough to understand controlling of resources, and conceiving of rivalry for survival, deducing tactical scenarios in implementing a strategy for dominance.

All I have seen, my witness to his methods, have supported my epiphany the lord minister is what the lord minister fears most. In his struggle for omnipotence, he struggles with omniscient and Omni liberum, as the former sheds guilt on his ambitions and the latter paradoxical to his senses.

What am I? What the lord minister knows, has the power to enforce his own will over others? Though relents in being all good by choosing to prevent omni liberum. Including myself, I am the preeminent example of a human form scientifically created to be a servant. Disallowed to have the empirical experience to form my ethical and moral views.

Only to conform and obey the Riverstrike enterprise, the ice breaker when needed to do the lord minister's dirty work, for dirty compensation. Making me dirty of conscience and soul if arguably I possess at least one if not both, as honed, despite being molded, forged by the Lord Minister Riverstrike to accumulate debts over hundreds of years, I will pay forward by stopping him in his tracks.

His show of contempt is predictable toward his EZS guard. When given the reason to commit such dishonor and betrayal, he delivers without hesitation. I have seen him use poison on whole families, as was the case of the murder of whole family trees like Catherine's and Jürgen's. It is ironic I find myself as his closest living relative, half-brothers I suppose, but it doesn't matter anymore ~

He walks into the nuclear fusion propulsion room, purposely secures the C-4 explosives wired, he detonates without hesitation.

Upon defeating the EZS on the flight deck and seeing Captain Junior flee in a RAKLAV intergalactic cruiser to join the treasonous caravan is of no surprise. The shuddering thunder of an explosion so enormous and powerful as to rock the Dark Eagle propelling its occupants to the ceiling, their bodies flailing back down as though a school of cod fish tangled in a dragnet hoisted onto a fishing boat's deck in rough seas, is shocking.

When the DE SS is rocking from a blast and unexpectedly lost its drive power, the disgraced Patrick Riverstrike did make his way to the cruiser Dark Eaglet. His effort to escape is complicated by the EZS attempting to embark on his cruiser. Brandishing an MG with a fire rate of seven thousand bullets per minute he does take delight in gunning down his own EZS troops in cold blood as not to interfere with his retreat. With the firepower that cuts limbs off, and some bodies severed in two pieces at the waist, a blood red with brownish yellow excretion occurs quickly forming puddles across the hangar deck, with large clumps of flesh, shattered skulls, and robotics material in layer on top of one another.

He takes to the cockpit and uses the automated launch setting:

"Proceed to Mosaic Caverns."

All cadets are equipped with Shuriken with nano-robotic capabilities and Double Antler Dragon Handle Tomahawks. These five cadets take down the one-hundred-fifty Elite Zealot Sentinels in less than ten minutes.

We take a moment to regroup, each of us saluting one another as others aid Jürgen to stay on his feet as we find our way to exiting from the flight deck on our way to the hangar bay where we can escape in our Nebula Drifter cruiser.

The path to the hangar bay is a few elevator trips and several pedestrian corridors where few people are present. The Dark Eagle SS is under lock down and all the population of scientist, and their research support staff, except crew members essential to assault the space stations, are quarantined to their private living units throughout the space station. Jürgen begins to recover lower body strength hoisted by the Cadets.

The stomping of EZS boots brings my attention forward down the corridor where we need to proceed on. Approaching in five lines of eight across, the forty EZS draw strange-looking guns, with a circular and extended bullet clip conjoined to their armor.

They commence firing. The ammunition explodes into fireballs that would incinerate the seven of us if we stood in the open.

Everyone curls down for cover behind the intrados of the fuselage hallway segment arches.

I can see the platoons of EZS are reloading, "Keep down, prepare for a second barrage."

Next, the ammunition is less formidable. We sense the futility of rubber bullets bouncing off the floor and walls, some reach us in the air with the velocity of a thrown snowball.

We all sort of laugh, "Please let me handle this, it's perfect for something I only dream about. I have a technique I trained with to give me an edge called, well watch me, cadets."

Making eye contact with each cadet to confirm my intention is heard, I peer around a fuselage beam, and I turn seeing the EZS running toward us. I loosen up my hips and vault into the air spinning upright, my feet connect with one EZS on the chest, the next on the shoulder and I paddle across their heads in sequential motion as I use their faces like bowling balls thrusting my fingers into the cyborgs eye-sockets.

The technique is to build upward momentum and execute

with precision contacting a bone on each step like kicking a foot into a crevice as if rock climbing. My hands grab onto the heads and shoulders of the enemy as I pinwheel and strike with my feet. Qyxzorina said my body is in outstanding fitness and form for the 'Twister' move, and I wish she was here to prove her right.

My friends come running up to me surrounded by forty EZS cyborg carcasses.

"What is that called, Catherine?" Lily asks breathlessly, overcome with excitement.

"Don't ask me when I learned it, but it's called the 'Twister' technique." I beam with pride as everyone offers a rousing cheer, slapping hands, offering me a variety of salutations and handshakes.

"You must train us with your advanced fighting skills," Lily says to me. How she has matured in six short years.

"We will. We have to move on ~ everyone with me?"

The young Elite Zealot Sentinels are the true embodiment of leadership, courage and strength displayed by their enthusiasm to carry on the fight.

We board the Nebula Drifter and can launch out of the hangar bay without hesitation.

The absence of the Dark Eaglet is not lost upon us as we set course for The Glass Planet SS to get the vivarium system Online and ramp up its and ramp up its AFS system, and to suppress the EZS from using the Dark Eagle SS to cause further destruction.

44

The GPPJ Counterattack

Shane Colston, this is Minister Riverstrike's senior officer Commander Janalake, over." She uses her former given name to avoid confusion.

"Commander Janalake, this is Shane Colston, I read you loud and clear," Shane reports looking to Olivia who displays a face riddled with anxiety.

Kariana directs an order, "Shane Colston prepare for recon-sabotage mission. I'm picking you up now."

Olivia stands confused before speaking, "I am going to get the shotgun for you to take with you, can I refresh our drinks?"

"I will take care of the drink," Shane assures calmly, "you would like a glass of wine?"

Olivia, "Yes please." She rushes up the stairs.

Shane is in the wet bar when an image catches his eyes at the Bay window, the picture from the year two-thousand-five when serving in special forces under then Captain Patrick Riverstrike in the jungles of Colombia. Surrounding Captain Riverstrike are the then leadership of the platoon including himself, Staff Sergeants Augur and Martinez, and Lieutenants Fricke and Robinson.

His thoughts resonate through his GPI, "The sacrifice made by poor 'lost' generations, are not to be forgotten. The freedoms, joys, abundance, love, and happiness are due to the multitudes of sacrifice, the ultimate sacrifice, especially of young soldiers eighteen, nineteen, twenty-years-of-age yet to experience and enjoy life with a young family, a spouse with a child, or children . . ."

"Countless orphans have been created by war." Kariana's voice is heard through the GPI private line, "No, they are gone, as humans on Earth to marvel at nature's truths and now there's a massacre happening that you facilitated. It's time to redeem them and De Oppressor Liber, Sergeant."

The RAKLAV cruiser creates a sonic boom in the Appalachia vivarium as Kariana plants a landing in front of the homestead in a matter of seconds in the direct sight line of Shane Colston.

Olivia returns to the parlor with the shotgun to find Shane missing. She calls out, "Shane? Shane Hons?" She turns to view Shane walking towards the RAKLAV cruiser, alone. She raises her voice, "Here's your shotgun Shane! Shane!"

Shane does not hear her even if her cries we're audible from the distance to reach him. His mind is captured by the dilemma Riverstrike has exploited him to further commit crimes by developing firearms to use against the GPPJ, and his focus is now on doing what is right.

Olivia runs to open the front double doors and looks out on the cruiser lifting off and she makes it out to the willow tree before helplessness descends on her as the cruiser disappears beyond the clear blue ceiling of the Appalachia vivarium sky.

"I know enough to be prepared for a double crossing from a son-of-a-greed fascist. It is an opportunity perceived by a courageous genius, to know better than not to have a quick strike plan in preparation."

The whole SSN hears this transmission: "Marcel, can you both return on the emergency craft?"

"I'm in the Blister ~ he responds ~ do you know what that is?"

"As long as you and Qyxzorina are safe."

"That's right, we're safe and we're in the docking bay of the Entrepreneur SS, ready to administer some whoop-ass."

As Marcel hustles his way into his offices, Qyxzorina follows adamantly questioning his actions, "Do you think it's a promising idea, Marcel? I mean we have a lot invested in these tour ships, but then again, they are already lost for certain."

"I didn't pay for them; he owns the Martian fleet by contract. He paid for them. If he knew better, he would not be compelled to hijack his fleet."

"I always said you are a smart businessman."

"You don't say it enough, though."

I have been listening along with the other twenty billion plus in the GPPJ, "Marcel Etrion, is that you?"

"Yes, it is Catherine; Qyxzo is here also."

"Hello Catherine, so nice to hear your voice."

"Thank you Qyxzorina, I'm glad you made it through, and you are safe."

"We are and so are you."

"Marcel, you know Riverstrike, unlike anyone."

"He'll get to know me better in about twelve hours," Marcel has his forefinger poised on a launch button. "OG detonation," he presses the button, pulls a lever, and receives a confirmation of his dubious action. "Ships away, going to be smashed into atoms."

"Marcel, what have you done?"

"I set off my counter-offensive against my 'business partner.' We had nuclear mines built-in to detonate the SGMT ships. Patrick's insistence on maintaining more than half of the fleet at a Mars docking facility I perceive as a red flag."

"No one who knows him would think any different." I feel Marcel's pain as he suffers through the trauma of the millions of innocent lives lost as a distraction for the SSN to be vulnerable to attack by the Dark Eagle SS. "Now his deceit is revealed, and we have him cornered at the Mosaic Caverns." I hope to alleviate Marcel's distraught condition.

"Marcel has done what is logical. That is if the SGMT ships have indeed been hijacked?"

"We feel they were successful in hijacking most of the SGMT ships." I reluctantly add, "This is because we have lost contact with the Martian colony, at last communique the EZS was mowing down the ZS defenses."

"Did you hear what Catherine said, Marcel? The ships were hijacked."

"That is good news, Qyxzo." Marcel looks at me on the brain screen and reacts to the confusion on my face, "We can be reasonably certain the nuclear explosions will occur millions of miles away from Mars."

"When?"

"In just under twelve hours the signal to detonate will reach them." Marcel adds, "Then kablooie, they're blistered."

"Qyxzorina, I think the both of you need to stay at your offices until the DE SS is secured to a lock-down. I'm on approach to The Glass Planet to end the aggression, I need to prepare."

"Catherine ~ I hear Qyxzorina's pleasant, optimistic voice ~ you are prepared young lady, take his ass out. Over."

"Loud and clear, Qyxzorina. By the way, that 'Twister' move paid off. Over."

"Tremendous, you pulled it off! How many, six, ten, don't tell me twelve? Over."

"It was a forty head count! Over."

"May the Lord have mercy! I can't wait to hear about it. Over and out."

Upon arriving at The Glass Planet, we are greeted by the Chief Station Officer of communications for the GPI, Fred Deininger. We exchange our introductions with his obligatory salutation and congratulations for who Jürgen and I are, "It's an honor to . . ."

We offer our greeting with a hand salute cutting him off.

He takes no time to ask, "What the hell is happening out there?"

As we approach the entry terminal, I inform him, "The situation is beyond explanation at the moment and we need to dial in all GPI conversations, as well as the prayers and thoughts of the Earth-landers to channel the immense volume to smother the Dark Eagle in the same fashion the audio fragmentation suppression system disables motor function from the brain."

Ofbyfor exclaims, "This is The Glass Planet? Never thought I would get to use this." He grabs a GPI and plugs in for rapid conditioning, as do Lily and Kanga, Triessence, and Auloi.

"Catherine and Jürgen, this is Kariana, over."

"Kariana, this is Catherine, go ahead, over."

"I'm escorting Shane Colston, he is on the cruiser, we're heading for the Dark Eagle committed to disabling the weapons systems he designed and claims to have installed against his will."

"Interesting he has a change of heart. A little too late for billions of fatalities, but better late than never."

"What is she doing?" Jürgen asks, "Is she on a suicide mission?"

Shane Colston is the sole architect of the massive arsenal he designed and manufactured to be placed on the Dark Eagle SS under the scrutiny and pressure of Patrick Riverstrike's quid pro quo.

"This is Shane, I did it as Riverstrike assured me this was for their deep space journey to the artificial solar system he is developing halfway between our solar system and Alpha Centauri. There was no talk about wielding this firepower against the space station network."

"Catherine, update me, what is happening?" Kariana asks.

"Jürgen, the Cadets, and I escape the Dark Eagle, against all odds, we fought our way tooth and nail, thanks to your superior training. Destroying their AFS undoubtedly aided our efforts so far, now we need to take down the arsenal on board, but there's no telling how many EZS remain active to defend the DE SS."

"What matters the most now is that you are all safe, isn't it?" She responds slyly, "Then we can secure the space station. Once Shane Colston disables the canon and machine gun turrets he designed and installed you can order Sergeant Gian and the remaining ZS available to board and secure the Dark Eagle. Your efforts will be perfect timing."

"It will be, the station's propulsion system is destroyed, looks like an explosion as the entire mechanical engineering room wall is gone, the entire apparatus was blown into space somehow."

"The MER you're talking about is where we have to go."

"Catherine, he says the explosion occurred in the same location as the munitions operating systems MER."

"The weapons fire at will and are indiscriminate in targeting."

"Yeah, it's been a while since I worked on targeting systems, nothing too modern anyway."

"We must signal out a message to the masses," I say reminded of how pivotal the AFS will be in our favor.

"You can do that through the GPI and get the GPPJ to inform the Earth-landers to pray. They will need you to inspire them, Catherine, you will need to generate a worldwide communique using The Glass Planet's instruments."

"Thank you, Kariana for your precious wisdom."

"My pleasure Catherine, you are an old soul yourself."

I suspect Riverstrike has something brewing, as he is always scheming, just didn't think he would go this far toward destroying the aesthetic he conceived to build.

"We have made it to The Glass Planet, Kariana. I know how we can neutralize the crew to preserve the Dark Eagle," I state expressing my plan for her approval. "We can get the entire GPPJ and the Earth-landers to channel their voices in prayer and meditation through The Glass Planet, then the sheer volume of billions of voices can be transmitted throughout the Dark Eagle subjecting the crew to neurological paralysis through audio fragmentation suppression."

The pulsation of spiritual energy blossoms into space, it emanates in auras of all colors, and the thousands of languages intertwine into one language: The hum of love. The ebb and flow of energy in a subatomic flow, the human union does grow also.

"Then we can decide if the repairs to The Glass Planet SS to re-establish the vivarium technology will be necessary or not."

45

A Balance of Liberty and Sacrifice

Roberto and the space truckers engage the largest pieces of free-falling space station debris using robotic arm clamps securing and guiding them harmlessly into the oceans.

The bodies of allegiance GPPJ and ZS are shattered and sucked into space suffering deaths without mercy, without preparation in innocence, as bullets, missiles, and cannon fire make the fine line between life and death, the fragility of the living into the permanence of death. Their severed bodies floating in space, pieces of human carnage from billions of victims of sacrifice forever wasted instead of the manipulations of the few entrenched in greed-fascism. It is the delusional obsession of their perceived righteous inheritance of all wealth and power over the mass populations of human existence, to secure their privilege, to inherit the Earth by the means of greed-fascism.

The maiming, crippling force expounded on the masses in the name of greed fascism dominates the minds of ill-willed psychopaths and sociopaths and of the haters too insignificant of valuing the miracle of life, blinded by the insecurity of their shortcomings, to know no other strength in life but weakness, to tear down, erode the aesthetic of other's lives as cause from their delusions of grandeur, power, superiority; suppositions which never come to be, are just hollow, empty promises wrapped in big lies.

Roberto hits acceleration to add momentum upon contact increasing the force of deflecting a massive portion of an exploded space station to break away from Earth's orbit sending it harmlessly on course to no-man's land, open space.

The SSNERT's commander's S.O.S. call to aid the tour ship fleet prompts Roberto to rouse space truckers into deep space, "We will make it right."

"Roberto, how can we leave the debris horizon to sacrifice innocent people to expedition out to the SGST ship fleet?"

"Divert all sizable structures capable of landfall to be demolished."

"Smash 'em, Bash 'em approach?" A space trucker with the handle 'Hopper' breaks in, a Texas twang to his voice. "The way of the good old days, no fuss!"

"As a last resort only. Let's try to hedge any debris capable of entering the atmosphere. It will require two thousand of us to assist the tour ship fleet."

"Copy that Roberto, the fleet in operations, get all three-hundred-thousand tow and hauling craft on alert. We must get aid to the SSNERT rescue effort; the fleet of tour ships has reportedly been sabotaged. All available short-range craft concentrate on debris management. Any craft with towing or hauling long-range ability set course at maximum speed to the stranded fleet. The Noah's Arc rescue crafts will be coming our way."

Kariana docks the RAKLAV cruiser in the Dark Eagle SS hangar and she leads Colston to the mechanical operations room to gain access to the control board to disable the machine gun turrets along with the rest of the ballistic missile weaponry.

"The obstacle of the EZS is the fact they are equipped with firearms, large numbers of them who have 'cyborg' themselves with performance automation controlled by synoptic patching directly into their forearms or mounted onto their shoulder blades.

"What are you going to do about the EZS?" I ask them with a conservative estimate of a few hundred thousand more or less to remain on board to defend the DE SS.

"They're trained to refrain from discharging firearms while aboard any space station unless the preservation of the space station requires the extreme measure of use of deadly force."

"Then we should do fine if we keep our mouths shut and avoid eye contact?" Shane is exuberant with a hint of lightness inappropriate for a man in his situation.

"I think I know a way we can get to the mechanical engineering rooms without detection." She sizes up Colston eying him from head to toe, "You'll have some tight squeezes along the way, the architectural design is slimline and sharp-edged."

"You'd be surprised where my body bends, how it is malleable," he speaks through his experience dating back to his service with the

Green Berets. "I always was comfortable with a rock climb, especially in the service of my country when your skills of maneuverability and stealth push your physical and mental strength to its limits."

She leads him around a corner, down a good stretch of the corridor they run when they hear the approach of ZSI units, recognizable by the synchronized marching of a platoon of magnetized boots.

He follows her through a service door that is accessed manually, once they make it to the mechanical engineering room, Colston will need to use his authorization as a project manager to gain access to the hardware where he easily shuts down the armament mechanisms by simply overriding the targeting systems by deprogramming them.

They enter a mechanical engineering room depressurizing from a blast hole in the fuselage. The force of the suction has cleared the room of any objects not secured to the hull. Bracing each other as they hold securely in the corridor just outside the door, the former commander speaks on her private GPI channel, "Good thing you found a helmet that fits ~"

Colston is looking around to find a way to get to the armament mechanism without being vacuumed into space. Realizing he does not have a GPI; she knocks on his helmet and gestures she will adjust his headgear.

In the next moment, two dozen EZS are perilously thrust through the service hallway screaming into the MER to their deaths as their hapless bodies are swept into the void of space through the breached wall.

"I'm going to have to climb into the MER and get to the command board for manual access. There's no other way to deprogram at this point."

"Voice and odor identification security clearance are 'out the window' as options," she implies the obvious pun with a smile that Colston returns to her with a look of trepidation.

"No other choice other than retina or fingerprints to clear security," he shakes his head, "That is before I can use the keyboard to enter the deprogram codes, as usual, I didn't bring the software chips with me."

"How long do you think it will take you to enter the codes?"

"It depends on how stable the workspace is. You make sure I am tacked in with these cables and the better you can help me from flailing around, the sooner we will be out of here."

Colston's long and lanky body with its maneuverability and angling skills enables him to scale into the MER by grappling with the components fixed to the wall of the hull. He gets in a position where he can stretch his dominant left arm towards a scanner to register his fingerprints for security access. The suction of the depressurizing corridor is at full force against him, but he extends his fingers to be successfully identified. The keyboard for manual input of the deprogramming codes appears from a console.

It is in a position that compromises his ability to see the keys on the keyboard, slowing his ability to type in the codes.

The tacked cables are holding strong in support of his weight from being sucked into oblivion. It seems like an eternity for him to finish a routine task normally performed in mere seconds, but under the conditions, the fact the task was accomplished without injury to either of them is considered a success.

"Sergeant Gian, this is Commander. Come in, over."

"Commander Catherine, this is Sergeant Gian, over."

"Sergeant, proceed with your troops to secure the DE SS and detain all personnel and crew to their living quarters. Keep an eye out for Commander Kariana, she will be escorting a ballistics expert by the name of Shane Colston from the mechanical engineering rooms. They are evacuating on a RAKLAV cruiser. Give them cover if you encounter any hostilities. Assist them if you cross paths to provide secured access, over."

"Heard and understood. Over and out."

Detection of the arsenal going off-line due to the deprogramming is depicted precariously near the 'catastrophic event' alert where the propulsion hull is compromised. Kariana and Colston are responsible for the arsenal off-line alert, but how did the hull breach occur? The security video files will provide clues, if not the answer to this question.

Kariana uses her RAKLAV credentials to close off the breached MER with sealant panels generated from the use of biophysics integrated into the steel-based materials forming the hull. The technology is like the biophysics pods used to establish infrastructure on distant habitable planets such as the Spark Creation Genesis solar system's three orbiting planet space stations. She views Colston from the corridor as he double-checks the disabled status of the arsenal before making his way out of the MER.

"Catherine, come in, this is Kariana, over."

"Go ahead Kariana, this is Catherine, over."

"The arsenal is disabled, over. You can instruct Sergeant Gian to lead the troops in and secure control of the DE SS, over."

"That's a copy, I thought you might overhear the orders I issued to Sergeant Gian just now. The ZS battalions are en route via exoskeleton propulsion gear and will start boarding immediately. Kariana, what is your next move, over?"

"The corridor was under emergency lock-down due to the breach in the MER hull. We are able to secure the area by the mending of the breach but were unable to maintain communication until coming in clearly now. I intend to lead Colston back to the cruiser via the service passageway, then exit from this incapacitated space station, over."

"Kariana, the security video reveals the explosion ignited from a device placed on the integration grid that controls and coordinates all propulsion mechanical systems, over."

"Catherine, can you identify what credentials the saboteur used to gain entry. Over?"

"Kariana, the credentials used are assigned to Simon Noir. How strange is that? Over."

"Catherine, I read you loud and clear. It is strange, but not a priority now; I will apprehend Colston and have him detained. You must track down Riverstrike to face justice. Over and out."

She disengages her communication link and hears a soft 'click' noise about eight inches from her head.

"Okay, you got me."

"Colston, I thought you said firearms are prohibited for use?"

"I did say the Elite Zealot Sentinels are under strict orders to disarm their weapons. Not me commander, it looks like we have some business to discuss."

"Do we?"

"Don't try to lead me by the nose. You damn well know that when all of this is said and done, there will be no mercy on me. There shouldn't be given what I've done."

"Listen, Colston, what was initiated by Riverstrike, you shut it down. Your defense is a solid clad alibi, a bit complicated, yes, but in the end, you did the right thing."

"I also enabled the mass murder of billions of GPPJ and three-hundred-million Zealot Sentinels."

Kariana shifts her view from standing with her back to him by adjusting slightly to her left, "You did not pull the trigger, Colston. It will be enough to keep you alive."

"I'm not able to take the chance. It is you or me that will fill the void left by Riverstrike. If it's you then I will have to stand trial. If it's me then no one will have the authority or evidence to prosecute me."

"What about Catherine or Jürgen?"

"Oh, they will be cast as traitors, attempting to take over the DEN SS, while the actual defectors of the nine space stations, and anything requiring explanation was destroyed amid chaos and conflict!"

"Then you destroy the communications recordings and security data figuring you will have a blank canvass for whatever story you conjure."

Kariana straightens herself facing away from Colston to contemplate the moment when she hears an utterance from him, a sense of disorientation, a thud on the floor with the scraping of his firearm landing and sliding in view in front of her. She abruptly spins around to face Sgt. Gian who clubbed Colston unconscious on the back of the head, "Colston the conspirator, eh General?"

My spirit shines with the initiative to access the GPPJ via the GPI and through them to reach out to the Earth-lander populations with a message of acceptance to peace addressing every living human on Earth, "We appreciate your thoughts and prayers in these apocalyptic times. I assure you we will pick up the pieces and rebuild the aesthetic for the 'wellbeing' of the human condition.

"What is most necessary going forward as we emerge from isolation is your mutual understanding of the categorical imperative of a 'wellbeing.' With our collective empathy for all who are in agony, we will heal through the support we provide each other.

"There is no reason to go through this world without high hopes and informed confidence in experiencing an ideal or innovation while attaining success in the contributions of everyone's unique skill set and ambitions.

"In this way, the concept of domination is marginalized as an archaic practice from the 'age of barbarism' and is put into practice currently as nothing more than a momentary dislocation of our collective consciousness of mutual interest.

"Everybody pray, whether you are of faith or not, through prayer we can heal and unite ourselves for the 'wellbeing' of the human condition."

As I look before me from The Glass Planet SS telescope screens upon all of Earth, I see billions more begin to meditate, to pray. Many are certainly thinking the apocalypse is upon them. There's no consoling for those who pray in earnest only when they are hopeless.

The Glass Planet hums with the beautiful tangle of voices emanating from the innocent peace-loving billions of people who emote their inner selves through several thousand languages.

It is more crying than ever occurring in human history on one given day. In these dire moments searching for survival, the complexities of thought are of the priority for survival, searching for heavy stone buildings, or underground facilities ranging from vehicle storage to other isolated areas like underground irrigation super structures, where enormous PVC piping and forms of acrylic tubing provide structure below ground to withstand the force of space station fuselage crashing onto Earth's surface.

For others unable to remain calm, they can only visualize what the moment of impact will result to in their certain Death. Will it be unnoticed and abrupt, or does some other unpredictable calamity befall their 'wellbeing'?

46

How Pathetic is War to be Had?

The instruments on The Glass Planet are intuitive, as I confidently assist Deininger and his communications operations staff.

"Is it possible to repair the vivarium vector shields?"

No Commander, not at the moment. It will require extensive component replacements, and a rigorous sequential configuring of the beacons for synchronizing to the space stations global positioning."

Once the message was sent out the response is as vast as the sound of billions of voices in random sequence creating quite a potent weapon harnessed by The Glass Planet AFS security system. The sound waves are broadcast via The Glass Planet to the Dark Eagle SS comms links of the crew members' GPIs.

"General Kariana, this is Admiral J. P. Jones. We have reached and evacuated the SGST flagship Soley Leve's crew members who are now on board the Freedom SS. They are all accounted for, and the fleet of space trucks are towing the stranded SGST ships to port, over and out."

"Some good news," I say to Jürgen.

"Good news for the moment. Poor Marcel and Qyxzorina, what a tragic betrayal by Riverstrike committing such acts of greed-fascism."

Jürgen's warm blue eyes are gently piercing, "He is a very sick man consumed with greed, narcissism, a highly functional sociopath to mobilize against his best interest, don't you think?"

My smile in reaction to his remarks offers a moment for us to connect with our eyes. At this moment glancing into each other's eyes is the trust and love I found missing in the impostor Simon Noir.

This is our chance to mobilize as well, "Sergeant Gian, this is Catherine, over."

There is silence.

"Can you read me, Sergeant Gian?"

"Catherine, this is Sergeant Gian, over."

"The Dark Eagle will be in your command once you enforce a lock-down, it's the only way to remedy our world order. You must secure the Dark Eagle."

"Catherine, our ranks are decimated, but our willpower remains undeterred. I have knocked out Colston, and General Kariana has taken him into custody."

"Your loyalty to the preservation of humankind is most honorable. Riverstrike and top command have abandoned the disabled Dark Eagle SS. The cadets are with us and were able to help eliminate EZS troops on the flight deck. The remaining occupants will be immobilized by Audio Fragmentation Suppression we are emitting from The Glass Planet SS. Once the vessel is on lock-down, the conditions will favor compliance to keep order. How many Zealot Sentinels do you have remaining?"

"Less than twenty million. Several triage are forming on operational space stations, and I ordered the remaining eighteen million to occupy and conduct aid on whichever space stations they can board." Sergeant Gian's tone is dismal and depressed, "The Dark Eagle's firepower wiped out everyone else. We were sitting ducks deployed within the self-contained flight suits, incapable of defense against the shower of bullets, explosive projectiles."

"You must carry on the fight Sergeant Gian, stay strong. The remaining civilian crew and personnel on the Dark Eagle will be neutralized by the AFS in time for you to secure the space station to keep order."

The sound is to be transmitted to The Glass Planet SS communications network of beacons and transmitter buoys dispersed within the perimeter of the SSN. When the signal is delivered to the Dark Eagle SS, the effect is as intended, detrimental to operations as the crew members are incapacitated by the sheer volume and diversity of the voices.

We attend to the AFS operations monitor to increase and sustain the frequency at optimal levels for at least thirty minutes.

As Sergeant Gian's ZS troops continue to approach using the propulsion exoskeleton space suits to board the Dark Eagle something goes wrong as the transmission of the sound waves breaks off.

"Sergeant Gian, this is Catherine, over."

"Commander, this is Sergeant Gian, over."

"There's been an interruption of the AFS transmission, can you hold your position?"

"Commander Catherine, we are nearing exhaustion of our oxygen and energy supply. We have seven-hundred-thousand troops boarded, while I have another seven-hundred thousand or more with mere minutes remaining before their oxygen reserves expire."

"Understood," I see how well trained they are forming in long lines, boarding as if a colony of bees swarming their honeycomb, crawling in as a continuous flow. I am enraptured by the strength and boldness of the troops as they embark on the DE SS. "As you continue boarding your troops, they must deactivate their GPIs to avoid affectation from the AFS transmission once we can restore it, copy?"

"Deactivation will eliminate our mechanical advantage, over."

"It's better having you fight it out hand-to-hand until all of your troops are safe from exposure and suffocation, over."

"I prefer an old-fashioned fistfight anyway. Over and out."

The cadets, Jürgen, and I adorn the exoskeleton propulsion space suits allowing for direct interaction and involvement in space without a tether to investigate the exterior of The Glass Planet SS.

We release and open a side hatch with ease, to exit slowly putting our bodies outside of the mighty space station, floating ten thousand miles from Earth, the enormity of it makes me feel out of place, as if in a dream.

There are body parts, pieces of dry flesh floating past us, immersing us in a cloud of human carnage. I am overwhelmed with the morbid conditions we encounter as we scale the sleek, solid, and slippery exterior surface, checking the multiple satellite dishes to locate any damage.

As I make my way to the primary transmitter satellite-dish I lay witness to the apparent issue as my mouth becomes agape to viewing the form of a human corpse impaled on the 'feed horn.'

"Oh my, Jürgen, the issue is on the main transmitter." Jürgen and the cadets close in on my position as the grotesque appearance of Simon Noir's scorched head and torso are pierced through the chest.

Ofbyfor and Auloi assist Jürgen to free the cadaver from the 'feed horn' and Kanga moves in to repair the mechanism. I hasten to return inside the cabin to assist Deininger in re-establishing the transmission."

Once the 'feed horn' is repaired, the two-million crew on board the Dark Eagle SS will be compromised neurologically to paralysis using the AFS. The remaining EZS combatants are engaging in a hand-to-hand battle with Sergeant Gian and his valiant two million regular ZS in a fight to the death to determine if the Dark Eagle SS can be declared secured.

How pathetic is a war to be had?

Captain Junior arrives at the DN SS where Admiral Barcarui is leading an armada of nine space stations, twenty-five SGMT ships, and over two million support craft transporting an array of goods, entrepreneur start-ups, and prospectors of the latest land rush.

"Progress is being made, my cabinet members, I welcome you to the beginnings of a major development in human history. As you are all aware of the itinerary implemented for transition into hibernation for the long journey to SCG solar light system. The time has arrived to initiate the processes for hibernation of your crew and human assets. Over and out."

"With all due respect Admiral, the SGMT ships are the only capable craft, most of the support caravan are interplanetary cruisers incapable on their own to get to Alpha Centauri. Their survival depends on the fleet."

"We will wait for all personnel to hibernate first before moving ahead."

"When does that happen?"

"Hibernation of thirty million people can pose delays, even with so many half-cyborgs."

"If we're going to be on hiatus for so long, I'd like to request a rest for non-essential personnel."

"Granted on one stipulation, Captain Junior."

"What's that Admiral?"

"That you spend your time searching for Minister Riverstrike, your father."

"I accept, but my father will join us if he is able. He does not want us to delay departure on his behalf. He will make his way on the Dark Eagle, if at all."

"By the way, I suggest you abstain from having sexual relations with the virtual bots. They are fully capable of impregnating and giving childbirth."

"What good is it to have them at all? Where is she?"

"Who?"

"You know who. Show me."

Admiral Barcarui follows two ensigns as his guard, a short walk to a medical lab with a sign along the top of the entrance 'Sensitive Equipment Hibernation Module.' The Admiral invites the Captain to step up to the door. He sees through a viewing window and recognizes the face of Catherine, with eight more Catherine's undoubtedly cloned during the five years she spent at the ZS Training Facility 'reconditioning.'

"The cloning was your father's idea. He felt her bloodline must survive as he believes the memory of the subterranean society is stored in her DNA. To ensure this her healthy clones created today will someday see technology advance to unlock hidden memories."

They both stand back ruminating privately for a moment before engaging by acknowledging the impact viewing nine cloned Catherine's in hibernation has on their meager minds.

"I suppose I can wait," Captain Junior yields.

"What do you mean, you can wait? The cloned specimens are for the Minister's indulgence."

"If he made it out of the Dark Eagle before it was destroyed."

Admiral Barcarui finds the Captain's tongue loose on the evidence of whether the Dark Eagle remains functional. "Would it be plausible the Minister is on his way to the rendezvous point?"

"If he made it to the Dark Eaglet, then maybe."

"Operations to Admiral Barcarui, over."

"This is Admiral Barcarui, go ahead Operations, over."

"Sir, while conducting role call with the fleet there are multiple sudden disconnects. We've lost contact with twenty of the SGMT ships, and about one percent of the support crafts."

"Is there an explanation?"

"We have multiple reports of nuclear explosion detonations and the blast radius of each taking a considerable number of the support crafts surrounding each of the twenty SGMT ships."

"Report the number of craft remaining in the armada after the roll call." Barcarui is deflated by the terrible developments.

"What could have happened?" Junior asks in earnest, "Certainly there are no weapon systems that could strike from the SSN accurately enough to hit twenty of the tour ships from this distance."

"No Captain, the CEO of the company is a former sapper."

"You suspect Marcel Etrion had remote nuclear mines installed during construction?"

"He knows your father very well, at least by having the forethought to create a 'failsafe' alternative. If any one of the ships lost their bearings, disaster can be averted with preemptive destruction."

Admiral Barcarui leads Captain Junior out of the containment area and the two ensigns take the lead walking their way leading to a heavily armored door. Captain Junior is looking over the Admiral's shoulder into the screen to view through. The screen is sourced from this security door, the entire door becomes transparent.

Three seconds elapse before an image of the occupants in the room reveals human bodies taller than seven feet; they have elongated skulls; their faces are of natural human skin tones; the crown of their bulbous skulls is bald with veins and stretch marks evidence of having had surgical alterations to the thin foreheads. The eyes are under eyelids stretching to cover the bulging eyeballs from the ridges of the eye sockets; the slender noses are long, narrow, and sharp-edged, distinguishable from the other features like the mouth; large full shape lips with the protrusion of incisors snug over the lower lip, an odd anomaly for a homosapiens descendant.

"Are these humans crossbred with a reptile species?"

"Your father intends to nurture their evolution as bionic-cybernetic organisms that can feed intravenously."

"Those are the cyborg-homo-Excelsior?" Junior peers in closely as if expecting to recognize someone.

"Yes." He bows his back to lean away from the door, "They are our overlords now." His eyes reflect on Juniors. "They take over the fleet two thousand years into our mission. They are to upgrade energy efficiency; thrust propulsion and science they develop will extend lifespans to survive thirty- to forty-thousand years."

"The absurdity of it all ~" Junior seems guided by Admiral Barcarui, his subtle emotional undertones speak volumes foretelling his concerns. "It will take twenty-thousand years to reach SCG solar light system by our current technological means. Didn't someone say 'two hundred years?"

"I believe we're reliant on the resourcefulness of our new overlords to conceive and develop light-speed technology."

The Dark Eagle SS has obliterated most of the major space stations from the Moon to the Earth leaving a few remaining isolated space stations, most importantly The Wishing Well SS, the headquarters for SSNERT.

The vivarium deactivates as the societies are met with multiple massive space station debris falling from the sky, burning through the atmosphere.

Admiral J. P. Jones deploys all SSNERT's fleet, over one million rescue craft, to save GPPJ citizens floating in open space in the recently developed propulsion suits. SSNERT shuttles have Robotic Orbiting Platform Encasement (R.O.P.E.) Devices that are saving tens of millions of lives from perilous death incinerated by descent through

Earth's atmosphere.

The falling of debris from destroyed space stations hurdling down to Earth will decimate and annihilate much of the environmental engineering technologies disabling the remaining surviving Earth population from stabilizing the health of the planet.

With the scientific infrastructure diminished the Condorcet procedure will not be widely available for future generations, therefore reducing the life spans over one generation from a potential seven-hundred-fifty-years of age to just one-hundred- twenty-five years of age maximum for the tens of billions of people remaining on Earth.

The survivors on Earth will have great conflict over food and medicine to counter the re-emergence of diseases, land, property claims, and procreation rights as the Earthlings instantly overpopulate and are scarce in resources. Everything will need to be reassessed. The death toll will be high amongst the eldest GPPJ, anyone aged over one-hundred-twenty-five years will crumble at the end of their Condorcet Procedure cycle has run its course. The rapid toxic density in the cellular make-up will cause over-stressed cells, unknown suffering to unrelenting death. Billions will suffer precipitous aging resulting in grueling painful deaths.

As Jürgen, the Cadets, and I board the Nebula Drifter we see the Dark Eaglet cruiser pass by at a distance approximately two miles below us heading toward Earth.

"Let's go!" I order as everyone responds as one unit each taking a seat and auto-strapping on their harnesses. What in this hour of defining actions has swayed Riverstrike from his grand plan of cutting ties with the GPPJ?"

"Is he going to destroy The Glass Planet?" Jürgen asks lacking full comprehension of what is happening. "Isn't he committed to a kamikaze attack as the Dark Eaglet is easily capable of obliterating The Glass Planet?"

"Who is to say he is not on a kamikaze mission? He's heading for Mosaic Caverns. Set course for Mosaic Caverns."

The Nebula Drifter lifts off and accelerates to twenty-five-hundred miles-per-hour toward earth only five hundred miles away, or twelve minutes travel time.

Jürgen is now a vestige of his former self, a cyborg of Riverstrike's creation, as are countless EZS cyborgs of the making from a desperate, tormented soul named Shane Colston, whose ability for creating robotics rivals his ballistics capabilities.

Humanity is greatly compromised in violent conflict, there are no winners, and no one benefits other than the oppressed with the elimination of the fascist, the curing of the disease, and the innovation in overcoming adversity.

And to the profit of the manufacturer of the utensils of death, the owner of patents and rights, the people who value the monetary unit over the 'wellbeing' of the human condition, they surely benefit.

We catch up with the Dark Eaglet in a matter of a few minutes to view the interplanetary cruiser hovering over Mosaic Caverns.

"Is it what I believe it is I see?" Asks Jürgen completely overwrought with emotion.

"Yes."

Lily enters the cockpit, "What is going on? Why are we hovering?" She looks to the surface viewing the apparitions from the legend of Mosaic Caverns, "It is the lost souls of the forgotten sacrifices?"

The emergence of the lost souls of forgotten sacrifices from Mosaic Caverns swells in a dense mass of sub-atomic material.

I need to persuade Lily to return to the safety of the cabin with the others, "Lily, dear, go back into the cabin right now."

"I want to watch the apparitions."

"You can watch them from the monitor inside with the others." Lily reluctantly exits, "The monitors don't show anything."

"Go on, hurry," I direct her out of the cockpit.

The apparitions are ancient human souls, spirits of the American Revolutionary War, Union soldiers of the American Civil War, millions of African souls subject to enslavement from greed-fascism, and their lives, as their descendants' lives strive for freedom.

African souls covered in tracer marks with multiple scars kinship on the back, necks cut, heads blown off, and grotesque disfigurements give proof of the price people have paid seeking freedom from vile greed-fascism enslavement, and unjustified persecution.

Freedom fighters from various countries from the 'Old World' defeated monarchy and autocracy, despotism as well it is dictatorships across the world, again and again. Souls from each war who died to fight for freedom, liberty, and the pursuit of happiness, continuously rise.

The impact of seeing the forgotten sacrifices appear from the Mosaic Caverns, lingering on to dismiss those who gave their lives to protect the 'wellbeing' of others to exercise freedom of will, defines valor in honor of the centuries of human struggle to form a better world union.

"He is obsessed with the past." My voice trembling in awe of the spectacle instantly brings into focus reasoning, "He knows there is a conflict he has been unable to win, and it defies his lifelong ambition to prevent progress towards human equality."

It is an obvious answer as the Dark Eaglet descends to a safe landing. Riverstrike must understand his destiny, at least in his mind's eye. Vengeance against the threat of the ancient subterranean populations dwelling in the deepest crevices of Earth proves no god could allow this.

Those who are not like him, are not worthy of equality in life, but if time has instructed him about his anger to defeat the alien threat for the 'wellbeing' of the human condition, he knows he has performed the ultimate act to help assure the preservation of wealth and power by creating the Spark Creation Genesis solar light system where the 'wellbeing' is assured for the greed-fascist to exploit and manipulate the innocent and vulnerable unwilling subjects under autocratic rule.

The will to relent is now justifiable, as an energy surge results in the apparitions swarming over Riverstrike, immersing his body until no longer visible.

"He is entombed in the past, a dark reminder of what is the 'worst-being' of the human condition." I believe for certain, "No one is omnipotent, no one will ever be."

"The Noah's Arc class rescue craft are being safely towed in by the fleet of space tow trucks."

"Roberto? This is Kariana. I'm coming home."

"You are amazing Kariana." Roberto comments while taking the task of leading the space trucks back to Earth to manage the debris of destroyed space stations about to enter the Earth's atmosphere, "To think what you have become hailing from the impoverished class of old-world Colombia. My heart is filled with pride for you."

"Thank you, Roberto, you mean everything to me, but you haven't seen anything yet!"

"What are you talking about Kariana?"

"Since Patrick Riverstrike owes me a favor for stealing my life, now is the time to give him his comeuppance."

"How do you mean, financially?"

"Come home Roberto," Kariana pleads seductively, "where we share our passions. I want to be with you, living free to choose as I like to do with my body. It's the greatest revenge against chauvinistic, misogynistic ghouls."

"Si, Te Quiero dulce Amor, Kariana. Roberto descends from the debris-filled exosphere in his STTU. He arrives in a flash of three-hundred-sixty-degree roll-overs in a near free fall, before stabilizing the craft to land safely in a clearing. He joins her on ACRES property overseeing Mosaic Caverns as the 'lost souls of the forgotten sacrifices' continue to flow around Mosaic Caverns.

The children of ACRES, who will know nothing of a prospective life span approaching a millennium or more, are equally curious about the apparitions. The question arising in most of their young developing minds is: Do these souls exist for eternity?

The way of the world through time and age did not escape us, nor will Riverstrike. If he survives, he will be suffering a slow, merciless decline in a dwelling not approving of him.

He will be denied medical treatment until disability and disease lead to an excruciating death.

His existence is absorbed into the cosmic fabric, his fate a transcendence carrying the burdens of his deceit against the 'wellbeing' of the human condition.

Devastated by the destruction, barbaric, lethal force Riverstrike has chosen to use against the people, this separation of the social contract is an example of greed-fascism to oppress the masses into subservience.

The generations of the deceased people who are the pillars of economic sustenance to accumulate the infrastructure of wealth the greed-fascist consolidated over centuries have transcended as the 'spirits of the forgotten sacrifices' continue to emerge from the Mosaic Caverns gorge.

Jürgen and I see the apparitions in metaphysical existential transcendence. They are many to form the one stream of an other-worldly portal leading to a dimension Jürgen and I have transcended as we intuitively see the macro in the micro.

The entire crew of the Tigris SS was decimated when a pellet size meteorite tore through the space station at over one-hundred-thousand miles per hour, they too emerge from Mosaic Caverns.

I notice many GPPJ in their space suits who hold facial expressions cherub-like in their appearance so graceful in bodily movements. I perceive closer a name badge below The Glass Planet SS emblem woven into the space suits tailored thin like scuba diving gear, and figures absent of any oxygen apparatus, begin to emerge.

There are thousands upon thousands of them, and as they

increasingly appear, I perceive a deeper pattern developing, a mark glowing on their feet as a branding signifying assimilated refugee."

"The other marks and disfigurements on each of the various enchantingly graceful apparitions indicate where the wound occurred upon instant death. Many without external wounds may have jettisoned into space, therefore, suffocating to hypoxia or experiencing an embolism, or from a lung puncture wound.

A meteorite shatters upon impact allowing the penetration of lethal shards of space rock through the hull wall grotesquely disfiguring tens of thousands of the crew piercing and slicing bodies into a shredded mass, with remaining shards passing on through the Tigris space station crew and GPPJ citizens on board, onto The Glass Planet SS taking in nearly eighty-seven-thousand more casualties who, at this moment emerge in a swell overcoming Patrick Riverstrike like a tsunami wave flushing him into the Mosaic Caverns portal.

The presence of the apparitions continues with the emergence taking shape into shining lit orbs of all colors of lights that dissipate as quickly into thin air as more spirits emerge in the next fold from Mosaic Caverns.

The thousands upon thousands rise as many military passersby come forth and recede again, then a procession of young females, mostly of Peruvian, and Inca ancient tribes. They possess a brave solemnity, partial skulls truncated by metal headdresses electrocuted as sacrifices to appease ancient gods.

There are two who appear, I perceive wearing green berets, their faces, my perception greatly deterred by the expressionless faces devoid of recognizable features, yet offering a sense of knowing the familiar uniform, the arm patches are the rank of Staff Sergeant, to the right my eyes lock on to their patches on the left side of each of their chests, my memory awoke, everything came back to me once seeing what is stitched upon the patches, their names, Augur, Martinez.

"No! Stop! Do not fire a shot! Stop it, madmen! We are defenseless you God damn ignorant animals."

The days, weeks, months, years, decades, centuries, millenniums of killing, murdering with deadly force and through less pervasive methods must come to an end!

My moment of epiphany creates a surge of energy, unlike anything I have ever experienced ~ our surroundings in the Nebula Drifter alter to the elasticity of shapes, and the hard components vibrate with sub-atomic energy. We perceive our bodies as billions of cells, molecules, atoms, quarks, and every identifiable and previously unknown content of the cosmic fabric envelopes us at speeds surpassing light.

"Catherine ~ are we seeing the depth of the universe?"

"I see the macro inside the micro ~ it is the beginning of and the content of light up to the present moment. The light coming at us reflects a time in the past before any of us were here."

"And the rest?"

"Is the past of us, the present times emanating away from us, our most recent history is nearest to us in this dimension. The distant emanations contain our history flowing eternally outward. The spectrum is one massive force of energy ~ Absolutely."

We look at each other, our molecular structure vibrates, our metaphysical state of being flows in the cosmic fabric of dark matter.

"I find my atoms move freely and can exist separately within the cosmic fabric light years away."

"Our atomic structure flows across dark matter covering great distances in split seconds ~ we can go as far as where dark matter takes us."

"Adding our life existential experience, our understanding of it, affects positively or negatively the 'wellbeing' of the universe by informing the cosmic fabric."

"What we do not understand on its terms will be perceived in terms we do understand."

"I feel like I am a part of something large and that it contains multitudes."

"Will we find out who we are?"

"Yes, I believe so. We can see more than just our life history; we will see all the history of life and the history of creation."

"Does that make us God's?"

"No, and no one is. Perception of this fourth spatial dimension, where there's complete physical integration, makes the distance to the Sun like a short walk down the street; the Milky Way is a celestial forest to be meandered about in a few hours; Dark matter is a conduit for energy to flow through the universe wherever it's found, allowing for cognitive capabilities to access the known existence of everything. We're equally a part of it all, the metaphysical as well the physical; we are the transcendent willpower of existence."

THE END

Epilogue

What is Metaphysical?

The branch of philosophy examines the fundamental nature of reality, including the relationship between mind and matter, substance and attribute, and potentiality. Greek words meaning 'After or behind or among' the natural.

What is Existential?

The four basic dimensions of human existence include the physical; the social; the psychological; and the spiritual. Independent attitudes are formed from the experience of their world.

What is Transcendental?

There are three kinds of transcendence, first, ego transcendence about self, beyond ego, secondly, self-transcendence that is beyond the self, and time. Thirdly the spiritual transcendence, beyond space and time.

Transcendent Value, a noun, is a value that surpasses all spiritualist differences and unifies a group.

ABOUT THE AUTHOR

Christopher Zyck has exercised and developed his writing skills ever since reading his first big word in an encyclopedia at the tender age of seven. Writing has always been a fascination, as has science fiction and in 1976, in the bicentennial of the United States of America, standing in the Elementary school library he read the word 'transcendentalism.'

On a Panasonic television featuring bunny ears, nine television channels, and a much-needed 'horizontal control' button, he learned the early science fiction literature and movie classics ranging from historical to future fantasy, everybody knows the list is long.

Christopher attended thirteen years of undergraduate semesters studying creative writing, American Literature, English Literature, print and broadcast Journalism, poetry intensives, and dramatic arts (acting.) He obtained multiple skills engaging in producing, fundraising for not-for-profit theaters, marketing, advertising, directing, and a few other hats, some larger than others, all of them about the work at hand.

On a transcendental journey through the deeply rooted societal-generational dysfunctions as examined in this epic space odyssey, Christopher was born in February near President's week 2/14-2/22, endearing him as a Patriot to the USA Constitution.

CONNECT

theglasspplanetlaunch.com

JOIN THE EMAIL LIST @ CJZMEDIAISLAND.NET

LIKE & FOLLOW page on FB/Meta: C J Z Media Island

SUBSCRIBE to the CJZ MEDIA ISLAND!

YouTube channel for video content short stories & profiles:

YouTube channel: https://www.you-tube.com/channel/UCHHNbHr

1qwOn-VdVZ278yIA

Cover Design by SusansArt: yuneekpix.com

Thank you for reading THE GLASS PLANET.

COMING SOON!

MOSAIC CAVERNS

(The prequel to THE GLASS PLANET)

Made in the USA
Columbia, SC
12 August 2023

20849533R30274